I0534659

Murder By Vote

Penrose & Pyke Mysteries, Book 3

Rose Pascoe

Published by Flax Bay Books, 2023

Copyright

MURDER BY VOTE

Copyright © 2023 Rose Pascoe. All rights reserved.
Written by Rose Pascoe
First edition February 20, 2023.

This is a work of fiction. Names, characters, places and incidents are either the product of the author's imagination or are used fictitiously.

ISBN: 978-1991181305 (Epub)
978-1991181312 (Softcover POD)

Publisher: Flax Bay Books, New Zealand

Cover design: Rose Pascoe
Cover images from Adobe Stock Images by Obsidian Fantasy, Flatman vector 24, and Irina Korsakova

Table of Contents

Acknowledgments & Dedication

A huge thank you to my fabulous beta readers – Mary, Jenny, Kathy and Ross – whose enthusiasm is very much appreciated. Thanks also to friends and family for their encouragement.

This novel is dedicated to all the women and men who worked tirelessly to achieve voting rights for women, putting our small country at the forefront of a peaceful social revolution. New Zealand became the first self-governing nation in the world where women won the right to vote.

While this story is fictional, it is set at a time of real drama in the struggle for women's suffrage in New Zealand, which was achieved with little violence, but great passion.

Lest we forget what the suffragists faced, here is the text of a poster from the era:

"Notice to Epicene Women. Electioneering women are requested not to call here. They are recommended to go home, to look after their children, cook their husband's dinners, empty the slops, and generally attend to the domestic affairs for which Nature designed them. By taking this advice, they will gain the respect of all right minded people – an end not to be attained by unsexing themselves and meddling in masculine concerns of which they are profoundly ignorant." (Source: National Library).

Distraction

Friday, 22 April 1892, Dunedin, New Zealand

Grace Penrose stared at *Gray's Anatomy*, willing the words to take root in her memory. The anatomical diagrams were exhibiting an alarming tendency to blur and dance in front of her eyes, turning the twenty-seven bones of the hand (plus muscles, ligaments, tendons, sheaths, arteries, veins and nerves) into a frolicking five-legged spider.

Grace prised herself out of her chair and went to the window, hoping for a worthy distraction. The cable car whirred its way up the steep incline of High Street. A chill wind rippled through the trees, sending a flurry of autumn leaves against the pane. Not exactly the excitement she longed for. Perhaps she ought to start her essay on … what was it again? She drifted back to her desk, unearthing a sheet of paper from deep within the "urgent" pile. Oh, yes, the toxic effects of common garden plants. Nibbling on hemlock seemed almost preferable to spending another hour closeted with her textbooks.

The tap-tap of a walking cane passed her door. Her great-aunt, Anne Macmillan, on route to her study.

Grace intercepted her outside the door. "Auntie, do you have any books on poisonous plants?"

"Not planning to murder your elderly relative with monkshood, I hope, Grace? Should I employ a taster to test my food?"

"I'd probably go for foxglove or deadly nightshade myself. I wouldn't worry though, if only because I'm too busy to spend my days in the kitchen, brewing lethal potions."

Anne shuffled close enough to peer into Grace's bloodshot eyes. "I shouldn't have let you go out so often to collect signatures

7

for the franchise petition, when you have so much study to do. When did you last get a full night's sleep?"

"Some time over the summer break, I expect, in between my little sojourn in the lunatic asylum and the start of the university term."

Grace had spent most of the summer break working for the police surgeon, which meant there had been precious few days to enjoy lazy mornings in bed. Despite the hazards of asylums and autopsies, she missed the excitement. Studying from books was all very well – she could hardly get her medical degree without them – but there was nothing like dabbling in real-life medical drama, with a thrilling dash of crime thrown in for good measure. Especially in the company of a certain rather attractive policeman.

"Grace, dear, your eyes have glazed over. Is it too much study, or are you pining for the emerald-eyed charms of Detective Constable Pyke?"

How did her great-aunt read her mind like that? It was most disconcerting. "Now, why would I be doing that? As a matter of fact, I haven't heard from Charlie for several weeks."

"Off on another secret foray into the dark corners of criminality, is he? Let's hope he stays out of trouble this time."

Grace let out an unladylike snort. "You might as well hope the sun fails to rise. Can we get back to toxic plants? I have essays to write about cholera, mental disorders, and diseases of the bones as well. It'll be a miracle if I find time to sleep before I graduate in 1895."

"Take a stroll in the fresh air and talk to Mr Todd about poisonous plants. You'll get far more sense out of him than any textbook on the subject. While you're there, gather some vegetables for the soup pot. If you're going to have a career and a family, you'd better learn to do at least two tasks at once, if not two dozen."

Given the size of her "urgent" pile, two dozen tasks would be an underestimate. Grace sighed. "Sometimes I think it would be much easier to live the life of a pampered lady."

Another woman might have patted her arm and told her all would be well, but not Anne Macmillan. "Chin up, Grace. Nothing worthwhile comes without sacrifice. Pampered lady? You would be bored to tears within a week. Think of all the excruciating afternoon teas one would have to endure with tedious society matrons. Diabolical! I'd rather attend a dozen breech births than any event involving crustless cucumber sandwiches and chit-chat about the latest fad for lace what-nots."

"But think of all the delicious petit fours I am missing out on," Grace grumbled, as she went to find Mr Todd, the gardener.

Anne was, of course, entirely correct. The fresh air did her good and she wouldn't swap her hectic life for anything (even petit fours). Mr Todd was happy to expound at length upon the fascinating, but sinister, properties of common plants in his slow drawl, full of ayes and arrs and age-old wisdom.

By the time Grace had a full basket of vegetables, she also had a new appreciation for the deadly killers lurking in plain sight. Even the humble potato deserved a skull-and-crossbones label, along with pretty assassins such as rhododendrons, daphne and arum lilies. Better yet, Mr Todd had supplied intriguing details of several toxic native plants, which, with luck, no other student would include in their assignment.

Grace returned to the house, ready to dash off a quick essay on death in the garden. Before she could lift her pen, she heard a familiar voice in the kitchen, frothing over with news by the sound of it.

"Molly! How lovely to see you." Grace took in the shining eyes and wayward locks of curly hair escaping from hairpins, and deduced a worthy distraction had arrived at last, in the form of her dear friend, Molly Sugden.

"I've come to see if you can spare me a few hours tomorrow, Grace. Are you still on your Easter break from medical school?"

"Break? More like an excuse to pile us high with extra work. But I could certainly use some excitement in my life. What have you to offer, Molly?" She joined them at the table, leaning forward eagerly.

"Miss Nicol has asked me to help her with an urgent task before the Women's Franchise League meeting next Thursday."

"I thought you had an essay to write, Grace," Anne said, although she leaned forward to hear the task every bit as eagerly as her great-niece.

"Getting women the vote is far more important. Besides, with Mr Todd's help, I can dash off my toxicology essay this evening."

All three of them were involved with the campaign to urge the New Zealand government to grant women the vote. The logic was undeniable. Women were subject to the laws of the land – why not allow them to have a say in the making of those laws? With women voting, there might even be a move towards some much-needed common sense and compassion in the political debate, instead of cigar-puffing self-interest.

"You know of Mr Fish's petition, I presume?" Molly began.

"May he fall into a cesspit full of ravenous eels, along with all the sycophants and boozers who support him," Anne muttered.

"A little cruel to the eels, don't you think, Auntie?" Grace said. "Besides, even an elected Member of the House of Representatives has as much democratic right to collect signatures for a petition as we do, as long as he does so fairly."

"I'd rather put my faith in the eels," Anne retorted.

"What does Helen Nicol want you to do, Molly?" Grace asked, before Anne got started on her reasons for loathing Henry Fish and his obnoxious tirades against women's rights.

Grace was impatient to hear their franchise superintendent's plan. Last year, over ten thousand women had signed the franchise petition, yet still the bill to enshrine their right to vote was overturned by a last-minute piece of political skulduggery. This year, they were aiming for twenty thousand signatures, by far the largest petition ever presented to parliament.

10

"You'll have heard rumours that the liquor lobby is funding Fish's petition," Molly continued.

"We all know Fish is a puppet dancing to the publicans' whims," Anne said. "Those evil purveyors of booze would do anything to stop women from getting the vote. They cannot seem to get it into their thick skulls that only a minority of women support prohibition."

"They are right to be worried, Mrs Macmillan," Molly said. "The prohibitionists have already taken the majority on some of the local licensing committees and closed down hotels across Dunedin."

"Not before time. There are more places to swill alcohol in this town than shops to buy food."

"Do tell us what Miss Nicol wants from us, Molly," Grace begged.

Molly explained rapidly to prevent further interruptions. "You'll also have heard the rumours that Fish's men are paying for signatures and using trickery to get people to sign. Now we have possible proof of it. Miss Nicol has received information from an anonymous source, including a list of names of women who have been duped into signing Fish's petition."

"That is good news, if the source can be trusted."

"That's what we are going to find out, Grace. If it is true, we're going to get the women to sign another petition to say that they signed under false pretences. Sir John Hall will take it to the Public Petitions Committee, so Fish's petition can be dismissed."

Anne rubbed her hands together. "Wonderful. Prove that allegation and Henry Fish will be fish paste."

"I was planning to go out tomorrow morning," Molly said. "Would you like to come with me, Grace?"

"I wouldn't miss it for the world!"

"I wish I was young again," Anne sighed. "I'd give anything to be out there with you, getting signatures for a petition against the counter-petition to our petition. Makes me dizzy thinking about it."

11

The Vote

The cask of ale oozed a cloying mix of malt and hops, as the pot man hoisted it to his shoulder. Rough staves rubbed against his unkempt beard and added another layer of grime to his tatty waistcoat, as he staggered up the cellar stairs.

In the bar, the airless fug hung with the stench of stale beer, fried liver and onion, and honest working-class sweat. A raucous chorus of men vying for attention added to the thump of the pot man's headache. Friday nights were always busy, with only a half day of work to worry about on the morrow. This Friday was worse, as men were making up for the lack of booze over Easter. The way some of them were knocking it back, their wives must have forced them to give up alcohol for the whole of Lent.

The pot man hefted the cask under the counter, with little apparent effort. In reality, his muscled shoulders ached from the unfamiliar work. He swept a thick lock of straggly black hair out of his eyes. "What next, Mr Vance?" The barman liked to tell him exactly what to do, in case he was too dim to have grasped the fundamentals of his job after several weeks of practice.

"There's a pile of tankards wanting rinsing out the back, Potts," the barman ordered, before turning to serve a customer.

"I hear a man can get a free drink here for signing that petition of Fish's." The customer was Irish and fresh off a ship, judging from his thick brogue. "Reckon that's a fair deal, since any right-thinking man would sign anyway."

The two men behind the bar eyed him warily, taking in his rough clothes, which were suspiciously lacking in the normal layer of sweat and grease. The Engineers' Arms did not welcome many strangers. They catered almost entirely to regulars from the

Caversham area, most of them straight from the Hillside railway workshop up the road. A clean man was a man to be distrusted.

The stranger met the barman's gaze without flinching. "I'm new in town. Looking for a local watering hole. Do you have a problem with that?"

The barman shoved a beer-soaked sheet of paper across the bar. Signatures filled the petition form almost to the bottom of the page, scrawled with minimal concern for literacy or legibility. The barman limped back to the other end of the bar to pull a half-pint of the cheapest ale for the newcomer.

The pot man knew from bitter experience that the pain in the barman's injured leg got worse as the night went on, making him increasingly surly. So far, Mr Vance had only reached the grumpy stage, so he leaned over to the barman and whispered in his ear. "That Irishman's a copper from Dunedin Central Station."

The barman pulled the rest of the beer, topping it expertly with foam, as if he hadn't heard. He moved back along the bar to where Detective Constable Kelly was waiting, sliding over the ale, but keeping his hand on it. "You heard wrong, fella. You can sign the petition, but don't expect no payment for it. Wouldn't be right and proper now, would it?"

Kelly sent a scorching look at the pot man. "I've heard more than one man say they've earned the price of an ale by helping you collect signatures. There's no cause to deny me because I'm new in town."

Potts moved around the bar, standing a foot away from Kelly, with his head almost touching the low ceiling of the tavern. He crossed his arms over his chest, displaying no-nonsense biceps and an expression that said I've seen it all before, and it ended badly. "You heard Mr Vance. No free ale. Do I have to show you out the door on the tip of my boot?"

Detective Constable Kelly blanched and pushed back the bar stool, scraping it across the sticky floor in his haste. He tossed a coin on the bar, where it landed in a puddle. "Keep your ale. I don't care for the company or the smell in here." He was out the door faster than a drunk could knock back a dram of moonshine whisky.

When the door banged shut, the barman slid the untouched ale towards his helper with a grin. "Nice work, Potts. How is it you know a central station copper?"

"Stupid bleater tried to arrest me once for intimidating a Chinaman. All I did was suggest politely that he wasn't wanted in our country. Didn't lay a finger on him. Not that anyone would swear to leastways." The pot man leaned against the bar, curling a fist around the ale, looking both relaxed and ready to go three rounds in a bare-knuckle ring. After several weeks on the job, he felt sure his slightly almond-shaped eyes had not given away his own Chinese ancestry, as most people looked no further than the tall stature inherited from his English father.

"You're new here, aren't you?"

Potts snapped to attention at the authority in the voice, standing straight as he took in the petulant jaw and expensive tailoring of the new arrival. "Yes, sir. Started a few weeks ago."

"Come with me." The man struggled to extract his flesh from the tailored overcoat. He discarded it into the arms of the young woman from the kitchen, who had appeared at his side as soon as he had made his entrance. Without so much as a glance or thank you, he headed through a swing door, along a corridor and around a corner, to a staircase. His barrel-shaped waistline brushed both sides of the narrow stairs as he puffed his way to the top.

The man gestured at Potts to follow him into a room on the first floor, which seemed to belong to a different realm from the squalid public bar below. Potts didn't flinch as the man ran a critical eye down his body, from head to toe, although the experience was by no means a pleasant one.

"I'm Mr Bertram, owner of the Engineers' Arms and three other hotels in Dunedin. I could use a man with your muscles, especially as it seems you have your wits about you too. What's your name, lad?"

"Charlie Potts, sir," Detective Constable Charlie Pyke replied. He stood under the repellent gaze of his boss without venturing any further comment, attempting to look neither intimidating nor intimidated. In his undercover role for the police, he aimed to project the strong silent type, who could be relied upon to keep a secret and do anything that was asked of him.

Charlie has seen the likes of Bertram before. The Otago goldfields, where Charlie had grown up as a policeman's son, were awash with hard, greedy men from all over the globe, all of whom craved wealth the easy way. The majority soon soured under the hard slog of reality. Those few who did succeed made more money than friends.

Bertram's accent hinted at the wrong side of London, by way of Australia, while his clothes stamped him as a successful self-made man. Charlie would have taken short odds that he had made his money running a grog shop, siphoning off what little gold the average miner scraped together.

Judging by the plush seats and mahogany tables in the room, Bertram had done well for himself. Charlie had never seen anyone come up here during his work hours, but he had seen lights behind the heavy curtains late at night. If the locked cupboards on the back wall didn't contain gaming equipment, he'd eat his truncheon.

This was what he had been sent to discover, but it was also the moment of maximum danger. Being so close to a breakthrough set his nerve endings alight. Detective Inspector Wallace would be pleased. There had been persistent rumours of illegal gambling and bootleg liquor, but they'd never proved who was behind it.

Sure enough, Bertram opened a drawer, lifted out its false bottom, and took out a couple of packs of cards, tossing them on the table. "Have you ever been in trouble with the law, Potts?"

"Not a single conviction, sir," Charlie replied, conveying a subtle not-for-want-of-trying subtext, while avoiding any hint of bragging.

"Good. Keep it that way. I can't afford to have the peelers sniffing around my business. What did that one want before you showed him the door?"

"He'd heard he could get an ale in exchange for signing Mr Fish's petition."

"And what business is it of the police that a Member of our esteemed House of Representatives wishes to canvass honest opinions on the women's franchise abomination? It's Mr Fish's democratic right and duty to convey his constituent's disgust at the very idea. Women voting? Ludicrous. I'd sooner give all the rabid dogs of the nation the vote."

"Yes, Mr Bertram." Charlie was not inclined to mention that bribing a man to sign and paying canvassers to secure votes by whatever means possible were not part of that democratic right.

Bertram adjusted the cuffs of his fine worsted suit with his coarse fingers. "I'm hosting some acquaintances for a round or two of cards tonight, Potts. We do not wish to be disturbed. Can I rely on you to ensure we are not interrupted?"

"Whatever you want, Mr Bertram."

"Good. Bring up a keg of our best bitter and a bottle of Highland malt. Vance will know what's needed."

By the time Charlie had made two trips to bring up the refreshments, three more men had arrived, their silk cravats looking out of place under faces as hard as a glacier. When he entered with the whisky and glasses, they were laughing at Bertram's exaggerated retelling of the ejection of the snooping policeman. The conversation switched to the wintery weather and its effect on the liquor trade, as he approached the table.

Charlie kept his eyes averted for the most part, after a quick glance to memorise what he could see of them. The tall man with dark hair, facing away from him, hung his hat and overcoat on a rack. Expensive clothes and a smooth voice, a rolling Scottish lilt with a hard edge.

16

The broad-shouldered man, who had already taken a seat, had his head down, his face hidden under unruly red hair. He shuffled cards with practised dexterity, speaking with a back alley Irish accent, which played havoc with his vowels. When he looked up, his heavy jaw was rigid under flint-hard eyes. Not a man to turn your back on.

The fourth man, who had kept out of Charlie's sight line, came up behind him and slapped him on the back, causing the whisky bottle to rattle on the tray. Vance, the barman, had impressed upon Charlie the need to treat the bottle like holy water. Any breakage and he could kiss his wages goodbye for months to come.

"Come work for me, Potts. I could use a muscleman to keep troublemakers in line." The man's voice had the rasp of a heavy smoker and the persistent remnants of an Emerald Isle past.

Charlie ignored the slap, but swivelled his head enough to note sandy blond hair and a body more suited to dark corners than honest labour. He must be confident of his position, if he went about slapping the backs of men twice his size. "Thank you, sir, but I am content with where I am."

Bertram gave him a nod of approval and waved at him to leave. "That will be all for now, Potts. Stay at the bottom of the stairs and make sure nobody comes up, no matter who they are and what they say. The girl has been told to bring supper in half an hour. Make sure you ring the bell before she brings it up."

Charlie put the tray down, surprised to be dismissed so soon. He had been hoping for a room full of gamblers to arrive. As he closed the door behind him, he saw Bertram take the only seat with a high back and leather upholstery. Even at a circular table, there always has to be a leader.

He gave silent thanks to DC Kelly, who had volunteered for the ignominious, but carefully planned, role of bumbling copper, so that the cask-lugging Potts could establish himself as a trusted employee. The operation was a delicately balanced one, as Bertram would play the outraged honest businessman if they attempted to arrest him without sufficient evidence of illegal activity – the usual trifecta of

17

gambling, after-hours drinking and liquor tax evasion. His connection to Henry Fish and other like-minded members of the House of Representatives made it especially problematic.

Charlie had been seconded from his position in Wellington to infiltrate Bertram's operation. He had lived in Dunedin before, so he knew the ground, without being widely recognisable as a member of the local police force, especially in his current hairy state. He had his own reasons for jumping at the chance to impress the Dunedin police with his capabilities. Charlie would have walked a tightrope over a shark-infested pool to get a permanent position here, although the knot in his gut told him the four men in the room tonight made a pool of sharks look like a basket of fluffy kittens.

Within days of scouting the Engineers' Arms, Charlie realised illegal gaming was only the tip of a very grubby iceberg. Harry Bertram was at the centre of the liquor lobby's fight against temperance and votes for women, spearheaded by Henry Fish. A fight that was being waged using dirty tactics.

Charlie had already reported back to DI Wallace that Bertram's men were using bribery to collect signatures. He had also witnessed many signatures been forged outright – hardly surprising when the canvassers were being paid seven shillings for every hundred signatures. The forger had sat at a table in the Engineers' Arms, in full view of the other patrons, supping an ale and scrawling name after name on the petition.

Furthermore, Charlie had been ordered by the barman to go out and collect signatures door-to-door. He had grumbled out loud about the extra work, while secretly relishing the chance to see what other dirty tricks the canvassers were using. What he saw was women being encouraged to sign the "suffrage petition", implying that it was in favour of votes for women rather than the opposite. He couldn't act on the information himself without risking his cover, but he had passed on the deceived women's names to DI Wallace, with an under-the-table copy to a leading suffrage campaigner for good measure.

Charlie clumped downstairs, his boots loud on the wooden steps. At the bottom, he turned and tiptoed up again, with surprising lightness, given his size. He picked up the glass he had left by the door and put the rim hard against the wall. Through the thin lining, the rising indignation in the room transmitted clearly to his ear.

"We cannot allow it to happen." Bertram's growling carried above the indignant rumble of the other men. "The time for words and petitions has passed. We must take direct action, as we discussed at our last meeting."

"Taking direct action against the suffrage women risks drawing the attention of the police to our other activities and setting the general opinion against us," the rasping voice of the sandy-haired Irishman countered.

"I agree," the smooth Scotsman said. "The likes of Fish and Seddon will make sure the Franchise Bill is defeated. The Liberals will lose the next election in a landslide if women get the vote."

"It was a close call last year, as you well know," Bertram shot back. "My sources say the Premier and his cronies have the numbers to pass the Women's Franchise Bill this session. We'd be fools to sit back and hope these maverick women will go away. We need to hit them hard and stop them right now."

"But women don't even want the vote," sandy-hair grumbled.

"Tell that to the tens of thousands of women who have already signed their cursed petition," the red-headed Irishman replied.

"Exactly. We've done our best with Fish's petition," Bertram said, "but a few thousand signatures against giving women the vote will look laughable when the women present their petition to parliament. I'm telling you, the only way to stop this travesty is to scare the fight out of them once and for all."

Charlie's ear burned as he crushed it against the glass, struggling to hear what appeared to be murmurs of agreement. A fist thumped on the table, rattling glasses and making him jump.

"The time for words is over. We risk losing our livelihoods without a penny in compensation. These suffragists must learn that politics is no place for women, no matter what it takes to convince them. We want them on their knees, begging for mercy."

"You're not suggesting outright violence against women, are you Harry?" the Scotsman asked.

"You can take my word for it, Mac. The little ladies will run squealing without the need for serious violence. All they need is some forceful encouragement to abandon their soapboxes in favour of returning to their homes, like proper women."

Bertram's voice dropped to a low murmur as he outlined his plan, frustrating Charlie's attempt to hear. All he caught was the odd word – "shame", "protest", "shock", "scare" amongst them.

"Time to vote. All those in favour of direct action?"

Threes ayes responded immediately. The reluctant Scotsman added his aye a fraction of a second later. Charlie pegged him as the weak link in this dangerous group.

"Excellent. You all know your roles. I look forward to seeing our scheme in action. I have already sent a letter to the press to get the battle started. If we can shake the men of Dunedin out of their apathy, their anger will do our work for us." Bertram paused. "Where is that useless girl with our supper?"

As Charlie fled down the stairs, he heard a bell ringing below. In less than a minute, the door to the barroom swung open, letting in the sound of men singing drunken ballads.

The sinews of the girl's thin arms strained under the weight of the platter of food. Although she looked no older than eighteen, and likely weighed little more than a cask of ale, the woman everyone referred to as "the girl" was actually Mrs Vance, the barman's wife. It had taken Charlie two weeks to realise this, as she must have been fifteen years his junior. Vance treated her with as much contempt as the dishrag she wielded.

She looked at Charlie with feral eyes, which softened when he attempted to take her tray. He didn't want to dwell on why the men upstairs scared her so. Perhaps he could help her when his work here was finished.

She pulled the tray out of his grasp. "It's me who has to take it up."

Charlie was caught between wanting to help her and needing to maintain his role. He took the tray. "Let me take it up the stairs. It looks heavy."

After Charlie delivered the food, Bertram dismissed him, but ordered the girl to stay. The barman soon had him working hard to make up for the time he had missed "hanging around like a pampered guard dog". Charlie's mood wasn't helped by the sight of the girl washing dishes late that night, her tears dropping silently into the filthy suds.

He let himself out long after the closing bell, exhausted by the long day, hunching in his ragged overcoat against the drizzling chill of an autumn night. He had forgotten how much colder it was in Dunedin, even though it was still only late April.

As Charlie trudged down the street towards the flats of South Dunedin, past sly-grog shops and brothels, the pervasive odour of poor drainage rose to meet him. Caversham, proudly working class as it was, was a cut above life on the flats, where the unskilled and destitute scraped a living, cheek by jowl with their neighbours.

He wished he had something more to look forward to than a lumpy bunk in a cheap boarding house. Not that he would be in bed anytime soon. He wanted to write up his notes on the meeting and sketch the men while they were fresh in his memory. DI Wallace would have to be informed of the threat as soon as possible. Even if Charlie hadn't overheard the precise plan, the words "direct action" were ominous, especially given the anger of the men towards women who only wanted to have the same rights as men.

Inevitably, his thoughts turned to Grace Penrose, who would be tucked in her warm bed in one of the better areas of Dunedin, not knowing that he was a couple of miles away, in a very different world. He had promised not to contact her, in case he blew his cover. It was driving him mad, especially now that he knew the four liquor barons were going to disrupt the suffrage campaign dear to Grace's heart.

False Pretences

Grace rose early on Saturday morning to give herself time to finish her poisonous plants essay before Molly arrived. Anne was already waiting for her at the kitchen table, eager to discuss the prospect of undermining Fish's petition. Molly joined them soon after, as she too had been unable to sleep.

"I feel in my heart that this might be a turning point," Anne enthused. "The whole anti-suffrage rhetoric will be shown as a sham if they are so desperate they must resort to deceit to get signatures."

"Fish will be kippered when he finds out how many signatures we have collected from the women of New Zealand," Molly added gleefully.

Grace shared their sentiments, but wanted action. "Do let's go, Molly. I can't wait to find out if the list from the anonymous source is genuine. Did Miss Nicol have any idea where it came from?"

"None at all, Grace. It came as a complete surprise."

Anne handed Grace her winter coat as she went out the door. "Don't give me that look, Grace. It may appear sunny, but there's a winter chill in the air. I can't have you expiring from pneumonia before you get your first chance to vote for a new government."

"I'll tell you all about it when I get home," Grace promised, as she vaulted over the steps to the path, one arm trailing out of her coat. "I hope there is fried Fish for dinner!"

"I'll make sure there is a Humble Pie to go with it," Anne called after them.

"Good to see you've got a glow back in your cheeks, Grace. And Mrs Macmillan looked ready to throw away her walking cane and sprint after us."

"Dedication to her causes is what keeps her young. I hope I'm still that passionate in my seventies."

22

"Talking of passion, have you heard from any eligible policemen lately?"

Grace strode down the path to avoid giving Molly the satisfaction of seeing her blush. The future of Detective Constable Charlie Pyke appeared to be as unclear to him as it was to her, unless he was keeping her in the dark. She paused at the gate for Molly to catch up. "Can I have a look at that list before we leave?"

When Molly handed it over, it seemed as if her eyes were playing tricks on her. The writing reminded her of Charlie Pyke's precise hand. As if it wasn't enough to be thinking of him all the time and seeing him every time a tall stranger passed in the street, now she was imagining his writing.

"Grace, you've drifted away again."

"I was merely thinking that several names on this list are definitely supporters of votes for women. This should be as easy as shooting fish in a barrel. Where shall we start?"

"Let's start in north Dunedin and work out way back."

A sour voice came from behind them. "I hope you young ladies are not out knocking on the doors of strangers again. It is unseemly. I wonder your fathers allow it."

Grace turned to her neighbour, smiling politely as she waited for the latest lecture on her many shortcomings. "Mrs Patterson, you gave me a start. Where did you spring from so suddenly?"

Mrs Patterson winched in her ramrod spine another inch and set her lips into the familiar downward curve over her square jaw. "I did not 'spring' from anywhere, Miss Penrose. I exited my own front gate."

"I do beg your pardon. And I agree with you, Mrs Patterson. I would much rather be attending to my medical studies than knocking on doors. But the leaders of our fair country refuse to acknowledge the right of women to vote, on the erroneous pretext that women do not wish to exercise that right. We have no option but to raise a petition to prove them wrong."

23

"You would do better to accept what God and nature intended. Women should restrict their interests to their domestic duties and caring for their husband and children. Heed my advice, Miss Penrose. Make a good match and leave the affairs of the wider world to your husband. Now, if you will excuse me, I have a meeting of the Orphans' Benevolent Society to attend. Good day to you." Mrs Patterson climbed into her carriage, with the aid of a step and a helping hand from the coachman, as if she was at Buckingham Palace, rather than the far reaches of the Antipodes.

Molly stared after the departing carriage. "Your neighbour appears rather formidable, Grace."

"She is an omnipresent force in our lives, always appearing when I am on some errand for the devil. She's the only person in the world Charlie is frightened of."

"Do you often run errands for the devil?"

"Mrs Patterson thinks a woman is in league with the devil if she is not in her rightful place, at home scolding the servants and churning out heirs. She is the president of the local chapter of the Homemakers' Association."

"Homemakers' Association? Sounds fairly benign, if rather dull."

"In theory perhaps, but Mrs Patterson and her accomplices think women do not need or want the vote, because they would only cast their vote wherever their husbands or ministers told them to. To do otherwise would be to 'sow discord within the sanctity of a man's home'. Women such as her do as much harm to the suffrage cause as all the devotees of Mr Fish combined. Although, to be fair, the Homemakers do refrain from violent abuse."

"Let me guess," Molly said. "She also thinks that it would be unseemly to be seen at a polling station. And that women do not have the interest or intellectual capacity for politics."

"Exactly, although I do have my suspicions that my neighbour has a greater intellectual capacity than she admits to. Perhaps that is why she is so cross at me for having the temerity to attend university."

Molly hoisted her satchel on her shoulder and took Grace's arm. "Fascinating as it is to dissect the characters of our neighbours, we'd better get going. I'd like to get a few signatures back to Miss Nicol at the meeting this afternoon. She is as eager as I am to see if this anonymous spy in the enemy camp is correct."

Two hours later, they had ample evidence from irate women who said they'd signed Fish's petition after being told the petition was in favour of women's franchise, not against it. Also, half a dozen abusive husbands ordering them off the premises and several women too ashamed to admit they had been fooled. One woman had hustled them outside and whispered that her husband had made her sign. She had cast a worried glance back at the curtained window, before scribbling a signature on their form and hurrying back indoors.

All the women said that two men had come to their door. One had been short and intimidating, the other as big and hairy as a bear, without the ferocity. "He had ever such lovely green eyes," five women said, which only made Grace more suspicious about the anonymous provider of the handwritten list. Charlie Pyke had unforgettable eyes – almond shaped, gold flecked emeralds.

"Well, I think we have proved the point," Molly said. "Twenty-two signatures in two hours. Makes you wonder how many other women were deceived. Let's take this back to Miss Nicol. She will want to contact the national franchise superintendent, Mrs Sheppard, to make sure this is not happening in other regions around the country."

Molly and Grace took a shortcut alongside the Water of Leith, too deep in conversation to notice the trio of young men slouching by the bridge until it was too late.

One of the men stepped into their path. "What do you two slatterns think you're up to? Women like you should be at home looking after your husbands, not out making a spectacle of yourselves." His voice slurred drunkenly, although it was not much past the noon hour.

"Women are people too," Molly retorted. "We deserve the same rights as men. More rights than drunks and street blackguards, for sure."

"Molly, come away," Grace pleaded. "They're not worth the aggravation."

Molly held her ground, her arms crossed. "Stand aside."

The man spat a stream of tobacco juice at her feet. "How dare you talk to me like that? Your husband ought to put you over his knee and thrash you." He lurched closer to Molly, grabbing for her arm. "If he won't, I reckon it's up to me to teach you some manners."

The other two men roused themselves, no doubt sensing easy prey for a little fun to enliven their day. One moved between Grace and Molly, the second seized Molly as she stumbled backwards.

He pulled Molly closer until their faces were inches apart. "How about we dunk the cheeky wench in the Leith to teach her that her place is in the washhouse."

"Leave her alone!" Grace swung around, looking for help, but there was none to be had. If that idiot threw Molly into the river, the weight of her clothes would surely drag her to her death.

The man in front of Grace grabbed at the crotch of his trousers. "I'd rather show them a woman's place is in the bedchamber."

Fortunately, he was the most inebriated of the three. His fumbling unbalanced him, landing him at Grace's feet. She took the opportunity to show him what she thought of his plan, leaving him rolling in the gutter shrieking unrepeatable oaths.

When she looked around again, she saw Molly had been dragged to the edge of the bridge. Her mouth was stifled by the second man's hand, but her eyes were wide with a plea for help. Her captor was the steadiest on his feet, using his greater weight to pin Molly against the railing.

Their initial tormentor urged him on. "Throw her in, Smitty. Let's see if the witch floats or sinks. That'll teach her to obey her betters."

Smitty was bending down to hoist Molly over the railing when Grace hit him full in the side of the head with Molly's dropped satchel. The extra force from the swing of the long shoulder strap, combined with the power of Grace's desperation, knocked him to the ground. He lay still, his head at an angle against the metal rail.

Grace hesitated between her instinct to flee and her duty as a doctor to check his vital signs. The rush of footsteps behind her caught her off guard. Molly charged past her, head down. Grace turned just in time to see Molly's head impacting the approaching man's soft belly. He spun around and retched up a morning's worth of cheap ale.

The man Grace had felled was now groaning and pushing himself semi-upright on the bridge railings. Grace grabbed Molly's arm. They hoisted their skirts to their ankles and fled to the next intersection, leaping onto a passing tram and collapsing into an empty seat with trembling relief.

The gut-punched lout was left panting a few paces behind, weaving across the pavement, clutching his belly. As the tram pulled away, their attacker yelled a final battle cry. "Vengeance against rabid Jezebels shall be ours!"

Outraged Gent

Charlie Pyke left his boarding house early on Saturday morning. He needed to brief his commanding officer on last night's meeting before he started work at the Engineers' Arms again at noon. He had to sprint to catch a departing tram, which gave him a chance to check if anyone was following him. Undercover work always came with a large helping of suspicion. It might not do his nerves much good, but it kept him alive.

On the tram, he grabbed a dangling leather strap to steady himself, as he listening to the conversations around him. There was nothing like a trip on public transport to reveal the mood of the populace.

A young woman was sitting ahead of him. Her dark hair and slim features reminded him slightly of Grace, except for the submissive dip of her head as the man beside her spoke. Many adjectives might be used to describe a complex woman like Grace Penrose, but submissive was not one of them.

"Don't let my arm go when we get to town," her husband ordered. "I saw several men abusing ladies yesterday. I'm not sure what has got into them, but I don't want you subjected to any untoward behaviour. Indeed, I think it might be better if you stayed at home, my dear…"

The rest of the sentence was cut off as the tram stopped to take on more passengers, forcing Charlie to move further along the aisle to where a group of men had their heads buried in the *Otago Daily Times*.

A man shook out a crease in his newspaper, letting out an annoyed grunt as he tapped a headline. "More anarchists in Europe, running riot with dynamite and bombs. Our government ought to be taking more notice of suspicious foreigners, instead of harassing ordinary working men."

"Aye," agreed the man beside him. "They'll not want for explosives if they come to our shores. Look, here's Briscoes advertising blasting powder and dynamite for sale to the public. Shouldn't be allowed. It's bad enough having to fend off temperance fanatics on every corner, without worrying about anarchists."

Charlie lost interest as the men began to discuss which public house they would drown their sorrows in after work. He knew from Detective Inspector Wallace that the politicians – and thus the police force – were on edge. The newspapers had been reporting almost daily on the latest anarchist bombings around the world. He'd been ordered to keep an ear to the ground for signs of suspicious activity, even if it was only the unions acting up. It struck Charlie as ironic that the Liberal government, which was meant to favour the working man over landed gentry, was worried about labour activism. Too many gentlemen in charge, in his opinion, and not enough true working-class men, like Seddon.

Despite the early hour on a Saturday morning, DI Wallace and DC Kelly were both at the police station, poring over a map together. The two men were cut from the same cloth, although their tartans were separated by the Irish Sea. Solid, dependable, dedicated policemen, who got the job done without fear or favour, although without the flair of his own commanding officer, DI Stewart.

Stewart had once told him that he and Wallace had gone to school together in Edinburgh and played for the same rugby football team. Charlie had no problem imagining the burly Wallace as the relentless player who won the ball from rucks and tackles, passing it on to the slim, fleet-footed Stewart to weave his magic to the try line.

Wallace looked up from the map. "Pyke, I didn't expect to see you here."

"I have information that I didn't want to entrust to a messenger."

"My office. You too, Kelly."

Kelly closed the door behind them. Nobody else, aside from the Chief Inspector, knew Charlie's real identity. The desk officers had been told that he was a valued police informant, who should be directed only to Kelly or Wallace. Charlie recognised a few policemen from when he had worked in Dunedin over two years ago, but none of them had recognised him under the unkempt beard and wild hair. Most people took one whiff of him and turned away.

Charlie addressed his designated mission first. "Thanks to Kelly's acting skills, I could finally see upstairs at the Engineers' Arms. Bertram keeps a well-appointed room up there, which I'm sure he uses for after-hours gambling. I saw him take a couple of packs of cards out of a concealed draw, but I didn't get a chance to look through the locked cupboards."

Wallace grunted. "It's a start at least, but we'll need more evidence to raid the place, especially with so many other matters claiming our attention. I suspect you didn't risk coming here to tell me that."

"We have another problem, sir," Charlie said. "Have you seen this letter published in the *Otago Workman*?"

Wallace reached across to take the newspaper clipping from him. "I hope you don't make a habit of reading that radical rag, Pyke."

"All part of the job, sir. Lister's paper is widely read amongst the working men of Dunedin. Lister himself is outspoken against temperance and the women's franchise movement and it seems he is gathering like-minded louts to his cause. The writer of this little gem calls himself Outraged Gent. He reckons Fish's petition doesn't go far enough, that direct action is needed to stop women getting the vote."

Wallace's face wrinkled with distaste as he read the letter. "Good heavens, I've never read such ridiculous inflammatory rhetoric. 'Rise up against the rabid Jezebels … vengeance shall be ours.' The man is a lunatic. If I can find out who this Outraged Gent is, I'll have him for inciting violence. I'm surprised Lister agreed to publish it. Even 'The Chiseler' would not go so far in his infamous columns."

It seemed as if Wallace did read the *Otago Workman* after all, if he knew of The Chiseler's satirical column, which delighted in sharp invective directed at the many causes despised by Lister, the publisher.

"It's highly provocative," Wallace continued. "So much so, I shouldn't wonder if it turns the general public away from Fish's cause. Even his own party has distanced themselves from him after his endless speeches in the House last year. He'd be far more successful if he didn't revel in giving offence to friend and foe alike."

Charlie agreed Fish was a fool for inflaming the suffragists, but that didn't make him less of a danger. "Fish has a following in South Dunedin amongst working men. They may well read this and take Outraged Gent at his word."

"Abuse and heckling at temperance meetings has been on the rise," Kelly noted, "and we've had reports of women being harassed on the streets. That petition of Mr Fish's seems to have stirred the scum in the pot to the surface. Outraged Gent sounds like the latest on the bandwagon."

"Kelly is right, sir," Charlie said. "The reason I risked meeting you this morning is that I overheard a meeting last night between four men associated with the liquor trade. The publican of the Engineers' Arms, Harry Bertram, called the meeting to discuss taking more forcible action against the women's franchise movement. I'm sure Bertram is Outraged Gent."

Wallace rubbed a hand over his chin. "Did Bertram say what type of action he was suggesting?"

"I could not hear the specifics, but his tone was aggressive. He was advocating direct action using shock tactics, saying that petitions and speeches were not enough. The publicans are terrified that, if women get the vote, the prohibition of alcohol will follow. The implication was that they would do anything to stop it."

31

"Do you have names for the four men?"

"Only Harry Bertram, not the others." Charlie pushed over a sheet of paper with sketches of the four men. "Best I could do, as I had little chance to look at them." He tapped the page. "This one is Bertram. This one is Irish, with pale hair and a rasp."

"The sketch is a good likeness. I know him all right," Wallace replied. "Owen Gilroy, a publican in west Dunedin. He was warned for threatening the five prohibitionists who got themselves elected to the Roslyn licensing committee and closed down one of his hotels last year. Gilroy is a nasty piece of work."

"The third man is shorter than average but makes up for it in bulk. Reddish hair, Irish, pugnacious attitude."

"What do you think, Kelly?"

"Sounds like Conor Sweeney. He's a tough customer, and two of his hotels are under threat of closure. We've dealt with frequent incidents of fighting and accusations of after-hours drinking, but Sweeney is as slippery as an eel."

Charlie's low opinion of the men wasn't improved by hearing more about them. "Number four was about my height and build, with dark hair. I never saw his face. More of a gentleman than the others and definitely the most reluctant of the four to commit to direct action. The only name I heard was 'Mac'. Not very useful in a town with so many Scottish immigrants."

"Doesn't ring any bells with me," Kelly said.

"Thank you for bringing this to my attention, Pyke." Wallace sat back in his chair, assessing the information. "I want you to keep a close watch on these men, but only if you are sure that your identity hasn't been compromised. I don't like all this subterfuge. In my experience, it often ends badly if we try to keep a man in place too long."

"Bertram is suspicious of outsiders, but I think he has accepted me. The barman, Vance, keeps a close watch on my every move. I'll try to be careful."

"See that you are. Kelly, let's get to work on these men and see what they are up to. Hopefully, we can stop them before they do anything stupid. And Pyke, I want you out of there if you get the faintest inkling that they are on to you."

Fireworks

Grace's heart was still pounding when she and Molly got off the tram in the Octagon. Suffragists were used to verbal abuse, but the brazen malevolence of this attack was in a league of its own. She and Molly both knew from experience the terror of having one's life threatened and that was exactly what those louts had made her feel. A few seconds later and Molly might have been drowned.

Grace glanced at her friend, who looked outwardly calm to a casual observer. Grace wasn't fooled. The signs were clear – pale, clammy skin, tight facial muscles, shallow breathing, twitching at any unexpected sound. But, try as she might, she had failed to convince Molly to go home and rest. Her friend was unwavering in her determination to tell Miss Nicol about their findings. Grace consented, but only because she felt their fellow suffragists should be made aware of this new level of intimidation as soon as possible.

They rounded the corner of Princes Street and walked up Moray Place to Choral Hall. Up and down the street, miserable looking horses huddled in their traces, while the coachmen slouched with raised collars and tightly wrapped scarves against the chill wind. A baker's dozen of women were gathered outside the entrance to the hall, stamping their feet to stay warm. One of the women saw them coming and stepped out to wave at Molly.

Molly hurried up the road to greet her, conveying her usual cheerfulness despite her brush with the grim reaper. "Mrs Creswell, how splendid to see you here again. Have you met Miss Grace Penrose yet? Grace, this is Mrs Violet Creswell, a new recruit to our cause."

"I have not had the pleasure, although I might venture to say that I have heard a great deal about you from Miss Sugden." Violet was as delicate as her name – a slight lass, with a fine bone structure

34

and blushing cheeks, who looked up at Grace demurely from beneath long lashes.

Grace banished thoughts of their attackers in favour of a smile. "Welcome to the 'shrieking sisterhood', as our detractors like to call us. We may be forced to adopt a fierce outward demeanour at times for the sake of the cause, but I hazard a guess that you will not find such amusing company or loyal friends anywhere else in Dunedin."

When Mrs Creswell raised her head, Grace realised she was not a young girl, but a woman of perhaps thirty, with sorrowful eyes and an eager-to-please smile. "I have no doubt of that, Miss Penrose. I only wish I had had the courage to join the suffrage cause earlier. There are many wrongs cast upon womanhood. I was blind not to realise that no one but women themselves could change that."

Molly smiled at her friend. "Well said, Mrs Creswell. Now then, can you tell me why we are stranded outside Choral Hall like a group of street urchins?"

"The caretaker says we must wait outside until the proper ladies have finished," Mrs Creswell replied. "I do not think he cares much for suffragists."

"Taylor is a curmudgeon, who cares for little but the bottle," Molly agreed. "But you are right, he has a special antipathy towards women who do not know their place in society."

"Perhaps we ought not cast aspersions on the man," Mrs Creswell ventured. "He may be cantankerous because of some terrible grief or pain."

"You are very charitable," Grace said, "but his ruddy face is ample evidence of drinking to excess. Whatever pain he suffers is as likely because of gout as any other cause. If you ladies would excuse me, I must greet a friend."

Tiny Tim huddled in a doorway across the street. Grace wondered how she had not noticed him before, as his bulk was never easy to miss. As she crossed the street, she reminded herself that he was no longer the young lad she had met over two years ago, who

35

had given up his job as an enforcer at a gambling den to help them at Lavender House.

"Mr Timothy Shorten, if my eyes do not deceive me. I have not seen you since your marriage."

His rugged face transformed into a smile. "Miss Penrose, how nice to see you. It's plain Tim to you, as you well know."

"How are you, Tim?"

"Never better, Miss Penrose. How could I be otherwise, with a wife as wonderful as Alice? I am a lucky man and no mistake. I'm working for Alice's father these days, delivering coal. It's a good job, though I miss the Lavender ladies."

"We miss you as well. Johnny Todd still does a fine job of transporting our aged and infirm to their medical appointments, but you two were a marvellous team. A friend of Mrs Macmillan's, Mr Drummond, has given Johnny the loan of a horse and buggy."

"Aye. I never hear the end of it. Johnny is as proud as Punch to be master of his own wheels. What the—"

The events of the next few seconds happened so fast that Grace was left gasping, yet so slowly that time passed at a fraction of the normal speed. Tim's wife noticed Grace talking to Tim and started across the street. The caretaker opened the door, demanding that the suffragists make way for the ladies of the Orphans' Benevolent Society. Mrs Creswell flinched at his gruff command and stepped backward into the street, pulling her hat low over her eyes.

And all around them, the air filled with the sharp tuk-tuk-tuk of a series of small explosions. Miserable horses transformed into frightened hulks of muscle, not knowing which way to flee, fighting their startled coachmen for control. The nearest horse, which was right on top of the noise, reared and plunged forward, tipping its driver from his perch and plunging into the paths of Mrs Shorten and Mrs Creswell.

Molly and Tim reacted with stunning speed. Molly yanked Mrs Creswell back onto the pavement, avoiding the edge of the wildly swinging buggy by a hair's breadth. Tim surged towards the terrified horse, grabbing its bridle and forcing it away from his wife by sheer brute strength.

The horse reared again, catching Mrs Shorten with a hoof. Tim pulled the horse's head down, all the while shushing it with calming words. The horse and buggy were almost at Princes Street by the time he had it under control.

Grace rushed to the spot where Alice Shorten had dropped to her knees, her eyes wide with shock and pain. "Where did the hoof hit you, Alice?"

Alice dragged her eyes away from her husband's fight to control the horse. "I'm fine, Grace. You'd better go to my Tim, in case he is hurt."

"It would take more than a bolting horse to hurt your Tim, Alice." Grace noted the way Alice was clutching her arm to her belly. "Is it your arm or your belly that the hoof struck?"

"Only a glancing blow to my arm." Alice held out her left arm.

Grace took it gently and rolled up her sleeve. She felt along the arm, which was already swelling. "Thanks heavens, it is not broken, but you will have a nasty bruise. It must hurt like the devil."

One of her fellow suffragists appeared beside them. "Is it bleeding? I found some clean muslin cloths and water, if you need them."

"No blood, but these are just what we need." Grace bandaged the arm to help reduce the swelling and fashioned a sling. "This will help to keep it elevated and rested, Alice."

The driver had picked himself off the ground and hastened to them. "Is the lass all right, Miss? I'm terribly sorry. It gave me such a shock, I couldn't hold our Bess to rights. Damnable little guttersnipe set off firecrackers right under us, if you'll pardon my language, ladies."

"We can see that it wasn't your fault. Fortunately, Mrs Shorten wasn't badly injured. Did you see the boy?"

"Not more'n a glimpse, Miss. Street urchin, I'll be bound. Ragged little toad only looked about nine or ten years old. He were

37

off like a greyhound as soon as the ruckus started. If you're not in need of my help, I'd best be seeing to my Bess. Thank the Lord that big fellow was so quick on his feet or there'd have been blood on the street."

"My husband," Alice said, with the fervent pride of a newlywed.

The object of her affections flung himself to his knees beside them a moment later. "Alice, my dearest, are you badly hurt?"

Alice scrambled to her feet, with Grace's help. "I'm right as rain, my darling, thanks to you. Thought I was a goner when I saw that hoof flying towards my noggin. Couldn't believe my eyes when you pulled the beast away. Can you take me home, Tim?"

"Try to rest your arm," Grace called out after her, but the two of them had set off down the street, with eyes only for each other.

Grace suddenly became aware of the crowd of onlookers, which included both suffragists and ladies from the Orphans' Benevolent Society. "All's well, ladies, no need to linger. Disaster was averted thanks to some quick thinking by Miss Sugden and Mr Shorten."

Her neighbour detached herself from the charity group and hurried towards Grace. "Might I offer you a ride home and a glass of sherry to fortify yourself, Miss Penrose? I imagine you must be feeling rather overcome by the shock."

"Mrs Patterson, how very kind of you, but I must attend my meeting." Grace was grateful for her thoughtfulness and of a mind to use the opportunity to improve their neighbourly relations. "Perhaps we could have that sherry another time? I have been meaning to ask you how you grow such impressive quantities of fruit in your garden, if you are willing to share your secrets."

"That would be delightful, Miss Penrose. I shall inquire of our gardener." Mrs Patterson departed up the street, fluttering her hand to summon her carriage.

Grace looked around for Molly, finding her huddled in a doorway, shivering uncontrollably and biting back tears. Grace took off her coat and wrapped it around her friend's shoulders.

"I'm sorry, Grace. I was a fool to take on those ruffians at the bridge. We might have been killed."

"You have no need to apologise, Molly. They were intent on harm, no matter what we did. Your courage in standing up to them will probably save other women from their harassment, as bullies only become emboldened if nobody takes a stand. And now you have saved another woman as well."

"Poor Mrs Creswell. She has been through quite enough in her life without being nearly trampled by a horse. It's … it's all been a bit much for one day."

"What is Mrs Creswell's story?" Grace asked, to keep Molly's mind off the day's traumatic events.

"Her husband died in a tunnel collapse. She told me she had been given a small pension, but not enough to survive the loss of her husband's income. She had to find a job to make ends meet. You can see why the two of us have formed a friendship."

"You're the perfect friend for her, Molly. I am in awe of your capacity to cope after losing a loved one."

"I had no choice but to go on after my fiancé died. Weeping did me no good, though it didn't stop me. And now here I am, on the verge of tears again." Molly took a shuddering breath. "How is Alice?"

"A nasty bruise, but not enough to stop Alice. She's tough, like you."

A familiar woman approached them from across the street. "Is Molly hurt?"

Grace struggled to recall the woman's name. Her brain seemed to be functioning at quarter speed. Finally, it came to her. "Molly's had two bad shocks this morning, Mrs Addison, but she is not injured."

"I will take her home in my buggy. If she needs a doctor, my husband can see her."

"Thank you, but I think her own home would be best. Mrs Addison, can you tell me if Mrs Creswell was hurt? She disappeared before I could see to her."

"She was uninjured. I'm not sure why she rushed off in such haste. Perhaps the shock was too much. I must say, I feel quite shaken myself after such a close call. What in the name of heaven was the frightful noise that set that horse off?"

"Firecrackers, according to the buggy driver." Grace pulled Molly to her feet. "Right, my friend, let's get you home."

"Grace, would you mind taking my satchel to Miss Nicol? I want her to know what we found as soon as possible."

"Of course, Molly. Now off you go and do as Mrs Addison says."

A buggy pulled in beside them. When Molly was seated, Mrs Addison wrapped her in a blanket and returned Grace's coat.

"I'll visit as soon as I can," Grace called after them.

The street was more or less empty now, as the remaining women had sought the shelter of Choral Hall. Grace searched the spot where the horse had taken fright, finding a string of two dozen blackened cylinders, with the last few squashed and unlit. The horse must have stood on the wick and put it out before the last crackers could go off. She wrapped them in a spare petition form, in case the police wanted them as evidence.

Helen Nicol, the franchise superintendent for Dunedin, was hurrying up the street, her face beet red. As she came closer, Grace saw that the flush was because of anger, not haste. The bottom of her skirts slopped around her legs as if she had waded through a stream.

"What has happened to you, Miss Nicol?" Grace asked. Helen Nicol was one of her heroines, a pioneer of the campaign to gain women the vote, who had devoted her life to the betterment of society. Not a woman to be swayed from her imperturbable determination by anything less than a hurricane.

"That rotten swine from the Golden Shamrock Hotel on Princes Street. The barman emptied his beer slops on me as I passed. If it hadn't been for a warning cry from a passer-by, I'd have been soaked from head to foot. Indeed, I was fortunate that the pail itself missed my head by a whisker. He pretended the pail had slipped from his fingers, but I could see from his malicious grin that it was no accident. I gave him a piece of my mind, I can tell you. And now I am both sopping wet and late for the meeting."

"I've a cloth you can use to wipe yourself down." Grace held out the muslin.

Miss Nicol pressed the cloth to the sodden skirt. "Is Miss Sugden here? I'm eager to hear how her door-knocking went."

Grace opened Molly's satchel and handed the signed sheets to Miss Nicol. "We got the signatures of over twenty women who were deceived into signing the Fish petition. Every name on the anonymous list, in fact, of the few we had time to speak to."

Miss Nicol's anger transformed into glee. "Excellent work. Sir John Hall has promised to take the matter up with the authorities if we can prove signatures are being collected under false pretences. It would appear the Mr Fish is about to be skewered by his own gaff. I, for one, will not be sorry to see it."

"Miss Nicol, before we go inside, I think you should know that Molly and I were threatened and physically attacked by a trio of drunken louts this morning. Molly was almost thrown off a bridge, which is why I sent her home. And two suffragists were nearly run over a moment ago, after a boy lit firecrackers under a horse."

"Oh, my goodness. Was anyone hurt?"

"Molly and I escaped only by the luck of a passing tram. Molly's quick thinking saved Mrs Creswell from the horse. Mr Shorten saved his wife, Alice, who escaped with a painful bruise. Any of us might have been injured or killed. Add your own attack and we have three potentially serious incidents in one day."

"Four incidents, in fact, Miss Penrose. I had a note from Mrs Rachel Reynolds this morning to say she came back from a

41

temperance meeting yesterday to find her prize rose bushes had been slashed and a threatening note left on her veranda."

"Has she notified the police, Miss Nicol?"

"No. She is not one to be cowed by a little spite. However, in light of these other incidents, perhaps we ought to inform the authorities, in addition to warning our ladies to be on guard against troublemakers."

"Shall I speak to the police?"

"Thank you, Miss Penrose. Yes, please do make use of your contacts in the force. I will convey the news to Harriet Morison and Marion Hatton. We must all take extra precautions."

Miss Nicol glanced down at her stained skirt. "Perhaps I should call a halt to our women canvassing for signatures. We have almost seven thousand already from our region. Kate Sheppard is in transports of delight at our success." Her voice trailed off. "I have no wish to put our women in harm's way, but I did have such hopes of reaching the full seven thousand."

Grace could understand her dilemma. The last thing any of them wanted was for their attackers to frighten the suffragists into inaction. "Perhaps we would be safer if we went about in teams of four, two to each side of a street?"

"Yes, that would be a most practical solution. I do believe this will be the last straw that will turn parliament against Mr Fish. His arrogance and deceit will be the making of our cause."

"Shall I visit the police immediately or go after the meeting?" Grace asked.

"The police should know straight away, given the serious nature of the incidents."

Miss Nicol sailed into Choral Hall, an elfin battleship sweeping forward on a wave of determination, while Grace headed to the police station on legs that refused to stop shaking.

The Source

The desk officer at the central police station recognised Grace and called DC Kelly, who hurried her up to Wallace's office as soon as Grace uttered her first sentence. Grace was taken aback by his show of concern, which surely must have stemmed from something more than their brief past acquaintance. She had half expected that she would be laughed at when she complained of childish pranks like thrown firecrackers and beer slops.

When Grace had gone through the incidents in detail, twice (leaving out the rose incident, as she had no authority to speak for Mrs Reynolds), Wallace leaned back in his chair, his powerful jaw rigid with dark thoughts. Kelly turned over the remnants of the firecrackers in his fingers, as if the answer lay within the charred remains.

"I confess I did not expect these incidents to be accorded such attention, Detective Inspector Wallace. Am I correct in discerning that you were expecting something of this sort to happen?"

"You are correct, Miss Penrose, although I confess I am alarmed by how quickly events have escalated. Serious threats of physical harm to you and Miss Sugden, a heavy wooden pail thrown at Miss Nicol's head, and two women nearly run over by a horse – all in the space of a few hours. I'd say we are lucky that nobody is in the hospital or worse." Wallace lapsed into silence, drumming his fingers on the desk, before coming to a decision. "I don't suppose you have seen this letter in the newspaper, written by a man calling himself Outraged Gent?"

Grace took the newspaper clipping. "No, the *Otago Workman* is not a favoured newspaper of suffragists such as myself. My great-aunt takes the *Otago Daily Times* out of habit and respect for her late husband. I prefer the *Evening Star*."

Her outer body froze as she read the letter, while her insides churned with revulsion at the tirade. The most obnoxious section of the extended rant read: "Men of Dunedin, do not let your wives and daughters be coerced into signing the women's franchise petition, which is being forced upon them by rabid Jezebels, led by a shrieking sisterhood of bitter old maids. For women to seek a vote is an abomination against our Lord. Be warned, the righteous husbands and fathers of this land shall rise up against the outrage. Vengeance shall be ours."

"I imagine even the egregious Mr Lister must have consulted his conscience before he published this venomous drivel." Grace dropped the clipping back on the desk, wiping her hands on her skirt as if she had touched a noxious substance. "One of the men who attacked Molly and I this morning yelled out 'vengeance against rabid Jezebels shall be ours', as we escaped on the tram. I believe they were serious in their threat to throw Molly from the King Street bridge into the Leith."

"I agree it is very disturbing, Miss Penrose. We have had reports of verbal abuse before, but never anything as serious as this. Do you know which hotel Miss Nicol was passing when the bucket was thrown?"

"The Golden Shamrock, on Princes Street."

"Owned by Conor Sweeney," Kelly said, with grim emphasis.

"Miss Nicol is a vocal supporter of temperance," Grace said. "She has also been instrumental in organising the franchise cause in Dunedin, along with her friend, Miss Morison, and others."

"Do you think Nicol and Morison are the bitter old maids of the letter?" Kelly asked.

"Probably. Neither of them is married, although they are hardly old, being in their thirties. The only bitterness in them is in their views on men who would suppress the rights of women. They are outspoken in their opposition to the Fish petition, without doubt, but thoroughly admirable women, in my opinion."

44

"Miss Morison has not been targeted, as far as you know?" Wallace asked.

"I have not heard of any attack on her. Miss Nicol will warn her and others. It may be a coincidence, but the woman who was injured outside Choral Hall works for Harriet Morison at the Dunedin Tailoresses' Union."

"I don't trust coincidences, Miss Penrose. I am relieved to hear that Miss Nicol is taking the threat seriously."

"Thank you, Detective Inspector. Your concern is appreciated."

"Did you see the boy who let off the crackers?"

"My attention was on the bolting horse and the injury to Mrs Shorten. The driver said that he was a small, ragged urchin, probably around nine to ten years old. Not the type of lad to have money to spare for firecrackers."

"Especially not these ones," Kelly said. "Not the sort of little bangers you can buy cheap."

"We'll find the boy. He'll have been paid to do this, I don't doubt, and any young lads with coins in their pockets tend to brag. The only problem is that lads like him won't talk to the police. Don't you worry, Miss Penrose, we have a fair idea who is behind this spate of attacks." Wallace let his gaze rest on her, his mouth quirking to the side. "We have a man on the case."

Grace frowned. "You appear to be amused, Detective Inspector Wallace."

"Why do you say that, Miss Penrose?"

"Because, if you will forgive my impertinence, you have a slight tic to the edge of your mouth when you are amused, but do not wish to show it."

Wallace's lips tightened on one side, before he caught the movement and stopped it. "Detective Inspector Stewart, did warn me about you."

"Oh dear. My reputation as a troublemaker is spreading."

"Quite the opposite. He warned me not to underestimate you, nor to ignore your views merely because you have the outward appearance of an innocent young lady. Have you seen Stewart or his detective constable lately?"

"Not since December last year. I have not even had so much as a letter from either of them for several weeks. I suspect they must be up to something that they would not wish an innocent young lady to know about. I do hope you are going to enlighten me, rather than sitting there like the Cheshire Cat."

Grace did not mention her suspicion that it was Charlie who had written the list of suspect signatories to the Fish petition. If he did not want to make his presence known to her, he must have a compelling reason. But if Wallace was ready to confess, she was eager to hear it.

"Alistair Stewart is one of my oldest friends, despite our differences in style. I prefer to go by the book, whereas Stewart works by instinct and cunning, with what some might call a reckless disregard for rules. However, he gets away with it because he has been extremely successful. I rather think Pyke is a man made in his image. What do you think, Miss Penrose?"

"I have little knowledge of policing methods, Detective Inspector Wallace, so I should not care to speculate."

His smile spread to his eyes. "Come now, Miss Penrose, I think we both know that is not true."

Grace couldn't help but return the smile. "If you insist on having my opinion, I would say that DC Pyke is willing to use his intelligence and initiative. But, above all else, he will do what he thinks is right and just, regardless of the consequences to himself. Rather like both Stewart and yourself, I believe. Any recklessness you may have perceived in him is entirely my fault, as I do have a tendency towards acting precipitously, forcing Charlie to come to my aid."

Wallace's lips skewed up again, but this time he let it flow into a deep chuckle. "As a matter of fact, I agreed to give Pyke a temporary assignment here in Dunedin, on the condition that he did not contact you or any of his other local acquaintances. The matter is highly sensitive, and I could not risk anyone finding out about it."

"Charlie's here, in Dunedin?" Even though she had suspected it, Grace couldn't control either her heartbeat or the rush of blood to her cheeks.

"It appears he has passed my little test of his ability to obey orders, even when faced with a strong inducement to do otherwise." Wallace rose from his seat. "I thank you again for bringing these incidents to my attention, Miss Penrose, and for gathering evidence. Be assured that the police force is taking action in the matter. I suggest you warn your fellow suffragists to take additional precautions to ensure their safety."

Grace rose as well. "It has already been done."

"I fear this is not the end of it. I only hope it does not spiral out of control." Wallace held the door open for her. "I will give Pyke leave to see you, when I see him next."

Grace's heart leapt, but her brain reeled it in. "Only if you are sure it will not compromise his safety. These are not men to be trifled with. I hope he knows what he has gotten himself into."

In truth, she wondered what all of them had gotten into.

Rescue

Charlie used the half hour he had to spare before he started work to prowl the local market for something more edible than his landlady's watery porridge, which tasted more like tea-tree sawdust than oats.

He was brushing Cornish pasty crumbs off his jacket when he spotted Mrs Vance buying vegetables. The vendor emptied a pile of potatoes from the scales into her basket, making her wince as the weight dragged her arm down.

"May I help you carry that basket back to the Engineers' Arms, Mrs Vance?"

"Oh, Mr Potts, you startled me." She hesitated. "Thank you for the offer, but it's best if I carry it."

"Perhaps if I take it to the corner of South Road. You can carry as soon as we are within sight of the hotel."

She scanned the crowd before replying. "Well, it is heavy." With a last glance around, she handed the basket over. "It's not that I'm ungrateful, but Mr Vance doesn't like me to accept help from other men."

Not that he ever gave his wife any help of his own, Charlie thought. What he did give her was obvious from the livid mark on her wrist under the checked gingham of her sleeve. "That's a nasty bruise. It must be painful to carry a heavy basket."

She yanked the sleeve down. "I'm terribly clumsy. Mr Vance says he's never seen such a one as me for bumping into things."

Charlie wanted to question her, but knew he had to treat her with kid gloves or she would stop talking altogether. He took the basket and followed her, keeping two steps behind so he would appear to be a lackey rather than a companion. "What do you think of Mr Bertram's friends? The ones who came to play cards last night," he asked, with the air of a man filling time with idle chatter.

Mrs Vance considered the question, before deciding it held no hint of rebuke. "The tall one is a gentleman. He speaks kindly to me and even brought me a nice bit of lace once. I reckon he must be foreign, cos he insists on kissing me. Seems improper to me, but he says it is the custom where he comes from, so not to allow it would be impolite." She turned to look up at Charlie with pleading eyes. "I can't afford to give offence to the publican's friends."

"No, indeed. Is that the one called Mac? I don't think I heard his full name."

"They only ever call him Mac, although I did once hear Mr Bertram call him Lenny."

"Are the others not as nice as Mac?"

She shivered, though she was wrapped in a heavy woollen shawl against the chill of the day. "Mr Gilroy and Mr Sweeney are uncommon free with their hands. I tell them I don't like it, but they just laugh. It ain't right, but Vance gets cross if I complain."

"And Mr Bertram?"

"Oh no, he never touches me, but he never stops them doing it neither. He looks away and tells me to get on with my job."

"A woman has the right to leave her home when it is not safe. There are places you can go."

"Only the Benny and I ain't going there. Vance would find me."

"The Benevolent Home is right in Caversham. I can see that wouldn't be a good idea. But I know a place further away, where I can guarantee you won't be found. It's called Lavender House. The women who run it are very caring and discreet. I promise you would be safe there."

They had almost reached the final corner. Mrs Vance took the basket and scurried away without another word. Charlie was relieved that he wouldn't have to risk getting into a dispute with the barman, though the better part of him wanted to whisk Mrs Vance

49

to safety at once. He took a turn around the block, arriving back at the Engineers' Arms from the opposite direction.

He was soon glad he had succumbed to the second pasty – lugging casks around all afternoon was hard work.

By evening, the hotel was filling up fast with the usual Saturday night crowd, eager to lose themselves in drink and companionship after their week's work, knowing they could sleep it off in church tomorrow morning.

Charlie saw one of the regulars talking to the barman, glancing his way. Their sly exchange had him bracing for trouble. With luck, he had only been spotted with Mrs Vance. If they had found out he was a policeman, he could well end up floating across the Pacific Ocean, sealed inside a beer barrel.

Vance strode over to Charlie and yanked him into the back room. The barman grabbed the front of his waistcoat and forced him against the wall. "What d'ya think you're playing at, Potts, talking to my wife in the market and walking her home?"

Charlie willed the tension in his muscles to fade into limpness and contrition, as he shrunk back against the wall. "I meant nothing by it, Mr Vance, honest. I happened on her and she had a heavy basket, so I thought it only polite to offer help. She said she could manage, but I insisted. My apologies if I have caused you any offence."

Vance let him go, though his fist hovered in the air. "See that it doesn't happen again, Potts."

Charlie was too busy for the rest of the evening to think any more of it. He followed orders until his body ached for the lumpy squalor of his bed. When the last drunk rolled out the door, well after the legal closing hour, all he wanted was to head back to his lodgings, knowing that tomorrow was a day of rest.

If only he had ignored the whimpering as he headed for the back door. But, of course, he couldn't. Mrs Vance was crouched in the corner of the cramped kitchen, crying. Even in the dim light, he could see she had been beaten.

"You're coming with me, right now," he commanded, reaching for her arm.

"Wait." She wriggled free of his grasp and stumbled to a tin of mustard on the highest shelf, popping the lid and taking a small roll of banknotes and a few coins out of it. She was back in seconds, pushing past him in her haste to escape.

They were within an arm's length of the back door when Vance stepped in front of them. The man who had informed on Charlie came up behind him, smelling of fresh Guinness and stale sweat.

"Where in hell do you think you are off to with my wife?" Vance snarled.

Mrs Vance ducked under his arm and fled out the door, showing an impressive turn of speed for one in so much pain. Sheer terror must have lent her wings. Charlie stopped the barman's punch with an open hand and wrenched his other arm from the grip of the man behind him, before he too fled into the night.

The footsteps behind them dropped away far more quickly than he'd dared to hope. Weeks of work building up trust at the Engineers' Arms had been destroyed in an instant, along with the chance of a permanent job in Dunedin. The one consolation was that the barman's wife was safe now. He caught up with her a block later.

She clutched at his arm like a woman drowning. "You'll look out for me, Mr Potts, as you promised? They're up to no good, I'm sure of it. I feared to say earlier, but last night I heard Mr Bertram saying, 'Before the week's out, those women will be too terrified to organise a tea party, let alone a revolution.' Fair made my blood run cold. I don't know who he meant and I don't want to hang around to find out."

The dreadful implications of those words stayed with Charlie long after her fingernail dents in his arm ceased to ache.

Sanctuary

Grace heard thumping on the front door through a haze of sleep. She pulled the covers over her head as Mrs Brown attempted to send the caller away with a flea in his ear. The man answered calmly, his voice loud enough to register in her reluctant ears. Grace's feet hit the floor of their own accord. With her dressing gown half wrapped and her hair falling over her face, she raced for the stairs.

As she entered the hallway, she had to agree with Mrs Brown's assessment. The figure at the door was no more than a flickering shape in the light of the candle, but that only enhanced the impression that they were being invaded by the shaggiest of wild bears. Yet the silhouette was achingly familiar at the same time. She ran along the hall, her pulse beating time with her steps.

Before she could say anything, the bear held up a grubby paw. "Would you be Miss Penrose?" he growled, in a not-quite-Pyke voice. "I'm Charlie Potts from the Engineers' Arms out Caversham way. Mrs Vance here needs help and I hear you're the lady to see about such matters." He gestured for the frail figure behind him to come forward.

Grace had seen that expression on a beaten woman's face far more times than she cared to recall. "Mrs Vance, welcome. Please come inside, where it is warm. You will stay with us tonight and I will see you are looked after properly tomorrow."

The woman-girl looked up at her, seemingly reluctant to leave the solid presence of Mr Charlie Potts for the unknown young lady offering refuge. "Mr Vance will come for me. I don't want to bring you no trouble."

"Don't you worry about that. We have a group of women all over the country who care for women in need. Kind women, who want nothing more than to see others safe." Grace stepped forward and took her arm, gently but firmly handing her over to the motherly Mrs Brown, who knew exactly what to do, based on decades of experience.

Mrs Brown steered Mrs Vance inside with an arm around her shoulders, a tugboat in a storm. "'Tis a raw night tonight, love. Come along, there's always a pot of soup simmering on my stove."

Grace remained at the door. "Mr Potts, would you care for a plate of hot soup – or something else – to ward off the chill?"

Charlie's eyes sparkled in the dim light. "I'm mighty tempted by your kind offer, Miss Penrose, but I ought not be seen here."

"There's always a warm welcome here for men such as yourself. There are few who would do so much for a woman in need." Grace leaned forward to whisper in his ear. "Though the welcome might be all the warmer if you'd reacquaint yourself with soap and razor."

Charlie rubbed his hand over his unkempt beard. "Not even one small kiss for a man sorely in need of affection after four months away?"

Grace screwed up her nose and planted a kiss on the least whiskery part of his cheek. "It's like kissing a hedgehog that's been swimming in beer."

"Whereas you, my dear Grace, are as fragrant as an angel dipped in rosewater." He reached out to smooth her hair, where it was rumpled from sleep. "As beautiful as ever, if perhaps a little wilder than usual, which only adds to the charm."

"I wish I could say the same about you, Mr Potts. Wilder, it is true, but hardly a picture of sartorial elegance."

He chuckled and turned into the night, throwing a few parting words over his shoulder. "By the way, if anyone asks, you never saw me."

"Mr Potts, wait." Grace ran after him, before she could ask herself, yet again, why she was so addicted to this infuriating man. "Please do not leave until I have answers to my questions."

"What questions would they be, Miss Penrose?"

"What happened to Mrs Vance?"

"Her husband beat her for talking to me. We were simply passing the time of day for a few minutes while I helped her with a heavy basket. I did not touch her or do anything untoward. She works in the tavern her husband runs in Caversham, as a barmaid and in the kitchen. I suspect he also allows the owner and his friends to abuse her, though it appears he does not go as far as prostituting her."

"Fiend. He must have been furious when you took her away. Are you injured?"

"No."

"Well, that is a pleasant change. Have you learned not to pick a fight with an angry mob?"

He smiled, showing white teeth that were entirely out of keeping with his general state of hygiene. "There were only two of them. I was the fastest runner. Mrs Vance also has an unexpected turn of speed when the situation warrants. Mind you, one was drunk, and the other had a limp, so it wasn't anything to brag about. Next question?"

"Have you somewhere to stay? Somewhere safe and warm, I mean."

"I'll be fine." Charlie glanced around as if he might be under observation. "I shan't be returning to Caversham in a hurry. Unfortunately, that also means that my temporary secondment to Dunedin might be at an end. I'm sorry I couldn't come to see you earlier, Grace."

"If you have nowhere to go, you must stay here tonight." She could see his hesitation, so she added an enticement he could not resist. "Mrs Brown made a delicious lamb hot pot tonight. It would be a shame to let the leftovers go to waste."

Still, he hesitated. As she opened her mouth to mention pudding, he sighed. "I give in. You had me convinced as soon as you said safe and warm. There is no need to mention that Mrs Brown made an apple pie too."

"How did you know I was about to say that?"

"She always does when she makes my favourite meal. It's as if she knew I was coming."

Grace shrugged her shoulders with what she hoped was a studied nonchalance. "I knew you would be here sooner or later."

"What? You knew I was in Dunedin? How…"

"Come now, DC Pyke, you know a good detective never reveals her sources. Charlie, dearest, I should close that gaping mouth if I were you, or you will be eating moths for supper. Why don't you take a seat in the garden, while I check that Mrs Vance has been tucked away safely."

She left him standing by the gate, his mouth still offering moths a sanctuary, while she glided up the path.

Mrs Vance had been put upstairs in the guest room with a basin of hot water and a bowl of soup. Grace explained Charlie's situation to Mrs Brown, who immediately put more water on the range to heat. Shaggy bear or not, Charlie had always been a favourite of their housekeeper.

Grace knocked on the door to the guest bedroom. "Mrs Vance? It is only Grace Penrose. May I come in?"

Mrs Vance was sitting on the bed in one of Grace's old nightgowns. Slim as Grace was, the nightgown swamped the frail girl. She did not meet Grace's eye as she took a seat nearby. "I don't want to be Mrs Vance anymore. My name is Ellen," she said, in a barely audible whisper.

"Do you want to go back to your maiden name or chose a new surname?"

Ellen considered the matter for a few seconds. "Could I be Mrs Ellen Potts?"

"Your husband will be looking for Mr Potts. It would be best to choose something else. How about Ellen Brown?"

"That would be grand. I wish Mrs Brown was my mother. You are both very kind, but I should not be here."

"Ellen, I know you are scared right now, but what if we could find you a situation in a kind, safe home away from your husband?"

"Vance won't find me?"

"Absolutely not. We have done this before, many times, for good women in a bad situation." She waited until Ellen nodded. "Would you be willing to let me examine your injuries? I am training to be a doctor. I realise it will be difficult for you, but it is a great help if the police should become involved."

"The police?"

"In case Vance reports you missing. Rather than waste police time, we would inform them you have been given refuge and the matter will be closed. However, we would have to justify that decision with medical evidence. If I can examine you, it will make you safer. Mrs Brown will be here as a witness."

Ellen nodded again. Grace hurried to get her bag and witness before Ellen could change her mind. When she and Mrs Brown returned, the soup bowl was empty and Ellen appeared fortified for her ordeal. Despite her initial reluctance, she submitted to the examination like a model patient. Grace found, with relief, that she had no broken bones or internal injuries. Not that the raft of bruises, new and old, was in any way trivial, but she had seen far worse.

With the examination complete, Mrs Brown tucked Ellen into bed as one might a child. When the housekeeper left, Grace sat beside Ellen and went through their standard list of questions, as calmly as if she was reciting a shopping list. Ellen responded in kind, answering all the intimate questions in a firm, if subdued, voice.

"Thank you, Ellen. The first step is the hardest, and you have managed that with courage. Sleep as long as you wish tomorrow morning." Grace kept her voice light, although inside she seethed with anger at the despicable Vance and his abusive cronies.

"It's such a soft bed, Miss Penrose. I might never wake up."

Grace left her to sleep, assured that Ellen had a strength of spirit that would blossom under the right care. Mrs Brown was back in the kitchen, clearing away an assortment of dishes, which looked as if they had been licked clean by a ravenous bear.

"I don't know why you stay with us, Mrs Brown, after all we put you through."

"I'd be bored to tears in a regular household, Miss Penrose. Helping such desperate women brings me joy."

Grace had long ago given up on getting the housekeeper to call her Grace. Amenable to midnight visitors she might be, but it came with an old-fashioned sense of position. There was no point in offering to help, so Grace settled down to write up her notes for the police, in case they were needed.

"Mr Pyke is taking a bath. I gave him the carbolic soap and some of Mrs Wu's nit lotion for his hair."

"Excellent. I hate to think where he has been living to have accumulated so much grime. Quite disgusting."

Mrs Brown's nose wrinkled in sympathy. "I had him throw his disreputable garments out the window. Mrs Macmillan supplied a respectable set of clothes from her dear departed husband's wardrobe. I've had Sadie make up the attic room for tonight. Mrs Macmillan says she will find him somewhere suitable to stay tomorrow."

"Wonderful, thank you. Do go to bed, Mrs Brown. You must be dead on your feet. I'll finish writing my report and direct Detective Constable Pyke to the attic."

"If you say so, Miss."

Grace waved away the housekeeper's uncertainty. She knew it wasn't appropriate for Charlie to stay, given their feelings for each other. He had stayed here two years ago, but only to be with his injured aunt, before they had become entangled in their first case together. But what were they to do now? Throw him out into the autumn chill to sleep under the stars, all for the sake of propriety?

She was finishing her report when a waft of carbolic warned her he had entered the kitchen. How such a big man could tread so quietly, she had never figured out. "Feeling better, Charlie?"

"Immeasurably. If I'd stayed in that foul boarding house much longer, I'd have turned rotten and decayed into earth." Charlie sat opposite her, still scratching his head. "Mrs Vance all settled?"

"Meek as a lamb. I've written a report on her injuries, if you think we should report her case to the police."

"The situation is delicate at the moment. I would rather not draw attention to my connection with the police at this point, but I will pass your report to DI Wallace. I'll see Mrs Vance gets justice when the time is right. If I am not kicked out of the force for abandoning my post."

"If you are no longer operating undercover, I suggest I take the hedge clippers to your hair and beard. Anne would have a fit if you infested her house with vermin."

"Nothing would make me happier than to get rid of both the hair and the insects. The itching has been driving me mad. Not to mention the fact that I will be unrecognisable to Vance and his mob once I get rid of the whiskers."

They swapped information on recent events as Grace cut his hair as short as he would allow her to. "Beard next. I'll trim what I can with the scissors. Do you have a shaving kit to finish the job?"

"In my bag. How are you at shaving, Grace? I'm so tired, I'd probably end up looking like one of Jack the Ripper's victims if I attempted a close shave tonight."

"I've shaved a few heads for medical reasons. If you trust me, I'll try to make you look presentable. Honestly, however inept I am with a blade, I couldn't make you look much worse."

"As long as you refrain from drawing blood, I'll be satisfied."

Charlie appeared to be asleep, or close to it, when she finished. Grace rubbed a hand lightly over his face to find any patches she had missed.

"Mm, that feels nice," he murmured.

"Farewell Charlie Potts. Welcome home Charlie Pyke." Grace patted his face with a towel, before giving in to the temptation to welcome him properly.

Charlie leaned into her kiss, running his hands around the back of her head to pull her closer. "I missed you," he whispered, as they pulled apart to catch their breath. His hand went to his face. "You left me with a moustache. It feels like one of those ridiculous thin ones that upper class dandies affect."

Grace stepped back to admire her handiwork in the dim gaslight. Not bad for a beginner, although the moustache wasn't quite straight, making him look rakish rather than distinguished. "I know you loathe that style, but I thought you ought to look as different from your normal self as possible, if you have an angry husband chasing you."

"I suppose you are right. I might forgive you for another kiss."

"No such luck, Pyke. It's past midnight. You might be a gentleman of leisure now, but I need my sleep. You're in the attic room again."

59

Amongst Friends

Charlie slipped out the next morning before anyone else was up. Except for Mrs Brown, of course, who was clattering around in the kitchen as usual. She caught him before he got to the door, nodding her approval at his new respectability, while sliding a bacon sandwich into his hand. The aroma drifted up, teasing his nostrils.

"Mrs Brown, you are an incomparable treasure."

"Get on with you, Mr Pyke. Make sure you're back for Sunday dinner."

"Roast with all the trimmings?" Saliva rushed to fill his mouth. "Tell me you're making Yorkshire puddings and I will weep at your feet."

She patted his cheek. "Noon sharp."

One night with the comforts and delights of Anne's house was akin to floating in paradise, but his mission for the morning would crash him back to earth soon enough. He had to report as soon as possible that he could no longer work in the Engineers' Arms. The only morsel he could offer in recompense was the tiny extra clue Mrs Vance had given him to the fourth man's identity.

As it was Sunday and he didn't know where DI Wallace lived, he would escape his commanding officer's wrath for failing to maintain his role at the Engineers' Arms. Kelly would have to break the news to Wallace.

Charlie kicked a stone, sending it clanging against an iron fence. This had been his one chance to impress DI Wallace enough to secure a position in his team. His own commanding officer in Wellington, DI Stewart, had told Charlie that he would be retiring soon, leaving Charlie desperate to return to Dunedin. Working for Wallace would not be as exhilarating as working for Stewart, but he was still a first-rate officer. And an hour in Grace's company had reminded him how much he was missing by living so far away.

Even DC Kelly, whom he had first thought of as a bit of a plodder, had grown on him. Kelly might not be flashy, but he was relentless and hard-working – a man who got the job done without fuss. It had been a novel pleasure to work as part of a team with a congenial man of similar age.

Kelly lived in a modest cottage at the north end of Dunedin. A young woman of about Grace's age answered the door, with a squalling infant in one arm and a toddler clinging to her skirts. Behind her, two older children ran along the corridor, yelling about pulled hair and a broken toy soldier. They were in their Sunday best, albeit with untucked shirts and jam-covered faces.

"Can I help you?" the woman asked, with motherly serenity, despite the chaos around her.

"Mrs Kelly? My apologies for interrupting you on a Sunday morning. Might DC Kelly spare me a minute? I'm DC Pyke."

"Come in. A pleasure to meet you. Declan has told me all about you, though he failed to mention that you were such a handsome gentleman."

Kelly appeared at the end of a corridor, tucking his shirt in. "Bryan, Moira, for the love of Mary, wash your faces and get your shoes on. We're leaving for Mass in five minutes." Kelly glanced towards the door. "Can we help you, sir?"

"That's a fine way to greet a fellow officer, Declan," his wife teased.

Kelly recoiled. "Pyke? By all that's holy, you're a new man without all the hair. Come in, come in."

"Only for a minute. I can see you're in a rush." Charlie picked up the toddler, who was about to fall off the doorstep, and came inside. Kelly must be older than he looked to have four children.

Kelly answered the unasked question. "The oldest two are my sister's children. She's about to give birth to her third. Come into the front room. Do call me Declan, by the way, as we're off duty."

"I might be permanently off duty, Declan. I had to make a call last night about keeping my cover or helping a woman who had been beaten." Charlie handed him an envelope. "Can you get this to Wallace as soon as possible?"

"Don't you be worrying yourself, Charlie. Wallace will be relieved to have you out of there. He can hardly take you to task for rescuing a woman in trouble."

"Good to know he takes such a lenient view of his men abandoning their posts."

"As I recall, his actual words were: 'Alistair Stewart will flay my hide if I have to pull Pyke out of the Leith with a knife in his back.'"

Charlie roared with laughter. "You have an odd way of cheering a man up, Declan, but it works."

Declan turned the envelope in his hand. "Can this wait until after church?"

"For sure. I wanted to let Wallace know I am no longer keeping an eye on the publicans' activities, but it'll wait for later. According to the barman's wife, they are planning at least a week of troublemaking. And she confirmed the third man was Mr Sweeney. Not a nice character. The fourth man was more of a gentleman than the others, she said, although I believe she was naïve in mistaking his charms. He sounded Scottish to me and they called him Mac in my hearing. She thinks he might also be called Lenny. Leonard, I presume. Ring any bells with you?"

"Not off the top of my head. I'll think about it." The sound of a minor stampede rolled in from the hallway. "We'd best be off to Mass or my darling wife will have my hide. Please join us if you wish."

"My mother would have a fit. We're C of E, although I'm not as regular as she would like."

Charlie suffered a momentary stab of envy as Kelly kissed his wife on the cheek, with his baby in one arm and his wife's arm in the other. "You've a fine family, Declan."

"I've the luck of the Irish, all right. See you at the station tomorrow morning, Charlie." He strolled off down the street.

Halfway down, he stopped and ran back to Charlie. "I forgot to ask. Have you seen Miss Penrose? Has she recovered from her ordeal?"

"Ordeal?"

"Didn't she tell you? She and Molly Sugden were attacked yesterday. No injuries, thank the Lord, but it could have been disastrous if she hadn't got the better of the three assailants. Reckon they'll think twice before harassing a couple of sweet innocents again. Give her our best."

Declan hurried back to his family, leaving Charlie frozen in place, his heart as heavy as a stone inside his chest.

Charlie forced himself to walk back to Anne's house at normal speed. There was nothing to be gained by rushing in, demanding to know why Grace hadn't told him of the attack. While he liked to think they were close enough to discuss anything, she was under no obligation. If he was honest, there were more than a few policing incidents he had kept to himself, not wanting to worry her.

As he walked up the path to the door, a deep voice and laughter drifted out the open window. The man's voice was unfamiliar alongside Grace's distinctive laugh. Not the polite titter of a society debutante, but the full-bodied laugh of a woman embracing life.

Anne ushered him into the drawing room. "Charlie, come and meet a friend of mine. He has offered you a room in his house for as long as you need it. He lives further up High Street, so I expect you will find it quite convenient."

"Thank you, Mrs Macmillan. You are too kind, especially on such short notice." Charlie's eyes sought out Grace, who was standing by the window with her back to him, engaged in a lively conversation with a tall stranger, perhaps a decade older than her. Too amusing, too smartly dressed, and far too male, in Charlie's instantly formed opinion. After a second glance, he noted that the stranger's suit was showing signs of wear and was older than the current style, while his strong hands and weathered face suggested he was no wealthy dandy. Molly Sugden was with them, also laughing and receiving a share of the man's attention.

"I had hoped to gather a few old acquaintances, who especially wished to see you again," Anne continued. "Tiny Tim was eager to attend, but his wife, Mrs Alice Shorten, was kicked by a horse yesterday, as you no doubt heard."

"Tiny Tim married. How much has changed since I last saw him." Charlie murmured, as he attempted to listen in on the conversation by the window, as well as Anne's words.

"Will Finlay asked me to send his apologies," Anne continued. "He wanted to be here to thank you properly for rescuing him from the gallows, but his wife is due to give birth to their firstborn any day."

Charlie's attention snapped back to his hostess. "Will Finlay married, and about to be a father! I have missed so much. It would have been nice to see him again."

"Will's worried about the baby, of course, but I told him that whatever the child looks like, a loving home is all it needs for a happy life. Besides, the baby is unlikely to inherit his father's facial defect. I've been reading some interesting new research published recently about heredity…" Anne must have noted Charlie's gaze roving the room. "But you don't want to be hearing about that now."

"Is my aunt not here, Mrs Macmillan?"

"Goodness, you have been out of touch, Charlie. Lily is in Wellington with Alistair Stewart. Making wedding preparations, I expect." Anne gave him an enigmatic smile, as she led him to a tall, stooping gentleman of advanced years. "Charlie, I would like you to meet Mr Kenneth Drummond, one of my dear departed husband's oldest friends."

The extended hand was wrinkled and age-spotted, but the handshake was firm. "Detective Constable Pyke, a pleasure to meet you at last. I have heard a great deal about you, young man. I'm looking forward to having your company for as long as you would care to stay."

"Thank you, Mr Drummond. I am most grateful." Charlie wasn't sure what to say, as he knew nothing of this man. This gathering was full of surprises, not least being the absence of his Aunt Lily. Coming out from an undercover mission often left him feeling disconnected from real life, but never more so than today.

Anne filled the conversational gap. "I should warn you, Kenneth is an attorney, so do not attempt to get the better of him in an argument. He'll have your brain so knotted, you won't know which way is up. Now, if you gentlemen will excuse me, I must see to the luncheon arrangements."

Charlie watched her go, leaving him with a brain already in knots. "I do hope Mrs Macmillan did not have to twist your arm too hard to extract such a generous offer."

"Don't worry about that, young Pyke. I expect you know as well as I that Anne Macmillan is an expert at getting people to do her bidding, in the nicest possible way. In truth, I am looking forward to some youthful company. I have been alone since my wife died a little over two years ago, with only a dour old housekeeper and an equally ancient valet to keep me company. I would steal away the estimable Mrs Brown if I dared."

On that, Charlie was on firmer ground. "Mrs Macmillan would never forgive you. Mrs Brown is quite the best cook and housekeeper I have come across, not that I have had much experience. I first came here from the police barracks, which was rather too far to the lower end of culinary and comfort standards. Since then, I have been in cheap lodgings. If I seem a glutton at the table today, you will understand why. I have not had a single decent meal since I left Wellington."

"In that case, we must hope for many invitations to Anne's table, as my own is nothing to excite the appetite." Drummond paused. "You have not asked me how I have heard so much about you."

"To be honest, Mr Drummond, my head is in a spin. I feel as if I have been away on a long journey, returning to find everything achingly familiar, yet utterly different at the same time. The young lads I once knew are now married and settled down. Even my aunt has gone to make arrangements for her own wedding. If Mrs Macmillan suddenly announced her engagement, I declare I should hardly be surprised."

Mr Drummond glanced towards the door Anne had gone through. "I have been working on that very matter these past few months, but to what effect I am as yet unable to say. I have admired Anne Godwin for half a century, but I made the fatal mistake of introducing her to my friend, Doctor Gordon Macmillan."

He paused, catching Charlie's furtive glance towards the window. "Dare I suggest it is not the marital state of Mrs Macmillan that you are most concerned with?"

Heat crept across Charlie's cheeks. "I have arrived back unexpectedly. The nature of my assignment meant I could not forewarn anyone of my presence in Dunedin. I feel as out of place as a cuckoo in a warbler's nest."

Charlie's gaze flicked back to the cheerful trio. The man was telling another story, complete with extravagant gestures, which had Molly and Grace doubled over with laughter. "Is the man by the window an acquaintance of Miss Sugden's? I haven't seen him before."

"He's the new doctor at Lavender House," Drummond replied. "A genial fellow, as you can see."

Far too genial, in Charlie's view.

"He's set more than a few local hearts aflutter," Drummond continued. "But he is a fine doctor, according to Miss Penrose, and dedicated to the work. The community is fortunate to have him. I know Anne is most relieved to be sharing the burden of work at Lavender House."

Before Charlie could decide whether it would be unpardonably rude to leave Mr Drummond in order to rescue Grace from this paragon of virtue, Anne appeared at the door.

"Ladies and gentlemen, luncheon is served."

Mr Drummond stepped forward to claim Anne's arm to escort her to the dining room. Charlie stood back until Molly and the new doctor disappeared through the doorway.

A familiar arm slipped through his. "Not like you to stand back when Mrs Brown has laid out a feast, Mr Potts."

He resisted her pull towards the dining room. "I wasn't expecting to have to fight for my place at the table, Miss Penrose."

"You know my great-aunt loves a diverse company at her table. Although even she might have drawn the line at the Mr Potts of last night."

"Was it only last night? I fear I am losing my grip on reality. How is Mrs Vance?"

"I took her to a safe house this morning. She seems to be a remarkably resilient young woman. You did a good deed to get her away, Charlie. I hope DI Wallace was not too upset?"

"I haven't seen him yet. Kelly thought he would be relieved to have me out of harm's way." Charlie lifted her chin, so his glare wouldn't go unnoticed. "It seems there has been a rash of violent behaviour lately – far more than I was aware of."

"Don't give me that look, Charlie. Neither Molly nor I was hurt, which is more than I can say for the three ruffians who tried to stop us from going about our lawful business. I was only trying to spare you the worry."

"It's my job to worry about violent criminals. And their victims."

"Before you arrest me for assaulting those charming young men, might I suggest we make haste to the table, as you are the guest of honour."

Grace seated him at the far end of the table and took the seat beside him, with the doctor on her other side. "Charlie, you wouldn't have met Doctor Rory Ravenwood, the new doctor at Lavender House. His sister, Isla, is the new nurse. Rory, this is Charlie Pyke."

"Detective Constable Pyke, pleased to meet you. I am only the temporary doctor, but I must say, everyone has been most welcoming."

"I hope you will make it permanent, Rory. Now that you are here, I cannot imagine how we coped without you." Grace turned back to Charlie to explain. "Anne is feeling her age, I'm afraid, and struggles to cope with long hours delivering medical care. And with Lily about to be married, we had rather a crisis on our hands at Lavender House."

"The good fortune is all on our side. Isla and I came out to New Zealand as nurse and surgeon on an immigrant ship, DC Pyke, driven by the lure of adventure, with no firm prospects in hand. Grace's father took us under his wing in Wellington and suggested that we might find a ready welcome here."

Grace returned the doctor's smile. "My father loves to help ship's surgeons establish themselves in New Zealand. As you know, my grandfather came over on a sailing ship as a doctor. We are most fortunate to get two experts with such experience. Isla Ravenwood nursed in a workhouse infirmary, where Rory also volunteered his services."

"Marvellous luck," Charlie mumbled, as a loaded plate of roast beef, Yorkshire puddings, roast potatoes and peas appeared over his shoulder.

Doctor Ravenwood turned to answer a question from Molly, across the table. They were soon engrossed in a conversation about workers' rights.

"Molly seems to have regained her old sparkle since Rory arrived," Grace whispered. "I have every hope he will help her come to terms with the loss of her fiancé two years ago."

"Now that would be marvellous," Charlie replied, with genuine enthusiasm. "It does appear to be a perfect solution on all counts. I know Aunt Lily was worried about how she would cope with her work at Lavender House, given her imminent marriage to Alistair Stewart."

"Do not tell Lily," Grace whispered over the gravy boat, "but her fiancé is secretly funding the new arrangement. Alistair does not want to look as if he is undermining her position, which, of course, she will keep for as many hours as she wishes. Goodness knows there is plenty of work for all."

The luncheon proceeded with all the ingredients for a successful gathering. Excellent food, lively company and a suspicious avoidance of any subject likely to cause upset. Charlie had the distinct impression that police matters came into the latter category, but he was enjoying himself too much to wonder why.

Union Strike

On Monday morning, Grace decided to call on Harriet Morison, to see if she too had been the target of an attack by the followers of the poisonous letter writer, Outraged Gent.

Alice Shorten arrived at the door from the other direction at the same time. "Grace, how lovely to see you again. My arm is much better, as you can see."

Grace could see nothing of the sort, as the arm was hidden by long, billowing sleeves, which suggested significant swelling. She held Alice's wrist gently and slid the sleeve up, revealing a livid horseshoe-shaped bruise. "Are you sure it's not too sore to be at work? Miss Morison would not wish you to be in pain."

Alice slid her sleeve down again. "I admit it aches, but it is not my writing hand. If I keep to light duties, it will be fine."

As they walked up the steps into the building, a delivery boy arrived with a parcel.

"Excuse me ladies, would you know where the Tailoresses' Union premises are? I have an urgent delivery for Miss Morison."

"I'll take it up. I work there." Alice tipped the boy and reached for the parcel, grimacing as a sharp edge caught on her forearm.

They were halfway up the stairs, with Alice carefully holding the parcel out in front of her, when a gentleman came rampaging down, pushing past them. Alice shrieked as his elbow jostled her arm. The parcel spiralled out of her hands, crashing onto the steps below. Grace registered a flash and boom, before she was knocked backwards by the blast.

Faces appeared above them in the drifting smoke. The steps vibrated with running feet, but all Grace could hear was thunder reverberating in her ears. Somebody lifted her off Alice's legs. She could see the woman's mouth move and the shock in her eyes, but Grace couldn't seem to take her words in.

The woman looked down the steps and screamed, so loudly it penetrated Grace's battered eardrums. She snapped out of her daze and turned to Alice, who was sitting on a higher step, shocked but uninjured. The gentleman who had pushed past them was not so lucky. He sprawled on a lower step, staring at his scorched trousers and blistered, bleeding lower legs.

"Get a large basin or two pails of water and bandages, as quick as you can," Grace shouted to the women gathered at the upper-level balustrade. "And send for the police."

She turned her attention to the gentleman, who looked up at her with stunned incomprehension. Carefully avoiding the debris of the bomb – even the word sent a shiver down her spine – she crouched on the next step down to examine his legs. To her relief, the damage was relatively minor.

"The steps blocked us from the worst of it," she said to him, keeping her voice calm and professional. "Superficial burns and cuts, although I imagine it is painful."

Faces began to appear in the doorway to the street, drawn, as people always are, to the scene of a disaster. "Stay outside," she ordered. "Nobody comes in except the police."

Two pails of water appeared beside her. Grace took off the gentleman's shoes, ignoring his protests, and submerged his lower legs, to his obvious relief. Three fine splinters of wood jutted out from his tibialis anterior muscle, which she removed with only a moderate welling of blood. In the dim light of the stairwell, still swirling with smoke and dust, she could see no further damage. A few days of discomfort and minor scarring, but no real harm done. An extraordinarily lucky escape.

The gentleman finally recovered his wits, then his tongue, and a sharp one it proved to be. "Take your hands off me, girl. I need to see a doctor."

"As you wish," Grace replied, "but you would be better off keeping your legs in cool water for a few more minutes to stop the burns causing any more damage."

"What would you know of it?" the man growled.

"I'd advise you to do as Doctor Penrose says. The lass might be young, but she knows what she is doing."

The deep voice came from behind Grace, but she recognised the Scottish accent immediately. She glanced over her shoulder. The police had arrived in force.

"Detective Inspector Wallace. You arrived with commendable speed. Good day to you too, DC Kelly, and to you, sir."

The latter greeting was for Charlie, as she wasn't sure of his status or what name he might be using today. He looked up from his notebook, in which he was scribbling with a ferocity detrimental to pencil lead, and nodded to her. His emerald eyes surveyed the damage with the same intensity that had reminded her of a large predator the first time they had met. He didn't look pleased to see her in the thick of it, although it was hardly her fault. Or only marginally her fault, given that her insatiable curiosity had brought her here.

"Haste seemed in order. I was told there was a bomb," Wallace replied. "Are there any other injuries?"

"Only this gentleman. Thanks to a stroke of divine intervention, the parcel was knocked to the bottom of the stairs, blocking us from the worst of it. It caused more noise and smoke than actual damage."

Wallace was already bending, inspecting the scene as he talked. "Judging from the state of the steps, you had a lucky escape. Pyke, bag the evidence. Constable Fletcher, make sure nobody enters or exits. Constable Evans, take statements from the onlookers. Kelly, come with me."

The gentleman was still sitting with his legs in the water. "I saw nothing. These girls bumped into me as I was coming down the stairs. Next thing I knew, there was a flash and my legs were hurting like the devil. Must be anarchists, come over from the Continent to spread their evil. If you ask me, the government shouldn't let them in the country."

"This is not the work of anarchists, sir. Most probably a foolish prank." Wallace spoke in his most authoritative voice, no doubt aware of the crowd behind him, eager to rush off to the newspapers with tales of mayhem and the imminent downfall of civilisation. Wallace looked up at Grace. "Is there somewhere we can talk?"

"Come to my office." The voice came from above. A calm, firm voice with an Irish lilt, emanating from a woman of about thirty, with a solid, no-nonsense look about her.

"And you are?"

"Miss Harriet Morison, Secretary of the Dunedin Tailoresses' Union."

They retreated up the stairs and into Miss Morison's office, where Alice Shorten told Wallace what had happened.

Charlie arrived a few minutes later, bringing a chair with him into the crowded room. He squeezed in beside Grace, so close their legs touched. A frisson of endocrine activity rushed through every cell of her body, unlike anything documented in her physiology textbook. Charlie's eyes slid sideways, the skin at the edges crinkling, as if he had read her mind. She dragged her attention back to DI Wallace, who was asking questions.

"Can you describe the messenger boy to me, Mrs Shorten?"

"I can't say I noticed, as I was looking at the address on the parcel. Just a boy. Brown cap, lots of freckles."

Grace cut in. "He was a delivery boy, rather than a messenger boy. Age about ten to twelve, ginger hair, well-fed, no sign of disease, but he was puffing, as if he had rushed to get here. Perhaps he had been offered a good reward for diverting from his normal duties. He was probably a baker's boy, by the name of Mitchell or Mitchener or something similar."

Kelly's pencil stopped its feverish scribbling as he gawped at her. "You know him? That's a lucky break, so it is."

"I've never seen him before, but he propped his bicycle against a nearby lamppost. I could see the first few letters of the shop's name on the delivery basket. From his healthy appearance, but slight dusting of flour, I'm guessing he is the son of a baker."

Wallace rose from his chair and opened the door to the work area. "Excuse me, ladies. Does anyone know of a baker called Mitchell or Mitchener or something similar?"

"There's Mitchem's bakery, near the intersection of the tramlines at South Road," a woman answered. "I often stop there on my way home to Caversham."

Wallace resumed his seat, his normally impassive face alight with the hunt. "Excellent. I did not expect to make such rapid progress. I do wish all witnesses could have your observation skills, Miss Penrose."

"It's the company I keep," Grace replied, as warm fingers brushed against her hand under the table.

Wallace's eyelids flickered, but he didn't rise to the bait. "I expect your work with the police surgeon is all about noticing details."

"Grace was the one who told everyone to keep away from the remains of the parcel," Alice Shorten added.

"I'm grateful for that, Miss Penrose," DI Wallace replied. "It's hard enough to stop my own men from trampling through the evidence, let alone the public. Can you describe the package, Mrs Shorten?"

"It was about the size and weight of a cigar box," Alice replied, holding her hands about ten inches apart, "Wrapped in brown paper with a typewritten address pasted on top. It was addressed to Miss H Morison, Secretary of the Dunedin Tailoresses' Union, with the street address, marked urgent."

"Would you have opened it yourself, Miss Morison?"

"One of the ladies usually opens the mail, unless it is marked as personal. But if it was marked urgent, it might have been brought straight to me." Miss Morison's brow wrinkled as she considered

74

the question. "In the circumstances, I believe I would have taken it and opened it with caution. I understand, Detective Inspector Wallace, that you are aware there have been several nasty incidents lately, targeting suffragists. I was expecting some unpleasantness, but nothing of this magnitude. It is most disturbing."

"I can only agree, Miss Morison. The severity of the incidents is escalating. We'll have to get an expert in to assess what caused the explosion. We've never had such a situation to deal with before."

"It was black powder, sir." Charlie opened a newspaper-wrapped bundle on the desk, pointing to a small amount of unburnt powder. "Based on the size of the box Mrs Shorten has described and the blast radius indicated on the stairs, it was a never intended to be a lethal device."

Grace added the three shards of wood to the evidence. "I extracted these three splinters from the victim. You'll note from the blood on the tips that they have not penetrated the tissue more than about a quarter of an inch, confirming DC Pyke's assessment of a relatively minor explosion." She held one up to Charlie's nose.

He leaned forward to smell the splinter, bumping heads with her. "A hint of tobacco? Is that what you're thinking, Grace?"

"Alice may well be correct with the cigar box comparison."

Wallace was observing them with a lopsided grin. "Do go on. Are you about to tell us the brand and provenance of the cigars or some irrefutable clue as to the owner?"

"No, sir," Charlie replied. "I'm not a smoker myself, and I doubt I could afford cigars on a constable's wage. Which rather suggests the maker of the bomb was a man of means."

"Or employed by somebody wealthy," Grace suggested.

"I suspect he designed the bomb to terrorise rather than to kill, although anyone who opened it might have been badly burned or injured by splinters of wood." Charlie used a pencil to sift through the charred remnants. "You can see there is no evidence of a metal casing or other means of concentrating the pressure and thus increasing the explosive force, only light wood consistent with the powder being loose inside a box."

"How is it you know about explosives, DC Pyke?" Wallace asked.

"My father is a policeman in a gold mining town. He had several mining accidents to deal with when I was growing up. I used to pester him until he told me about his more interesting cases."

"How fortunate you followed your father into policing." Wallace turned to Miss Morison. "Who was the injured gentleman?"

"He owns a clothing factory. He had come to speak with me about his workers threatening to walk off the job over factory conditions and wages. I was unable to resolve his problem on the spot, so he was a mite cross."

"Just as well," Alice said. "If that man hadn't barged past me so rudely, the parcel would have been opened by one of us. Oh, I almost forgot with the shock of it all. It came with a note taped to it. Fortunately, I removed it as soon as the boy gave it to me."

Alice passed the note across to DI Wallace, who examined it carefully before opening it.

"Typewritten, no signature," Wallace murmured, before reading it out. "'Your activities will not be tolerated. A woman's place is in her husband's home. Be warned, the righteous husbands and fathers of this land shall rise up against the outrage.' That last sentence is from the Outraged Gent letter in the *Otago Workman*."

"Usual sentiment, unusual way of expressing it," was all Miss Morison said.

"You are being remarkably calm, Miss Morison. I have to ask, do you have any enemies?" DI Wallace raised an eyebrow, no doubt well aware that the first female union leader in the country had more detractors than she could count.

"If you want a list, Inspector, it may take some time. Many of the local clothing factory owners do not take kindly to the activities of the Dunedin Tailoresses' Union, although they are unlikely to speak of wanting women to stay home. Their profits are bloated by using women, who are more productive than men, yet earn far less than a man's wage."

"You are also a member of the Women's Christian Temperance Union, I understand? I expect you are not a favourite of the publicans and brewers."

"It is fair to say they detest me," she replied with pride. "Nor am I popular amongst the legions of ordinary men who cling to the right to drink as much alcohol as they can pour down their throats, regardless of the consequences. You might as well add to the suspect list every person who quails at the thought of women getting the vote. Thus, every man who believes his wife should think of nothing but her husband and home, and the not insubstantial number of women who feel the same. Not to mention politicians who fear for their positions if women get the vote."

"Outraged Gent referred specifically to the women's franchise issue," Kelly noted.

"Miss Morison and Miss Helen Nicol can take much of the credit for advancing the cause of women's suffrage," Alice explained. "The women's suffrage petition would be a far flimsier document without Harriet's advocacy amongst the working women of Dunedin. You will be aware the support of working women is a crucial issue for the Liberal government, as a conservative vote by wealthy women voters would oust them."

Wallace shook his head. "Perhaps it might be quicker to list all the people who do not wish you harm. Although few would have the skills or desire to construct an explosive device, however crude, knowing it might maim or even kill whoever opened it."

Miss Morison didn't respond. Grace knew she had endured many threats and abuses before now, with impressive stoicism.

"I admire your bravery, Miss Morison. There are many among us who believe the country would be better managed if women had the vote." Wallace acknowledged their surprise with a shrug. "It is the police who have to deal with the carnage caused by drunken men. It is far from pleasant, I assure you, especially when women and children are the victims."

77

"What action do you suggest we take, Detective Inspector Wallace? While I do not want to curtail our activities, I must consider the risk to the women working here."

Wallace rubbed his jaw as the seconds passed. Finally, he said, "I'm not sure what to advise, Miss Morison, other than the obvious need to treat every package as suspicious. Perhaps you might also restrict visitors to those you trust, for a few days at least. I hope this is nothing but a brief flurry of threats from a crackpot, who has now made his point known. Rest assured, we are working with all diligence on the case, with possible suspects already identified."

Harriet Morison smiled. "I feel we are in safe hands, for which I thank you."

"Are there other women in the franchise movement who might be seen as potential targets?" Wallace asked.

"There are many, but I expect Mrs Marion Hatton would be foremost. Her vivid turn of phrase has enlivened many a suffrage speech at the expense of our detractors. She shows up Henry Fish for what he really is, and he does not care for it."

Grace smiled to herself as she recalled Mrs Hatton's dismissal of Fish's petition: "How does Mr Fish go about finding out whether women want the franchise? Why, by paying a lot of lazy, drinking men to ask another lot of similarly minded men to say whether they are willing it should be granted to us."

Out loud, she said, "Detective Inspector Wallace, are you aware that there is a significant event in three days' time, on the twenty-eighth of April? The inaugural meeting of the Women's Franchise League will be held in Choral Hall at two o'clock. The league aims to further the cause of women's suffrage by offering an independent organisation, not linked to the temperance movement or religion. It will be a united and powerful force for achieving the vote and thus a tempting target."

Wallace turned a sickly shade of white. "I do recall hearing of it. Will it be a large meeting?"

Grace thought he should know the full extent of what he was up against. "City Hall was packed to overflowing on the twelfth of April to hear the proposal for a Women's Franchise League. Mrs Hatton and Sir Robert Stout addressed the meeting, amongst other eminent persons. We expect perhaps one hundred to two hundred suffragists to attend the inaugural Women's Franchise League meeting on Thursday."

"Oh my Lord," Kelly muttered.

Miss Morison pursed her lips. "Surely these scoundrels would not strike at the meeting, with so many in attendance."

"We cannot risk it," Wallace said. "You'd better get me a list of prominent attendees."

"Alice, could you attend to that as soon as possible?" Miss Morison asked. "Inspector, I ought to tell you that Lady Stout herself has agreed to become our president, alongside Mrs Marion Hatton. Miss Helen Nicol will be the secretary and several of us, including myself, have agreed to put our names forward as vice-presidents. A great many important supporters will be there, including Members of the House of Representatives."

All colour had now vanished from Wallace's face. "We can muster a strong police presence, but I beseech you to consider postponing this event until we have apprehended the culprits."

Harriet Morison puffed out her chest and fixed him with a steely glare.

Wallace stood. "I thought not. Perhaps I can persuade Lady Stout to send a representative."

Wallace's resigned sigh told Grace that he knew his odds of success were slim. She sympathised with his position, as any threat to Lady Stout would be a terrifying prospect. Sir Robert Stout, the former Premier (and probable successor to the current Premier), and Lady Stout were both strong advocates of extending the right to vote to women.

"We had better get to work finding this bomber as soon as possible. I ask you, for your own safety, to refrain from any activity

79

that may endanger you," Wallace's gaze settled on Grace as he said this. "It is a police matter now. Thank you for your time, ladies."

When the policemen had left, Harriet Morison called a meeting of her helpers.

"Ladies, I know we are all shocked by events. The inspector is hopeful it may be a short-lived protest against our cause, but there are grounds to be concerned that the Women's Franchise League meeting could be a target. I would ask you all to take extra care. I am shutting the office for the rest of the day and will advise Helen Nicol to halt all door-to-door canvassing for the time being. Please spread the word amongst your acquaintances. Tomorrow we will focus our efforts on letter-writing and preparing for the meeting, as well as dealing with the day-to-day business of the union, behind locked doors. If anyone does not wish to return, I will applaud your common sense, especially for those of you with children."

Grace hurried home. If they weren't allowed to canvass for signatures today, the time would be well spent catching up on her medical studies.

She had an all too familiar gnawing sensation in the pit of her stomach, warning her that today's bomb wouldn't be the end of it.

Liquor Barons

Charlie sat at a requisitioned desk in the bowels of the police station, in a small room that had previously been used as a prison cell. After protests by prison reformers over inhumane conditions, the windowless space had been turned into a storage room. By stacking boxes and clearing out junk, he had fashioned a temporary workspace.

The remains of the package sat in front of him. The bomb sent to Harriet Morison had caught them all off guard. It was one thing to throw beer and firecrackers, unpleasant as those acts were, but quite another to risk a person's life or limb.

If he was honest with himself, it was Grace's proximity to the explosion that shook Charlie the most, although he knew his personal feelings should not intrude into an investigation. He assessed his chances of getting her to stay at home on the day of the inaugural Women's Franchise League meeting and concluded he had more chance of holding back the tide on St Clair beach.

Which was exactly the expression DI Wallace had used when he went off to convince Mrs Hatton to call off Thursday's meeting. If she refused, Wallace's back-up plan was to arrange for as many policemen as they could round up to provide protection at the meeting. In order to convince the Chief Inspector to reassign his limited force, they had to provide strong evidence of a credible threat.

DC Kelly had gone out to track down the delivery boy at Mitchem's bakery, which was not much more than a stone's throw from both the building where Lister's *Otago Workman* was printed and the Engineers' Arms. The publican, Harry Bertram, had some explaining to do, but that would not be an interview Charlie could attend, however much he wanted to.

Instead, Charlie had been assigned to desk work. His first job was to work out how the bomb had been put together. They would give the fragments to an explosives expert, but that would take time they didn't have, as they had never had call for such a specialty in a city police force. Thanks to his father's indulgence of his curiosity, he had enough knowledge of explosives to get the investigation started.

The problem was, although he was sure the damage was caused by black powder, there appeared to be no detonator or fuse to set it off. Black powder needed to be packed tightly into something to create an explosive force, such as the pipe of a pipe bomb or the barrel of a firearm. Loosely packed into a box as it was, it wasn't so much an explosive as a firebomb. But it still needed an ignition source.

Charlie attempted to put the myriad pieces of the box back together, but he could not fathom the method for a while, until he brushed through the debris and noted what appeared to be burnt stubs of matches. Along the inside edge of the lid, he found traces of the type of striker plate used to ignite the matches. If the matches had been attached to the inside of the box, they could have rubbed against this friction source as the lid was opened, or the box was dropped. The burst of flame would have ignited the loose black powder.

Simple, but ingenious. Probably not intended to be deadly, although the perpetrator must have known that whoever opened it would receive severe burns, with a small risk of fatality if a sharp fragment of the wooden box had sliced through an artery or the recipient had leaned over the box when she opened it.

He switched his attention to the remains of the firecrackers that Grace had dropped off on Saturday. Fortunately, the last few in the string had not gone off. The crackers were fairly basic – not much more than black powder tightly wrapped in stiff paper. But the fuse appeared to be of superior quality and thus it was unlikely the crackers had been constructed at home by a person with no experience or limited means. Certainly, the urchin who set the string of firecrackers off must have been given them and instructed on what to do.

Charlie was writing his report when Mr Peters appeared, bearing a pile of papers and a bag wafting an exquisite aroma, triggering a ravenous hunger. Surely the records clerk would not eat his lunch in front of him while droning on about cross-referencing systems until Charlie expired of starvation?

Peters looked at the mess on Charlie's desk and deposited the bag on the floor. "Your Miss Penrose dropped this off at the front desk for you, DC Pyke. She's quite a lass, by all accounts."

"One in a million, Mr Peters. Thank you for bringing this down." Charlie extracted a casserole dish from the bag. He tipped the lid, inhaling deeply of Mrs Brown's cottage pie. Grace had even thought to include a fork, wrapped in a napkin, together with a note. "Sorry, no pudding. Someone ate it all last night." Charlie chuckled. He held the note to his nose, detecting a hint of rosewater, before realising that Mr Peters was still standing in front of him, trying to suppress a grin.

"DI Wallace asked me to access criminal records for three men and pass the information on to you, DC Pyke. He also asked for a fourth man, known only as Mac or Lenny, but miracles are not my department."

"I'm all ears, Mr Peters, even if my mouth is otherwise engaged. Have you eaten?"

"I have. Now, DI Wallace said the men were probably in the liquor trade, so I cross-referenced my files on liquor licensing matters, with criminal records, and counter-checked the gaming and alcohol-related infringements to provide a complete picture…"

Charlie had scraped the casserole clean by the time Peters had finished. "Mr Peters, you are a miracle worker. I've never known a system as efficient as yours. I hope the Dunedin force appreciates your work."

83

Peters' face lit up. "As a matter of fact, after your DI Stewart had a word on my behalf when he was last here, I was promoted to Senior Records Officer. I do hope he received my letter of thanks."

Charlie was saved from replying by the arrival of DC Kelly.

"There you are Charlie. I didn't even know this basement room existed. Mary and Joseph, what is that delicious smell?"

"Cottage pie. All gone, I'm afraid. Pity you didn't arrive ten minutes earlier, Declan. Did you find the delivery boy?"

"Miss Penrose hit the bullseye. The lad delivers bread for Mitchem's Bakery. Little blighter turned mute at the sight of me, but his father soon had him talking. The boy was offered a week's wages to make the extra delivery to Miss Morison. He had the time to spare and saw no harm in it."

"Please tell me he recognised the man."

"He gave an excellent description of the coins the man was tempting him with, but the best he could do with the man himself was that he was a tall, well-to-do gentleman. Bowler hat firmly pulled down, gloves on, face covered by a scarf. He thought nothing of that, as the wind was blowing from the south with a fierce chill."

"Still, it tends to rule out Bertram, who is fat, and Sweeney, who is shorter than average. I wouldn't describe Gilroy as tall, but he might seem so to a small boy. The most likely candidate is our fourth man, whom we only know as Lenny or Mac."

"Or someone else entirely," Kelly countered. "Being prosperous men, they might well use others to do their foul deeds. Fortunately, I had a lucky break on the black powder. Arthur Briscoes keeps a record of all sales. Who do you think bought black powder eleven days ago?"

"I'm all ears."

"Owen Gilroy. Or his gardener, to be precise, but it was charged to Gilroy's account."

"Great work, Kelly. Wallace will be overjoyed."

"Speaking of Wallace, he is back and wants us both in his office. I've found out some other titbits through the Kelly grapevine too." He registered Charlie's raised eyebrows. "Irish Catholic family – there's one of us in every nook and cranny of this town. I sent out word on Saturday."

"I don't know why I bothered to go undercover in that case."

"Perhaps not quite every nook, especially amongst the top hat and bowler set. And there are some crannies that not even the Kelly clan would sink into."

Wallace glowered at them when they entered his office. "What are you two so cheerful about? We have a bomber on the loose and a group of women who are the most pig-headed, cavalier bunch you could ever wish to meet. Not only did Mrs Hatton refuse to delay their meeting, but she refused to insist that Lady Stout stay away if the lady wished to attend. It was only with the greatest reluctance that she agreed to police protection. 'Nothing will be achieved without fortitude and sacrifice,' is what Mrs Hatton said to me. Who do they think they are – soldiers going into battle?"

Charlie kept his mouth shut. Perhaps Mrs Wallace was a more biddable sort, but the women in Charlie's life were every bit as brave and determined as a soldier marching to war.

"I've wasted enough time on the potential victims. Time to concentrate on the perpetrators. We'll tackle Conor Sweeney first, as he's closest."

Wallace had arranged for the use of a four-seater brougham so they could move fast and talk in privacy.

"What do we know so far, lads?" Wallace asked, before their rear ends had touched the leather seats. "It had better be good news after the morning I've had."

Charlie settled back as the coachman slapped the reins on the horses' flanks. "The bomb was a simple affair of black powder in a box, set off using matches against a striker plate when the box was opened. Or in this case, dropped. The firecrackers were also simple, but well made with a high-quality fuse."

"Not an amateur. What of our suspects?"

"Mr Peters confirmed that Owen Gilroy has been warned for threatening the five prohibition members of the licensing committee who closed down the Roslyn hotels. He is also suspected of running illegal gambling, dog fighting and unlicensed drinking after the closure of his hotels, but no charges have been laid. The good news is that DC Kelly had the foresight to check purchases of black powder at Briscoes' store."

"Gilroy's gardener bought black powder eleven days ago, on the morning of the fourteenth of April," Kelly said.

Wallace rubbed his hands together. "Excellent. Not long after the City Hall meeting on the franchise issue on the twelfth of April, which likely was the trigger for their actions. Gilroy has jumped to the top of our suspect list for the bombing."

"Gilroy also had a grudge against Miss Harriet Morison and her Tailoresses' Union, according to my cousin, who lives in Roslyn and used to drink at Gilroy's hotel before it was closed down," Kelly said. "Gilroy's older brother owned a clothing factory, which was closed after the union took a case against him for insanitary conditions and underpaying the union rate. The brother sold up and went back to Ireland."

"Conor Sweeney and Harry Bertram only have hotels, as far as we know," Charlie added. "Mr Peters said they have the usual string of fines for operating outside licensing hours. Police have been called to break up fights. The usual for that type of establishment. No criminal record for serious offences."

"Harry Bertram made his money on the goldfields, selling grog," Kelly said. "Likes to put on grand airs according to my sister's brother-in-law, who is also in the liquor trade, but he says Bertram is really as common as muck and a nasty creep to boot. Conor Sweeney is handy with his fists and not a man to cross, but I couldn't find out anything about his background, as it seems he hasn't been in the country for very long. Irish, by way of Australia."

Wallace's eyes were alight with the thrill of the chase. "You two make a fine team. Let's visit Conor Sweeney first and see if we can get him to squeal on Gilroy. Pyke, we can't risk you being recognised by Sweeney, so you talk to the barman. Kelly, talk to the patrons. I'll take Sweeney."

Wallace came back down the stairs twenty minutes later with his eyes gleaming from a successful hunt. As they walked out of the hotel, a drunk yelled, "vengeance shall be ours".

"I have a feeling we will be sick of hearing that expression before this case is done," Charlie grumbled, as he and Kelly climbed back into the carriage. He felt eyes upon him and made the mistake of looking up. Conor Sweeney was staring at them with ill-disguised hatred. Without his beard, long hair and grimy work clothes, there was little chance that Sweeney would recognise him as the man who had served him at the Friday night meeting, but he should have known better than to take the risk.

"Makes me want to knock their stupid heads together," Kelly agreed. "Don't they know the Bible says the exact opposite? 'Vengeance is mine, I will repay, says the Lord'. It is not for us to seek vengeance, but to turn the other cheek and leave vengeance to God."

Wallace finished his instructions to the coachman and joined them in the carriage. "They try to make it sound like God's will to justify their actions. It has always been the same with fanatics. Outraged Gent's message does seem to have taken a hold on the drunk and disorderly element of the city. He probably paid men to spread the word."

"Wouldn't take much to get that lot in a fighting mood," Kelly said. "One of the regulars at the hotel saw the beer throwing incident and could hardly contain his mirth." He flipped open his notebook and read, "'These bitter old maids who try to stop a man from his right to an ale after a hard day's work – they have it coming to them.' Most of the other patrons took the same view."

"A hard day's work? That's rich, coming from a man propping up a bar on a Monday afternoon."

"The barman admitted to throwing the beer slops," Charlie added, "but he said it was an accident. His words were: 'I was clearing out the slops and didn't think to check the street first. I must

87

have slipped, and the bucket went flying.' When I asked him more about the incident, he looked me right in the eye and said, 'accidents do happen. Shouldn't wonder if there are more to come. A man can get clumsy when his mind is distracted.' They must know that more trouble is planned."

"They got their story straight all right. Conor Sweeney used almost exactly the same words. 'My barman was clearing out the slops and didn't think to check the street first. He must have slipped, and the bucket went flying.' Sweeney's a smug little weasel. He claims to have been visiting another of his businesses out of town this morning when the bomb was delivered. We'll have to check his alibi, of course. If he has his own horse, he might have come back."

"Did Sweeney admit to attending the meeting of the four liquor barons on Friday night?" Charlie asked.

"Not at first. He's not the type of man who would admit to a policeman that the sun rises in the east if he can come up with a believable alternative. But he did look mighty shocked that I knew of his meeting with his co-conspirators, Bertram, Gilroy and Mac. When I mentioned he was under investigation for conspiracy to commit murder over the bomb sent to Miss Morison, his tongue soon loosened."

Charlie and Kelly leaned forward, eager to hear Sweeney's confession.

"Sweeney said the meeting was no more than a bit of light banter amongst card-playing acquaintances. In his words, 'the government is allowing womenfolk to take over. No man wants a petticoat government'. According to Sweeney, they only wanted to show the 'pushy womenfolk forcing their views on parliament' that men will not stand for it. Nothing violent, only 'putting the wind up their skirts'. He said we cannot arrest him because his barman accidentally spilt beer slops on the street. He insisted he had nothing to do with any bomb and it was not part of their agreed plan."

"These publicans do seem fond of getting their lackeys to do their dirty work for them," Kelly said. "Sweeney gets his barman to target Miss Nicol, a lad paid to set off crackers, another to deliver the package to Miss Morison."

"It's the bomber who worries me the most. We need to see Owen Gilroy as soon as possible. Sweeney admitted that they each had targets. Bertram was keen to teach Mrs Reynolds to keep her nose out of his business. We'll have to check whether Mrs Reynolds has been targeted yet. Conor Sweeney took Miss Nicol, as she passes his hotel regularly. Gilroy was eager to claim the hated Miss Morison as his victim."

"And the fourth man? Lenny or Mac?" Charlie asked.

"Not Leonard, but Lennox. Lennox MacDonald, brewer. Sweeney didn't think much of him. MacDonald was reluctant to commit to any action at the meeting, although he promised not to let them down."

"That corresponds with what I overheard," Charlie said. "Perhaps MacDonald organised the firecrackers, since that did not appear to target anyone in particular, although a woman was injured."

"So, what now, sir?" Kelly asked. "Sweeney will send a message to the others to warn them we are onto them. Should we split up in order to interview them all before they are forewarned?"

"Bertram will never admit anything to us, regardless. Lennox MacDonald might be the weak link in the group. All the better for being left to stew for a while, knowing that we are coming for him." Wallace leaned back in his seat, his eyes taking on the faraway look he got when he was thinking. "Owen Gilroy is our priority. Pyke, I want you to talk to the gardener who purchased the black powder and any other servants. Kelly, you come with me to interview Gilroy. With what we know so far, we'll have cause to search the premises to prevent further offending."

Charlie would have loved to be at the interview, but he couldn't risk being identified. Besides, he was determined to obey orders to the letter. Wallace had been open about the fact that there were no vacant positions in Dunedin, but if he made himself useful, perhaps that could be changed.

The drumming of hoofbeats interrupted his thoughts. A powerful horse surged up beside them, the rider's long coat flapping around his leather boots in the wind. Curious to see what sort of man would risk his horse's legs galloping on a hard road, Charlie stuck his head out the window.

Sweeney's hard eyes glittered with recognition. "Filthy snooping copper." He spat at the carriage, before yanking his horse's head around and heading south, towards Caversham.

90

Black Powder

As Sweeney rode away, Charlie cursed himself for allowing Sweeney the chance to recognise him.

Wallace caught his eye. "We'll let him go, for now. Might be for the best that he knows you are a policeman. If they believe we are onto them, it might stop them from going ahead with their plan. It does place you in danger, though, Pyke. Watch your back and don't take any risks."

They drove on in silence to Gilroy's residence on the western outskirts of the city. The house was a sizeable structure, with an unkempt look about it, set in an acre or two of grounds. Charlie tracked the gardener down in the kitchen garden, digging out carrots with slow and methodical thrusts of his garden fork.

He tipped his cap as Charlie approached. "Morning."

"I'm Detective Constable Pyke, with the Dunedin police. I need to ask you about a purchase you made eleven days ago at Briscoes. Black powder, to be specific."

"Aye."

The gardener was clearly a man of few words. Charlie rephrased his statement as a question. "Did you make that purchase?"

"Aye."

"For what purpose?"

"Stump."

"Can you show me?"

Head jerk. "Around the back."

Charlie followed the gardener around to the far side of the house, where the man pointed out a blackened tree stump next to a pile of logs waiting to be chopped for firewood. He continued on, stopping again in the middle of a freshly gravelled path, leading to a newly planted flower garden.

The gardener tapped his muddy boot on the middle of the path. "The stump were in the way."

The hole was filled in, but Charlie could see evidence of a dug-out system of tree roots radiated from the spot. "Was all the black powder used?"

"Most of it."

"Can you show me what was left over?"

The gardener led him back towards the vegetable garden, showing no overt curiosity about the line of questioning. He stopped at a locked shed and reached under the eaves to unhook a key.

"Is the shed always kept padlocked?"

"Aye, since the young'uns came along." He removed the lock and pointed to a shelf. "Rat poison and such."

"Has any black powder been taken since the stump was removed?"

The gardener leaned forward to check. "No."

"Are you sure?"

"Aye."

Charlie took a good look around, to no effect. It had seemed such a promising lead, but the gardener showed every sign of being as incapable of lying as he was of stringing together a sentence of more than a few words. On the other hand, the gardener was not the sort to volunteer information unless he was asked a direct and specific question. Charlie took a moment to identify any gaps in his questioning, while the gardener locked up the shed.

"Did Mr Gilroy have any involvement in blowing up the tree stump? Did he, for example, assist with setting off the explosion or have access to the black powder at any time?"

The gardener appeared ill at ease for the first time. He chose his words carefully. "Mr Gilroy is not an outdoors type of man."

"By which you mean?"

"He wanted to let off the explosion, but he didn't have the first idea of what to do. He was smoking when he held out his hand for the black powder." The gardener uttered the last sentence with a shake of his head. His eyes pleaded his case. "He'd a blown his hands off if I'd let him help. He was cross, but what's a man to do?"

After this epic sentence, the gardener sunk back into silence.

"You did the right thing by him. Explosives are not for amateurs."

The gardener took up his garden fork again, with a nod of agreement.

"Just one more question, if you will. Did you happen to see Mr Gilroy this morning?"

The gardener stared at him as if he was a madman. "Never do afore noon."

"He didn't ask for a horse or carriage earlier today?"

"Best ask at the stable."

"Of course. Thank you for your time."

The gardener tipped his cap again and trudged back to his carrots.

The stable boy was dozing in a pile of hay. Charlie let him sleep on, while he examined the stable. A single horse stood in a stall, still muddy from its last outing. Charlie patted her neck, finding no trace of dampness or dried sweat. Next, he lifted her foot, noting that the mud was dry. When he scrapped out her hoof, he found only mud. If the mare had last been used on the drive or road, there would have been gravel embedded in the mud.

"Oi, you there, what 'yer doing with our Peggy?"

"I'm Detective Constable Pyke. What's your name, lad? I need to ask you a few questions."

"Sam. What yer wanna know then?"

"How many horses does Mr Gilroy keep, Sam?"

"Only Peggy here. He calls her Pegasus, but that's a right daft name, if you ask me."

Peggy was a fine mare, but as she was not white, winged, or a stallion, Charlie was inclined to agree with Sam. "How do they manage with a single horse?"

"Mrs Gilroy has Peggy put in the trap to go to church and ladies' meetings. Groceries and such are delivered. Mr Gilroy never needs a horse until his work starts of an evening. Used to have three horses here when times was good."

"What if Mr Gilroy goes away?"

"He'll borrow Cassius from Mr Blackett, down the road. I suppose he might hire a nag if he has to."

"Do the Gilroy children live at home?"

The boy sniffed. "Boarding school."

"They don't have a horse to use when they come home?"

"Oh, aye, there's a couple of ponies in the back field. I ride 'em regular to keep them in shape."

Charlie was about ready to pull his hair out, but there was no point getting cross with the help. They were answering the questions he put, if not the questions he implied. He tried again. "Did anyone use Peggy today, or any other available horse or pony, borrowed, hired or otherwise?"

"Nah. Missus took Peggy to church yesterday. I gave her a good brush and feed after. Mr Gilroy said to let her into the field, cos he didn't need her until tonight." He saw Charlie looking at the mud. "She musta got into the creek. I'll give her a good brush before he leaves. Won't be for an hour or more."

"Who else lives here, Sam? And who would be most likely to know Mr Gilroy's comings and goings?"

"Mrs Gillespie, the housekeeper, keeps an eye on everything. It be no use talking to the cook, who is always in the kitchen on the other side of the house. The maid's not right in the head and, like as not, won't recall her own name. Mrs Gilroy is poorly. She has a nurse what comes in of a morning to help her. There ain't much to do in the stables, so I help in the garden and do odd jobs too."

"Thank you, Sam. That's all for now."

94

Charlie headed for the house. He heard a raised voice in one of the side rooms, so he went around to the front door. An age-wizened woman in a white pinafore answered his knock.

"I'm Detective Constable Pyke. Would you be the housekeeper?"

"Aye, sir. I'll take you through to the other gentlemen."

"Actually, I need to have a quick word with you, Mrs Gillespie."

Her eyes darted nervously. "You'd best come through to the parlour."

Charlie followed her through to a cosy room, which appeared to be untouched since its original decoration several decades ago. He sat down and gestured for her to do the same. "No need to be concerned, Mrs Gillespie. I merely wish to know about Mr Gilroy's movements over the last few days. Most particularly, whether he went to the city this morning."

Mrs Gillespie perched on the edge of a faded armchair. "This morning? I hardly think so, sir. It would be a rare day indeed before the master is out of bed before the luncheon hour. I don't mean no disrespect, you understand. His business interests take him out of an evening, sir, oftentimes not arriving back until the wee hours."

"Did he come home late yesterday?"

"Oh no, sir. It were Sunday!"

"Is Mr Gilroy devout?"

The housekeeper's nostrils flared. "Only Mrs Gilroy goes to church. What I meant was that his business is closed on a Sunday."

"What line of business is he in?"

Her mouth formed a tight line. "Drinking and gambling. If it were not for me age, I'd look for a more suitable situation."

Charlie gave her a sympathetic nod. "When did Mr Gilroy last go out?"

"Saturday night. He weren't back until nearly daybreak, according to Cook, who got a terrible fright when he walked past the kitchen window looking like a ghoul. Ain't right, if you ask me."

95

"Thank you, Mrs Gillespie, you have been most helpful."

Charlie heard a door opening along the corridor, so he returned to the brougham, where Wallace and Kelly joined him a couple of minutes later.

Kelly stowed a box between his feet. "We've seized his records, on suspicion of conducting illegal gaming. Gilroy says the black powder was to get rid of a tree stump. You should have seen his eyes light up when he described the stump exploding upwards. I'd wager he was the type of child who loved to play with fire and pull the wings off flies."

Wallace thumped on the ceiling of the carriage and they rattled off down the driveway. "But Gilroy denied all knowledge of the bomb sent to Harriet Morison. He appeared to be telling the truth."

"Thought he was going to have heart failure when you told him we knew he intended to target Miss Morison," Kelly said. "He claimed he got cold feet. Reading between the lines, I think he didn't want to draw any attention to his illegal gambling business. Like Sweeney, he said there was never any intention of hurting the women."

Charlie wasn't convinced by their pleas of innocence, but he had found nothing incriminating to say otherwise. "Gilroy had no idea how to use explosives and no opportunity to take any black powder, according to the gardener, who is a simple, honest fellow. Nor did he leave the house yesterday or today, according to the stable boy and the housekeeper."

"We can confirm he is in the clear for this morning," Wallace agreed. "Mrs Gilroy took a turn and her husband was there to tend to her. She's got consumption, poor woman, and bad too. Her nurse has Sunday off, so Mr Gilroy never leaves his wife until the nurse gets back at midday on Monday." Wallace slumped in his seat. "Damnation. I was sure we had our man."

"Did he say anything about Lennox MacDonald?" Charlie asked.

"He agreed with Sweeney's assessment," Kelly answered. "Lennox MacDonald didn't say much at the meeting and appeared reluctant to be involved. MacDonald owns a brewery out Caversham way. Gilroy's view is that MacDonald is not worried about all the hotels being closed, as that will only make men drink more beer from his brewery in their own homes. It's a fair point, although MacDonald must be as worried as the others at the prospect of total prohibition of alcohol."

"Men always find a way to make and drink alcohol, regardless of the law," Wallace said. "I cannot believe that they think the government would allow prohibition, whether or not women get the vote. Any politician who supported such an extreme stance would be voted out on a tide of outrage at the next election."

"Does he think Lennox MacDonald did nothing?"

"Oh no, he agreed to give the women a fright too," Kelly said. "He wasn't specific at the meeting, but, according to Gilroy, MacDonald said 'he would have them jumping to his tune'. As you said earlier, Pyke, that sounds like MacDonald could have been responsible for the firecracker incident. He is also a good fit for the man who paid for the bomb to be delivered, unlike Gilroy. Perhaps he was more enthusiastic about the plan than he let on."

Wallace pulled his watch from his waistcoat pocket. "It's getting late. Let's call it a day. Kelly, you and I will visit MacDonald and Bertram tomorrow. Pyke, you'll stay behind tomorrow and go through this box of evidence. We may as well get Gilroy for illegal gambling as nothing. Might give these scoundrels second thoughts about their plot."

They travelled in silence until they were within sight of the central city.

"What worries me most is their future intentions," Wallace said. "It seems they each had a single target, so one might assume their campaign is nearly over. But when I asked each man specifically about the meeting to establish the Women's Franchise League, this coming Thursday, I got a creeping tingle up my spine that they were

97

lying in their denial of any plans to disrupt it. Both Gilroy and Sweeney flinched when I mentioned Lady Stout and Mrs Hatton."

Charlie and Kelly glanced at each other. Neither stated the obvious, that they only had two days left to prevent an attack on Sir Robert Stout's wife. If Lady Stout was harmed, or even threatened, they'd be lucky to be demoted to the graveyard shift in the Devil's Half Acre.

"It couldn't have happened at a worse time. With DS Elliot working on a case out of town and a DC laid up with a broken leg, I haven't the men to spare." Wallace cracked his knuckles and stared out the window with ill-disguised apprehension. "If Lady Stout is injured, it might be the spark that sets this revolution of womanhood aflame."

"Let's pray that any flame does not involve black powder," Charlie muttered, as he got out of the carriage and watched it disappear into the gathering gloom of an overcast evening.

Noose of Thorns

Grace had returned to Anne's house after the bombing with the firm intention of doing as she was told, by leaving investigations to the police. She rose early on Tuesday morning, made a strong cup of tea and settled down to her medical studies.

Despite having an essay due on the causes and symptoms of cholera, her attention strayed to treatments for burns and traumatic injuries. Before she knew it, her thoughts drifted to firecrackers, bombs and the Reynolds incident, which hadn't been followed up. Should she send a message to DI Wallace to interview Mrs Reynolds? He was a busy man, and the incident had sounded trivial. It would only take an hour of her time to satisfy her curiosity, then she would return to her essay.

Grace sent off two messages. One to Johnny Todd, who had a buggy on loan for transporting patients to Lavender House, and the second to Mrs Rachel Reynolds, requesting an appointment.

Johnny arrived with the buggy at half-past ten. Grace climbed up beside him, settling her plain grey skirt on the leather seat. Her fingers itched to take the reins, but she left it to him, knowing how much he relished his job as a driver.

"Do you know Montecillo house on Eglinton Road, Johnny?"

"Would you be visiting Mrs Reynolds?" His eyes widened. "Rather you than me. I hear she can crack a stock whip better than most men."

"And where did you hear that?"

"My sister has a friend who knows the scullery maid, who heard it from the cook, who was told by the lady's maid."

Grace laughed. "In that case, it is bound to be true. As a matter of fact, I know she grew up on a farm in the middle of nowhere in

Australia, so perhaps it is true. But she is a fine lady now, who has achieved more good deeds for this city than almost any other."

"Aye, I know. She and her daughters, and her ladies at St Andrew's, taught my sisters to sew on a machine. Helped them to get their jobs an' all."

"And I would not be at university if Mrs Reynolds hadn't advocated for the admission of women."

Grace closed her eyes and let the April sunshine warm her face. The buggy wheels crunched through autumn leaves, sending up a delicious, earthy scent. Far too nice a day to waste time indoors, especially with winter upon them in another five weeks. Far too nice to be thinking about bombs, but the fact remained that the men behind it must be stopped.

"Johnny, I imagine you have heard of the bomb delivered to Miss Morison yesterday and the firecracker incident on Saturday?"

"Aye, Miss Penrose. My pa reckons it must be anarchists, over from the Continent to spread their mischief."

"I fear we will find the culprits rather closer to home. The police have been unable to find the boy who set off the firecrackers. Someone will have paid him to do it. Do you think you might be able to find out?"

"No problem. My lot may not talk to the coppers, but they sure love to prattle amongst themselves, 'specially for something as exciting as that."

"If you find out who he is, ask the lad to describe the person who paid him, then take the information to DC Pyke at the police station."

"Do I have to go to the police station?" He shot her a pleading look, as if she was asking him to infiltrate a den of cutthroat pirates. "What if Copper Charlie ain't there?"

"In that case, ask for DC Kelly. Do you know him?"

"Declan Kelly. My cousin knows the Kelly boys. She was sweet on one of them, but it came to nothing, what with him being one of the Pope's lot."

Johnny directed the horse into a gateway, his hands light on the reins, as an expert ought to be. "What time shall I be back for you, Miss Penrose?"

"I can drive the buggy home. It is important that the police hear from you as soon as possible."

"If you say so." He sunk into uncharacteristic gloom as they trotted up the driveway. The fine view over the lush green of the town belt to South Dunedin and the ocean beyond should have banished the gloom from any face.

Grace prepared herself to meet one of the most formidable characters Dunedin had to offer. Had she the time and the daring, she would have loved nothing more than the opportunity to question Mrs Reynolds at length, to learn how she had achieved so much for so many worthy causes, while raising nine children of her own and supporting her husband's political career. Another day, perhaps.

Mrs Reynolds rose from her seat on the terrace, looking as formidable as her reputation, in her tall hat and furs. She strode forward with a welcoming smile. "Miss Penrose. We have not been formally introduced, although I am acquainted with Mrs Macmillan."

Grace jumped down from the buggy. "My great-aunt is a great admirer of your work, Mrs Reynolds, as am I."

"You are to be a doctor, I understand. It will be a fine day when women are attended by one of their own. A certified practitioner, I mean. I would not wish to diminish the excellent service provided by Mrs Macmillan at Lavender House."

"I count myself fortunate to have been given opportunities that were not open to my great-aunt."

Mrs Reynolds' eyes sparkled with understanding. "Given? I heard you put up a staunch fight for a place at medical school against considerable opposition. I would have loved to have been present when you convinced the hospital trustees."

"I'm sure you've faced far worse than that coven of stiff-necks, Mrs Reynolds. I suppose each generation must forge new paths."

101

"Indeed, they must, for there is always more to achieve." Mrs Reynolds offered her arm. "Come along, Miss Penrose. Much as I would enjoy a lively conversation with you, I am sure you are a busy young woman. We shall have tea on the veranda while you tell me what you wish to see me about."

They strolled around the side of the house, on a sunny path lined with bright orange marigolds, on their last gasp before the frosts set in. "Miss Nicol told me there had been an incident involving your roses. I am not sure if you know that there have been several other attacks targeting supporters of the franchise for women, of increasing seriousness."

"I saw the article in the *Times* this morning about an explosive device sent to the Tailoresses' Union yesterday. I can scarcely believe it to be true. A foolish prank, perhaps?"

"Unfortunately, it was no prank. I was there. The bomb was a warning, we think, but it could have caused serious injury to the woman who opened it. Miss Nicol was also the target of a spiteful attack, and another lady was kicked by a runaway horse, while two others were assaulted by a trio of ruffians."

"I see. That does rather change my view on the matter. Come. I can see you have more important matters to attend to than tea and cake."

Mrs Reynolds led Grace to an enclosed rose garden, where several roses bushes had been savaged. Grace examined the severed plants, noting a series of footprints, which were made by a man's work boot. Two pairs of boots, in fact. No doubt one pair belonged to the irate gardener.

"The damage to my roses pains me, but I saw no point in reporting it to the police at the time."

"Who do you think might have done this, Mrs Reynolds?"

"As an advocate of alcohol prohibition and other unpopular causes, I imagine the list of suspects would be a long one. The liquor merchants who gather around the coat-tails of Mr Henry Fish would be my first inclination. Although the present incident goes beyond their usual *modus operandi*, of vitriolic verbal abuse."

"I take it nobody saw the person who did this?"

"My husband and I were not at home. Our gardener recalled seeing a man loitering on Eglinton Road as we left. All the gardener could recall was that the man had a slight limp, a large nose and the attire of a working man. The man walked away, so the gardener thought no more of it and continued on to the other end of the property to fix a fence. None of the household staff saw anything. The rose garden is overlooked by the main bedrooms, not the staff areas."

"Aside from your lovely roses, did the perpetrator do any other mischief?"

"The scoundrel left an unpleasant message." Mrs Reynolds turned and walked to a vine-covered veranda, perfectly angled for shelter in the summer and sun in the winter. She reached into an alcove and drew out a crude noose, fashioned from plant stems, with a note affixed.

Her hostess handed it to her with a grimace. Grace took it carefully to avoid the thorns and the greenery twisted around the rose stems, which she knew to be hemlock from her recent foray into toxic plants.

The note itself was as repulsive as the noose. A newspaper clipping had been stuck onto the paper. Another copy of the letter penned by Outraged Gent. The note was splattered with drops of red. The drops were too pale and orange-red to be blood, but they were sufficiently similar to make the implications obvious.

"Rosehip juice," Mrs Reynolds remarked. "I have had my share of abuse from all manner of men in the past, but I must admit I cannot recall anything that made me angrier than this. My prize roses, hacked to pieces, right when they are putting on a beautiful display of hips."

Grace admired her fortitude, but surely anger at losing one's roses cannot have been her first emotion at seeing this blatant threat.

"I would suggest that you do not ignore its chilling warning, Mrs Reynolds. The imagery of the red drops is suggestive, as is the hemlock entwined with the rose stems to form the noose."

The lady bristled. "I will not be intimidated by an odious coward who is not man enough to argue his case against me in person."

"Nevertheless, it would be best to take extra care. There is a malicious mind behind this."

"Or an idiot spurred into hasty action by this poisonous letter in the *Otago Workman*. Have you read it?"

"I have. It is a vile rant against womanhood and good sense. But also a clear incitement to rise against us. The police are aware of it and are taking action."

Grace skimmed through the newspaper clipping again, feeling every bit as sick as when she first read it. The use of phrases such as "an abomination against our Lord" and "righteous husbands and fathers of this land shall rise up against the outrage" gave it a spurious biblical quality, suggesting that right was on their side, no matter what they did.

Underneath the newspaper clipping, the culprit had appended his own handwritten message. "Men hav the rite to sup ail. Deny us over yore ded bodie." Perhaps Mrs Reynolds was right. The malicious mind was more likely to be Outraged Gent than the illiterate idiot who had acted upon his advice.

"I concede your point. The illiteracy of the handwritten message seems at odds with the overall message, which is vicious but cleverly conceived."

"Especially as the handwritten message refers to temperance, while the other is against the franchise for women."

"May I take this to the police, Mrs Reynolds?"

"In view of recent events, I think it would be wise. In fact, I was planning to do so myself, as I received a message from Detective Inspector Wallace this morning, warning me to be careful. They appear to be taking the matter seriously."

"Very much so, especially with the first meeting of the Women's Franchise League in two days' time."

"Then I shall detain you no longer."

"Thank you for your time, Mrs Reynolds. Might I venture to suggest that you do not attend the meeting?"

"Will you be attending, Miss Penrose?" Her head tilted to the side as she watched Grace's hesitation. A smile twitched at her lips. "Splendid. I shall see you on Thursday afternoon, two o'clock sharp."

Prime Suspect

Charlie arrived at the police station early on Tuesday morning and got to work sorting through the documents seized from Gilroy. The man was cunning. He'd used a coding system to disguise the nature of his business, although he couldn't disguise the extent of his dealings. Well before Charlie had choked down the first cup of the stewed beverage the station claimed was tea, he'd found a list of debts owed. One or two influential names were in debt to Gilroy for substantial sums, alongside a raft of lesser names. By the second cup of the evil brew, he had cracked the code and had the makings of a case against Gilroy.

The closure of Gilroy's hotels must have been a hard blow to his finances, but Charlie still wondered why the Gilroy household struggled to make ends meet, when he operated a lucrative illegal gaming enterprise. He discovered the reason at the bottom of the pile. Gilroy had bailed out his brother when his clothing business was forced to close down. All the more reason he must harbour deep resentment against Harriet Morison and the Dunedin Tailoresses' Union, as well as the temperance movement.

As he neared the end of the paperwork, Charlie got a call from the desk officer. He ran up the stairs, hoping it might be Grace, but he was faced with a young man who looked both vaguely familiar and relieved to see him.

"Johnny Todd?" He was scarcely recognisable as the small, ragged boy Charlie had first met over two years ago. Johnny had sprouted up and out until all that remained the same were his bright eyes and cheeky grin. "Come with me."

"Miss Penrose sent me," Johnny said, when they were safely in his basement lair. "She asked me to find the lad who set off the firecrackers and come tell you."

"You did better than us if you found him, Johnny."

"Aye, well, lads on the street don't take to coppers asking their business, especially when their business ends up hurting ladies. But they sure do like to brag about it around their own. He told me a man came up to him near the Octagon, offering him tuppence to let off the firecrackers. What a halfwit. He ought to have known the lad would have jumped at the chance to do it for nothing."

"The man cannot have known much about the enthusiasms of young boys," Charlie agreed.

"At any rate, the man stood across the road and signalled when he wanted the boy to light the fuse. When he looked up again, the man had disappeared. As soon as the horse bolted, so did he, and no wonder. Reckon he was feeling a mite ashamed, knowing a lady could have been killed."

"Did the lad give a description of the man?"

"Tall gent, fancy clothes, wearing a scarf over his face. The lad didn't set much store on recognising him again."

Same story as the baker's delivery boy, thought Charlie. No surprise there. Charlie flipped a coin to Johnny, who caught it with unerring accuracy. "Good work, Johnny. We might need the lad to come in and look at some pictures. Would you be able to find him again?"

"Sure, but I reckon I'd have to hog-tie him to get him into a police station, and I don't reckon it would do much good, anyway."

Charlie let Johnny out of the rear exit and went back to his desk. Not five minutes later, his thoughts were interrupted by the distinctive tread of Mr Peters upon the stairs, a rapid but tentative patter, accompanied by a slight wheezing. Peters was carrying a slim file. Charlie couldn't recall ever seeing the records clerk without a document in hand.

"This is all I have been able to find on Mr Lennox MacDonald."

"Splendid. Please have a seat, Mr Peters, and give me a brief summary of facts."

"Lennox MacDonald, age thirty-six, married Emily Bertram six years ago. The marriage was witnessed by Harold Bertram, Emily's brother."

Charlie felt the jolt of excitement that always accompanied a minor breakthrough. "Excellent work, Mr Peters. This may well be the reason that the reluctant Lennox is part of Harry Bertram's group of intimate friends and conspirators."

Peters grinned, which was so uncharacteristic, Charlie couldn't wait to hear what was to come next.

"I haven't got to the best part, DC Pyke. Lennox MacDonald is the part-owner of the Southside Brewery in Caversham. His father, Mr Fergus MacDonald, purchased it for him two years ago, retaining a controlling share. Lennox also holds a share in his father's company, MacDonald Roading, which is notable for its work constructing roads and railway lines. Work which, without a doubt, requires substantial quantities of explosive material."

"Better and better. Wallace will be ecstatic."

"One other matter that might be of interest," Peters continued with barely restrained glee. "Two years ago, before the purchase of the brewery, Lennox was investigated by the police for his part in an explosion which took the life of an employee. No charge was ever laid. The official version was that the employee was at fault. However, two workers came forward claiming Lennox MacDonald was negligent. Their accusations were dismissed as grudges against the son of the boss. Reading between the lines, it is possible Fergus MacDonald paid off the deceased's family and the accusers to make the charges go away, before finding a less dangerous line of work for his son."

Charlie shoved his chair back and took the folder in one quick movement. "Great work, Mr Peters. Please excuse my haste. Wallace will want to have this information before he interviews Lennox MacDonald." He left Peters straightening the files on his desk, as he raced up the stairs.

Charlie intercepted Wallace and Kelly as they emerged from the Engineers' Arms. Wallace hurried him away, not uttering a word until they found a private spot in the gardens of the Benny.

"I know you told me to stay at the station," Charlie explained, "but you need to hear what Mr Peters has found out. Lennox MacDonald is the brother-in-law of Harry Bertram and the son of Fergus MacDonald, of MacDonald Roading, specialising in roads and railway lines. Lennox was hustled out of the business two years ago after killing a worker with his careless use of explosives. Allegedly, never proved."

Wallace's tight irritation dissolved into a predatory smile. "So Lennox MacDonald had access to black powder and the expertise to use it, while Bertram could have gotten hold of the bomb makings through his brother-in-law. Perhaps Gilroy is not our man after all."

"We'll get Gilroy on the illegal gambling regardless," Charlie replied. "He's in desperate need of funds to pay off his brother's debt. Did you get any information out of Harry Bertram?"

"Bertram admitted writing the Outraged Gent letter to the paper. Indeed, he showed every sign of being proud of it. He did not admit to any intention of attacking Mrs Reynolds, but he left us in little doubt that he hates her. In fact, he appears to hate all women, especially those who show any spark of independence. He refused to comment on the other three men at the meeting. He was, however, adamant in his denial of the bomb sent to Miss Morison, and in this he seemed sincere, as far as one can judge sincerity in such a man. What was your take, Kelly?"

"I agree. He was convincing in his denial of the bomb, but he is an expert poker player, so I suppose that leaves room for doubt."

"This new information suggests MacDonald had the means to make the bomb and firecrackers, if not the strongest motive," Wallace continued. "But we know Gilroy also had black powder and the other two could have bought some easily enough too. Which still leaves us with a minimum of four suspects and who knows how many other accomplices, with an unspecified but likely high-profile

109

future target, and any method of attack from pea shooters to a barrel of dynamite." Wallace paced back and forth. "If we can't break MacDonald, all I can do is beg for enough men to put all the suspects under day and night surveillance."

"Then let's go and squeeze the truth out of our reckless explosives expert," Kelly said.

As they walked the half mile to the brewery, Wallace outlined his plan. "Pyke, you take the brewery staff. Kelly, you search his office. I'll tackle Mr Lennox MacDonald. If he won't talk, I'll bring you in, Pyke, to ruffle his feathers. He'll know by now that the police had a man at the meeting the four of them attended last Friday. We must leave him with the impression that he will be left taking the blame, if he does not tell us the truth."

Charlie interviewed staff members at the brewery and came away with the impression that Lennox MacDonald had a very easy life indeed. The brewery manager claimed, with a distinct lack of conviction, that Mr MacDonald was a busy man, who could spare little time from his personal affairs to spend time at the brewery.

The foreman was less tactful. "Stumbles in at noon, after the rest of us have been working for hours, looking like hell and smelling of expensive cigars and cheap perfume, if you get my drift. Life of a toff, eh? All right for some."

The alibis of all four suspects would have to be checked via a lot of tedious interviewing of wives and domestics, though Charlie had a strong feeling it would make little difference. The wives of such men would certainly have their own rooms rather than waiting until the wee hours of the morning, only to be awoken by husbands smelling of cheap perfume. What a hideous life. He hoped the wives thought the financial benefits of the marriage were worth it.

Kelly came to say Wallace wanted him in the interview with Lennox.

Despite it being early afternoon on a Tuesday, the man lounging behind the desk appeared exactly as the staff described – bleary eyed, reeking of tobacco and full of the kind of self-satisfaction known only to indolent rich men who did not deserve to feel anything but shame. Nevertheless, his valet had ensured his fashionable clothes were pressed and his handsome face was closely shaved, which kept Mr Lennox MacDonald on the right side of the line between well-to-do and dissolute.

"Ah, Detective Constable Pyke. Mr MacDonald was telling me he was tucked up in bed last Friday night and has never attended a meeting with Bertram, Gilroy, and Sweeney."

Charlie walked up to the desk, planting his rear end on its pristine surface. MacDonald glared at him, but the glare was soon followed by a frown. Charlie rubbed his hand over his clean-shaven jaw as he stared the man down, giving him a good look at his distinctive green eyes. His foot swung back and forth, drumming gently against the desk.

"Nice cravat you're wearing, Mr MacDonald. Exactly the same colour and pattern as the gentleman attending that very meeting last Friday. Your height and build he was too, with the same oddly shaped ears. Funny how some men have one ear lower than the other – attached lobes too. What a coincidence."

The frown hardened into suspicious silence.

Wallace took his turn with bland assurance. "Perhaps we could ask Mrs Lennox MacDonald whether her husband was with her brother on Friday night?"

"We might do better to ask the barman's wife at the Engineers' Arms, sir," Charlie replied. "Mrs Ellen Vance has a clear memory of events, as the suspects abused her in a way no true gentleman would countenance. It's all in the official medical report, along with the names of her abusers."

The silence was broken only by his kicking against MacDonald's desk – thump, thump, thump … thump, thump, thump – until MacDonald appeared to be on the verge of using the fists he had been clenching for the last five minutes.

"Of course, Mrs Vance was not present when the suspects were talking about their plot to terrify the suffragists into stopping their campaign to get the vote for women."

"You slimy, snooping blackguard," MacDonald hissed, rising to his feet and towering over his tormentor.

Charlie stood up too, crossing his arms over his chest and meeting his glare, showing Lennox MacDonald that, for all his size and arrogance, he came a poor second in both musculature and authority compared to the man in front of him. "Detective Inspector Wallace is waiting for answers to his questions, Mr MacDonald. I wouldn't advise lying to him. You are aware, I take it, that statements have already been made by the other three men at that meeting. You have some explaining to do."

MacDonald resumed his seat, almost missing the chair in his haste. "I demand to have my attorney present."

"That is your right, Mr MacDonald," Wallace conceded. "While you arrange that, I will return to the station and peruse the files on past charges laid against you, which appear to have been dropped rather prematurely. Wilful negligence causing death, wasn't it? What do you think, Pyke? Shall we resurrect the charge and upgrade it to manslaughter?"

"That would certainly make an impression on the jury, should the suspect be charged with the attempted murder of Miss Harriet Morison on Monday morning, as well as the woman injured in the firecracker incident outside Choral Hall on Saturday. Unless you have anything further to say upon the matter, Mr MacDonald?"

Lennox MacDonald shrank back into his chair, his jaws clamped so tight his lips turned white. He glared at them defiantly, refusing to say another word. They left him to stew.

"Damnation," Wallace growled when they were clear of the brewery. "I was sure he would be the weak link, but he must be too terrified of Bertram to give an inch. His attorney will tell him we don't have sufficient grounds to arrest him."

"Did he give anything away?" Charlie asked.

"No admissions, but he's not as good at lying as the others. The muscles in the corner of his eyes definitely tightened when I asked if he was responsible for the fireworks. His reaction to the Morison bomb was interesting – genuine shock, followed by a less than convincing denial of any involvement. If I had to put a wager on it, I'd say he is peripherally involved in it, perhaps as supplier of the black powder, without knowing what it was intended for."

"Did you ask about the Women's Franchise League meeting?"

"His eyes flicked sideways like a cornered rat searching for a dark hole to escape into. They are planning something, I'm sure of it. My guess is that he is regretting being part of Bertram's band. Probably thought of it merely as a prank, to unnerve the suffragists."

An hour later, Charlie was back in the basement cell that he was beginning to think of as his office, be it ever so humble. A soft step behind him and the faint scent of roses sent his pulse racing. "Have you brought me information, Grace, or is this a social call? Either way, you are most welcome."

"You have the hearing of a canine, Charlie. The desk officer appears to be quite resigned to my frequent visits, but I feared he had misdirected me to the dungeons, until I found your lair."

Grace ran a hand over his shoulder, sending the nerve endings on a merry dance, and deposited a tin in front of him. How perfect life would be if he worked in Dunedin and he could see her every day. Every night too, if he had his way.

"More bomb fragments?" Charlie opened the tin eagerly. It contained a slice of seed cake, so fresh from the oven it was still steaming.

"You look as if you are in a state of bliss, DC Pyke. Is it Mrs Brown's baking, or the evidence piled on your desk?"

"Both." He caught hold of her hand and held it for a moment, before guiding her to a chair. "And a third reason even more delightful. Unfortunately, I can see from the gleam in your eyes that this is not a social visit, more's the pity."

"I come with information about an attack directed against Mrs Rachel Reynolds."

"In that case, social niceties will have to wait." Charlie put the lid back on the tin and stood up. "Wallace will want to know immediately, as we'd been expecting something of the sort. I hope the lady is unharmed?"

"She is more cross than upset. The incident was malicious rather than an actual assault, but nasty enough to turn the stomach."

Charlie took Grace upstairs to Wallace's office. "Miss Penrose has news about Mrs Reynolds, sir. I'll get DC Kelly."

When they were all seated, Wallace gestured for Grace to go ahead.

"Mrs Reynolds received your note before I arrived at her house this morning. She had not reported the incident to the police, but wanted to do so as soon as she heard about the bomb sent to Harriet Morison. She agreed to let me convey the details, which was that she received a warning message on Friday, while she was out at a temperance meeting with her husband. The likely suspect was a working man with a slight limp and a large nose. Judging from the boot print in the garden, his left leg is the problem, as the boot was unevenly worn."

Grace withdrew the vile noose from her satchel and dropped it on the desk. "The greenery is hemlock. The drops of red are rosehip juice."

Three heads bent forward. Kelly lurched back with a gasp, Wallace prodded it with his pencil as if it might be a venomous snake, and Charlie struggled to suppress an inappropriate laugh. Three faces turned on him.

"Good detective work on the boot print in the garden, Grace, but this particular criminal will be easy to unmask. Vance, the barman at the Engineers' Arms, has a slight limp in his left leg and a large nose. He is also barely literate and a terrible speller, who writes the word 'ale' as 'ail'. I had to take an order to the brewery, and the clerk made a joke about it."

"Vance is Bertram's man, isn't he?" Wallace said. "That's good news indeed. Thank you, Miss Penrose. We had been expecting an attack on Mrs Reynolds after hearing that one of our suspects planned to target her. Harry Bertram, owner of the Engineers' Arms. This is exactly the evidence we need to break his silence."

"I'm pleased to hear you know who is behind this repulsive threat," Grace replied. "The handwritten note struck me as out of step with the broader message."

"I agree," Charlie said. "I have little doubt that Bertram was behind this, using Vance as his delivery boy. How typical of Vance to be unable to do a simple job without putting his own vicious stamp on it."

Wallace poked the thorny noose with the tip of a pencil again. "Their motive appears to be to frighten women into giving up the suffrage cause, so that women cannot vote in favour of prohibition. Each of the targeted women supports both temperance and suffrage."

"They are each associated with the Dunedin Tailoresses' Union as well," Kelly noted.

"The message is explicitly against allowing women the vote," Charlie countered.

Grace shuffled in her chair, her collar itching as the heat of the room intensified. "Each of the women targeted is also critical to the establishment of the Women's Franchise League."

Wallace bent the pencil between his hands until it started to splinter. "I have arranged a contingent of constables to protect the meeting attendees. I will make sure there is a special detail to protect the presumptive presidents, Lady Stout and Mrs Hatton. I hardly need tell you of the political ramifications if the wife of Sir Robert Stout is attacked."

"Shall I leave you gentlemen to your discussions? I have an essay due on cholera that won't write itself."

"You may as well stay, Miss Penrose, if you wish. Your knowledge of the suffragists might be useful. However, I must insist on two things. First, that what we say is not discussed outside this

115

room. And second, that you promise to keep out of the investigation of these incidents from this point on. These men are dangerous."

Charlie noticed Grace wasted no time in resuming her seat, the cholera essay notwithstanding. "So, what now, sir?"

"I've half a mind to bring all four men into the station for further questioning. The problem is that they have probably already organised whatever disruption they are intending for the Women's Franchise League meeting. I'm inclined to leave them under surveillance, to see if we can't get a hint at exactly what they have planned. I wish I had the time and manpower to interview all their associates, family, household staff and so forth, to see if we cannot shake a few apples off their tree."

The Chief Inspector appeared in the doorway, catching sight of Grace as he did so. "Pardon me, Miss."

She smiled angelically at him. "I was about to leave. I was only here to deliver a witness statement to your fine officers." Grace slipped out the door before he could ask further questions.

The Chief Inspector stood aside to let her out. "Wallace, a moment of your time."

Wallace left the office, returning five minutes later and several shades paler. "A problem has arisen, DC Pyke. The Chief Inspector has received a letter accusing Charlie Potts of abducting Mrs Vance. The letter identifies Potts as a policeman. It is the work of the barman, Vance, and his puppet-master, Bertram, without a doubt. The letter is, I hardly need add, inflammatory. They didn't waste any time seeking revenge on you."

"What was the Chief Inspector's reaction, sir, if I might ask?" Charlie choked out the words, with little help from his overstrung vocal cords.

"He reminded me that he had not been in favour of your secondment and placement in South Dunedin, owing to the sensitivity around investigating prominent members of the business community. What was I to do?" Wallace demanded. "The Chief wanted action on rumours of illegal gambling and liquor license violations. Putting an out-of-town man undercover was the only sensible and discreet method to tackle the issue."

"I'm sorry, sir. I realise this does not reflect well on you. It was a mistake on my part to assist Mrs Vance and jeopardise my position. Does the Chief want me stood down?"

"I managed to convince him the letter was a misrepresentation of the facts," Wallace said. "I told him that I am completely satisfied that no abduction took place, as verified by an independent medical expert. He didn't order me to stand you down, not in so many words. But we need to be careful. You're to have no further contact with Vance or anyone else who might recognise you as Charlie Potts. Rather like shutting the stable door after the horse has bolted, but I have no other choice."

Charlie kept his emotions rigidly under control. "Yes, sir. I understand."

"It's no fault of yours, Pyke. I read Miss Penrose's report on the extent of injuries and abuses to Mrs Vance. You made the right call." Wallace paced around the small office, which was not much bigger than his desk. "I can ill afford to lose an experienced man at this point of the investigation, but I agree with the Chief Inspector that you must keep your head down."

"I still want to be of assistance, at least until the Women's Franchise League meeting has safely passed." Especially as Grace and her great-aunt would be there.

"Take tomorrow off, Pyke. You must be owed leave, after all the time undercover. We will have no time to conduct further investigations anyway, as we will be fully occupied putting a plan in place to keep the suffragists safe on Thursday."

"And the franchise meeting, sir?"

"You cannot be seen by any of the men who know you as Potts, but perhaps you could be inside Choral Hall, keeping a watchful eye on what is happening."

"Thank you, sir."

"But don't come outside. Even if Miss Penrose is threatened."

Charlie's jaw tightened. "I would rather lose my position entirely, sir, than stand back when a friend is threatened."

Wallace's shoulders slumped. "Of course. Forget I said it and, for the love of God, try to stay out of trouble for a few days."

Wallace waved at the door. Charlie took the hint and departed before he could be asked to make any other promises he couldn't keep.

Vultures Circling

Grace put the final full stop on her cholera essay, knowing it would scrape her a pass at best. She flapped the final page to dry the ink, before folding it into an envelope. Shame at her pathetic effort almost stayed her hand, but she didn't have the heart to rework it. Besides, it was due tomorrow, the day of the inaugural Women's Franchise League meeting. If ever there was a time to let her medical degree take second place in her life, it was now.

Despite DI Wallace's assurance that they had their suspects at bay, with every knock on the door she feared word of some new outrage. Two days had passed since the attack on Harriet Morison, but the lull gave her no comfort. Indeed, it only made her more convinced that the next attack would be tomorrow at the meeting.

She had agreed to stay out of police business, but that didn't stop her worrying about what was to come. Aside from the threat to her friends, she was concerned about Charlie. The problem was, she possessed information that he did not. She had promised not to tell him until the time was right, but she had a strong sense that he was being dragged into a situation that he did not fully comprehend.

"Grace, may I have a moment of your time?" Anne called up the stairs.

Grace deposited her essay in the post tray in the hall and found her great-aunt with Mr Drummond, seated together cosily on the sofa in the drawing room. Drummond stood to greet her, bowing over her hand with a charming old-fashioned civility.

"Kenneth has come to see us, as he is concerned about Charlie," Anne explained.

"I share your concerns, Mr Drummond. Charlie has the right to know what is happening in Wellington, despite DI Stewart's desire to shield him."

"I agree, Miss Penrose," Drummond said. "I find myself in a difficult position. Your young man asked me not to tell you about his current situation in Dunedin. Equally, Alistair Stewart asked me not to discuss events in Wellington. As an attorney, I am obliged to respect their confidences. However, as a friend, I cannot remain silent. Young Pyke is heading for trouble and he does not yet know it."

Grace perched on the edge of an armchair, trying to remain calm. "His situation in Dunedin?"

Drummond paced across the room, his hands clasped behind his back, looking every inch the barrister conveying weighty matters to a jury. When he reached the fireplace, he seemed to have come to a decision. "Pyke has been accused of kidnapping Mrs Vance. Wallace has given him his full support, naturally, but you will appreciate that another false accusation is the last thing he needs. It begins to look like 'no smoke without fire', even though the evidence in his favour is compelling. Wallace has asked him to take the day off and to ensure he has no further contact with Vance and the other suspects."

Grace was on her feet in an instant. "In that case, there is nothing more to discuss. Charlie must be told immediately. Wallace ought to have sent him far away at the first sign of trouble."

"I'm sure it cannot be so bad as you think, Grace," Anne said, "although I agree he should be told."

"His career is in jeopardy, and that means everything to Charlie. Please excuse me. I am extremely grateful for your visit, Mr Drummond."

"You'll find Pyke in my garden, savaging weeds with a slasher. That lad has an extraordinary capacity for hard work, as well as a fine mind. I wish he could stay on with me indefinitely. I have so enjoyed his company."

Grace grabbed her coat and hat as she dashed out the door. Five minutes later, she reached the gate of Mr Drummond's overgrown garden.

Charlie paused in mid-slash at the sound of the creaking gate, leaving a devastation of weeds all around him. "Grace, what are you doing here? I was beginning to think I was the last person left on earth, aside from Mr Drummond and his housekeeper."

"I promised I would stay away. The thing is…"

"You couldn't bear to be away from me?" He leaned on a post, crinkling his emerald eyes at her in that beguiling way he had.

She raised an eyebrow. "How could I resist you, dripping sweat in those filthy old gardening clothes? Are you beginning your transformation back to Mr Potts?"

"Give me a minute to wash and change back into Mr Charles Pyke, esquire. There's a path into the town belt beyond that apple tree."

"I'd rather have the regular Charlie Pyke," she called after him.

The regular Charlie Pyke returned dirt free, with a clean shirt and a wide grin. She knew that would not last, but perhaps they could have a few minutes of uninterrupted normality first. He appeared to feel the same, because they strolled up the woodland path in companionable silence.

When they reached the lookout at the top of the hill, he took her in his arms and kissed her with unhurried tenderness. Grace would have been happy to stay there forever, locked within his arms, but he released her and stepped away, putting a literal and figurative distance between them.

"Now, what dire news are you here to torment me with, Grace?"

She didn't bother to ask him how he knew. They had sensed each other's thoughts from almost the first time they had met. It was only when they were apart – which was almost always – that she gave in to doubt. "Charlie, I want you to stay away from the Women's Franchise League meeting tomorrow. Anne and I will be safe inside Choral Hall. We'll be there before the meeting, counting signatures on the petition so we can announce a final tally."

"Why should I stay away, Grace? I have agreed not to show my face outside, but Wallace has assigned me to be on guard inside the hall. I cannot let him down and I'll be perfectly placed to ensure your safety."

"And I know you have a sixth sense for danger. Do not give into it. Not because you might put yourself at risk, but so as not to endanger your career."

"Why the concern about my career? Is this about the accusation that I abducted Mrs Vance? We have your medical evidence in my favour. Besides, I doubt Vance would risk his wife giving evidence of his brutality towards her. I'm sure the barman and his boss are simply trying to stir up trouble for me."

"Charlie, it's not that." She took his arm and propelled him to a bench seat overlooking the city. When they were seated so close she could feel the heat radiating from him, she continued. "It's about the vultures circling in Wellington. I promised DI Stewart I would say nothing, but I think you should know the extent of it, in case word leaks out and exacerbates your position here."

"I'm not sure I know what you mean, Grace. What vultures?"

"That gang of anti-immigrant louts you arrested last December–"

The tension in his shoulders gave way to relief. "That's old news, Grace. I know the ringleader hasn't been charged because he is the nephew of a Member of the House of Representatives. I'm not happy about it, naturally, but there is little I can do. The accepted position is that they were a merry group of well-bred young gentlemen, out for a night on the town, who never so much as glanced at the Chinese shopkeepers, who were later beaten by persons unknown. I've been reprimanded. End of story."

"I wish it was that simple, Charlie. After you left for Dunedin, the ringleader decided to extract his revenge on you, for having the gall to arrest him."

"I didn't even know who he was at the time."

"And if you had known, would you have stood back and watched him and his fancy friends beat those Chinese shopkeepers to a pulp?" Grace stared him down. He didn't need to answer.

"Exactly how is he planning to get his revenge?"

"He has demanded that you be charged with assault. DI Stewart didn't want to worry you, as you had already gone undercover."

"Assault? Are you joking? As you well know, it was me who ended up with boot marks all over my back, not him."

"He says you kicked him in the kidneys and he suffers continuing internal pain because of it. Very hard to prove either way, medically speaking."

"But I didn't kick him in the kidneys. The shopkeeper's wife did manage to land a blow before I dragged her off, but she was such a tiny woman, she could hardly squash a fly."

"Charlie, this is serious. All the Chinese shopkeepers withdrew their evidence. They are now saying that there was no mob attack, only your assault on an innocent man walking home after a night on the town. Naturally, his friends rushed to his aid, which is all the other policemen saw when they finally arrived on the scene."

"The swine must have intimidated the shopkeepers. Why am I not surprised?"

"The truth will be buried if they are too frightened to testify, especially with sworn evidence from the associates of the ringleader, who are part of the same mob of attackers. DI Stewart argued your case and got the authorities to hold off on a formal charge of assault. As you know, that would have automatically ended your career."

"Saints preserve us. What a mess. So, what happens now, Grace?"

"There will be a disciplinary hearing to establish the facts."

He jumped up. "I have to get back to Wellington to defend myself."

Grace pulled him back onto the seat. "Charlie, DI Stewart wanted you to remain here. With you undercover on secondment to Dunedin, he could argue you are doing your duty as a fine upstanding police officer, whereas your presence at the hearing might count against you, given your obvious size and strength. You are rather intimidating, you have to admit."

Charlie groaned as the implications sunk home. "But now I am no longer undercover. I am accused of abduction. If Vance hears I am also under investigation in Wellington, he will demand the abduction be investigated and probably claim I assaulted him too. And if the Wellington disciplinary hearing becomes aware of the accusations against me here, which the Chief Inspector is bound to report, I will certainly lose my position, if not my liberty. Of all the rotten luck. Sometimes I think I am cursed."

Grace slid her arm through his and pulled him close. "You are a diligent policeman, who never hesitates to choose the right path, rather than the easy path. Everyone admires you for that."

"Not everyone, evidently. Is that the extent of it, or have you more wounds to inflict?" He shook her arm loose, then thought better of it, gripping her hand tightly. "I'm sorry, Grace. I didn't mean that as it sounded. I know you are trying to help."

"There is one more unfortunate twist. Well, two twists, if you wish to know the worst of it."

"I'm not sure it could get much worse."

"DI Stewart agreed to your secondment to investigate illegal gambling. He is angry with himself now for not perceiving the complication that gambling and liquor go hand in hand. Even he could not have foreseen that you would uncover a plot by the liquor lobby to use violent means to stop the women's franchise movement."

"And?" Charlie grimaced, waiting for the blow to fall.

"The young lout who wants you charged with assault is not the nephew of any old member of parliament. His uncle is a rabid supporter of the liquor lobby and fervently against giving women the vote."

Charlie emitted the plaintive whimper of a wounded animal as his head slumped into his hands. "If they get an inkling of my undercover activities here, their desire for revenge will know no bounds. Do I have any support within the police force, aside from DI Stewart?"

"Of course. However, the other unfortunate complication is that one of the young louts arrested – not the ringleader, thank heavens – is the godson of the Deputy Commissioner of Police, who is inclined to accept the word of the young 'gentlemen' over his own men."

Grace's heart went out to him. She could see why he thought himself cursed right at this moment, and hoped he would remember his outstanding record as a policeman when he collected himself. Meanwhile, it was up to her to help him see that dark clouds always passed.

"Charlie, I am only telling you this because it is imperative that you stay completely out of the police investigation here in Dunedin. Wallace is a fine officer, but he does not appreciate what you are facing. In particular, you cannot be seen, in case anyone outside the police force makes the connection between Charlie Pyke and Charlie Potts."

"I'm sorry to say it is too late to keep that horse from bolting. The four liquor barons already know exactly who I am."

"Oh."

"I appreciate your kindness in being open with me, Grace. But you must see that such accusations stick like mud. My reputation and career will be over, even if I am ultimately cleared of all the allegations."

"You will be cleared, Charlie. I have left the good news until last."

"There is some good news? Pray tell me quickly."

"We have all been working hard to clear your name. Mr Drummond has been giving legal advice. I am not sure if Anne has told you, but he was one of the leading barristers of his generation and still as sharp as a scalpel. Lily is in Wellington using her contacts in the Chinese community to convince them to tell what really happened that night."

"She is? I thought Aunt Lily was making wedding preparations."

"I expect she is happy to see Alistair Stewart and discuss their wedding, but that is not her main aim. Even my family has become involved. They tracked down the only eyewitness who was neither a victim nor an attacker. They found him just before his ship sailed and convinced him to stay. You met him on Sunday."

"Doctor Ravenwood?"

"Rory saw the whole incident and gave a compelling witness statement highlighting your heroism in saving the Chinese shopkeepers from the mob." Grace squeezed his hand. "And the assistant police surgeon sent a report on the extensive injuries you sustained during the mob attack."

"But I wasn't examined by…" Realisation dawned. He clutched her hand to his chest. "And to think how I grumbled when you insisted on checking my injuries. Thank you, Grace. How can I repay everyone for their kindness?"

"I don't know about the others, but my devotion to you can be bought very easily."

"Jewels? Gold? Furs? Anything you want, dearest Grace."

"Idiot," she said, as she raised her lips to his, hoping to regain the earlier feeling of untroubled bliss.

But Charlie was not an idiot. He was a man bailed up in a corner and smart enough to know it. He kept the kiss brief, without a trace of his earlier passion. She was grateful that he hadn't walked away from her as soon as he heard the bad news, based on some cursedly honourable attempt to save her reputation from being dragged through the mud too.

Choral Hall

Charlie had considered Grace's request that he stay away from Choral Hall for all of ten seconds. Not that he thought she was wrong, but because it seemed inevitable that these lying troublemakers would take him down eventually and he was not about to walk away without a fight. Which was why he was at Choral Hall on Thursday morning, as planned, to stand guard until the Women's Franchise League meeting was over.

Besides, he wouldn't have been able to live with himself if a suffragist was injured when he might have prevented it. He had enormous respect for the way they held their heads high and forged ahead for what was right and proper, in the face of an unprincipled and often venomous opposition. How could it be right that an intelligent, compassionate woman like Grace Penrose was barred from having her say in how the country was run, when even the most degenerate brute of a man had that right?

As if conjured by his thoughts, a waft of stale sweat and whisky assailed his nostrils.

"Ye're still here?" the caretaker muttered, as he swept a broom across the foyer of Choral Hall with all the vigour of a geriatric slug – or a man with a thumping hangover.

"Yes, Mr Taylor, I'll be here all day, as Detective Inspector Wallace notified you." Charlie wondered how much whisky it took to sink a burly man like Taylor into such a state. His ruddy face suggested he'd had plenty of practice.

"Lot of feckin' fuss over nothin'," Taylor grumbled.

The caretaker had hauled himself out of bed to let Charlie in through the locked front door at nine o'clock, as had been agreed. The door was to remain locked, with Charlie patrolling the premises and only letting in those who had a reason to be there. As far as he was concerned, that list included only the women attending the Women's Franchise League meeting at two o'clock this afternoon and the Homemakers' Association at ten o'clock this morning.

Wallace had worked hard to convince the Homemakers to postpone their committee meeting, but he had met with the same implacable refusal as he had suffered at the hands of the Women's Franchise League organisers. You had to hand it to these women – they were indomitable when it came to their respective causes, even if their causes were as different as fire and ice.

Charlie returned to his circuit of the building's interior. The sun streamed through a round-arched window above the stairs like a ray from heaven, lighting his path upstairs. The upper hall stretched out before him, with room to seat hundreds of people. His eyes were drawn to the ceiling, a remarkable elliptical structure of polished kauri wood, with skylights of stained glass adding to the grandeur. A most fitting location for the inaugural meeting of the Women's Franchise League.

He checked every nook and cranny. Everything appeared to be in order, so he went back downstairs to the smaller lower hall, where the Homemakers' Association committee would meet. Aside from chairs and a table, it too was empty. He exited back into the foyer and across to the corridor along the western side of the building. The main office was adjacent to the foyer, overlooking Moray Place. Next was a kitchen area and adjoining storage room, the back entrance, and the caretaker's poky bed-sitting room.

Charlie checked that the back door was securely locked before continuing his tour along the rear side of the building, which comprised two smaller meeting rooms. One of these rooms showed signs of recent use. The place reeked of tobacco. A set of chairs surrounded the table haphazardly, with ash, crumbs, glasses, plates and bottles strewn across the table. Charlie bent to pick up a bright object from the floor. A gaming chip. Mr Taylor, the caretaker, had some explaining to do.

The man himself shuffled into the room. "No need to be poking yer nose in here, Constable."

"It is my job to be thorough. When was this room last used, Mr Taylor?"

Taylor's eyes flicked to the side under hooded lids. "Couple of days ago. A gentlemen's group meets regular to discuss charitable matters."

Charlie held up the gaming chip. "Charitable matters?"

"One of them gents must've dropped it from his pocket. Ain't no gambling on these premises."

"What time of the day do these 'charitable gentlemen' meet?"

"Evenings. After work."

"The smell of tobacco is overwhelming. Are you sure they didn't meet last night?"

"Aye. I've been that busy, I must've forgot to clean up. Tobacco smell do linger in a closed room. Ain't been no one in the hall since four o'clock yesterday afternoon, when the Scottish dancing lasses were here." The caretaker started sweeping the mess into one corner of the table, before brushing it into a dustpan. "I'll finish up here, Constable. The Homemaker ladies will be here soon."

"I'll see to the front door. Nobody is to enter without me present."

"You can't expect to have trouble from them, surely. Grand bunch of ladies, always courteous to me, always a slice of cake left for my supper. Proper ladies, if you ask me, looking after their husbands and doing their charity work, not like them so-called ladies coming this afternoon. I'll wager those franchise radicals wouldn't know a Victoria sponge from Victoria Station."

"Perhaps the suffragists have more important matters to attend to than cakes, Mr Taylor." Charlie left before he lost his temper or got dragged into a pointless argument.

The sound of a fist hammering on the main door hastened his step. The Homemakers' Association ladies clearly didn't care to be kept waiting, even though it was still ten minutes before their meeting time. He unlocked the door, intending to let them in one at a time.

129

That naïve plan evaporated as a surge of fashionably dressed ladies burst into the hall on a wave of indignant chatter, accompanied by maids, footmen, coachmen and a husband or two, carrying trays, baskets, tins and boxes. The wave ebbed as quickly as it had surged, leaving him alone in the entrance, as helpless as a stranded whale.

He waited a few minutes for latecomers, but it seemed the Homemakers' Association ladies were excellent timekeepers, besides being an unstoppable force. He was beginning to understand the concerns expressed by some politicians that allowing women the vote would soon lead to a petticoat government.

Charlie was about to close and lock the door when the tidal surge returned in the opposite direction, although this time it was a silent outflow of functionaries, their loads safely delivered. Charlie locked the door and set off for the lower meeting room, which had already been set out with chairs facing a head table.

The woman at the centre of the table looked familiar. With dismay, he recognised her as Anne's neighbour, a woman who lost no chance in telling anyone remotely attached to Grace that DC Charlie Pyke was not an appropriate sort of acquaintance for a young lady seeking a respectable, wealthy match. He lived in fear of her influence rubbing off on Grace. The worst of it was that Mrs Patterson was right. Grace Penrose deserved far better than he could offer.

He reversed out of the doorway with unseemly haste. What was he to do, after all? Demand that these ladies subject themselves to a search and interrogation? The caretaker was right. A respectable group of charity matrons would not cause any problems of the criminal type. He would do better to keep a close watch on the street.

Instead, he followed voices to the kitchen. Two young maids in starched caps and aprons paused when he entered, before returning to their task with occasional glances in his direction and giggling nudges of elbows. They were preparing a large pot of tea and setting out morning tea on platters. Tiny triangular sandwiches with the crusts removed, itsy-bitsy pastries, Lilliputian petit fours …. call that food? A man would lose such trifles between his thumb and finger if he tried to eat one. A whole plateful of the darned things would scarcely be the makings of a proper tea.

One of the girls opened a box and brought out a plump Victoria sponge. Now that was more like it. For a fleeting instant, the thought passed through his mind that he ought to cut it open to check for a hidden bomb, before he realised the tension of the day was making his imagination run riot over common sense. Besides, the girl was now slicing the cake, with no adverse effect other than a delicious oozing of cream and jam.

The other maid loaded the plates, cups, and pot onto a trolley with a combination of brisk efficiency and a flirtatious pouting of her lips. She brushed past him, so close they would have had an intimate encounter if he hadn't taken a step back. "Excuse me, sir, I need to take the tea out. It's a bit of a squeeze, with you being so big and all."

The second girl shook with suppressed laughter, putting the Victoria sponge at risk. "Don't you mind her, sir. But if you do fancy something sweet, I get off work at noon for my half day out."

Both girls collapsed into giggles. Evidently, they expected no reply, which was just as well. Charlie had never felt so old and staid as he did at that moment. Still, the girls knew nothing of the threat. Another time, he might have laughed along with them. Instead, he followed them along the corridor, watching on as they delivered the morning tea to the meeting room.

Grace's neighbour was speaking about the importance of women maintaining their proper place in society. He lingered at the door, intrigued to hear what views the Homemakers' Association espoused.

"Ladies, would we wish to live in a world where men no longer place women on a pedestal of the highest regard? Would we wish to lose the gallantry and protection our husbands afford us? We risk losing our honoured status as their helpmeet, the mother of their children, the guardian of their home and hearth, where they seek sanctuary after a hard day's work. The suffragists would have us surrender our God-given place in society … and for what? The right to vote! I ask you, ought a lady vote against her husband's wishes? What rancour that would sow! What intolerable strain upon the holy bond between husband and wife …"

One of the maids started giggling again. She clapped her hand to her mouth and hurried away, her job done. Charlie followed, to see them off the premises.

When they reached the foyer, the maid said, "Anyone would think them ladies was down on their knees cleaning their husband's home and hearth with their own fair hands. The mother of his children? Hah! That's a laugh. My mistress hardly sees her children, except to check that the governess and nanny are teaching them how to be proper little lords and ladies."

"Reckon they're afraid that us working girls will get the vote and demand a few rights of our own. Decent pay for a start." She saw Charlie watching them and turned on him. "And what are you staring at, Mr Policeman? Ain't you never heard a girl with thoughts of her own before?"

That sent the girls into another round of hilarity as Charlie chivvied them out the door. No wonder the women's franchise issue was so fraught with divided opinions, if even the women could not agree. He stood at the entrance, looking out onto the everyday activity on Moray Place, wondering what the afternoon would bring. The Women's Franchise League meeting wasn't for another three hours. This was the part of policing he disliked the most – the watching and waiting, the calm before the storm.

Charlie went back inside to make another pointless circuit of the premises. As he strolled towards the staircase, trying to eke out the activity for as long as possible, he felt a draught on his cheek. He turned along the corridor towards the back door to the building, which was propped open. The caretaker came up behind him with a crate of empty bottles. He stood aside as Taylor deposited the crate outside, with a rattle of glass and a grunt of effort.

"Mr Taylor, did I not make it absolutely clear that Choral Hall was to be locked at all times today?" For the love of God, could not a single man nor woman do as they were asked, this one day?

"Had to tidy up that mess in the meeting room, didn't I?" the caretaker replied, with an aggrieved undertone, as if his job came above the orders of a mere constable.

"Leave it. This door stays locked. Anyone might have come in while you were busy."

"Keep your shirt on. It were only open a minute, guv." Taylor shuffled off with a long-suffering sigh.

Charlie restrained his impulse to arrest the man. If only there was a law against stupidity. Before locking the back door, he stepped out into the narrow alley beside the building, looking up the steps leading to the street above, then down to Moray Place. Nothing stirred but a fat ship rat, which was whiskering its way through the rubbish pile, sniffing at an empty brandy bottle.

The steps were so steep that they passed the upper storey windows of Choral Hall.

Charlie resumed his patrol around the interior of the building. He checked the latches on the upper storey windows and gazed out the window to the street for a time, before returning to the Homemakers' Association meeting.

Another woman was speaking now. Her voice was raised, whipping the respectable ladies into a righteous fervour. "We cannot allow this small minority of suffragists to believe they are speaking for all women. The time has come to set aside our feminine delicacy for a brief moment in history, to show our fellow citizens that we do not want the vote."

She signalled to two younger women, who unfurled a painted banner saying "Women Against The Vote". The speaker's voice reached a crescendo. "We must gather as many right-thinking women as we can to come here at two o'clock this afternoon to protest against this abomination."

Charlie groaned inwardly. The last thing they needed was another group of protestors for Wallace and his men to worry about. He pictured the stalwart ladies of Homemakers' Association mixing with the liquored-up mob of Fish supporters outside Choral Hall, as the Women's Franchise League women arrived surrounded by their police escort. No cigar box of black powder would be needed to set that volatile mix aflame.

He had no time to come to terms with this new threat, as the Homemakers' Association women had given three rousing cheers and were now surging for the door, a horde of genteel Boudicas on the warpath.

When Declan Kelly arrived half an hour later, Charlie could have cheered at the sight of a sane face.

Declan slumped onto one of the bench seats in the foyer. "What a relief to be in a place of calm. It's crazy out there, Charlie. Men are gathering in hotels all around the central city, not least at Conor Sweeney's dubious establishment. They're being liquored up on cheap gut-rot and exhorted to come to Choral Hall to stop 'the evil harpies trying to take away a man's right to control his own life'. Wallace is in a lather. There is no way we will be able to control them all. It's going to be carnage if we cannot stop the Women's Franchise League meeting from going ahead."

"I'm afraid I have no good news to dull the blow, Declan. The Homemakers' Association ladies are planning a protest of their own. A peaceful one, by intent, but they are not a group to back down when their principles are under threat."

"Mary and Joseph! Can this day get any worse?"

"If the Women's Franchise League will not cancel their meeting, perhaps they might be persuaded to change the time?"

"Wallace begged and pleaded until he was blue in the face. They will not be intimidated."

"The unstoppable force meets the immovable object," Charlie groaned.

"At least we know what the men's plan is. Their aim is to stop the meeting going ahead by blocking access to Choral Hall. When Lady Stout's carriage appears, they will surround it and give her a good shaking up. If there is one silver lining, it is that no physical harm is intended to her ladyship, according to the men we have planted in the bars. With luck, the women will see that their route is blocked and beat a tactical retreat."

"All very well to say no harm is meant, but when a mob is fired up, anything might happen. If a few firecrackers can risk a woman's death underneath a panicked horse, how can we guarantee the safety of a large group of women surrounded by hundreds of drunken, angry men, fighting for their right to dominate womankind?"

Kelly sunk his head into his hands. "I know it. So does Wallace. But what can we do, if we can neither stop the unstoppable force, nor move the immovable object? All we can do is hope we have enough policemen to prevent the worst of it. I must be getting back. I only came to warn you to guard the door to Choral Hall with all your strength."

"Good luck, Declan. I'll pray for a hailstorm to cool their ardour."

Kelly stood at the door, looking up at the blue sky. "Reckon it'd take the second Great Flood to hold back that lot, complete with Noah's Ark and a pair of ravenous tigers. Good luck yourself, Charlie." With that, Kelly disappeared at a jog.

Charlie pulled his watch from his waistcoat pocket. Ten minutes to noon. Only two hours to go.

Signature Move

Grace and Anne arrived at noon to find Charlie waiting at the door to Choral Hall. He helped Anne from the buggy, while Grace pulled her red silk shawl tighter around her shoulders and gathered their basket and bags.

Charlie relieved her of the laden basket in the foyer. "By all the saints, I'm pleased to see you, Grace. I'm in sore need of an agreeable distraction from the troubles of the day."

Grace rolled her eyes. "What a surprise to see you here, Charlie, despite my best advice. Are you going to search my basket, in case I'm concealing an explosive device?"

He lifted the cloth. "Tiny sandwiches and savouries again. I don't see the point of food so small I have to get out a magnifying glass to see it."

"Just as well the afternoon tea is not for the likes of you." She brushed his hand away from the cloth, allowing her fingers to linger over his. "Are you required to search the meeting attendees as well?"

Charlie's eyes gleamed as he stepped closer. "I've no orders to that effect, but I would be willing to make an exception in your case."

The tap-tap of Anne's walking stick interrupted them. "Detective Constable Pyke, don't you have work to do? I thought you were here to protect us."

"That I am, Mrs MacMillan. I am ready to give my life for either of you at the first sign of trouble."

"Very noble, I'm sure. I notice you didn't ask to search my bag or person. Don't you think I have the wits or gumption to be an anarchist? Or am I not pretty enough?" Anne opened her drawstring bag and produced a parcel about the size of a large cigar box.

Grace laughed. "Don't look so alarmed, Charlie. It's only a couple of Cornish pasties for your lunch. Although I cannot vouch for the filling, I'm guessing it's not black powder."

"You two ladies and your sense of humour will be the death of me," Charlie replied, "although they do say the way to a man's heart is by way of his stomach."

"You'll die a heart-broken man if you wait for Grace to feed you. It's Mrs Brown you have to thank for the pasties, though not in the hope of finding a way to your heart, I trust."

"Besides," Grace added, "the way to the heart is not through the stomach, but through the ribcage and pericardium, with the help of a razor-sharp scalpel and large retractors."

"Thank you for that, Doctor Penrose. Now I don't feel hungry anymore."

"Excellent," Anne said. "In that case, you can help Grace get the boxes of petitions for us to count. We haven't got all day to sit around waiting for Fish's mob to shout obscenities at us. The front office will be most convenient."

"With pleasure, Mrs Macmillan. However, I would prefer you to do the counting upstairs. This afternoon is shaping up to be even worse than we imagined. I want you two ladies to be as far from the entrance as possible. If necessary, barricade yourselves in with the table."

Anne eyed up the staircase. "I've not known you to exaggerate the danger in the past, Charlie, so I suppose we ought to do as you suggest."

"I can help you up the stairs, Mrs Macmillan. Grace, can you make sure the door is locked?"

Charlie supported Anne up the staircase and into the large meeting room, while Grace headed in the opposite direction with her basket and the parcel. After a slight detour to investigate an odd sound in the back room – the caretaker snoring – she dropped the basket in the kitchen. Fortunately, it had been left clean by the last group. She set about organising teapots and cups until Charlie returned.

"We stored the petition boxes in there," Grace said, pointing to the adjoining room, "so we could do a final count of signatures to announce at the meeting."

The storage room was lined with shelves and cupboards, containing everything from large tins of tea and sugar, to stationery supplies and cleaning equipment. The boxes of petitions were stacked in the rear corner.

Charlie whistled. "So many!"

"The women of Dunedin have been busy while you have been away, Charlie. Harriet Morison and her team have worked wonders in getting so many working women to support the cause."

"I take my hat off to the lot of you. Mr Fish and his ragtag bunch of malcontents will be brought to their knees when your petition is presented to parliament."

Grace allowed herself a moment to bask in his delight. For all the hard work of the women, she knew it could not have been achieved without the support of good men – fathers, husbands, brothers, friends, and the many Members of the House of Representatives who championed their cause.

Charlie turned the emerald glow of his eyes on her. The skin around them crinkled in the way it always did when he was about to tease her. "How about you make me a nice cup of tea, while I lug these boxes upstairs? I oughtn't dare ask in the circumstances, but I'm absolutely parched and I don't know where everything is in this kitchen."

"I'll let it pass this once, Pyke, as you are being kind enough to help. But don't expect me to join Homemakers' Association anytime soon."

"I'd rather face Fish's mob than dare suggest such an outrage, Grace."

Charlie lifted the first two boxes and whistled his way up the stairs, leaving her to domestic duties. He returned for the next load as she arranged three cups on a tray, next to the Cornish pasties, and a plate of petit fours.

"This is by way of bribery. As you have nothing better to do, perhaps you could spare a little time to help us with the counting."

"I'll have to be near the main entrance in case anyone arrives, but I suppose I can count as well as listen for intruders." Charlie shifted aside a large tin of tea with a fancy gold label to get access to the next two petition boxes.

She marvelled at his good humour, despite the enormous pressure he must be under. "Charlie..."

"Yes, Grace?"

"My mother has told me about all the help you gave to the suffrage cause in Wellington. Collecting signatures in your free time, providing the necessary brawn to evict hecklers at meetings. Charlie, I ... what I mean is ..."

"No need for your thanks, Grace. A policeman's job is to see that justice is done, after all."

His whistling faded up the stairs again. Grace tamped down a gush of emotion and followed him with the tray, reminding herself for the millionth time that she only had two and a half more years of study at medical school before she would be free to move wherever she pleased. She could only hope that the wait wouldn't prove too long for him.

They were counting the final box of forms when she heard Charlie calling her from the foyer.

Grace raced down the stairs, not knowing what horrors he might be facing. But it was only one of their own, the woman Molly Sugden had rescued from the path of the bolting horse. Goodness, was it only five days ago? Grace racked her brain for the woman's name. Violet something or other. Charwell? Creswell.

Grace took one of the two bulky baskets the woman was lugging. "Mrs Creswell, welcome. Have I lost track of the time?"

"I came early, Miss Penrose. I volunteered for tea duty."

"Follow me. I'll show you to the kitchen."

Grace returned alone to find Charlie at the window. She and Anne had been concentrating so hard on counting signatures in the upstairs hall that she had failed to hear the growing clamour outside. Standing beside the window, the noise was unmistakable.

Out in the street, a crowd was gathering, growing by the minute. The ladies of Homemakers' Association had established a stronghold on the upper end of the street, gathered under a banner proclaiming "Women Against The Vote". Grace was unsurprised to see her neighbour front and centre, leading her supporters in a rousing hymn.

The lower end of the street, right up to the entrance to Choral Hall, was awash with glazed-eyed men, harassing any woman who dared pass. A line of policemen struggled to keep a narrow path clear along the middle of the street.

"Charlie, there aren't nearly enough policemen to stop those men if they are determined."

"It was all Wallace could muster." Charlie glanced at his pocket watch. "Ten minutes to two o'clock. Prepare for mayhem."

Grace hovered at his shoulder, watching the men surge at the line of policemen, while taunting the trickle of brave women attempting to walk up to the hall. "I would have expected more of our Franchise League women to have arrived by now."

"I doubt they can get through."

Half a dozen men surged towards the door and began hammering on it. Two policemen ran to pull them away, taking up station beside the entrance to Choral Hall to deter further attack. The noise outside had risen to an eardrum-quaking intensity.

A procession of carriages turned from Princes Street into Moray Place, surrounded by more policemen. A man mounted a set of steps on the far side of the street and yelled at the mob to let them through.

"Oh no, that's Conor Sweeney," Charlie groaned. "They're luring them into a trap." He ran to the door. "Grace, bolt the door behind me, then go upstairs. This is going to get dangerous."

He dashed through the door before she could tell him, entirely pointlessly, to be careful. She bolted the door, before returning to the window, drawn like a mosquito to blood.

Charlie shouted for the carriages to turn back, but it was too late. Sweeney waved his arm. A bugler blew a short blast, triggering an orchestrated wave of angry, drunken men to lunge forward, sweeping through the police cordon as if it wasn't there.

Sweeney yelled to his supporters from his vantage point, "When women's rights have come to stay, oh, who will rock the cradle?"

Grace recognised the line from an anti-franchise ditty that had been published the previous year. But the men in the mob recognised it as a call to arms. They poured, en masse, around the carriages, blocking their path to the front and rear. Dozens of jubilant drunkards leapt onto the sides of the carriages, rocking them and banging at the windows, terrifying the horses and the occupants.

"Who will rock the cradle? Who will rock the cradle?" the mob chanted, as the carriages rocked back and forth.

The sounds of women shrieking and the coachmen's whips raining down on their attackers only seemed to spur the mob into a frenzy.

"Who will rock the cradle? Who will rock the cradle?"

Grace watched in horror, terrified that one of the carriages would topple and injure its occupants. Without warning, a group of men peeled off the mob and ran up the street. They surrounded the hall, shattering the side windows and battering the back door.

Grace belatedly acted on Charlie's last order, to get upstairs. At the foot of the stairs, she remembered Violet Creswell, alone in the kitchen, near the back door. Grace sprinted along the corridor to get her to safety.

She glanced at the stately grandfather clock in the foyer – five minutes to two o'clock. A futile thought crossed her mind – the much-anticipated inaugural meeting of the Women's Franchise League would not take place today – then the hall exploded in a simultaneous sensory overload of flashing, booming and splintering.

An almighty whump of scorching air flung Grace backwards. The world went black.

142

Chaos

Charlie, Declan Kelly and three other policemen were hauling a mass of protestors off Lady Stout's carriage when the bomb detonated. All eyes turned to Choral Hall, where men were screaming and running from the shattered glass. Men in the street stood gaping at them, unable to comprehend what had happened, while the Homemaker ladies shrieked and pointed at the side of the hall.

Charlie sprinted up the street, with Kelly at his heels. All the windows were blown out on the uphill side of the building. Flames danced behind the shattered kitchen window. Two men were lying in the alleyway, bleeding from multiple glass cuts. Charlie battered on the back door, cursing its solid construction.

The door crashed open. The caretaker stumbled out, coughing, chased by a cloud of smoke. Charlie pushed past him, into a scene straight from Dante's Inferno. Behind him, he could hear Kelly ordering men to help the injured and form a bucket chain to put the fire out. Further away, Wallace's voice could be heard commanding his men to summon medical help and a fire pump.

None of that mattered to Charlie. He ran to the kitchen, where a twisted body lay just inside the storage room, amidst a swath of debris and a swirl of ashes. He vaulted over the kitchen door, which was lying askew across the corridor. A blast of heat struck him from the flames surrounding the overturned stove.

Bile rose in his throat as he forced himself to check the woman. Her hat had been flung backwards under a chair, miraculously spared from damage. Not Grace's hat, but the hat of the woman who had arrived early. Mrs Creswell. She must have run to the shelter of the storage room when the men attacked the back door. Her face and clothes had been sliced by the shards of metal and wood that littered the room, but her eyelids fluttered briefly as he kneeled beside her.

Kelly ran up behind him, his boots crunching on glass and debris, a handkerchief wound around his mouth and nose.

"She's still alive," Charlie choked out, the ash and soot and searing heat playing havoc with his lungs. "Grace and Anne must be upstairs. Caretaker out. Nobody else."

Kelly pulled him out of the kitchen. "I'll get her to the hospital. You see to Grace." Kelly didn't wait for his reply. He was already running for the exit, yelling for help.

Charlie found Grace further along the corridor, lying motionless against a wall, legs askew, arms curled around her head. She must have had an instant to react, throwing the shawl over her head as protection.

He stumbled to his knees beside her, barely registering the splinter tearing through his trousers, as he eased the ruby silk – his present to her – from her lifeless face. "Grace, can you hear me?" Stupid. Of course she couldn't. He searched for a pulse and found it, erratic but still beating. Relief overwhelmed him for an instant, before he pulled himself together.

Anne stumbled up behind him, her walking cane unsteady in a trembling hand. "Charlie, is she…"

"Alive, but unconscious. I was about to check for injuries."

"Help me down."

Charlie helped Anne sink to the floor. She winced as her hip twisted, but she ignored the pain. Her quick, capable hands ran over Grace's body with expert efficiency. Only when they had made a complete circuit did the hands go back to Grace's face, brushing away flakes of ash and plaster.

"She appears unharmed, but for some minor cuts and bruises. I can't tell the extent of any damage with her clothes on. We need to get her to the hospital immediately."

144

Charlie pulled Anne up as gently as he could, shocked at how thin and fragile she felt. Her personality was such a dominant force that he forgot it was housed in the body of an old lady.

Anne clung to him with surprising strength. "I couldn't have borne it if I had lost Grace."

"Nor I."

Anne was crying. Charlie was so used to Anne's unshakable confidence and wicked sense of humour that her anguish momentarily shocked him until he realised tears ran down his own cheeks too. "Is it safe for me to pick Grace up?"

Anne nodded, so he scooped Grace off the floor. She felt lifeless and light in his arms, sparking a feeling of such intense protectiveness within him that he staggered under its weight. He commandeered a nearby policeman to take Anne and open the main door, so he could carry Grace out as quickly as possible.

Stepping out onto the street was like stepping into a palace-sized painting of the aftermath of an epic battle. The frenzy that had preceded the bomb had given way to a street-full of stunned, motionless figures and empty carriages. Suffragists stood amongst their oppressors, with both sides shocked into horrified silence. The only movement was the frantic activity of a handful of policemen, radiating out from DI Wallace, who was directing activity in front of Choral Hall with all his years of gravitas.

The effect of the still-life tableau was broken when a group of men appeared around the corner, dragging a fire pump up the street. Behind them came a tidal wave of women, who must have congregated in Princes Street when the mob blocked their path.

As the women passed through the chastened mob, one of their leaders broke into song, her high voice floating above the throng like a lark over the battlefield. Other women joined in until Moray Place swelled with female voices.

Despite the urgency of his task, Charlie found himself rooted to the spot for precious seconds by the power of their voices. Behind him, the cluster of Homemakers' Association women joined the chorus, quietly at first, then with increasing fervour.

Molly rushed forward from a cluster of women gathered by the nearest carriage, breaking the spell. "Charlie, over here. We have readied the carriages to take the injured to the hospital. Saints alive, is that Grace? Hurry, this way. Is she alive?"

"Yes. What about the others?"

"Mrs Addison, the doctor's wife, has taken the injured woman to the hospital. Two men have been taken away too. It's a miracle it's not worse."

He submitted with relief to Molly's competence in a crisis. She directed him to the grandest carriage. A lady's maid helped them to get Grace's body onto the padded leather seat. He was about to climb into the carriage beside her when Wallace's voice barked his name.

"Pyke, I need you here, now."

Lady Stout appeared beside him and laid a gloved hand on his arm. "Hughes will look after her, young man. I'm afraid you have work to do. As do I."

Charlie reluctantly saw that she was right. Besides, his weight would only slow the carriage down.

Debris

Charlie watched Lady Stout's carriage depart with its precious burden. When it rounded the corner, he refocussed his attention on the situation unfolding around him, moving up to the cluster of police officers around Wallace.

Policemen had herded the factions into separate clusters, guarded by uniformed constables. Women's Franchise League supporters gathered in front of their leaders, close to the entrance to Choral Hall. The Homemakers' Association women were holding each other in a tight circle further up the street. The violent mob was now as subdued as a herd of sheep waiting to be shorn. Silence descended on the street again.

Wallace issued orders with grim-faced efficiency. "Sergeant Dawson, take those men into the Criterion Hotel. Get your constables to take a name, address and statement from each and every one of them."

Wallace searched the assembled faces. "Sergeant Watts, take the lady protestors to the Queen's Theatre. Name, address, statement, no matter who they are or how important their husband is. DC Kelly, are you here?"

A soot-smeared face emerged from the hall. "Yes, sir. Fire's out. All injured parties transported to hospital. I've had a team search the building for casualties and other explosive devices, but they found nothing. Significant damage to the kitchen area, but not as much as you might expect from the noise of the explosion. Choral Hall appears safe and structurally sound. I've got two constables guarding the scene. The caretaker has scarpered."

"Good work, Kelly."

Kelly stepped close to Wallace to deliver the rest of his report in a low voice. "One woman is seriously injured."

"Mrs Violet Creswell," Charlie added, "the suffragist who was in the kitchen. Miss Penrose is unconscious too, but she doesn't appear to be badly hurt."

"Right. I've called Detective Sergeant Elliot back into town, as you can see." Wallace turned to an older man with the gnarled face and dour expression of a man who has seen it all. "Elliot, DC Kelly will be with you on the case. Take as many constables as the two of you need to arrest our four suspects. Sweeney was here, whipping the mob into a frenzy, so check if he has been taken to the Criterion. Find and arrest the caretaker too. Does anyone know his name?"

"Patrick Taylor, sir," Charlie replied. "I suspect he let the bomber in."

"Right. Kelly, make Taylor a priority. Pyke, I want you here to sift through the debris and establish what happened."

Charlie stepped behind Wallace to the entrance to the hall.

"Detective Inspector Wallace, would you care to make a statement to the *Evening Star*?" a bowler-hatted man called out.

"And the *Times*," another man shouted.

"Hold your horses, gentlemen. Give me a moment to get the situation under control, then I promise I will talk to you briefly."

Wallace turned his attention to the ladies of the Women's Franchise League. "All the women here for the Franchise League meeting may now go home, unless any of you have anything of significance to report. Tomorrow, I would ask that you come to the station to make a statement regarding any violence or damage sustained during this … incident."

A group of five women stepped forward, their faces set with a mixture of shock and determination. Charlie recognised Lady Stout, Harriet Morison and Helen Nicol, as well as two older women he presumed were Mrs Rachel Reynolds and Mrs Marion Hatton.

"Detective Inspector Wallace," one of the older women said, "I need to know if any of my ladies were hurt."

"Two, Mrs Hatton. Mrs Creswell is in a serious condition and Miss Penrose is unconscious. Both have been taken to the hospital."

The tension in Mrs Hatton's face eased slightly, suggesting she must have been bracing for news of fatalities. "I understand the upper meeting room is undamaged?"

Wallace observed her through narrowed eyes. "I believe so, Mrs Hatton. You will be able to reschedule your meeting within a few days, I expect."

Mrs Hatton held up her hand. "I wish to make a statement to those present and to our esteemed members of the press. She turned to address the crowd of suffragists. An enterprising woman retrieved a stepping box from the nearest carriage, to elevate Mrs Hatton above the crowd.

"Ladies and gentlemen, your attention, please." Mrs Hatton spoke quietly and calmly, but her voice carried clearly, silencing the low rumble of chatter in the crowd. "We have witnessed dreadful events here today. I have been informed that two of our number have been injured by men who would subvert democracy and right for their own vile interests. Men who will surely burn in Hell for the evil they have committed."

Her grim words set off a ripple of shock and outrage through the crowd, men and women alike.

"I ask everyone here to observe a minute of silent prayer for the two women in hospital, Mrs Violet Creswell and Miss Grace Penrose."

In the hush that followed, not a word could be heard, not a rustle of a skirt, not even the shuffling footfalls of shamefaced men. At the end of the minute, Mrs Hatton's voice cracked the silence like a pistol shot.

"Ladies, I would not wish it to be said that we are women who lack courage in the face of adversity. No change as great as that we seek is made without a determination to succeed, no matter the odds, whether it be a mob, a bomb, or a biblical plague. Women have risked their lives for this cause today, and we must honour that by not giving in to this tyranny."

Murmurs of approval swelled through the women assembled in front of the hall. At least a hundred and fifty women, at Charlie's estimate, and a few men, including at least one Member of the House of Representatives.

Mrs Hatton's voice rose another notch. "Mrs Anne Macmillan, who has devoted her life to the welfare of women, has spared time from her own suffering to give news to Miss Nicol that our petition has passed seven thousand signatures in Dunedin, and we must honour that."

The crowd gasped as one at this news.

"*Twenty thousand* signatures nationwide – one in every six women in this fair country. How can we not honour that!"

The ladies in the crowd erupted into a rousing cheer.

DI Wallace stood next to the impromptu speaker's platform with a look of growing disbelief creeping across his normally passive features. Charlie teetered between pride at the stoicism of these women, relief that the precious boxes of signed petition forms had been moved to the upstairs meeting room, and gut-churning concern for Grace.

Mrs Hatton raised a hand to still the crowd. "We have gathered in numbers here today to advance the cause of votes for all women, as is our right. And we must honour that!" With each statement her voice had risen, ending with an impassioned rallying cry. "Therefore, I welcome you to the inaugural meeting of the Women's Franchise League."

For the second time that day, a wave of unstoppable women surged past Charlie, through the doors to Choral Hall, and up the stairs. He looked to Wallace for direction, but his only response was a triple gesture of hopelessness – a rolling of the eyes, a shrug and a shake of the head. Charlie thought he caught a few mumbled words about Moses and the Red Sea, before Wallace turned his back and gave a short statement to the gentlemen of the press, making it sound as if he had the situation entirely under control.

Charlie hurried inside to start sifting evidence. The sooner he finished, the sooner he could be by Grace's side, if Wallace could be convinced to release him from duty.

Fortunately, Kelly had blocked off the corridor and set a guard to stop anyone going that way. The bucket brigade and firemen had departed, leaving the kitchen a sodden, blackened, chaotic mess. The kitchen door was propped up against the opposite wall. From its splintered and charred inner surface, Grace may well have been spared serious injury because the door had been closed as she walked towards it.

He paused in the doorway, taking in the scene with slow and deliberate attention. The fire had started around the stove and must have spread rapidly before being extinguished. Without the quick actions of DC Kelly and the firemen in putting the fire out, the entire building might have gone up in flames.

Aside from the charring from the flames and the blown-out windows, the damage was concentrated in an arc, converging on the storage room, whose door stood open. Within the arc, every surface was pitted from the debris flung by the blast – splinters from wooden shelving, twisted shards of tin, sharp pieces of crockery, dented pots and tiny bits of metal. The remains of petit fours and little triangular sandwiches were plastered against the wall.

Charlie picked up a piece of metal, realising it was a small nail, twisted by the force of the explosion, but still rapier sharp.

Kelly had marked off the area where the injured woman had fallen. Mrs Creswell had been by the door to the storage room, right in the path of the blast. Charlie forced the image of her body from his mind. Now was not the time for emotion – that would come later. He knew without a doubt that the scene would be seared into his memory until his dying day.

When Charlie had memorised the general layout of the scene, he took out his notebook, sketching and noting every detail. Having completed his sketch, he stepped into the kitchen, focussing on picking up suspicious fragments and putting them into an empty tin, which had been flung into a corner beyond the arc of destruction.

He moved methodically towards the storage room, slowly but surely. Inside, the charred hole in the wall and the direction of debris showed the explosion had originated in the corner where the petition boxes had been stacked. The walls were of solid construction, which had directed most of the explosive force out into the room, while limiting damage to the structure of the building. The room and its contents were almost unrecognisable.

Whoever had set the explosives had been expert enough to create a blast of exactly the right size to destroy this room, without damaging the entire building.

As Charlie gathered more fragments, he noted that some of the twisted bits of tin had patches of colour on one side where fire hadn't blackened the surface. With sudden clarity, he visualised the tin of tea he had moved earlier to get to the petition boxes, and realised that the puzzling flakes of black covering every surface were a mix of soot and tea leaves.

Few parts of the room had been spared the puncture wounds inflicted by the vicious little nails. The tea tin must have been packed with a handful or two of nails in amongst the tea leaves in order to achieve the maximum damage. If the petition boxes hadn't been moved, the precious signatures would certainly have been destroyed by the explosion or shredded by the nails, if not burned in the fire.

Unless the placement of the bomb had been an unfortunate coincidence, the petition boxes must have been the real target of the attack. The destruction of hundreds of hours of work, canvassing for signatures, combined with the terror of the physical assaults on suffragists, would surely have dealt the suffrage cause a terrible blow.

Charlie swallowed back the gush of bile that rose in his throat at the thought of what might have happened, when he had unknowingly shifted the tea tin with Grace in the room. If he had bumped the bomb, or dropped it ...

He blocked the thought from his mind and concentrated on sifting through the debris, setting aside anything that might hold a clue. The breakthrough came when he reached under a pile of shattered shelving and drew out a mangled disc of metal, a melted round of glass, and a collection of twisted cogs and springs. The remains of a clock.

Charlie continued to search every inch of the room until his knees ached and his nose was clogged with ash. By the time he had finished, he had a pile of tiny fragments, which he sorted by type. After staring at them for a full minute, the pieces rearranged in his mind into a long-forgotten pattern. He was looking at the remains of a stick of dynamite, complete with fragments of a blast cap.

There could be no doubting the conclusion. The bomb was sophisticated – the work of a professional or experienced hand – set to go off by a timing device as the hall filled with women, minutes before the meeting. Wallace needed to know right away. Charlie packed the critical fragments into an empty tin and pushed himself wearily to his feet, noting that he had left a smear of blood behind, where he must have cut his knee on a sharp fragment. Right now, it was the least of his worries, by a long shot.

DI Wallace had taken up residence in the front office. "Pyke, I was just coming to see you. Good heavens, man, you look as if you've been down a coal pit. Take a seat."

Charlie laid a newspaper on the chair to prevent it from turning black, before dropping onto it with a groan. "Undoubtedly a professional job, sir. A stick of dynamite, complete with blast cap, set off using a clock as a timer." He opened the tin, pointing out the tiny cogs, springs and dial. "Probably a small desk clock. The bomb exploded at five minutes to two, so we can be sure the bomber was specifically targeting the Women's Franchise League meeting, which was due to start at two o'clock."

Wallace ran a grubby hand over his face, leaving a smear in the grime. "If that mob hadn't blocked the road, the women would have been coming into the building at that time. And if we hadn't had the warning of their earlier attacks, the fire might well have gotten out of control and killed them all." He wiped his hands on a handkerchief, frowning. "It doesn't make sense."

153

"I see what you mean, sir. If one of our four suspects planted the bomb, why organise a mob to nullify the impact of it?"

"Nor does it fit with our intelligence that Lady Stout was to be the target. There is no chance she would have been relegated to kitchen duties. Was it mean as another scare tactic?"

"There's another possible motive, sir. The bomb was planted within the boxes of signed petitions. If Miss Penrose and I had not removed the boxes earlier to make a final count of signatures, the petitions would have been reduced to ash or shreds. I myself moved the tin in which the bomb was likely concealed – a tin of tea."

Wallace looked up sharply. "A lucky escape indeed. I can see the suffrage petition would make a tempting target, but there would be no need to time the explosion. Far easier to set fire to the place in the middle of the night."

"A dual motive, perhaps? Destroy the petition and terrify the suffragists at the same time. The timing and location suggest that the bomb may not have been intended to kill or injure. If it hadn't been for the delay because of the mob, at five minutes to two o'clock, all the women would probably have been in the upstairs meeting room. On the other hand, the bomb was packed with sharp nails, which might have been lethal to anyone in blast range. If the bomber hadn't intended to hurt anyone, he certainly took a massive risk that nobody would be in or near the kitchen."

Charlie handed over a twisted piece of metal. "The nails look familiar, but I can't place them."

"Horseshoe nails. Small, sharp and widely available." Wallace rubbed his chin again, as he thought through the possibilities. "Any chance the victim could have been specifically targeted, Pyke? What do we know of the injured woman?"

"Mrs Violet Creswell, the same woman who was nearly run over by a horse in the firecracker incident on Saturday. However, I cannot see how either incident could have targeted her specifically. The bomber cannot have foreseen she would be in the kitchen when the bomb went off."

"We'll have to check for any connection between the victim and our suspects, although I agree she is far more likely to have been in the wrong place at the worst possible time. The escalation of violence against the suffragists is frankly alarming. What next? A case of dynamite at their next meeting? We need to get to the bottom of this fast."

"The planting of the bomb may prove a useful avenue of inquiry. It must have been in place no earlier than two o'clock in the morning. The caretaker swears the hall was locked up from late afternoon yesterday until my arrival at nine o'clock this morning. I am sure he is lying. There is evidence to suggest he may have let in a group of men to gamble last night. If they left after two o'clock, one of them could have placed the bomb. What's more, the caretaker left the back door open this morning for a period, despite specific orders not to do so. It may have been unintentional. He was so much the worse for drink this morning, he could hardly stand."

"We cannot overlook the caretaker himself," Wallace said. "He may have been paid to place the tin, without knowing what was in it. Kelly is tracking him down. Apart from the caretaker or someone he let in, who else could have set the bomb?"

Charlie shifted his weight on the hard chair, crinkling the newspaper, as he considered the possibilities. "The only other people known to be in the hall are unlikely suspects. A group of women from an organisation called the Homemakers' Association met in the lower meeting room for about an hour and a half, starting just before ten o'clock this morning. Grace Penrose and her elderly great-aunt, Anne Macmillan, arrived at noon. Aside from them, the only people who were here were myself, DC Kelly and Violet Creswell. Two maids associated with the Homemakers were in the kitchen until about twenty past ten, preparing their morning tea, so the bomb could not have been planted then, unless one of them did it. The Homemakers' Association are against women having the vote, so in theory they had a reason to want the petition destroyed."

"But ladies of their sort are hardly likely to have the means or desire to use a bomb. We'll look into the servants, in case one of

155

them holds a grudge, but the caretaker and the liquor barons must take priority at this stage. Destroying the petition would benefit Fish's anti-suffrage group more than anyone else. Have you finished gathering all the evidence, Pyke?"

"Yes, sir."

"I expect you would like to take a short break to see Miss Penrose."

Charlie was out of his seat in a flash. "I would, very much. Thank you, sir."

"Please pass on my best wishes to Miss Penrose, if she is conscious."

"Thank you, that is kind of you." Charlie was already at the door when a harrumph from Wallace stayed his hand on the doorknob.

"I'm afraid it will not be simply a social visit, Pyke. If she is well enough, interview her. Miss Penrose has a good eye for detail and knows all the women involved in the franchise cause. Report back to the station when you've finished."

"I'll be there as soon as I can, sir. I'll check on Mrs Creswell too, but I suspect she was too badly hurt to be in any condition to talk."

Wallace leaned back in his chair, his mouth ticking up on one side as he looked Charlie straight in the eye. "I've recalled DS Elliot to take the lead on arresting our suspects. He's a good man at the end of a long career. I shouldn't wonder if he doesn't tire of it soon, what with his rheumatism playing up. Give him whatever assistance he asks for. Any other thoughts you have, however ludicrous, I want to know as soon as possible."

"Yes, sir."

"Don't linger at the station, Pyke. I want you well rested by tomorrow morning. You know these men better than anyone. I'll be relying on that when we interrogate them."

Charlie sped off with winged boots, scarcely daring to hope that Wallace had given him a hint that a place may soon become available in his team after all. A detective sergeant at that.

Consciousness

The first sensation Grace became aware of, through the thrumming agony of her head, was a bright light, turning the inside of her eyelids red. She couldn't seem to open her eyes or move at all, although she was aware of something pressing on her hand. She slipped back into oblivion.

"Grace, Grace! Can you hear me?"

The words fell as a dull thud on her pummelled eardrums. She wanted to tell the person to leave her alone, and let her die in peace, but the confused thoughts banging around in her brain coalesced into two vital recollections. The hall had exploded. And Charlie had been there.

"Charlie?" She wasn't sure if the sound had come out. Her throat was parched. Everything ached.

"Grace, it's James."

James? She had a brother called James, didn't she? Why was it so hard to remember? Why was he squeezing her hand so hard?

"James Cranston-Hartfield. Grace, can you hear me?"

"Don't shout. Head hurts." What was the police surgeon doing here? Was she dead?

"Thank heavens you are alive. Do you remember what happened?"

Grace shook her head. Mistake. She hovered on the edge of consciousness, kept awake only by the pain. "Bomb. Anyone hurt?"

"Don't worry about that, my dear. All that matters is that you are safe."

She wanted to tell him that it did matter. Her great-aunt was there, Charlie, her friends. All the people that mattered. A wave of nausea overcame her. An angel shoved an enamel bowl at her just in time.

"That's enough now, sir. The poor girl is in pain and not ready to be peppered with questions."

"I'll come back later, nurse. Take care of my girl, won't you?"

"You may be sure of it."

Grace sank back into the pillow with her eyes closed. A teaspoon of liquid drizzled into her mouth, bitter on her tongue. Soothing water followed, dripped in slowly, so that it slithered gently down her parched throat, as smooth as nectar from the gods. After a while, the pain receded. She dozed.

The next sensation she was aware of was the nurse wiping her face with a soft cloth. The nurse had strong, gentle hands. She sighed as the cool water soothed her burning skin and aching head. "Thank you, nurse. That feels heavenly."

"It's good to see you awake, Grace. You had us all worried for a while."

"Charlie?" She forced open her eyelids to ensure she hadn't dreamed his voice.

The cool cloth lifted from her forehead, replaced by warm lips. "I had a hard time convincing the nurse to let me in. Apparently, your devoted gentleman admirer insisted he should be the only visitor. I had to show my police badge to persuade her. She made me wash before she let me in, but I fear I still look disreputable."

He looked like a tramp who had taken shelter in a coal bin, but all that mattered was that he was alive. "Are you hurt, Charlie? What happened?"

"A timed dynamite bomb and a fire. I got a little grimy while sifting through the evidence. Anne and all the suffrage ladies escaped unharmed, except for Mrs Creswell."

"Is she badly injured?"

"I went to see her as soon as I arrived at the hospital, but they wouldn't let me in. They are doing all they can for her, but Mrs

Creswell was right in the path of the explosion. It might be days or weeks before we know if she will recover."

Grace closed her eyes, picturing the lively woman she had known so briefly. "I was going to find her when the explosion happened. A moment later and I would have been in the kitchen too."

His grip on her hand tightened. "A close call. Too close. You were saved by the closed kitchen door. The nurse told me that you haven't any major injuries other than being knocked out, although I imagine your head must feel like a stamper-battery right now. I will leave you in peace, if you would prefer."

"Don't leave me." The words sounded pathetically desperate to her ears, but he clasped her hand in both of his and held it to his lips.

The curtain around the bed flicked back. "Is this man troubling you, Miss Penrose? He told me he was a policeman, but he appears to be taking liberties that your young man would not approve of."

"This man is my beau, and a policeman as well. The previous man was only my employer."

The nurse had her hands firmly on her hips. "You ought to be resting, Miss Penrose."

Grace took in the dark bags under the young nurse's eyes, aware of the twelve-hour shifts these angels of mercy worked. "I suspect you need the rest more than me. Honestly, I am feeling much better. I want DC Pyke to stay. Perhaps I might be discharged as soon as the doctor has done his rounds?"

"I wouldn't advise it, but I know what you doctors are like. It's an age-old saying that doctors make the worst patients, but none the less true in my experience." The nurse's face crinkled into a brief smile, before she flicked the curtain closed and hurried off to see to her other patients.

Charlie laid the cool cloth over Grace's forehead again. "Doctor Cranston-Hartfield thinks I am a bad influence on you."

"You are, Charlie. A terrible influence. What the police surgeon fails to realise is that I enjoy the thrill of our adventures together, except for the times one of us ends up in hospital."

He stroked her hair, being careful to avoid the swelling where she had been thrown against the wall. "The police surgeon is a steady fellow, with a good job, from a wealthy family. Is it any wonder he cannot understand why you waste your time on a penniless policeman with an uncertain future. I cannot fathom it myself, yet you told the nurse I was your beau."

Grace lifted the cloth from her eyes. "Do you not wish to be?"

"Grace, it's all I've ever wanted, from the moment we bumped heads over our first corpse, on the dissecting table at the medical school."

"It took you so long? I was smitten the moment you allowed me to accompany you into the mortuary."

"What do you mean, so long? It can't have been more than half an hour since I first clapped eyes on you, Grace. And, in my defence, I had had little sleep and was having a terrible day. You certainly made an impression from the first instant I saw you. I would have run away in terror at so assertive a young lady back then, had my way not been blocked."

"I'm glad you didn't run away, Charlie."

He smiled and leaned closer, his breath warm on her cheek.

The tap-tap of a walking cane interrupted them. "Grace, are you here?"

Charlie pulled the curtain back. "In here, Mrs Macmillan."

"Suffering souls, Charlie. Have you taken up a new occupation as a chimney sweep? You shouldn't have shaved your beard off. It would have made a fine chimney brush."

"Good to see you are back to your old self, Mrs Macmillan. Are you feeling well?"

"Those pushy nurses made me lie down for a while. I must have fallen asleep. Quite foolish behaviour on my part. I cannot account for it. You must tell me everything, starting with your condition, Grace."

"Concussion and a few bruises and scratches. Now that I am floating on a cloud of laudanum, all is well with the world. Except that Charlie has just told me that Mrs Creswell was critically injured in the explosion."

Anne sank into the chair vacated by Charlie, her head drooping as the devastating news sunk in. "How awful. I didn't know she was in the hall. I will arrange for one of our ladies to be at her bedside at all times, so she won't be alone."

"Mrs Addison is waiting for the doctors to finish their work on her injuries," Charlie said. "She told me she would stay with Mrs Creswell as long as needed."

"In that case, I will stay with Grace," Anne said. "You'll tell me if you feel dizzy or in pain. Concussion can be a wily beast, as you know. They will keep you overnight, I expect."

"Not if I have anything to do with it. Charlie was about to tell me what happened, as my memory is rather hazy. I expect he has only come to interrogate us both." Grace lay back on the pillow and tried to focus, as he launching into an account of the explosion. His words triggered her own memories.

When he mentioned the tin the bomb had been in, Grace interrupted. "I remember that tin. A large tin, considering it was an expensive blend of tea. The tin had a green and gold label, with Darjeeling in large letters. I recall thinking it was out of place amongst the cheap tea that is served at most meetings. If only I had mentioned it at the time."

"I'm glad you did not, Grace. If I had opened the tin, we might both be dead." He must have seen the shock on her face, because he hurried to fill the silence. "Well spotted. I would never have known that it was expensive tea if you hadn't noticed."

"Tea is as sure an indicator of social status as the number of servants one keeps," Anne said. "Poor households must ration out the cheapest of teas, reusing the leaves until there is little taste left.

162

Society matrons vie with each other to secure rare blends from the most obscure plantations in India or Ceylon or China, handpicked by maidens from the first flush of new leaves by the light of the moon."

"You're joking, I take it, Mrs Macmillan."

"Stretching the truth a little to make the point, Charlie, but only a very little. You would be astounded by the cost of the rarest varieties of tea."

"Would you recognise the label again, Grace? If it is rare, it may provide a clue to who did this."

"I'm not sure, Charlie, but I will certainly visit every purveyor of tea in Dunedin if necessary. The only problem is that tea tins are often reused. More than once, I have seen a discarded tin of an expensive variety in the poorest of households, rescued from the scrapheap of a wealthy home, I suppose. You wouldn't believe the number of ways they can be put to use, from buckets to basins, or hammered together to cover holes in the roof."

"Did either of you see anything else that struck you as suspicious or out of place?" Charlie asked.

Both women frowned as they thought, their eyes flicking up and to the side as they visualised the events of the day.

"I cannot think of a thing, Charlie," Anne replied. "We came in. I went upstairs. We had tea and started counting. Nobody else came upstairs and I did not come down again until I heard the blast. I did go to the window twice, to observe the commotion in the street, but I expect you saw that better than me."

"The same goes for me, except for when we carried the boxes up," Grace said, "and when I came down to attend to Mrs Creswell. When you left, I watched until the men started attacking the hall, then I ran along the corridor to take Mrs Creswell upstairs. I remember looking at the clock and seeing it was five minutes to two, right before the explosion. I was thrown back against the wall. That's all I remember."

Charlie laid his hand on hers. "I'll do everything in my power to find the man or men who did this, Grace. Meanwhile, I need you to rest and recover."

Anne pushed herself to her feet. "I ought to let Mrs Patterson know about Mrs Creswell. She will be devastated."

"Does she know Mrs Creswell, Auntie?"

"I have heard Mrs Patterson talk of her several times. Have you not heard her do so?"

"Our neighbour does not share her thoughts with me, Auntie. She does not approve of my choices."

"Oh, you mustn't mind Mrs Patterson. She's more bark than bite. Her views on women's rights may be archaic, but she has a kind heart. Mrs Creswell works for Mrs Patterson's father. In fact, Mr and Mrs Patterson arranged for her to take up the position, so that she would have an income after her husband's death. They gave her a pension too."

"Why would they be so generous?"

"Guilt, I expect. Mrs Patterson's brother was responsible for the death of Mrs Creswell's husband. No, I shouldn't say that, as nothing was proved. Rumour had it that her brother was negligent, but no charge was laid against him. Another explosion, as it happens. Road construction is such a dangerous business, what with tunnels to be made and inconvenient boulders to be removed."

Charlie expelled a breath with such force that both women stared at him. "Mrs Macmillan, is Mrs Patterson's brother Lennox MacDonald?"

"Yes, I think that's his name. Certainly, her maiden name is MacDonald. Her father founded MacDonald Roading, a successful business by all accounts. Mr Patterson is in charge of it now. The brother was found some other occupation after Mr Creswell's death. What a dreadful coincidence that his wife has been injured in an explosion as well."

Charlie leapt to his feet and planted a kiss on Anne's cheek. "Mrs Macmillan, you're a treasure. I'll be back as soon as I can, Grace. Sorry to leave you so abruptly."

He raced out the door before she could respond.

"Do you have any idea what that was about?" Anne asked.

Grace shrugged. "We'll find out in due course, I suppose. Auntie Anne, can you hunt down a doctor to discharge me? I won't take no for an answer."

Vital Links

The sun was sinking towards the hills when Charlie emerged from the hospital at a sprint.

Wallace was back in his office at the police station, the bags under his eyes accentuated by the soot still embedded in the creases. "Spare me the youthful exuberance, Pyke. God knows, I'm getting too old for this lark."

"What's happened, sir?"

Wallace sank back into his chair with a prolonged sigh. "Sweeney, Bertram, and the caretaker, Taylor, were all detained in the Criterion Hotel, along with dozens of other men. We've charged Sweeney with inciting a riot."

"He'll have a hard job wiggling his way out of that one. Several hundred people witnessed him urging the mob to attack Lady Stout's carriage. I'm sure Bertram's barman, Vance, was one of them."

"Vance was the first one to jump on the carriage and hurl insults, but he managed to slip through the net. Once we have a man to spare, we'll bring Vance in and charge him with rioting, criminal damage, and threatening behaviour. When we spoke to him yesterday, he denied delivering the threatening note and noose to Mrs Reynolds, but we've got the evidence of his writing and the gardener's description. He tried to put the blame on you, Pyke – imitating his writing and so forth. We should have him to rights, unless Bertram pays for a top attorney for him."

Attorney or not, Charlie vowed that Vance wouldn't escape arrest on his watch. "What about Harry Bertram?"

"Cunning as a weasel, that one. He was having a meeting and lunch with his attorney the whole time, in an upstairs room on the Moray Place side of the Criterion Hotel. Thus, Bertram had a ringside seat and an iron-clad alibi in one. We've no proof yet that

166

he had anything to do with the mob attack or bombing. We had to let Bertram go."

Every shred of Charlie's instinct screamed that Bertram was behind the mob attack, if not the bomb. The very idea that the scoundrel might escape justice appalled him. "I take it all of them deny any knowledge of the dynamite?"

"Absolutely and unequivocally, as you'd expect," Wallace replied. "Much as I hate to admit it, I am inclined to believe them. Bertram was of the firm opinion that the Women's Franchise League set the bomb off themselves, to garner sympathy for their cause and incite outrage against the liquor lobby. I've no doubt an article will duly appear in the *Otago Workman* to that effect."

"'Oh, what a tangled web we weave, when first we practice to deceive.'"

"Walter Scott certainly hit the nail on the head, although I suspect even he would throw his hands in the air in this case. I haven't got to the best part yet."

Charlie leaned forward expectantly. "The caretaker, Taylor? A dubious character, that one."

"He was on the edge of nervous collapse by the time Kelly brought him to me. By then, I'd had his room searched, so I'm not surprised he was terrified. Taylor's real name is Patrick Tynan."

Wallace paused to let it sink in, but the name meant nothing to Charlie. "Not sure I follow, sir."

"I suppose you're too young to remember the Fenian bombing campaign in the early 1880s. Irish republicans hit targets all over England with dynamite bombs, set off by timers. Patrick Tynan was one of the most notorious of the group."

Charlie rocked back in his chair, stunned by this startling revelation. "The caretaker is a known bomber?"

"No, not a chance. Wrong age, wrong description, but he is Irish, and he did live in London. The name was so notorious, our man fled the country, persecuted for the misfortune of sharing the same name as a ruthless bomber. I vividly recall hearing about the

167

Fenian attack on London Bridge. Several deaths and dozens injured – it was news for weeks."

"I do have a vague memory of it. I would have been about fifteen."

"Gads, lad, sometimes you and Kelly make me feel as old as Methuselah. As you might imagine, the caretaker is falling over himself to deny any connection to our dynamite bomb. He has admitted that he is in debt to Owen Gilroy. Taylor-Tynan has no money, so he was repaying the debt by allowing Gilroy to use Choral Hall for illegal gambling after hours."

"Were Gilroy and his gamblers there last night?"

"Only until midnight. The caretaker said the gamblers had a dispute over cheating and Gilroy shut down proceedings early. He's sure of the time, because the grandfather clock stuck twelve after the gamblers had left. Apparently, the clock drives the caretaker crazy, chiming out the hours throughout the night."

Charlie was beginning to feel like a rat in a maze, running as fast as he could, only to end up in a series of dead ends. "If that's true, none of the gamblers could have planted the bomb. There's no way the timer could have been set more than twelve hours in advance, assuming the wiring was triggered by the hour hand. I take it the caretaker denied letting anyone else in later?"

"So he says. I've sent DS Elliot out to arrest Gilroy all the same. We'll hold the illegal gaming charge over him until he tells us what he knows. I can't say I hold out much hope. Gilroy would have been a fool to draw attention to Choral Hall by bombing it, if he was using it for illegal gaming. The same goes for the caretaker. All our suspects seemed credible when they denied anything to do with the explosions."

"The bombings do appear out of character with the rest of their campaign against the women suffragists. The incidents they admit to are malicious and spiteful, but not murderous. A noose of roses, thrown beer, firecrackers, rocking Lady Stout's carriage."

"I agree, Pyke. Dynamite, timer, commercial detonator cap, nails ... that's the work of a professional who doesn't care who might be hurt. I shouldn't care to be better acquainted with any of our four liquor barons, but they have too much to lose to take such risks. Once the newspapers come out, the public will be baying for blood."

DS Elliot and DC Kelly chose that moment to stumble through the door, looking every bit as exhausted as Charlie felt.

"Well?" Wallace barked.

"Gilroy came quietly. He's in custody downstairs," Elliot reported. "He was out last night, but returned home shortly after midnight. His sick wife has taken a turn for the worse, so he hasn't been out again. The wife's nurse was willing to swear he never left her side after midnight."

Wallace dropped his elbows onto his desk with a thump. "Curses. Seems we are running around in circles, biting on our own tails. Go home and get some sleep, men. We'll tackle them again tomorrow morning. No, wait. Pyke, what was it you came to tell me?"

"Miss Penrose remembered seeing the tin of tea in which the bomb was hidden. An expensive Darjeeling tea with a green and gold label, likely to be found in only the most well-to-do households. When she is out of hospital, she will go to the local grocery stores and importers' warehouses to see if she can identify it."

"All our suspects are wealthy, but with luck, only one of them uses that variety of tea. Good. Anything else?"

"The man killed by Lennox MacDonald two years ago in the explosives accident was Mr Creswell, husband of our bomb victim, Violet Creswell. Grace's great-aunt, Anne Macmillan, knew this because her neighbour, Mrs Patterson, is Lennox's sister."

This had Wallace sitting upright at his desk, his nose quivering. "Excellent. It's a fine thing to police a small city like Dunedin, where everyone knows everyone else's business."

169

"That's not all, sir. Mrs Patterson is a leading light in the Homemakers' Association group, who met at ten o'clock this morning at Choral Hall. It's not outside the bounds of possibility that she let her brother Lennox into the hall with her legion of helpers. I was at the main door and didn't see him come in, but she might have arranged for someone to let him in the back door while I was patrolling upstairs. Perhaps the caretaker?"

"Elliot, Kelly, get the caretaker back to the interview room." When they had gone, Wallace turned to Charlie. "Tynan knows you were at Choral Hall, so best you ask the questions."

Tynan recoiled when he saw Charlie waiting for him in the interview room.

"Remember me, Mr Taylor? Or is it Mr Tynan?" Charlie rose and went around the table, pulling out a chair for the caretaker. "Please, have a seat. I have a few additional questions about the sequence of events at Choral Hall."

Tynan sat, casting a nervous backward glance at the man holding the chair. "I've already told the police everything I know."

"Details may be missed, memories resurface. We will keep asking question until we are sure we can account for every minute. Is that clear, Mr Tynan?" Charlie waited for his grudging nod. "I want you to take your time and think carefully. Do you recall seeing or hearing anyone in the kitchen?"

"Those noisy girls were in there, organising morning tea for the ladies. You were there too, Constable."

"And after that?"

"Nobody."

"You didn't see a woman go in alone right before the bomb exploded?"

"No. I was in my room. Wasn't feeling too good, so I had a lie down."

Charlie wasn't surprised, as the caretaker was very much the worse for drink that morning. "Did you see anyone carrying a large tin of tea with a green and gold label?"

"No. The ladies brought a lot of boxes and plates of food. Ain't my job to take note of them."

"Did you open the back door at any time before or after I told you to keep it locked?" Charlie caught the twitch at the corner of the caretaker's mouth.

Wallace must have seen it too. "Mr Tynan, it is vital that you tell the truth. Catching the bomber is far more important to us than catching you out in a minor lapse of judgement."

Tynan squirmed for a moment, his eyes flicking to the door, but seeing no way of escape. "I ... I felt sick. Needed a bit of fresh air. It wasn't more than a minute or two, I swear. He couldn't have done anything in that time."

"He? Who? Are you saying a man went into Choral Hall?" Wallace thrust his chair back and loomed over the table. "Tell me exactly what happened, without leaving a single thing out, or I'll have you charged with being an accessory."

Tynan shrunk back into his chair, as if making himself smaller would make his problems vanish. "God's truth, Inspector, there's not much to tell. I stepped out for a short spell. When I went back in, a man was in the corridor, near the back door. He can't have gotten any further in than that. I yelled at him to get out, that nobody was allowed in. He left. That's it. I've never seen him before."

"Did someone let him in?" Wallace asked.

Tynan hesitated. His hands rose to cover his face for an instant, before dropping again. "I left the door open. I only wanted a breath of air, but I felt dizzy. Must have sat down for a moment. I didn't see anyone else. I swear I locked the door after he left and never opened it again until after the explosion."

"What time was this?" Charlie asked.

"Maybe about twenty minutes before the Homemaker ladies went home."

Charlie went over the sequence of events in his memory. "That would make it about eleven o'clock. The maids were gone. I was checking that all the upstairs windows were closed. With all the noise the Homemakers' Association was making, nobody else would have heard anything."

"Describe the man," Wallace snapped. "What did he look like? Was he carrying a bag or parcel?"

Tynan's face scrunched as he took a few moments to visualise the scene. "He had a bag, but it looked empty. Ordinary sort of fellow – fairly tall, lean but strong looking."

"What size and type of bag?"

"I dunno. Dark colour, about this big." Tynan's hands sketched the shape, which was big enough for the tea tin.

"Clothes?"

"He looked like a man who worked for his living. But fairly well-to-do – tidy, not scruffy or dirty. He stepped out so quick, I hardly saw him. He had his cap pulled low, I remember that."

"He must have said something to you."

"Not much. Let out an oath when I caught hold of him, apologised, said something about looking for someone. I didn't take much notice."

"Accent?"

"Not Irish, that's for sure. Scots or English maybe."

"Distinguishing features? Facial hair, limp, scars, memorable features?"

"Not that I recall. I really can't tell you anything more, Inspector. I only saw him for a moment and I was not feeling well at the time."

Wallace persisted, with more desperation than hope. "Would you recognise him again?"

"I'm not sure."

"Could it have been Owen Gilroy?"

"Definitely not. I'm sure I had never seen the man before."

"Do you know Conor Sweeney, Harry Bertram or Lennox MacDonald?"

"Only Sweeney. It wasn't him. Definitely taller and leaner."

172

Charlie put his notebook in front of the caretaker and flipped slowly through the pages of sketches he had made to record all witnesses, suspects, and other people involved in his cases. Tynan paused at a dozen pictures, but none with any certainty. In the end, he turned up his hands and shrugged.

"If you recall anything else about this man, Tynan, tell us immediately," Wallace said. "I'll see you're not dismissed from your position, unless we find you had any part in this attack."

"Thank you, sir. I swear I didn't."

Kelly and Elliot took Tynan away, with orders to show the caretaker the men being held in the cells, in the forlorn hope he might identify the intruder at the hall.

Wallace paced the room. "I don't want to jump to conclusions, but it seems probable that the man the caretaker saw was the bomber. It wouldn't have taken him more than a few seconds to plant the tea tin. Tynan must have met him coming out again with the empty bag."

"Seems a reasonable conclusion," Charlie agreed. "The man wasn't Gilroy or Sweeney and the description doesn't match Bertram, so that leaves Lennox MacDonald or an unknown person. Tynan did pause for a moment at the sketch of MacDonald, but he also showed signs of recognising a few others."

"Which other sketches did he pause at?"

"Vance, one of Sweeney's men, the foreman of MacDonald's brewery, four suspects from previous cases in Wellington, Constable Fletcher, and two men who happened to be playing football at the park when I was practising my drawing a few weeks ago."

Wallace groaned. "In other words, he has no idea. He might be making the intruder up to deflect suspicion from himself."

"You think the caretaker was in on it?"

"I'm not sure. He gave a fair impression of panicked innocence. I don't think he would have admitted to leaving the door open if he was part of the plot, especially as he was so eager to avoid notoriety.

On the other hand, a man like him would do anything for money, as he's already proved by allowing the gamblers to use the hall. I'll have his finances checked." Wallace stopped pacing and slumped into the chair. "We need to get Lennox MacDonald in for questioning. He matches the description of both the man at the hall and the man who arranged for the boy to deliver the first bomb."

"I've been thinking about the bomb, sir. The petition forms would probably have been destroyed by the dynamite alone. The addition of nails suggests a more deadly purpose. What if Mrs Creswell was told to be in the kitchen at that specific time? If Lennox was responsible for her husband's death, perhaps she had been threatening to disclose the fact or she was seeking compensation directly from him. That might give him motive to kill her."

"Why wait two years after her husband's death?"

"I gather she was a recent convert to the concept of women's rights. Perhaps she finally realised she had been hard done by. The MacDonalds gave Mrs Creswell a small pension, but she was forced out to work after her husband's death. In fact, she was working for Fergus MacDonald's business."

"That rather suggests she didn't hold a grudge."

"Perhaps it was the only position she could get. Or MacDonald was paying her over the odds to make up for her loss."

Wallace rubbed his hand over his chin. "We'll need proof. Pyke, I want you to work on the Creswell connection. Talk to her friends and relations. Tomorrow morning, I want you to come with me to interview Fergus MacDonald, Lennox's father and owner of the roading construction company."

"And Lennox MacDonald?"

"Left yesterday to stay with a friend out of town, according to his housekeeper. I've got men out checking his alibi. We'll talk to his father first, but if Lennox's alibi holds, it wasn't him who placed the bomb at Choral Hall. We might be looking at a paid job, in which

174

case, there is one very nervous man out there, terrified he's been set up for the bombing and knowing he was seen by the caretaker."

Forget Me Not

Grace awoke in a cold sweat, convinced she was trussed up beside a bomb with seconds left on the timer. Instead of ropes and ticking explosive devices, she found herself tangled in the starched white sheets of a hospital bed, with the benign sounds of creaking trolley wheels and the clatter of trays. A blob of stew and potato sat on a tray beside her, bringing back unpleasant memories of her time in a lunatic asylum four months ago.

She turned her head away. Her last memory was attempting to get out of bed, determined to go home. Obviously, she had been a little overconfident in her recovery from the concussion.

"Miss Penrose, awake again, are you? I did tell you not to get up. I sent your grandmother home. She will return to take you home tomorrow morning."

"Thank you, nurse. Could you help me sit, please?"

The nurse helped her upright, plumping the pillow as if it was made of feathers rather than some type of soft rock. "Try to eat to keep your strength up. The doctor said you're not to go home until you can stand by yourself." She consulted a list, before striding off down the ward.

All Grace wanted was a drink and a head that didn't feel as if it was on the losing side of three rounds in a boxing ring. The water tasted disgusting, but that might have been because of the persistent taste of soot in her throat. Tea would have been better, but she couldn't face the stewed hospital variety.

"That bad is it, Grace? Would you prefer some freshly pressed apple juice?"

"Molly Sugden, you're an angel. I can't think of anything I'd like more, except to be out of here."

"I know that awful feeling of waking up dizzy and dehydrated in hospital. People bring flowers, when all you want is something to drink that doesn't taste like the inside of a rusty pipe."

Grace sipped at the flask of juice, which washed away both soot and thirst. "Bliss, thank you Molly. You shouldn't have come. You must be terribly worried about your friend."

"Dearest Grace, you've been my best friend for over two years. How could I not visit you? I hardly knew Violet and I will visit her as soon as I have assured myself that you are truly as well as you pretend to be."

Grace brushed off her concerns with a wave of her hand. "Mild concussion. No cause for concern. I am worried about Mrs Creswell, though."

"Poor Violet. For such a tragedy to happen, especially when she had begun to believe the future would be brighter."

"Was she coming to terms with her husband's death, do you think?"

"Not exactly, but the healing had begun. I think joining the women's rights movement was helping her to discover new strength within herself. I understand she was coming into some money too, which must have been a blessing for a widow with an elderly mother-in-law to look after."

Grace recapped the flask and set it down with a satisfied sigh. "Do you know the source of the money Violet was getting?"

"I don't. I only hope it is enough to see her through what might be a long convalescence."

"What an awful day. Not an auspicious start to the Women's Franchise League. Have they rescheduled the meeting, Molly?"

"Oh, Grace, haven't you heard? Marion Hatton and Lady Stout insisted the meeting go ahead. We shall not be overcome, courage in adversity, and all that glorious sallying forth rhetoric. After a desperately sad minute of silent prayer for the injured, of course. The gentlemen of the press were lapping it up. I shouldn't wonder if Fish's mob is portrayed as a pitiful bunch of vicious, murdering thugs. What a contrast to the splendour of Mrs Hatton, Lady Stout, Miss Morison and Miss Nicol arm-in arm, leading the Women's Franchise League ladies into Choral Hall even as the smoke still drifted around them. Honestly, Grace, I have never been prouder of my fellow suffragists. Mrs Reynolds gave such a rousing speech. I do wish you had been there."

Grace smiled at her friend's jubilation. "Molly, my dear friend, you have done me more good than all the doctors in the hospital combined. I only wish I had been there to see it."

"I will have to tell you all about it another day. I must visit Violent and take news of her condition back to her mother-in-law. She is in a state of collapse, poor dear. To have to bury one's only child and then to have her daughter-in-law critically injured in such a short period – what could be worse?"

An imperious voice interrupted her train of thought. Cranston-Hartfield.

"Grace, my dear, you ought to be resting, not receiving visitors." The police surgeon deposited half a dozen out of season red roses in a vase on the bedside table.

Grace tried to send a silent message to her friend to stay, but Molly got up. "I must be going. Do try to get some rest, Grace." Molly blew her a kiss and fled.

Grace pulled the covers to her neck and counted to ten. It wasn't that she disliked the police surgeon, but he was her employer. Pleasant conversation was acceptable, roses were not. As the first female medical student, she had steeled herself for abuse, but she had never considered the need to protect her reputation from unexpected advances. But how could she admonish one of the few medical professionals who had been willing to give her a job where she could actually advance her skills, instead of making tea and doing filing?

He thrust a rose towards her nose. "I send a note to our gardener to liberate these from the hot-house for you. Mater won't mind if it is for a worthy cause."

"Thank you, Doctor Cranston-Hartfield. You should not have brought them. You would not think to give flowers to any other medical student."

"I insist you call me Jamie, Grace. Why should I not bring flowers to a fallen comrade, especially one so pretty? Do tell me how you are feeling."

"Better, although I am still shaken by the bombing."

"I would have come back sooner, but the hospital requested an immediate autopsy on the bombing victim."

Grace's breath caught in her throat. "What victim? Has Mrs Creswell not survived?"

Cranston-Hartfield's face fell into a comic parody of shocked dismay. "Oh, Grace, I'm so very sorry. She passed away after I saw you earlier. What a fool I am – I thought you would know."

Grace accepted the handkerchief he held out for her, grateful for its man-sized expanse of cotton to hide her distress. In her heart, she wanted Charlie back and the police surgeon gone, but she also wanted to know the truth. "How did she die?"

"Grace, you ought to be resting, not worrying. I don't know what came over me, telling you tragic news at such a difficult time."

"We all need to know as soon as possible, Doctor Cranston-Hartfield," a deeper voice interrupted, "since we are now dealing with a murder inquiry."

"Pyke! What are you doing here? Grace didn't tell me you were back in Dunedin." The police surgeon recovered his composure enough to glare at Charlie. "I might have known you'd be mixed up in this atrocity."

Charlie ignored the question and got straight to the point. "You were about to tell us about Mrs Creswell's death."

A professional mask slid over the police surgeon's annoyance. "A splinter pierced her skin and punctured a blood vessel. Violet Creswell died of internal bleeding, combined with the general trauma of being subjected to the shockwave from the explosion and multiple wounds from flying debris. There was nothing the doctors could do to save her."

"Did you find a reticule or any other items about her person?" Charlie asked. "I am curious as to why she was in the kitchen at that particular time."

"As a matter of fact, I found a note which suggests she was meeting someone there. The note was far from intact, as you might imagine, but I could discern enough words to identify a meeting time and place."

Charlie's nostrils flared. "Detective Inspector Wallace will want to see that note as a matter of urgency, but I would be obliged if you could tell me exactly what it said."

"I was intending to give it to DI Wallace on my way home." The police surgeon withdrew an envelope from his overcoat, extracting a charred piece of paper.

Grace leaned forward to see it. Many of the words and parts of words were illegible, but the message was clear enough. "….rswell, meet me ….itchen stora….five minu…ock…ur advant…."

"Mrs Creswell, meet me in the kitchen storage room at five minutes before two o'clock, to your advantage," Charlie read. "Could you make out anything else?"

"I thought I discerned the word 'alone' when I held it to the light, but it wasn't at all clear. I believe that is the gist of it. It was only a short note. No discernible signature."

"Not even an initial?" Charlie asked.

"No. Everything before and after the words you see was destroyed."

"This note is vital to the case. Thank you for making sure it gets to DI Wallace so promptly."

The police surgeon wavered for a moment. "It would seem that duty calls, Grace. I will call upon you tomorrow morning, if I may."

"No need. I shall be gone. I do appreciate you taking the time to bring me the autopsy results, Doctor Cranston-Hartfield. Please thank your mother for the lovely roses."

When the police surgeon had left, Charlie held up a small bunch of scraggly flowers. "I'll dispose of these pathetic specimens. A persuasive little waif was selling them on the hospital steps, but they pale beside a half dozen perfect red roses."

"You will do no such thing, Charlie Pyke. How amusing of you to buy me forget-me-nots. As if I would forget you."

"I assure you it wasn't intended as a cleverly coded floral message, Grace. If it's not a rose, I have no idea what the darn things are called." He pulled the curtain around them and kissed her tenderly on the cheek. "I'm deeply sorry for the loss of your friend, Grace, but I am also relieved that you're not quite as cross-eyed and pale as you were when I last saw you."

"Can you get me out of here, Charlie? I hate being a patient. It's too noisy and uncomfortable."

"The nurse told me you must rest and definitely not leave until you can stand on your own. I don't think she is pleased at the number of visitors invading her ward."

"Charlie, you might be interested in what Molly had to say. She thought Violet Creswell was about to come into some money."

"Interesting. We will certainly follow that up. The news that Mrs Creswell had a note to meet somebody is critical evidence too, as is the information on Lennox MacDonald, who is a prime suspect. It's possible Mrs Creswell demanded compensation from Lennox and was expecting him to show up at Choral Hall to meet her. Perhaps I should suggest that Wallace moves to your bedside to gather the latest intelligence?"

"That would really have the nurse up in arms. Besides, I only know a few bits and pieces. I'm relying on you to fill in the details."

"Let's see if you are fit to go home first."

"Are you thinking of my welfare, Charlie, or angling for an invitation to dinner?"

"Your welfare, naturally. And the chance to question Mrs Macmillan about the MacDonald family. If the peerless Mrs Brown happens to have a little food to spare, I expect I could oblige on that count too."

Grace slipped out of bed. Once the dizziness passed, she could more or less stand on her own. While she would never have allowed any patient of hers to leave in such a state, she considered herself exempt from doctor's orders. Only one problem remained. "I can't leave in a hospital gown. It's indecent. The clothes I was in are ruined."

Charlie held up a bag. "I sent a message to your great-aunt to the effect that I was about to abduct you. She replied with clothes, delivered by Johnny in the buggy. He awaits us outside."

"Two abductions in less than a week?"

He shrugged. "It's been a hectic few days. Shall I ask one of the nurses to assist you with dressing? I'd offer to help you myself, but I wouldn't care to upset your other admirers."

"Charlie Pyke, I sincerely hope you are not so forward with all young ladies. Off with you, or I shall be obliged to defend my honour. And take those roses away."

When Grace emerged from behind the curtain ten minutes later, clutching her forget-me-nots, she found Charlie deep in conversation with a patient further along the ward. The roses were sitting on her bedside table and the woman was giggling. To her amazement, he bent and kissed her on the cheek as he departed. Not for the first time, Grace marvelled at his ability to charm women from all walks of life.

Charlie took Grace's arm. "I can carry you, if you are feeling unsteady."

"No need, as long as I can hold your arm." Grace glanced along the ward to see the object of his attention. A shrivelled old lady with white hair waved back. "Let's go, Charlie. I'm longing to be return to the comforts of home."

"And the opportunity to interrogate me?"

"I expect I could oblige on that count too, if you can spare the time from wooing every pretty woman between the ages of eighteen and eighty."

Old MacDonald

On Friday morning, the streets rang with the calls of newspaper boys. Every person Charlie passed was carrying a copy of the *Otago Daily Times* and talking about the bombing. Sentiment on the street ran the gamut from fearful whispers to strident outrage. Anyone carrying a parcel found their way miraculously clear as other pedestrians gave them anxious glances and a wide berth.

Charlie arrived at the police station before eight o'clock to find it buzzing with activity. Every available man had been recruited to the case – checking alibis, following up Gilroy's gamblers, tracking down Lennox MacDonald and Vance the barman, interviewing witnesses, and investigating all known sources of dynamite.

Charlie escaped to the relative quiet of his basement desk to go over his notes. He hadn't had the opportunity to talk to Mrs Macmillan last night about the MacDonald family, as Anne was fast asleep in her favourite armchair when he brought Grace back from the hospital. Grace had been overcome with tears at the sight of her great-aunt, transformed by exhaustion into a pale, fragile old lady. Mrs Brown and her daughter had helped Grace to bed, while Charlie watched on helplessly, wretched with guilt that he had taken her from the hospital too soon.

He imagined the scene being repeated all over Dunedin. Strong, passionate women, finally giving way to grief and shock behind closed doors, after their show of defiance at the Franchise League meeting. Their bravery had not gone unnoticed. Today's editorial in the *Otago Daily Times* left no adjective unturned in praise of the suffragists and condemnation of the mob, who were dismissed as pitiful, drunken pawns of the liquor interests associated with Henry Fish. Bertram would be apoplectic.

At nine o'clock, Charlie and Wallace took the cable car up High Street to Mornington. Fergus MacDonald owned a large parcel of land and a grand house away from other residences, backing on to the wide swathe of trees forming the town belt.

The estate had a pair of driveways diverging from the arched gateway – a sweeping, tree-lined central drive and a gravel track to the left. As they arrived at the gate, a cart laden with boxes and tools approached on the latter and exited. A signboard on the side of the cart announced "MacDonald Roading" in plain lettering.

The man at the gate approached them. "Do you have business with MacDonald Roading, gentlemen?"

"I'm Detective Inspector Wallace. We are visiting every business with access to explosive materials. I am here to see Mr Fergus MacDonald."

"That'll be about the bomb at Choral Hall, I expect. Shocking thing to happen so close to home. Anarchists, I don't doubt, whatever lies the newspapers print about Mr Fish. It's Mr Patterson you'll want to talk to, Inspector. He is in charge of running the business. Up the central drive to the house. The office is on the left-hand side of the main house."

"Does Mr MacDonald's son not run the business?"

The gate man didn't blink, but a slight flaring of his nostrils answered for him. "Mr Lennox MacDonald has other business interests, sir. He only comes here for meetings and social events."

"Has he been here recently?" Wallace inquired.

"Oh, aye. Came last week for the Board of Directors' meeting. Thursday it must have been. Showed up early for a change."

Wallace and Charlie walked along the drive, heading straight to the main entrance of the house.

"If Lennox MacDonald got hold of black powder, it must have been before the meeting the liquor barons held on Friday night," Wallace said. "He had to have time to make the firecrackers by Saturday afternoon."

185

Charlie nodded. "Bertram had been planning to take action against the suffragists ever since the meeting at City Hall on the twelfth of April, when the Women's Franchise League was proposed. The directors' meeting would have been the perfect opportunity to steal the explosives."

"I wonder if they know Mrs Creswell was killed in the explosion. I asked the newspapers not to print her name until her next of kin had been informed."

"MacDonald's daughter, Mrs Patterson, was outside Choral Hall at the time of the bombing," Charlie reminded him. "I believe Mrs Macmillan informed her of the death yesterday, as they are neighbours."

Sure enough, the butler who answered the door wore a band of black crepe on his arm. When Fergus MacDonald entered the library, he wore a sombre expression and a dark suit. The elegant cut of the suit could not disguise his stocky figure, which looked as if it would be better suited to homespun clothes and a clay pipe. His whole demeanour suggested a self-made man. Charlie laid a wager with himself that MacDonald would allude to it before the interview was over.

Fergus MacDonald sank into an armchair with a wheezing cough, waving for the two visitors to join him. His white hair, deeply lined face and sickly pallor marked him as a man with little time left on this earth. "You'll be here about the bombing. I hope you catch the devils who did this, Inspector. They deserve to burn in Hell."

"Every available man is working on it, I assure you, Mr MacDonald."

"I expect you are wondering about the signs of mourning. The truth is, Mrs Creswell was more to us that simply a girl who did the typing. For all the success of my business, I'm still a self-made man who remembers the tough years. I think of my workers as a family, not simply employees. Mrs Creswell was a valued member of that family."

"She must have been grateful for that consideration, Mr MacDonald. It cannot have been easy for her, after being widowed at such a young age."

MacDonald had the grace to blush and the honesty to admit to the cause. "Her husband was a valued worker, the foreman of our tunnel construction team. After his death at work, we naturally felt obliged to see to his widow's welfare, even though it was a tragic accident. We gave her a pension, as well as a wage."

"Was Mrs Creswell a good worker?"

"Excellent, I understand. Mr Patterson, my son-in-law, insisted on raising her wage a few months ago. He reckoned she was better than any man at doing her job, so why should she be paid half as much. Very modern ideas, Mr Patterson. Nothing was too much, even the latest model of typewriting machine. I never believed a woman could do such work, but I now see that all those little buttons on the typewriter suit a delicate hand. Her fingers fairly flew over it."

MacDonald succumbed to a fit of coughing, which came from deep within congested lungs. A maid entered with a tray. She handed him a glass of water and a fresh handkerchief, before pouring coffee into three cups and handing them around. The maid glided silently out of the library before Charlie could thank her.

MacDonald took a sip of water and sank deeper into the armchair. "My apologies. Too many years breathing in dust and tar. It's made an old man of me in my sixties. I'm lucky to have a such an able son-in-law to take the reins."

"You have a son, I understand." Wallace let the sentence hang.

A small, derisive puff of air escaped MacDonald's nostrils, but he didn't rise to the bait. "Lennox is a successful businessman in his own right. He owns a brewery. I'd have preferred him to follow in my footsteps, of course, but a father must accept that a son may have other interests."

"When was the last time your son was here?"

"Last Thursday, for the Board of Directors' meeting and luncheon. Late, of course, as usual. Come to think of it, Mrs Creswell was absent. Perhaps because of her invalid mother-in-law."

Wallace didn't react to this discrepancy from the gatekeeper's account of Lennox's early arrival. "I understand you purchased the brewery for your son two years ago, after the accident."

A "how the hell did you know that" scowl darkened MacDonald's face, but he answered civilly. "It seemed best to direct my son's talents in a more suitable direction."

"You retained a controlling interest, I understand."

"If you know it, why are you asking?" MacDonald coughed again, spilling coffee on the arm of the chair. He swiped at it with his sleeve. "Detective Inspector Wallace, I am eager to assist you in any way with the apprehension of the villain who killed Mrs Creswell. However, I fail to see the relevance of your questions about my business interests."

"I apologise for any offence caused, Mr MacDonald. However, it is an unfortunate reality that police investigations into such serious incidents must be wide-ranging in order to sift through the many irrelevant details in search of the truth. Do you have any objection to discussing the financial structure of the brewery and your own business? We can do it in the privacy of your library today, or I can make an official request for the documents, if you would prefer."

"You're a nosy fellow, Inspector, but my affairs are no secret. While I still breathe," he said, with a wry grimace, "I own fifty-one percent of the brewery. I also appoint the staff at the brewery and my son's household to ensure that everything is run efficiently." He paused, daring them to comment on this lack of trust in his own son's business skills.

When no comment was forthcoming, Fergus MacDonald continued. "As for MacDonald Roading, I own seventy percent. I have gifted fifteen percent to my son, Lennox, and an equal share to my daughter, Abigail Patterson, so they may enjoy some dividends during their lifetimes. When I die, which won't be long, I expect,

Lennox will receive the entire brewery and a fifty-one percent share of MacDonald Roading."

"Your daughter and her husband will become the minority shareholder?"

They had to wait for their answer, as another coughing fit racked Fergus MacDonald's body. Nevertheless, he rasped out an answer as if nothing had happened. "I am an old-fashioned man, Inspector. I am well aware that Mr Patterson has been an extremely able manager of the business, but my son is my rightful heir. I purchased the Patterson's house in High Street as a wedding gift to them, and Patterson earns a salary, so they have no cause for complaint."

"It is more than many fathers would do for their daughter," Wallace agreed.

"I am uncommonly fond of my daughter, I admit. I always thought it a great shame she was not a born a boy. She has a good head for business, my Abigail. Used to come with me around the construction sites as a child, always wanting to know how everything worked. Naturally, she grew out of it when she matured into a lovely young lady. I had great hopes of her marrying well, but she set her sights on my head foreman, John Patterson, and that was that. Well, I've no regrets on that score. He is a hard worker and a model husband. I am not too proud to admit they have made the business far more of a success than I ever did. And Abigail puts her skills to good use in her charity work, as befits her situation."

"I thank you for being so accommodating to my questioning, Mr MacDonald. I assure you the information will be held in the strictest confidence. We are obliged to investigate all businesses in Dunedin that have access to explosive material. As part of that, we must satisfy ourselves that your stocks of explosives are all in order."

"We are scrupulous on that score, Inspector. We have a man on the gate night and day, in addition to employing a storeman and keeping the explosives shed locked tight at all times."

Wallace's eyebrow shot up. "You store the explosives on site, here?"

"It's a large property, with high fencing. We keep a lot of valuable equipment here, where we can keep a close eye on it. We undergo regular safety inspections."

"Perhaps Mr Patterson would be so kind as to show us."

"I don't think he is back yet. Patterson is often out at the construction sites in his role as overall supervisor of operations." Fergus MacDonald reached for a diary, then stopped to pat his pockets. "Darned eyeglasses, always getting lost."

"Why don't I take a look, sir," Charlie said, taking the diary from the side table. He flicked through the diary to the current day, noting that Mr Patterson was due back today from a two-day trip around various construction sites in the North Taieri area. He had also been away on the day the bomb had been sent to Harriet Morison. Charlie shook his head at Wallace.

"Thank you for your cooperation, Mr MacDonald. We will have a word with your storeman, then be on our way."

"You will find him in the building at the side of the house. I hope you catch the devil who did this, Inspector."

Charlie exchanged a glance with DI Wallace. Would Fergus MacDonald be so eager for the culprit to be punished if he knew his own son was a suspect? Frankly, by the look of the man, his son's arrest might be a death blow.

They left to the sound of a hacking cough, the sight of a blood-stained handkerchief, and the memory of a pallid, trembling old man.

New Roads

"Must be hard for a successful man like Fergus MacDonald to be so ill," Wallace remarked, as they walked around the side of the house to the office. "He was more forthcoming that I expected."

"Mr Patterson sounds like a paragon of virtue compared to Lennox MacDonald. He is due back today, after two days out of town. He was also away the day the first bomb was delivered."

"Thanks goodness. One less potential suspect to worry about. I'm eager to get away from here, so we can focus on Lennox MacDonald. The more I hear of him, the less I like it."

As they rounded the corner, they saw a tall, muscular man coming towards them from the stables at the fast lope of a busy man. He wore a long canvas duster coat, splattered with mud, and sweat-stained leggings, with saddlebags slung over his shoulder. When he came closer, Charlie could see two-day-old stubble, weary eyes, and the wide-legged gait of a man who is used to long hours on a horse.

Nevertheless, Patterson was already stretching his hand out for a handshake as he neared them, his open smile rendering a rugged face attractive. "Good morning, gentlemen. Can I help you?"

"I'm Detective Inspector Wallace."

The man pumped Wallace's hand with the vigour typical of a country man. "John Patterson, at your service."

Charlie found himself returning the smile, which was one of those genial smiles that immediately set a man at ease. With a start, he realised that this man was the husband of Grace's neighbour, Mrs Abigail Patterson, who had been forthright in her attempts to push Grace into the arms of a wealthy gentleman. The prim and proper Mrs Patterson seemed an unlikely match for him.

"We are here about Mrs Creswell," Wallace said.

The smile faltered and dropped away. "Mrs Creswell?"

"Mr Patterson, I had quite forgotten that you have been out of town. I'm terribly sorry to have to inform you that Mrs Creswell died yesterday."

Patterson stared at him for a few moments, before his face cleared. "Oh, you must mean old Mrs Creswell. For a moment there, I thought our Mrs Creswell must have had an accident. Violet did say her mother-in-law was very ill. She hasn't been able to come to work lately because of it. How terribly sad for her."

"I'm afraid it is Mrs Violet Creswell I am referring to. She was killed in an explosion at Choral Hall yesterday."

"An explosion? A gas leak?"

"Dynamite."

"Dynamite? I ... I don't know what to say. How shocking. Poor Abigail will be devastated. I wonder if she knows. Choral Hall, you say? I think my wife may have been there yesterday morning. An explosion ..."

In Charlie's experience, people shocked with unexpected news often reacted with a disjointed outpouring of words, as if all their thoughts were jumbled, one on top of the other, until they reached the single thought that mattered the most. He waited, and it came.

"Abigail! My wife ... is she–?"

Wallace laid a hand on his shoulder. "Mrs Patterson is unharmed, although she did witness the incident from the street. Mrs Creswell was the only fatality."

Patterson jigged on the spot like a horse eager to be let loose. "I must go home straight away. My wife was fond of Mrs Creswell. And to be present at such a terrible scene, without me by her side to comfort her."

Wallace guided him by the arm towards the office. "She had the support of friends, Mr Patterson. We must beg a few minutes of your time to answer some vital questions. You would want the perpetrator to be caught quickly, I am sure."

Patterson subsided. "Yes, yes, of course. My apologies. Mrs Creswell's death has come as a shock. What do you need to know?"

"We are investigating all businesses that use dynamite, blasting caps and black powder. I trust you keep a sharp eye on your inventory?"

"Of course. I'll get our storeman onto it immediately."

The office was quiet. The only sign of life was a man with his feet on a desk, reading the *Otago Daily Times*. He removed his boots from the furniture at the sight of Mr Patterson, but showed no signs of panic at being caught out. Patterson was clearly no tyrant as a boss.

"Have you heard about the bomb, John? Shocking business." The man caught sight of the policemen and straightened his back. "Excuse me, sirs, didn't see you there."

Patterson slung his saddlebags over a chair and stretched his muscles. "Bert, these men are from the police. They are checking whether any of our explosives are missing. Dynamite cartridges, blast caps, fuse, black powder – anything explosive."

"There's been nothing signed out in the last ten days, Mr Patterson. Most of the current work is finishing work – laying gravel on the finished sub-surface and such like – so there has been no need for dynamite."

"Please check the inventory anyway, Bert."

The other man got up and disappeared out of the office.

"Won't it take a while to count the stock?" Wallace asked.

"No. We have a tight system for managing stores. Boxes locked away and opened one at a time, and so on. You were interested in black powder as well as the dynamite cartridges, is that right?"

"Have you not read about an earlier incident, involving an explosive device made from black powder?"

Patterson dropped into a chair behind a tidy desk, gesturing them to take a seat too. "I have been busy of late, trying to get the inland roading projects finished before winter sets in. I rarely have time to read the newspaper. My wife is a saint to put up with all my absences."

193

"Also a minor incident last Saturday involving firecrackers, which caused a horse to bolt, injuring a lady," Charlie added.

Patterson jerked slightly. "Firecrackers?"

"You have heard of the incident, Mr Patterson?"

"No. It's nothing, a trivial coincidence."

"I need to hear it, all the same," Wallace said.

"We had been talking about firecrackers last week. Honestly, it is nothing. My wife and her brother tease each other about the pranks they got up to as children. Apparently, Lennox stole a bit of black powder and gave the cook a fright. An exploding chicken. Silly really, but it must have been quite amusing to the children." He caught the look on their faces. "A dead and plucked chicken, not a live one, and only enough powder to make a small bang. Their mother was furious, of course. I gather their father thought it a grand joke."

"Was Mr Lennox MacDonald a bit of a wild lad, do you think, Mr Patterson?"

"I wouldn't care to speculate on my wife's brother. Many young lads enjoy the odd prank, as I'm sure you know."

"Lennox was here for the Directors' meeting, we understand," Charlie said.

"Yes. That was all about the business. The chicken incident was recalled at the family luncheon after the meeting. Lennox had rather a lot to drink, I'm sorry to say. He made some rather tasteless jokes about firecrackers being the very thing to teach self-righteous troublemakers a lesson."

"Did he mention any particular troublemakers?"

"Oh no, I don't think so. Merely foolish bluster, if you ask me. We try not to encourage him, especially when he has been drinking." Patterson paused. "Now I come to think on it, he was rather scathing of temperance activists. His unpleasant jibes were in poor taste, given the fact my wife and I are strong advocates of temperance."

"Lennox MacDonald arrived late, I gather," Charlie said.

"No more than usual." Patterson was showing signs of agitation, or perhaps he was not a man who could sit still for long.

"Could Lennox have accessed the explosives storehouse?"

"The only people who have access to the explosives storehouse are myself, as overall manager of operations, the three works' foremen, and the storeman."

"Is there a spare key?"

"Locked away in the safe in the back office. The explosives store is in an isolated spot, away from the house, naturally. We are meticulous in keeping our records, as required. I am sure you will find everything is in order."

Bert arrived back, red-faced and quivering. "We're short, Mr Patterson."

Patterson rose from his chair so fast it toppled backwards. "We cannot be, Bert. None of the foremen have been here. Check again."

"I did, twice. We're short two packets of black powder, fuses, and half a dozen cartridges of dynamite and detonators. None of it signed out."

Patterson gripped the edge of his desk with enough force to turn his fingers white. He drew in a deep breath and let it out slowly. "Do me a favour, Bert. Check again," he said, in the same politely calm tone one might use to ask for the salt to be passed.

Charlie and Wallace exchanged a glance. Patterson was the type of man you'd want around you in a crisis. Fergus was a lucky man to have such a son-in-law, especially with a son like Lennox. Bert headed off without a word.

"Who had access to the spare key in the safe, Mr Patterson?" Wallace asked, in an equally calm voice.

"Only myself, my wife, and Mrs Creswell. My father-in-law too, but in practice he is rarely in the office. Sadly, his health is not good. He has not been involved in the day to day running of the business for some time."

"And the storeman and works' foremen?" Charlie asked.

"They don't have access to the safe. We run a large operation, and as such, we hold substantial sums of cash."

"Mrs Creswell is the typist, is she not, yet she has a key?"

"She is – was – much more than that. Mrs Creswell does all manner of office work, such as sending out invoices and notifying me of expenses to be paid. She has a splendid head for figures, like my wife. Our bookkeeper left a few months ago. Useless man, I was happy to see him go. My wife stepped into the breach. Supposed to be a temporary arrangement, of course, but between her and Mrs Creswell, the work was done in no time. I tried to convince my wife it was not appropriate for a lady to work, but, to own the truth, I think she enjoyed it. It took little of her time, as she already knew everything about the business."

"How so?"

Patterson's gaze drifted up and sideways and his expression softened, recalling happy memories. "She was born to it, Inspector. I don't mind admitting I was astounded that Abigail MacDonald ever looked twice at me. I worshipped her – what man wouldn't? – but she could have had any man she desired. It is not false modesty to confess that it was a significant step up for me, from works foreman to manager of the entire operation after our marriage. She was beside me every step of the way. My wife is a true MacDonald, devoted to this company, in a way Lennox could never be."

Patterson's modesty and devotion to his wife made Charlie like the man all the more. The contrast between him and his brother-in-law could not have been starker. "Lennox is still a director and shareholder in the company, despite that, isn't he, Mr Patterson?"

"Yes, of course. There is no ill will on either side, I assure you. Lennox is happy to pursue his other interests and we are proud to run this company. I consider myself the most fortunate of men, Inspector, in work, love and home life. No man could ask for more."

"Fortunate, indeed," Charlie agreed. "May I ask where Mrs Creswell worked?"

"There is a smaller room along the corridor." Patterson pointed at the inner door. "We cannot have the ladies working in here, with gentlemen and workmen about. The safe is in that room too."

Charlie could see Bert striding their way. "I'll go and have a look for myself, while you talk to the storeman. You ought to tell him about Mrs Creswell, Mr Patterson. From his attitude earlier, I suspect he does not know that she was the bombing victim." His concern was part compassion, part desire to have time in the back office away from Patterson's scrutiny.

Mr Patterson's instinct was all for compassion. He hurried to meet Bert at the door, as Charlie slipped out the back.

The rear room was filled with two small desks and a large Chubb safe. It took Charlie less than a minute to find the key to the safe hidden in Mrs Patterson's desk and only a little longer to find a second key in Mrs Creswell's domain. The safe contained a stack of banknotes, important documents and keys, presumably to the explosives store. Charlie locked the safe again and returned the key to its hiding place.

He turned his attention to Mrs Creswell's desk, the top of which held only a stationery tray, a fine porcelain teacup and saucer, and a large case. He removed the cover to reveal a shiny new typewriting machine. It looked hopelessly inefficient to his eye, but the machines were spreading like wildfire, so he supposed they must be quick once one got the hang of it. He hoped he would never have to master the beast – all those little keys were not made for hands like his.

A partially complete letter sat in the roller at the top, requesting a list of supplies from a shipping agent. He read it quickly, noting the neat, evenly spaced letters. It was certainly an improvement in terms of legibility over most of the handwriting he had to decipher.

Charlie switched his attention to the filing drawers arranged beside the safe, flicking through a few files at random. In the short time he had, he got the sense of a business managed with an impressive degree of order and efficiency. The accounts were enumerated in a neat, clear hand in precise columns, totalled with care at the bottom of each page. The roading construction business was generating a robust income, if rather up and down over time, but also high expenses. Thus, the business was successful and growing, but not especially profitable.

The door to the front office opened, leaving him enough time to shut the filing draw and return to the desk, before the footsteps reached the end of the corridor.

"Was there something you wanted to see...?" Patterson was struggling to recall the name of this silent second policeman, but Charlie didn't enlighten him.

"I only wanted to see where Mrs Creswell worked, sir. She was acquainted with a friend, so I feel touched by her passing. A fine woman, by all accounts."

"She was. We shall miss her. My wife most of all." Patterson reached out to touch the handle of the teacup, twisting it slightly on its saucer so it faced the empty chair of Mrs Creswell's desk.

"Extraordinary devices, these typewriting machines. This one appears to be near new."

"What? Oh, yes, only the best for our Mrs Creswell. She can type so fast, I swear her fingers are a blur. I don't know how she does it. I tried it once – hopeless." Patterson held up a scarred, calloused hand with fingers as thick as sausages.

"Have you kept the old typewriting machine, by any chance? I have an acquaintance interested in purchasing one, but he cannot afford a new one."

"I'm not sure what we did with the old one. My wife probably gave it to one of her charities. No, wait, I think she said Lennox took it for the brewery."

"Does her brother come by the office often?"

"No, and we don't encourage it."

"And why is that, Mr Patterson?"

"I ... I hardly like to say."

198

Wallace entered the room behind him. The three men filled the small space with their bulk. "You are obligated to speak, Mr Patterson, or you may be charged with obstruction of justice."

Patterson backed into a corner. "We had noticed sums of money missing from the safe on several occasions. Always when Lennox had visited. The only other people with access to the safe are beyond reproach. Mrs Creswell, myself, my wife and Old Mac."

"Mr Lennox is an independently wealthy man, is he not? I understand his father purchased the brewery on his behalf when he ceased his work at MacDonald Roading. He also receives a share of the profits from the construction business."

"We return most of the earnings into the business. One needs to invest to grow. But yes, my brother-in-law certainly has a healthy income. He also has expensive tastes."

"Expensive tastes?"

"The usual for a man of his inclinations. Fine liquor, fancy women, gambling. Only rumours, you must understand. We do not socialise in the same circles."

"The black sheep of the family?"

Mr Patterson did not reply, but his shrug was answer enough.

"Why have you not tackled him about the theft of money?"

"To be honest, we cannot be absolutely sure it was him. All the invoices and receipts are in order, but the outgoings on wages are difficult to keep track of, as the workers on site are constantly coming and going. Itinerant labour is a real problem, especially if there is any hint of a new gold discovery or some new business venture offering better wages and less arduous work. And, naturally, the work itself is up and down. More workers are needed when tunnelling is required or hard rock is encountered, often at short notice."

"So, how do you arrange it, Mr Patterson?"

"We keep plenty of cash in the safe, topping it up as necessary when the payroll is due. I take the pay out to each site personally, with enough extra to cover the comings and goings of any extra workers. The site managers are responsible for keeping a tally of numbers and hours. Wait a moment and I'll show you."

Patterson returned with the saddlebags, taking out a battered logbook and opening it to show Charlie. "See here? The site foreman fills in the number of men and hours. I check it against the work sheets and calculate the pay. We both sign to show the cash has been delivered."

Charlie took the logbook from him and checked the entries. A payroll delivery had been made on the day before the bombing at five o'clock in the afternoon, counter-signed by the foreman. Far too late for Patterson to have come back to Dunedin. The next delivery was late morning on the day of the bombing, some distance from the previous works site.

"You ride out alone? With all that cash?" Wallace asked.

"I travel armed on a fast horse. Besides, I visit different areas on rotation, carrying only enough for the teams I am visiting. We have several work teams engaged across the region."

"So there would be a lot of cash in the safe on a regular basis?"

"Yes."

"I am grateful for your assistance, Mr Patterson. I appreciate that this is a difficult matter, given the family connection. One last question. Could Lennox MacDonald have accessed the safe on the day of the directors' meeting? Last Thursday."

"I don't want to get Lennox into trouble, Inspector,"

"But?"

"He did arrive a little late to the meeting. My wife went to retrieve a document from her desk and found Lennox in here. She did not see him access the safe, so we could not accuse him."

"And the key to the explosives store is in that safe?"

"It is. But you must understand, I gave no thought to that at the time. He said he only looked in to see if any of us were here." A sudden wave of horror swept across his face, suggesting he had only just realised the implications of the questions. "You cannot think Lennox had anything to do with the bombing. He would never condone such an atrocity. He may be lazy and foolish, but he is not violent."

"We must pursue all avenues, Mr Patterson. I ask you not to tell anyone at all about our discussion here today."

"Of course," he murmured, but his wrinkled brow suggested his thoughts were elsewhere. He would have made a lousy poker player.

"What is it, Mr Patterson? Better to tell us all."

"I was only thinking that Lennox's brother-in-law is a bad influence on him. If there's trouble afoot, you ought to be looking at Harry Bertram and his associates, not Lennox."

"We will bear that in mind. Thank you for your time."

On the way back to the cable car terminus at Mornington, Wallace confirmed that the storeman's second count still showed a shortfall of explosives. "You were right, Pyke. Lennox MacDonald may be our man, after all, with or without his troublesome brother-in-law, Harry Bertram. Not that we've got much in the way of proof. We'll have to crack his alibi or prove he paid someone to plant the bomb. Did you find anything?"

"I found two keys to the safe in under two minutes. If Lennox had time alone in that office, he could easily have accessed the key to the explosives store. The typewriter was interesting too."

"How so?"

"They have recently bought a new machine for Mrs Creswell. Patterson thinks Lennox took the old typewriter to the brewery. All the older letters filed in the office had a blurred 'e' and a misaligned 't'."

"You've lost me, Pyke."

"Old machines develop unique faults over time. The typewritten note and address on the parcel sent to Harriet Morison had the same blurred 'e' and angled 't'. If Lennox MacDonald has the old typewriter, he must either be the bomber or he is an accessory."

Wallace slapped him on the back. "By God, Pyke, I'll have you on my team even if I have to challenge my penny-pinching Chief Inspector to a duel to achieve it."

"Truly, sir? That would be absolutely marvellous."

Charlie floated up the road on champagne bubbles of joy. Finally, the strands of his life were coming together. He knew exactly what the contented Mr Patterson meant when he said he was the most fortunate of men, happy in work, love and home. No man could ask for more.

But one barrier still blocked his dreams. "Sir, there is something you ought to know. I found out on Wednesday that an offender I arrested a few months ago in Wellington is trying to have me charged with assault. I am to face a disciplinary hearing to establish the facts."

Wallace walked on, unperturbed. "Yes, I know. Alistair Stewart is keeping me fully informed. He is certain you will be cleared of the accusation. Competent policemen face this type of claim from time to time. We take it seriously, of course. There's always the odd rotten apple in any barrel. I cannot ask the Chief Inspector to take you on until you are cleared, of course. He is a stickler for only accepting men with a clean record."

"I understand. Thank you, sir." Wallace went up another notch in his estimation.

"Best not say anything to your young lady until the deal is done. The Chief may still refuse me the extra man. We're supposed to be cutting numbers, not adding to them. This damnable recession will have us on our knees if it doesn't end soon. Perhaps I could argue that we will have two for the price of one, as you and Miss Penrose seem to operate as an impressive team."

Charlie grinned at his potential future boss. "As long as you don't expect me to control her, sir."

Maids and Motives

Grace awoke on Friday morning at the appallingly late hour of ten o'clock, with a mouth full of fur and a thumping headache. A jug of water stood at the ready on her nightstand. Mrs Brown always managed to pre-empt her needs. Grace pushed herself upright and glugged down the water, straight from the jug, hoping that their housekeeper's sixth and seventh senses didn't detect this outrage.

Sure enough, light knuckles rapped on her door. Grace put the jug down, wiped the drips from her chin, and smoothed her hair as best she could. At least all her limbs were in working order, albeit rather leaden. "Come in."

"Thought you might want a nice cup of tea, Miss Penrose, and something soft for your throat."

Mrs Brown placed a bed-tray over her lap, laid with the best china and silverware. The aroma of special-occasion tea wafted from a teapot commemorating the Queen's marriage to Prince Albert, which rarely saw the outside of the china cabinet. Bottled raspberries created a lush swirl of colour in whipped cream, bringing Grace close to tears.

Mrs Brown passed her a lace-edged handkerchief. "Now, now, my dear girl, you rest in bed. The shock of such terrible events takes time to work its way out of the body. Mrs Macmillan says you must not get up today, no matter how well you think you feel. She says you will not be well again by Monday if you rush about, as young ladies are wont to do these days."

"Monday?"

"Start of term, Miss Penrose. I'm sure the medical school will grant you a few days off if need be."

Medical school was the last thing on her mind, but life went on. She could not afford to miss a single lecture. "No need. I will be fine. Thank you, Mrs Brown. Tea and raspberries are exactly what I feel like."

Mrs Brown finished straightening the bedclothes. "Miss Sugden called by earlier and said she would be back. Call me if you need anything."

"Might I talk to Sadie for a moment?"

"By all means, Miss Penrose. She'll be pleased to have a break from cleaning out the hearths."

Grace was well on the way to recovery, thanks to hot tea and cool raspberries, by the time Sadie came up.

"Begging your pardon for being tardy, Miss Penrose. I dropped the scuttle and made ever such a mess. What was it you wanted to see me about?"

"I'm not sure how to ask this, Sadie. I wouldn't want you to think I am being indiscreet, but it is important that I find out about Mrs Patterson's brother, Mr Lennox MacDonald. You are good friends with the Patterson's maid, are you not?"

"I am, Miss. Meg and me have the same days off and often spend time together."

"Have you heard her talk about Mr MacDonald?"

"Oh yes, Miss. Meg gets a wee bit weary of the way Mr and Mrs Patterson prattle on about Mrs Patterson's brother, and her father too. The elder Mr MacDonald keeps a tight hand on the purse-strings. Fair drives Mrs Patterson potty at times, though I do believe she adores her father. Mr Lennox now, he couldn't be more different. Spends money like water, so they say."

"Do you know what sort of things he spends money on?"

"Oh, the usual things for that type of gentlemen, I expect. I couldn't say, I'm sure, although I recall Meg accompanied Mrs Patterson to a house party one time. She was all aflutter when she told me about it. French wine and fancy food 'til the tables were fair groaning under the weight. And the gowns! Meg must have described every inch of silk and lace, not to mention the jewels and hats and gloves, and I don't know what else. And the men, playing cards with piles of money and only the best cigars and brandy. Meg talked of nothing else for weeks."

"And what does Meg think of Mr Lennox MacDonald as a person?"

"Well, Meg does blush rather when she talks of him. A charmer he is, and handsome, but I told her to wipe the stars out of her eyes. A man like him means only one thing to a pretty maid like Meg – trouble. Besides, he's married, not that you'd know it from how he is here, there and everywhere without his wife."

"I can see why Mr and Mrs Patterson find his behaviour unacceptable. Quite the opposite of their views of the sanctity of the home and temperance in all things."

"Yes, Miss. Meg is loyal to them, for they are respectable folk, even if Mrs Patterson can be a little scary. I expect they would not throw their money around on fripperies, even if they had it to spare. It does seem unfair that Mr Patterson must work so hard, while Mr Lennox never lifts a finger if he can help it. There now, perhaps I have said too much. I wouldn't want you to think I talk of Mrs Macmillan's household the way Meg spouts on about hers."

"Not in the least, Sadie. Mrs Macmillan is full of praise for you and your mother. I do appreciate your candour, but I would urge you not to tell anyone that I was asking about Lennox MacDonald, including Meg."

Grace had little opportunity to dwell on the differences between the MacDonald brother and sister, because Molly arrived as soon as Sadie left.

"Grace, I did not think I would find you sitting up in bed at home like a grand duchess. The nurse at the hospital said you were not to leave until today."

"I hate being a patient in hospital. Why would I wish to stay a minute longer than necessary when I can come home to the medical care of my great-aunt and the superior culinary skills of Mrs Brown?"

"A fair point. I can see from the dab of raspberry cream on your upper lip that you are being well treated at home."

Grace rescued it promptly. "Molly, have you heard the news about Violet Creswell?"

Molly heaved a sigh. "I heard last night. I've just visited Mrs Creswell's mother-in-law."

"The poor woman. How is she coping?"

"She is quite elderly and frail. Her daughter-in-law's death has taken her to the edge of despair. I am sure it has recalled the ordeal of losing her son. She speaks of nothing else but how they have both been taken by the same demon. I don't wonder at her shock. Fortunately, one of her daughters is on her way to Dunedin to look after her."

"Do you know anything of her son's death – the younger Mrs Creswell's husband?" Grace asked.

"Violet's husband died in a tunnel collapse. When I first met her a few weeks ago, Violet was angry that she had been misled as to the cause. She didn't know who to turn to, so she asked at the Tailoresses' Union, being the only union run by women, for women. I happened to be the duty volunteer when she came to us, so I advised her to talk to the Miners' Union about her rights. In fact, I wrote a letter on her behalf."

"And what was their reply?"

"They used their contacts to look into the circumstances. It was their view that Violet was owed compensation. Apparently, there was sworn evidence from two workers that the son of the business owner was responsible for letting the explosives off, not her own husband, as she had been led to believe. The son was never charged. Violet Creswell was told none of this at the time."

"Violet must have been furious to have been deceived." Grace could see that Molly was angry too, on her friend's behalf.

"She was, especially as she had been pathetically grateful to receive a small pension despite her husband being at fault, when she ought to have received proper compensation because someone else had been negligent. Violet was so outraged that she gave her notice and asked if she might leave straight away."

"Wasn't it rather a rash move to leave her position? It must have been a dreadful struggle to make ends meet as it was, with her mother-in-law to provide for as well."

"I'm sure it was. Indeed, I believe she regretted leaving at first, as it caused a great deal of ill will with her employers, with whom she had been on good terms. She wanted to pursue compensation from the man at fault, but that isn't how it is done. To rub salt in the wound, Mrs Creswell had reason to believe the negligent son was taking money from the business, but nobody was willing to act against him, as he was the only son and heir. I tried to get her to focus on the compensation issue, as she would get nowhere by accusing the son of theft."

"And did she progress the compensation bid?" Grace asked.

"I think she would have, had she not been killed, although I did wonder if she had reached a private settlement as she had recently talked of being about to come into some money."

Grace slid out of bed, her determination quelling any residual wobbling of her legs. "Molly, have you got time to write out a statement outlining what you have told me. This is exactly the sort of motive the police need to know about immediately."

Molly knew Grace well enough not to question her or press her to stay in bed. She sat herself at the writing table by the window and dipped the pen in ink without further ado, while Grace donned the dark dress and hat hanging on the front of her armoire. She added a jet brooch and looked in the mirror. The dark colour gave an unflattering emphasis to her pallor, but matched her mood. Add a pair of wings and she might sally forth as the goddess of divine vengeance.

Goddess or not, her great-aunt refused to let her leave the house without a full medical examination. "I'll bet Nemesis never waited around for Zeus to give her the once-over," Grace mumbled, but Anne was undeterred.

An hour later, Johnny helped Grace from the buggy at the police station and said he had been instructed to wait for her. She found the place nearly deserted of policemen, although bursting at the seams with angry wives hauling shamefaced men out of overnight custody. Grace slipped past the overwhelmed desk officer and made her own way to Charlie's basement hideaway.

She lay her head on his desk while she waited. The next thing she knew, a gentle hand was shaking her shoulder.

"Grace? What are you doing out of bed?"

Good question. Her groggy state suggested she had been asleep for a considerable period. Grace straightened her hair and her thoughts. "I needed to see you, Charlie, about Violet Creswell and Lennox MacDonald."

"We're about to have a meeting upstairs. I only came down for my notebook."

The meeting was in the common area, DI Wallace's office being too small for the number of policemen gathered.

"Miss Penrose has information to report, sir." Charlie found a chair for her and the other men cleared a space.

Grace didn't waste time with pleasantries. "Mrs Violet Creswell, the bombing victim, had only recently become aware that her husband's death was caused by the son of the owner of MacDonald Roading."

"Lennox MacDonald," Charlie supplied.

"She was pursuing compensation for Lennox MacDonald's negligence, with the assistance of the Tailoresses' Union and the Miners' Union. She was expecting to receive some money imminently, suggesting the possibility of a private settlement. Mrs Creswell also believed that Lennox MacDonald was taking money from the company. According to Mrs Patterson's maid, Lennox lives an extravagant lifestyle, all play and no work."

"Thank you, Miss Penrose," Wallace replied. "Your information confirms our inquiries and provides the motive we were seeking for the specific targeting of Mrs Creswell. For those of you

208

who have not heard the latest, Mrs Creswell received a note to tell her to be in the kitchen at the time the bomb exploded. The bomb was probably designed to kill, as well as to cause damage to property."

Wallace waited for pencils to stop scribbling. "MacDonald Roading is missing explosives and Lennox MacDonald had the opportunity to take them. We may be able to pin the first bomb on him too, especially if we can find the old typewriter that was used to type the note and address. What we do not have is evidence that he was the one who planted the Choral Hall bomb, although he matches the description."

A constable at the back of the room cleared his throat. "Lennox MacDonald has been out of town since Wednesday. I verified his alibi with his wife, coachman, household staff and at the railway station. Then I telegraphed to the local constable who did the same with the acquaintance with whom he was staying. I have never seen a tighter alibi, sir. It was as if he was determined to have as many witnesses as possible to the fact he was out of town on the day of the bombing. With such a good alibi, I wanted to check with you before we risked an arrest."

"Confound it. He must have found a way to get back to town on Thursday morning or else he paid someone else to plant the explosive device. Lennox is the man with the strongest motive. Two motives, in fact, as he had reason to stop the Women's Franchise League, as well as to get rid of Mrs Creswell. Where is Lennox MacDonald now?"

"His intention was to stay out of town for a week, but his host says he received two telegrams early this afternoon and took the train back to Dunedin. The host said one of the messages was from MacDonald's father and the other from a man called Burnham or something similar. Could be Mr Bertram."

"Good work, Fletcher. Has anyone else got anything to report?"

There was a great deal to report, but all of it was unhelpful. All dynamite was accounted for, as far as they could ascertain, although a disturbing quantity was stockpiled around the region. Various

209

gamblers and their long-suffering wives had all agreed that Gilroy's gaming party broke up around midnight. Nobody had seen anything suspicious around Choral Hall. The men who had been at the protest had crumpled without the support of mob fervour, but none admitted to anything beyond disrupting the arrival of the franchise supporters.

The meeting was winding to a close when the Chief Inspector stalked in, his blood pressure so close to boiling point that Grace's hand automatically reached for her medical bag, even though she hadn't brought it with her. The only sound was the shuffling of men's boots as they retreated from his warpath.

"Detective Constable Pyke. Detective Inspector Wallace. Interview room, now." The Chief Inspector clapped a hand on Kelly's shoulder. "DC Kelly, I want you to escort Pyke and make sure he comes quietly. Cuff him if you have to. DS Elliot, you'd better come too."

Charlie froze in place beside her, all colour drained from his face. As Kelly moved to Charlie's side, Grace whispered, "Kelly, what's happening?"

"No idea, but it can't be good."

"I'll get Drummond," Grace whispered to Charlie, as he was led away.

Interrogation

Charlie was marched out of the room under the stunned gaze of his colleagues. A buzz of voices broke out as soon as he left the room. What would they be saying? Words of support? Or words that started a man on the slippery slope to perdition … *I always wondered about that one. Never trust an undercover man, too many temptations. The slant of his eyes is so sinister.* He had heard it before, when other policeman had been accused. Trust, once lost, was hard to regain.

A solitary figure stood as they entered the interview room.

The Chief Inspector took the lead. "This is Sergeant Young, South Dunedin Police. Young, this is DI Wallace and DC Pyke. DS Elliot will take notes. DC Kelly standing guard."

Charlie knew better than to ask what misunderstanding had led him here. He waited in silence for the show to begin. Wallace took the seat beside him, which he took as a positive sign. The detective sergeant was at the end of the table, the other two opposite.

"Do you read the newspaper, Pyke?" the Chief Inspector began.

"Yes, sir, when I have time."

"Do you read the *Otago Workman*?"

"Only since I was put undercover in South Dunedin, sir."

"You are a socialist, Pyke? An anarchist?"

"No, sir. I support the right of the all men and women to make a decent living, but hold no radical views."

"Yet you cut this article out of the *Otago Workman*." The Chief Inspector pushed across a cutting of the letter penned by Outraged Gent. "Would you not call this radical? An incitement to violence?"

211

"Yes, sir, I would agree. I cut it out to show DI Wallace, to illustrate my concern for how violent the situation was becoming. But this is not my cutting."

"I can verify that," Wallace cut in. "Pyke left his cutting with me."

"But you do have a history of violence, DC Pyke, especially against men of wealth and even women."

"No, sir, that is untrue."

"You have been named as the man who abducted Mrs Vance from the Engineers' Arms in Caversham." The Chief Inspector held up his hand as Wallace opened his mouth. "I know what you are about to say. We have a report that the woman was beaten by her husband. But her husband denies it and I am now told that the woman who wrote the report is a close confidant of Pyke's. But that is by the way. The more important issue is that Pyke is under investigation for assault in Wellington. The victim was a young gentleman with high connections, was he not? I'm told you joined a group of Chinese immigrants in attacking him, Pyke."

"It was quite the opposite, sir. The young gentlemen and his friends attacked the Chinese shopkeepers, not the other way around. It was my duty to arrest him. The allegation he has raised against me is about to be dismissed."

"Do you have a particular reason to side with the Chinese, Pyke? A reason that makes you especially sensitive to any suggestion as to the natural superiority of the European race?"

Charlie recognised the tactic. Wind the suspect up until he was so angry, he blurted out something he would later regret. But he wasn't about to lie about his ancestry, either.

Wallace saved him from answering. "Chief Inspector, I'm not sure this line of questioning is helpful, as Pyke has been investigating threats against the Women's Franchise League, not Chinese immigrants."

"Oh? I was led to believe Pyke was here to investigate illegal gambling."

Wallace's lips compressed into a thin line. "Yes, sir, that is correct. However, Pyke overheard a plan against the Women's Franchise League, which has proven to be accurate. The bombing–"

"As I understand it, Pyke raised the issue of a few minor protests by owners of liquor establishments, whose livelihood was threatened by the temperance movement. But did he warn you of a bombing, Detective Inspector Wallace?"

"Not specifically a bombing, but–"

"And have any of the men arrested admitted to the bombing? Did they not all have alibis?"

Wallace clenched his hands under the table. "It only occurred yesterday, sir. We are working on it. There is compelling evidence against one of them."

The Chief Inspector paused for a moment, his gaze drifting between the two men opposite him. "It has been brought to my attention by DS Elliot that the only men known to have had the opportunity to plant the bomb at Choral Hall are DC Pyke and the caretaker."

"Pyke was guarding the hall, not bombing it," Wallace answered.

"Yet a bomb was planted under his nose?"

"The caretaker has not yet been cleared, and another man was seen in the hall. DC Pyke has worked tirelessly to help the investigation, providing significant new leads, sir."

"Ah, yes, leads which demonstrate his own familiarity with explosives. I recall that the man who gave the bomb to the Mitchem's bakery boy to deliver was described as a tall, muscular man." The Chief Inspector turned back to Charlie. "And where are you residing, DC Pyke?"

"With a gentleman of my acquaintance in High Street, sir." Charlie was at a loss to see where this was leading, but he had a nasty feeling he was about to find out.

"Are you not residing at Mrs Doyle's boarding house on Prince Albert Road, South Dunedin?" the Chief Inspector continued.

"I was there until last Saturday night, sir, but not since."

"Room number?"

"Seven."

"According to Sergeant Young, Mrs Doyle says you have paid for your room until the end of next week. Your bag is still in the room, is it not?"

"No, sir. My bag is not there. I had already paid for the room until the end of this week, by which I mean today, and did not have time to seek a refund when I left on Saturday night."

"And yet, when Sergeant Young received an anonymous tip-off at the South Dunedin Station, he visited the room and found your bag."

"Not my bag, I assure you."

"Sergeant Young, perhaps you would care to tell us what you found in room seven of Mrs Doyle's boarding house on Prince Albert Road."

"Yes, sir." Young flipped his notebook open. "One bag with an NZR tag labelled 'Charlie Potts'. In said bag, wrapped in copies of the *Otago Workman*, two blasting caps, fuses, and a packet of black powder. Pinned to the wall, clippings of articles from various newspapers about anarchist bombing plots in Europe and England. In the waste bin, a wrapper from Mitchem's Bakery, a sketch of the interior layout of Choral Hall, and two sheets of paper upon which the occupant of the room had practiced the handwriting from an order form, taken from the Engineers' Arms. On proceeding to that establishment, the barman, Mr Vance, recognised the writing as an imitation of his own."

Charlie wanted to scream that it was all a set-up. He wanted to run from the room and not stop. He wanted to find that scumbag Vance and wrap his neck in a noose of rose stems. He wanted many, many things, but he sat there, bolt upright, trying not to let them see his panic.

The Chief Inspector cleared his throat in the officious manner used by all policemen about to arrest a suspect. "Detective Constable Charles Pyke, also known as Charlie Potts, did you enter the premises of Choral Hall on the morning of Thursday 28 April 1892 and plant an explosive device that took the life of Mrs Violet Creswell?"

"No, sir. I categorically deny all allegations made against me. The evidence has been planted in a malicious attempt to deflect attention from the real culprits."

Through the roaring in his ears, he heard a drone of incomprehensible words. "Charles Thomas Lee Pyke, I am detaining you–".

Prisoner

On Saturday morning, Grace awoke feeling even worse than when she had been knocked out by the bomb blast. Bile rose in her throat at the thought of Charlie, accused of murder and mayhem, waking up on a hard bench in a police cell. Not that she believed his guilt for a second, but she knew what a crushing blow it would be to his reputation and career. The stench of corruption lingers long after the corpse is buried.

Mr Drummond had arrived at the police station not long after Charlie had been detained, while Grace waited at home, wearing a groove in the floorboards with her pacing. The attorney returned not much more than an hour later with the news that the Chief Inspector had had no option but to place DC Pyke under arrest, given the evidence against him. Bertram and Vance had clearly done a comprehensive job of implicating Charlie.

But Drummond had not been without hope. As he had said last night, "there is always a loose thread, which, when pulled hard enough, unravels even the most tightly wound skein of lies."

Anne was waiting at the kitchen table, with a copy of the *Otago Daily Times* spread out before her. On seeing Grace's expression, she said, "It could be worse. At least nobody will recognise him."

Grace turned the newspaper around. The article was titled: "The Face of a Killer". The accompanying sketch would have been laughable, if she had been in a laughing mood. Charlie Potts was pictured as more hair than man. "I'd certainly believe that vagabond capable of mischief. The *ODT* got this into print surprisingly quickly."

"Read the article, Grace. They were tipped off."

"The *Otago Daily Times* received information from a reliable source to indicate that a former hotel worker from Caversham has

216

been arrested for the Choral Hall bombing, in which Mrs Violet Creswell tragically perished. The man, identified as Charlie Potts, is also suspected of the attempted bombing at the Dunedin Tailoresses' Union and the abduction of Mrs Ellen Vance. Chief Inspector Alford would only confirm that an arrest had been made of an unnamed person. He praised the hard work of the Dunedin Police Force, whose entire attention has been focussed upon the bombing. He would not confirm the nature of the arrested man's motive, nor whether the man had links to the anarchists currently terrorising Europe."

Anne pushed her breakfast away, uneaten. "They must know he is an undercover policeman. I suspect the *ODT* decided not to publish his real name until they can verify it. Read on, Grace. The next paragraph will cheer you up a little."

"Mrs Marion Hatton, President of the Women's Franchise League, confirmed that the bomb would have destroyed thousands of signatures in favour of extending the franchise to women, had not the boxes been moved shortly before the explosion. Readers of this newspaper will already know that Mrs Hatton's courageous women braved the smoking ruins of Choral Hall to attend the inaugural meeting of the League. Mr Fish and his loutish followers have been put on notice; nothing will deter these ladies from achieving the vote. Further revelations are expected imminently."

Grace put the newspaper down. "We haven't much time to prove that Charlie is innocent. He will be crucified by the public when it becomes known that a policeman has been arrested for attacking Lady Stout and the Women's Franchise League, as well as killing a supporter."

"Isn't proving his innocence the police's job, Grace? DI Wallace and DC Kelly are good men. They won't let Charlie down. You ought to be resting, not slaying dragons."

"Even if the dragons are threatening my future happiness?"

"Grace, dearest, you know I am the last person in the world to step back from a cause worth fighting for. But think how Charlie would feel if you destroy your own reputation defending his."

"Would that have stopped you if Uncle Gordon had been wrongly imprisoned?"

"Oh, for heaven's sake, you know I am only saying it out of obligation as your nominal guardian. At least have a decent breakfast before you charge off like Saint George."

"Are you quite sure that Saint George stopped to fill his stomach before slaying his dragon, Auntie?"

"Don't be difficult, child, just do as I say for once."

Grace reached for the toast rack. Her great-aunt had succeeded at one impossible task this morning – putting a smile on her face. "Auntie, I hope you know how much I adore you. I may act like a petulant child at times, but I do value your advice and support."

"Even if you ignore it." Anne passed her the butter, letting her arthritic fingers linger on Grace's hand. "You remind me so much of your grandmother, my dear. Who else would put up with my dragonesque ways?"

"I rather think Mr Kenneth Drummond would be willing to try." Grace didn't bother to hide her smirk as she reached for the strawberry preserves. "Auntie Anne, are you blushing?"

"Nonsense, girl, it's merely a little hot in here. So, tell me, what is your plan?"

"Visit the police station. Interrogate DC Kelly. Take in the sea air at St Kilda beach, where a certain landlady has some explaining to do. After that, I rather thought I might go shopping for expensive tea."

"Not alone, I trust?"

"I am hoping Wallace will allow me to accompany Kelly. He will surely wish to talk to the landlady, since the evidence against Charlie hinges on the mystery bag that appeared in his room after he left."

Less than an hour later, Grace was waiting at the front desk of the police station for DC Kelly.

"Miss Penrose. You shouldn't be here."

"DC Kelly, good morning. I came to deliver some fresh clothes to the prisoner. I hoped I might have a word with you too."

Kelly glanced around, but no one with stripes on his shoulder was watching. "Follow me. We'll have to be quick."

She hurried after him towards the stairs. "Is he in the police cells?" She had a nightmarish vision of Charlie sharing a cell with the remnants of the mob and the arrested suspects, Sweeney and Gilroy.

"Mr Drummond demanded Charlie be held separately for his safety. Rightly so. We would never put a policeman in with criminals."

"Thank goodness. What happens now?"

"The Chief has assigned DS Elliot to assist at the formal interview, as he is considered independent, unlike Wallace and I. The interview will start in about half an hour."

"Is this Elliot a good man?"

"To own the truth, I suspect he is worried Charlie is angling for his position, but I'm sure he wouldn't let that influence him, not with Charlie's life on the line." Kelly glanced back at her with a stricken expression. "My apologies, Miss Penrose, I didn't mean—"

"He has been arrested for murder, Declan. I know precisely what that means, and I intend to prove him innocent. Can I count on your help?"

"Yes, of course. I know he has been set up. I'll prove it if I have to strangle it out of that scoundrel Vance and his slimy boss."

Kelly stopped outside the room Charlie had been using as an office. "Unfortunately, we are short of space. This was all we had. I'm afraid I will have to search your bag, Miss Penrose."

As Kelly searched, she heard scuffling in the room. The prisoner was tidying his residence in order to receive visitors. Having seen the miniscule room before, she wondered how he had made enough space to sleep.

The warder shuffled along the corridor. "Ah, DC Kelly. Has this visitor been cleared?"

"Good morning, warder. I am an official welfare visitor." Grace showed him her member's card of the Ladies' Society for the Advancement of Prison Reform.

"I've searched her bag," Kelly added, "and will be present at the visit to ensure they both abide by the rules."

The warder nodded and returned to his cubicle at the end of the row of police cells.

"Prisoner Pyke, step away from the door." Kelly mouthed "protocol" to Grace and jerked his head toward the retreating warder.

"Door clear," Charlie replied. "I don't want Miss Penrose to come in."

Miss Penrose ignored him. She stepped into the airless space and wished for a moment that she hadn't. With no ventilation, the smell of sweat mingled with the odour from the covered bucket in the corner to form a stench as solid as a wall. Charlie was huddled in the other corner, glowering at her like a cornered animal.

Kelly went to close the door, but she stayed his hand. "For pity's sake, Declan, he'll suffocate if he doesn't get some air."

Kelly left the door open. What's more, he retrieved the bucket and disappeared with it along the corridor.

"Grace, I don't want you here."

"It's not about what you want, Charlie, it's about what you need. And right now you need to be a man of dignity facing false accusations you will soon be cleared of." Grace pulled a set of clean clothes out of the bag and laid them on the top of a stack of boxes, before handing him a bar of Pears soap, a washcloth and a flask of water.

He stared at the soap. "Not the foul red soap this time?"

Grace smiled at this first hint of the old Charlie's sense of humour. "I thought the Pears might leave a more distinguished

220

impression on your interrogators than the carbolic. Shall I turn my back, or do I have to scrub your stubborn hide myself?"

"Under the circumstances, I suggest you turn your back."

She emptied the rest of the bag onto another box. "Bacon sandwich, flask of tea, apples. Now, tell me what lies have been told that we can unravel. The sooner we have you out of here, the better."

"Dearest Grace, what have I done to deserve such loyalty? Any sane woman would have run a mile by now."

"You underestimate the female of the species at your peril. Enough prattle. Tell me what you know."

Between Charlie and Declan Kelly, who had returned with the empty bucket, Grace confirmed what Drummond had told her last night, as well as a few extra scraps of information.

"And you haven't been back to Mrs Doyle's lodgings since Saturday night?"

"No. You can turn around now, Grace."

Grace ran her eyes down the smartly dressed young man in front of her, approving of his newly straightened spine and the determined set of his jaw. She stepped up to him and adjusted his tie. "What's Mrs Doyle like, Charlie?"

"She's the usual type of landlady in a poor neighbourhood. A decent woman, but tough, as you'd expect, given all she must have to put up with. The residents are a motley bunch, often coming home the worse for drink, having poured their rent money down their throats. She's staunch Irish Catholic."

"Does Mrs Doyle have any reason to disapprove of you?"

"Not that I know of. She appeared to like me well enough, and she certainly approved of the timely arrival of my rent money each week. That's another oddity. She told the South Dunedin sergeant I was paid to the end of next week, but I only paid until yesterday."

"Declan, has Mrs Doyle's evidence been verified by you or DI Wallace?"

"I'm going out to see her this morning," Kelly replied. "She's the weak link in this whole setup. The only problem is that such women would rather be strung out on a rack than divulge the time of day to a copper."

"I thought as much. What you need is a woman's touch."

Both Charlie and Declan Kelly protested, knowing full well what she was hinting at.

"Would you rather have me wandering around South Dunedin on my own or under the escort of Detective Constable Kelly? Make no mistake, those are the only two choices, Charlie."

"Shouldn't you be resting at home, Grace?" Charlie pleaded.

They stood at either end of the small room, glaring at each other, until Kelly broke the stand-off. "I have to take Charlie upstairs to the interview room now."

Grace turned her back again, so she wouldn't have to see the handcuffs go on. "I will meet you in the waiting area, DC Kelly."

Reluctant Witness

By the time they stepped off the tram in South Dunedin, into the sharp tang of salt air from St Kilda beach, Grace had convinced Declan Kelly to use her first name. Quite apart from the fact that she liked him, she needed him to consider her a friend and ally.

Kelly had devised a cunning plan, which involved convincing the local priest to accompany them to the lodging house. Mrs Doyle might refuse to talk to a policeman, but no devout Catholic would refuse the advice of her priest. Convincing the priest was surprisingly easy, as he was a relative of Declan's – the cousin of Mrs Kelly's sister's husband, or some such connection.

"Father Brady, I was wondering if we might ask a favour of you."

"Well now, Declan, I'm in the middle of writing my sermon, but I know you wouldn't ask if it wasn't important."

"It is Father," Grace explained, trying to look her most winsome. "My sweetheart has been arrested for a murder he did not commit and I'll not see him hanged. One of your parishioners may have evidence that would clear him."

"Could you not spare us half an hour to come with us to talk to Mrs Doyle?" Declan pleaded.

Father Brady put his pen down, spilling ink across the blank page in front of him. "How could I say no to saving an innocent man? Perhaps a good deed will inspire some thoughts for tomorrow's sermon."

They found Mrs Doyle arguing with a ruddy-faced man over the amount of rent owed.

The priest laid a hand on the man's arm. "Good morning to you, Mr Donnelly. Sure and you know that Mrs Doyle here is an honest woman trying to make ends meet. She'll not be overcharging you."

The man hung his head and opened his purse. "As you say, Father Brady. I'll be seeing you tomorrow at church."

Mrs Doyle smiled at the priest, exposing a row of rotten teeth between thin lips. "Father Brady, 'tis a fine thing to have you visit. Will you take tea?"

"That would be grand, Mrs Doyle. We'll not be keeping you from your work for long, but the matter is terrible urgent. This young lady's sweetheart is accused of a crime he did not commit. Detective Constable Kelly here needs to have a word with you."

"The police is it?" Mrs Doyle's smile disappeared, while her eyes narrowed, her lips pursed and her arms crossed her chest. She could not have made her refusal to cooperate clearer if she had slammed the door in their faces.

"Now then, Mrs Doyle," DC Kelly crooned, as if he was fresh off the boat from Dublin, "do I have to get me mam to come over to have words?"

Rheumy eyes peered at him over the counter. "You're never Maureen Kelly's lad? I heard you'd become a copper, but never believed it on account of you being such a scrap of a wean. Look at you now, fillin' up me hall. Come through to the sitting room."

"Thank you, Mrs Doyle, and right grateful I would be for a cup of tea and a wee chat." They entered a tiny room with a single gas ring and two ancient chairs. "This is Miss Grace Penrose, the sweetheart of Charlie Potts."

Father Brady and Mrs Doyle reacted to the name with equal and opposite reactions. Father Brady looked horrified, presumably because he had read the morning newspaper and now knew exactly what accusation Grace's sweetheart was facing.

Mrs Doyle's eyes widened in astonishment. "Is she now? I'd not have thought Potts to have such a lady for a sweetheart. Lovely young man and all, he is, but a bit rough round the edges for the likes of you. I was sorry to see him go. Take a seat now, dear, while I get the water on."

"When did you last see my Charlie, Mrs Doyle?" Grace asked.

"Rushed out late last Saturday night with a bag on his shoulder and never seen him since." The landlady measured an exact spoonful of leaves into a battered pot.

"Did you check his room when he didn't come back?" Kelly asked.

"I looked in on the Monday, to see if he were all right. Neat as a pin, his room was, and no sign of him. Not so much as a speck of dirt or a forgotten handkerchief. Wish the rest of them were half so tidy."

"Were you concerned that you hadn't seen him?"

"I'm his landlady, not his mam. My lodgers are free to come and go as they please, as long as their rent is paid up."

"To be absolutely clear, Mrs Doyle," Kelly said, "You saw no bag, no rubbish, no newspapers, nothing at all in the room?"

"Are ye not listening, Declan Kelly? There was not so much as stray hair in his room."

"His rent would have been due yesterday, wouldn't it?" Grace took the offered tea, noting that she had been given the best cup. Mrs Doyle might not have fancy china and expensive tea, but she had her pride.

"Every Friday night. I insist on it. Let it be late once and you'll never see the colour of their money, sure as you like. But the man who brought his bag over on Thursday night, he paid for another week."

"Did you tell the police about the man with the bag, Mrs Doyle?" Grace said, willing herself to remain calm as she sipped weak, bitter tea.

"I told them nothing, because they didn't ask nothing. The coppers barged in here on Friday morning, demanded a key to Mr Potts' room. Stormed up the stairs, never mind their muddy boots on me clean floors. Came back down looking like the cat that got the cream. Asked if I knew where Potts was. Well now, I'm not hiding him under me skirts, I says. Then he tells me they was keeping the key, and I was not to enter the room, as if it were not me

225

own property! I didn't come halfway around the world to be lorded over by some English copper with his head up his arse. I run a respectable lodging house."

Father Brady reached forward to pat her hand. "Now then, Mrs Doyle, calm yerself. Everyone knows you run a fine establishment here. I expect it is all a misunderstanding, which you can help us clear up."

"Well now, Father, I'm sure I'll do what I can to help. Potts was a nice young man. I wouldn't have said anything against him to the copper, even if he'd asked, because I could see he must be innocent – plain as the nose on me face."

"You're a good judge of character, Mrs Doyle," Grace said. "My Charlie is a fine man. Perhaps you can describe the man who brought the bag and paid you for the extra week."

"I can tell you exactly who he is, Miss Penrose. Vance, what's the barman from a hotel up Caversham way. What's it called now? The Engineers' Arms. Mr Potts works there, you know, and the barman was kind enough to drop off a bag what Mr Potts must have left behind at work by mistake. You see, they must think well of him to go to such trouble and pay his rent too."

"You must have been surprised when the police turned up the next day," Declan said.

"Don't nothing surprise me at my age. Who knows why the coppers take it into their heads to harass us honest folks."

Grace caught Declan's eye. "Thank you for your help and hospitality, Mrs Doyle. If I save my sweetheart, it will be thanks to you."

"Delighted, I'm sure. I'll be seeing you tomorrow, Father Brady. You'll have a rousing sermon for us, I trust."

Father Brady's eyes twinkled. "Yes, Mrs Doyle, I believe I will."

Grace ushered the two men out before her, so she could slip a pound into Mrs Doyle's hand. "My Charlie would want you to have

226

this. No need to mention it to the police." She was out the door before Mrs Doyle's rotten teeth could clamp her gaping mouth shut.

Grace and Declan walked with Father Brady back to his church.

"Thank you, Father Brady," Declan said. "I doubt Mrs Doyle would have been so free with her thoughts without you there."

Grace looked up at the sagging roof. "It's a fine church, Father, but perhaps you could do with a little help towards the maintenance?"

"As it happens, Miss Penrose, there is a collection box by the door in aid of the roof, if you feel so inclined. I do hope you save your young man."

"So do I, Father, so do I. We couldn't have done it without you." She went off in search of the collection box, while Declan exchanged family news.

"That went better than I dared hope," Grace said, when they were alone again. "What next, Declan?"

"Back to the station, so I can inform Wallace of developments. Mrs Doyle's evidence will surely be enough to get Charlie released from custody. The Chief is desperate to make an arrest, but he is a fair man. Vance is in a tight spot, with charges of rioting and criminal damage pending, not to mention a possible charge of assault and the threat of being implicated in murder. He'll be talking soon enough, I warrant, even if only to lay the blame on Bertram."

"Vance took a big risk that the landlady wouldn't talk."

"Perhaps he intended the money he gave her as a bribe to purchase her silence, while she thought he was helping a friend by paying his rent."

"Who do you think planted the bomb, Declan?"

"Wallace is convinced Lennox MacDonald stole the explosives and made the bomb, but paid someone else to plant it. One of Gilroy's men or Vance, maybe – we don't know. If you ask me, I'd say Bertram is the big, fat spider in the middle of this web, pulling on the strands of silk to get everyone else to do his bidding, without being implicated himself."

"Let me know if I can help, Declan. I know Charlie feels he has found a valued friend in you."

"The feeling is mutual. We'll clear his name, never you fear, Grace." He paused. "You've done more than enough. He made me promise to keep you out of trouble."

"Can I ask one more favour? May I be there when Charlie is released?"

Repercussions

Charlie was back in his cell, stretching his limbs after a long morning of denying the accusations levelled at him. How many ways could a man say no before he lost his temper? He'd kept his anger in check, but only at the expense of appearing sullen. It was an eye-opening experience to be on the other side of the interview table. He knew the tactics – the wearing down, the repeating of the same question in different ways, the forceful attacks followed by wheedling persuasion.

For the first time, he understood such tactics wore away an innocent man more surely than a guilty man, because an innocent man had far more to lose – the ruin of his reputation if he was acquitted, undeserved punishment if he was convicted. For an innocent man accused of murder, the cost of a false conviction was the loss of his life by the barbaric practice of hanging.

Being arrested, even wrongfully, would run a sabre through his hopes of advancement, even if he kept his job. To his surprise, he was beginning to wonder if policing had ever been the right career choice for him.

Charlie took off his jacket, tie and waistcoat, laying them neatly over the back of the chair. Grace had been right. If he had had to face the inquisition tired, rumpled, hungry and smelling like the hind end of a ferret, he would have struggled to retain a dignified state of outraged denial of the lies levelled against him. He had always considered himself a fair man, but how many times had he too judged a man by the cut of his clothes? He had seen it in the Chief Inspector's rapid reassessment of his status, as soon as he had walked in with a straight back and a freshly starched collar, alongside a barrister as renowned as Kenneth Drummond.

Mr Drummond had been magnificent, pointing out the weaknesses of their case and citing DC Pyke's exemplary record. Charlie had hardly recognised himself in the flow of praise, which Drummond must have had to hand after helping DI Stewart with the Wellington case. Drummond, who had retired long ago, had hooked his thumbs under his lapels in true oratorical style, relishing the opportunity to ply his trade again.

Charlie's recollections of the Chief Inspector apologising for gaps in the evidence were cut short by the arrival of the warder, calling for him to step back. The door swung open. The warder put a plate of bread and cheese on the floor, along with a mug of water. "Chef's day off." He sniggered and closed the door.

Charlie poked at the stale bread and hardened rind of cheese. Grace's bacon sandwich was long gone, but he wasn't hungry.

He had ripped the bread into three pieces and was practicing his juggling, when he heard Vance's voice in the corridor. Despite his complaints, the door of the cell next door opened and shut again. What wouldn't he give to be at Vance's interrogation. On second thoughts, he might be facing a second count of murder if he got within an arm's length of the scoundrel.

How did men endure years of captivity, Charlie wondered, as the time dragged on? He was regretting the wasted bread when he remembered the apples Grace had brought in that morning. He'd no sooner bit into one when the door opened again, with no one demanding that he step away.

Grace slipped into the room, holding her finger to her lips to warn him not to react. The person who let her in didn't lock the door behind her. What was this – a secret jail break? As they stood in silence, the adjacent cell was opened and Vance was taken away. As soon as the corridor was empty again, Grace stepped forward and wrapped her arms around him. His own arms wasted no time in enveloping her, crushing her in his embrace, not knowing when he might next have the chance, if ever.

They stood in a silent embrace as the minutes passed until Grace lifted her head from his chest. "Aren't you going to ask me what's happening?"

"Do I want to know?"

"Definitely. Declan Kelly is upstairs informing Wallace that your rogue barman, Mr Vance, delivered a bag to your room the evening before the police raided the lodging house. Vance also paid the extra week of rent. Your landlady seems to have quite a soft spot for Mr Potts."

"Mrs Doyle can talk the hind leg off a donkey, but I admit I am astonished she spoke to the police. How did you manage to get her to talk?"

"Declan turned on the Irish charm, threatened her with his mother, and presented me as the devastated sweetheart of Charlie Potts."

"Devastated sweetheart?" Charlie pulled her closer. "I would have loved to see that performance. I cannot believe the two of you convinced her that a lady such as yourself was the sweetheart of the down-at-heel Charlie Potts."

"She did seem a mite surprised. We took the precaution of bringing the local priest to remind Mrs Doyle of the value of a clear conscience. The priest is a fine fellow, who is a distant Kelly relation."

"Of course he is. What would I do without you two?"

Grace was saved from answering by a discreet knock on the door. Charlie stepped away from her to the far wall.

Declan opened the door and gestured them to follow him. "Vance broke in five minutes flat. Most disappointing. I thought he'd be more of a challenge."

They met Vance in the corridor, being taken back to his cell. His scowl bloomed into fury when he saw Charlie. "You! You sneaky, rotten plague rat. I ought to have knocked your two-faced block off the moment I saw you."

231

Vance spat at his face, but Charlie dodged the venom with ease. "Your fists may have kept your wife under control, Vance, but you will find them a poor weapon against the hardened inmates of Dunedin gaol."

The Chief Inspector was the next to cross his path. "DC Pyke. Darned glad to clear up this little misunderstanding so quickly. Knew you were being set up, of course, but we had to go by the book and show no favour, as I am sure you will appreciate."

"Of course, sir. Thank you, sir."

"You're free to return to Wellington, Pyke. Your work here is done, and I know you have other matters to attend to. DI Wallace wants to have a quick word with you before you depart."

The Chief hurried off along the corridor, having never quite met his eye. Charlie held his tongue. It may have been more of a dismissal than an apology, but at least he was free.

Wallace was standing by the door, waiting for him, with his hand already extended. "Pyke, so sorry about this mess. If–"

Charlie cut him off with a smile. "You had to act on the evidence, sir. The press would have crucified you if it had come out that you hadn't acted against one of your own."

"By Jove, lad, you're taking it better than I would have at your age."

"I only hope it doesn't tarnish my future career in the police force. Having an arrest against my name, even if it is revoked … To be honest, I'm grateful I haven't been dismissed on the spot."

"Ah, well, it seems that I was remiss in doing my duty. With all that was happening, I quite forgot to file the arrest warrant, so there's no worry on that score." Wallace turned away, covering his discomfort by returning to his seat behind his desk. "Sit down, all of you. Yes, you too, Miss Penrose, as you appear to be an honorary constable for this matter. I suppose you want to hear what Vance had to say."

"Please tell me he confessed to planting the bomb," Charlie pleaded.

"No such luck. He has a solid alibi for the period in which the bomb could have been planted. It'll want checking, naturally, but Vance seemed confident. He agreed to talk only after we agreed to drop charges in relation to the threat against Mrs Reynolds and the assault on Mrs Vance."

"Neither of whom wished to press charges anyway," Grace noted.

Wallace smiled. "Vance was not to know that. He admitted his part in the mob attack on Lady Stout's carriage, excusing it as a moment of foolishness after becoming carried away by the excitement of the crowd. He was as quick to lay blame on Conor Sweeney for inciting the mob as he was adamant that Harry Bertram had nothing to do with it."

"Bertram has him on a short leash," Charlie agreed.

"He also admitted to taking the incriminating bag to your room in Mrs Doyle's lodging house, but he swears he did not know it contained explosive materials."

"I suppose he claimed to have had his eyes closed when he pinned up all those newspaper clippings on the wall and left the evidence in the wastebasket," Grace said.

"Vance said he was doing as he was told, being too intimidated to refuse."

"By whom?" Charlie said.

"Lennox MacDonald." Wallace paused. "I can see you are sceptical, Pyke, and I share your view. In all probability, Bertram and Vance got together and decided to save themselves by laying the blame on MacDonald. A good strategy, as they probably got the black powder and fuses from him. However, it might also be the truth. We have nothing at all on Bertram, and still no idea who planted the Choral Hall bomb."

"The caretaker is not budging from his version of events," Kelly added. "Gilroy, Sweeney, Bertram, MacDonald and Vance all have alibis. We're doing all we can to break them. Every source we've ever used has their ears pinned for rumours of someone being paid to plant the bomb."

"We need to track down Lennox MacDonald urgently," Wallace continued. "The fact that he is still missing suggests that he is either guilty or he knows who did this and is lying low."

"His sudden departure from his friend's house yesterday afternoon after receiving a telegram from Bertram is suggestive," Kelly said. "If I was him, I'd be running a mile from Bertram, not rushing back to town to do his brother-in-law's bidding."

"If only we had something on Bertram, we could pull him in for questioning." Wallace rubbed his chin, filling the silence with the rasp of day-old bristles. "Kelly, you and I need to shake Bertram's tree. We'll stop by MacDonald's brewery, his house, and MacDonald Roading on the way back. Somebody must have an idea where Lennox MacDonald is hiding. Pyke, it would be best if you stayed out of this until we resolve the issue of who planted the bomb. And Miss Penrose, if you don't mind me saying so, you look as if you need to be in hospital."

Charlie glanced at Grace. Wallace was right. Her pallor and glazed eyes told him she needed bed rest, at the very least. "I'll take Miss Penrose home straight away, sir. Good luck with your pursuit."

Neighbourly Woes

Grace leaned against Charlie in the tight confines of the hansom cab, grateful he had insisted that she was in no condition to walk the short distance home. The urgency of her mission to ensure his release had long since faded, leaving a wretched pounding in her brain.

To Grace's dismay, Mrs Patterson's carriage was standing at her gate, blocking their escape route to the tranquillity of home. Their own cab stopped further along the street, leaving them to walk past her. Mrs Patterson leaned heavily on her coachman as he helped her down. She made no move to enter her realm.

Her disapproving neighbour was the last person Grace wanted to face right now, but the sight of Mrs Patterson's limp body propped against the gatepost pricked her conscience, recalling her great-aunt's admonition to treat neighbours with respect. Whatever their differences in opinion, she was a woman in obvious distress.

"Charlie, would you please get my medical bag from the table in the hall?"

Up close, she saw that Mrs Patterson was red-eyed and shaking. "Let me help you inside, Mrs Patterson."

The door opened as they struggled up the path. The housekeeper rushed forward to take Mrs Patterson's other arm. Once inside, the housekeeper relieved her mistress of her hat. "Where are your gloves, ma'am?"

Mrs Patterson stared straight ahead with glazed eyes. "I expect I left them at my father's house." She stumbled out of the entrance hall, before the housekeeper could take her cloak.

Grace addressed the housekeeper, who seemed uncertain what to do in the absence of the usual orders. "Why don't you see to Mrs Patterson, while I wait in the drawing room. I can give her a sedative, if she needs it."

"Thank you, Miss. I'll ring for tea."

"I'll see to it. If I cannot be of assistance, I will not stay. I daresay Mrs Patterson needs bed rest."

The housekeeper nodded and hurried after Mrs Patterson. Grace's head was pounding too hard to bother with protocol. She knocked on the kitchen door and asked for a glass of water, explaining that she had a headache.

If the cook thought her presence a breach of etiquette, she didn't let it show. She put down the caddy she was filling from a large tin of tea and went to draw a glass of water. "I'm making tea, Miss, if you would care to wait in the drawing room."

Grace nodded dumbly, unable to take her eyes off the tin of tea. Its exotic label was an exact match to the one used for the Choral Hall bomb. "My apologies for disturbing you, but I must ask what type of tea that is. Mrs Macmillan always praises it when she visits Mrs Patterson. I thought I might purchase some for her."

The cook's sullen expression cleared. "Ah, Miss, you wouldn't be the first. All the ladies praise her tea, but it is a secret the mistress prefers to keep to herself. It's more than my job is worth to tell you, but perhaps you would care to step closer, while I turn my back and get the cups out."

Grace took the hint, hurrying forward to note the name and supplier.

"A special blend it is," the cook continued. "I warn you, it's terribly expensive. She could afford to employ a scullery maid for the price of it, though I ought not to say so. A gift from Mrs Patterson's brother it was originally, but she and her ladies adored it so much she kept on buying it."

"I must get back to the drawing room," Grace said. "Thank you for the water."

She spotted Charlie on the path with her medical bag and let him in.

"Grace, shouldn't you be going home? I'm no doctor, but even I can see you need a dose of laudanum and a soft bed."

236

"I'll have to make do with water and a strong cup of tea for the moment. Come into the drawing room." When Grace had closed the door behind her, she whispered her news about the tin of tea.

"It's certainly interesting that Lennox MacDonald gave the tea to her," Charlie agreed. "I suppose it is not in widespread use if it is so expensive."

"It seems to me an unlikely gift to be chosen by a brother. I wonder if Lennox's wife bought it."

"Which might suggest that the same tea is used by the Bertram household."

They were interrupted by the appearance of Mrs Patterson, freshly powdered and wearing a different gown and shoes. "My apologies for keeping you waiting, Miss Penrose. And Constable …"

"Detective Constable Pyke, Mrs Patterson," Grace said. "We have no wish to detain you. I stayed only to offer my services, if you wish to avail yourself of them. A mild sedative, perhaps?"

"That is kind of you, Miss Penrose. I am merely in a state of distress. It will pass."

"The death of Mrs Creswell must have come as a terrible shock."

Mrs Patterson looked at her as if she couldn't quite recall her worker's recent death. "Oh, yes, I suppose so. My husband and I did our best by her."

"I applaud your charity, Mrs Patterson. To lose a husband must be a terrible blow to a young lady."

"We did our best to help," Mrs Patterson repeated. "You must excuse my flustered state. I cannot believe she is gone."

The arrival of the tea left their neighbour with a social dilemma. She solved it by asking, "Will you stay to tea?" as a reluctant question rather than a gracious invitation.

Grace was about to demur, but Charlie – to her surprise – declared that he would love to. She sat in an armchair and watched on as he took the tray from the housekeeper and began the ritual of pouring tea, inquiring about milk and sugar, and generally acting like a charming host. It said much for Mrs Patterson's state of mind that she allowed it.

"I do hope you forgive me, Mrs Patterson, for usurping your place, but you ought not exert yourself when you have suffered a shock," Charlie said, as he handed her the first cup.

Grace was content to leave him to it. When she took a grateful slurp from the cup, she had to agree that it was the most delicious tea, although her recent experiences had rather coloured her judgement. The offerings of the police station, hospital and Mrs Doyle had almost put her off the beverage altogether.

As for Charlie, he wore his thin moustache and tailored suit as if he drank nothing other than the rarest of blends, handpicked by maidens from the first new leaves of the season by the light of the full moon. Her headache dimmed to a dull thud, as she sat back in the comfortable armchair, taking pleasure in watching him at work.

"I'm pleased to see you appreciate good manners, despite pursuing a career in the police force, Constable Pyke. Perhaps I have underestimated you. Do you come from a good family on your father's side, perchance?"

Really, Mrs Patterson was too awful, emphasising "father's side" just enough to hint at a slight to his mother, yet not enough to warrant outright offence. Grace braced for Charlie's inevitable defence of his mother's Chinese family, but he didn't so much as flinch.

"Family connections are so very important, are they not, Mrs Patterson?" Charlie nodded sagely, neatly avoiding her question. His little finger stuck out at an angle to the teacup as he lifted the delicate porcelain.

Grace struggled to hold her tea down as it threatened to snort up through her nose. To her astonishment, Mrs Patterson burst into tears. Grace took her cup from her, before her trembling spilled the tea.

"Forgive me," Mrs Patterson spluttered, when she had drawn herself back to a semblance of her usual rigid control. "Your mention of family was a reminder of how dreadful it has been for us all."

"There now, Mrs Patterson," Grace said, handing her back her tea. "Your family is very upset, I imagine."

"It's dreadful, Miss Penrose. I blame Mrs Creswell entirely. How could she have been so foolish as to allow the union to manipulate her into demanding money from Lennox? After all my family did for her! I cannot abide disloyalty. My brother is at his wit's end, being hounded by the police, and now my father is threatening to disown him because of a scandalous rumour that he was involved in the bombing. It's all the fault of that dreadful Bertram man. I begged Lennox not to marry his sister. He never loved her, only her trust fund."

Grace was knocked for six by this unexpected venting of spleen. As she tried to unpick the many disparate strands of the tirade, Charlie went straight to the crux. "Why do you think Bertram is to blame?"

"One only has to look at the man to know he is a low scoundrel, for all the trappings of new wealth. He is a viper, whispering poison into the ears of others. He has Lennox dancing to his ungodly tune. Lennox warned me that he had seen Mrs Creswell acting most inappropriately with Bertram. She denied it, naturally, knowing that Mr Patterson and I would never condone any hint of impropriety with a married man." Mrs Patterson blew her nose loudly into her handkerchief. "I no longer know what or whom to believe."

"Your brother would be well advised to come forward and present his case to the police, Mrs Patterson," Charlie said. "If he is innocent, he will be exonerated. To disappear like this makes it all the worse for him."

"Lennox did not 'disappear'," Mrs Patterson snapped. "He was simply visiting acquaintances out of town when it happened."

"Is he back home now?" Charlie queried.

"My father demanded he come to the house to explain himself. Poor Lennox, he was always such a sensitive boy. I fear his fragile nerves are shattered almost beyond repair by these malicious rumours. To make matters worse, my husband discovered the safe had been emptied of the payroll this morning and accused Lennox of that crime as well. It is all too, too horrible."

"All the more reason for him to come forward and clear his name. I could arrange for a sympathetic police officer to visit him at your father's house."

"I do wish you would, Constable Pyke. My brother knows he must speak to the constabulary, but he's so distraught, he is incapable of making a sensible decision. He's back at his own house now, after storming out of a meeting with our father before luncheon." Mrs Patterson dabbed at her eyes. "I should not have said anything to you. It is unforgivable to speak of private family matters so openly, but I am truly worried he will do something reckless. He was so terribly upset. He … he…" Mrs Patterson dissolved into tears again. Between sobs, she gasped out the reason for her distress. "He … he has a gun."

Charlie reacted with admirable calm. He thanked her for sharing her concerns, assuring her that he would go to her brother immediately. Within seconds, he had called the housekeeper to see to her mistress and whisked Grace out the front door. She was propelled into the afternoon sunshine before she knew which way was up.

"Grace, go home and lock your door. I have to warn Wallace and Kelly that Lennox is armed and dangerous."

"And what if one of them has been shot, Charlie? You'll need a doctor. I promise to stay away from the house unless you call for my help."

At that moment, the cable car approached. Charlie picked her up and dumped her on board, before leaping on himself, muttering something about her being impossible and ruing the day he met her.

The Prodigal Son

When they reached the terminus, Charlie settled Grace into a hansom cab and gave the driver the address of Lennox MacDonald's house.

The journey was over within minutes. Charlie hadn't been to Lennox MacDonald's house before, only the brewery, and hadn't realised how close he lived to his father. Both the MacDonald men had large houses backing onto the town belt, making for a tranquil backdrop to their own extensive gardens. Mr and Mrs Patterson's home, elegant as it was, was decidedly inferior.

Charlie had the cab stop outside, away from the gate, so their arrival wouldn't be seen. He peered through a gap in the hedge. "Wallace and Kelly are already here. Grace, stay behind their carriage and do not move until I call you."

"I promise. I assure you, I have no wish to be shot by a madman." She gripped his hand for a moment. "Charlie…"

"I'll be careful too, Grace."

The house was eerily quiet. As Charlie approached the steps, the front door opened. He assessed his options for cover, which amounted to crouching behind a straggly ngaio tree or throwing himself under the veranda. A familiar figure emerged before he hit the dirt.

"Declan, what a relief to see you. I've come to warn you that Lennox is unstable and has a gun."

"Unfortunately, we already know. He shot himself." Kelly looked past him to the carriage. "Good heavens, Charlie, you didn't bring Grace with you?"

"As if I had a choice. I take it there is no need for her medical skills?"

Kelly shook his head. "Her post-mortem experience may be useful. Come inside."

Grace joined them as they entered the grand foyer. "It's as quiet as a tomb in here."

"The elderly housekeeper is the only one home," Kelly explained. "She says that Lennox MacDonald was intending to be away for a week, while his wife went to stay with her mother. The remaining staff were given extended time off."

Charlie looked up from a display case of silver cigar cases and snuff boxes, each likely worth enough to feed a family for a month. "Did the housekeeper hear the shot?"

"She says not," Kelly replied. "Apparently, she was having a nap, as well as being hard of hearing. She didn't know Lennox was home until we came knocking. She showed us into the library and there he was, sprawled in a pool of blood."

"Does the housekeeper need my assistance?" Grace asked. "She must have had a dreadful shock."

"She's tougher than she looks. After a momentary dizzy turn, the housekeeper answered our questions, asked us if we wanted coffee, then went back to bed. No love lost for her master, that's for sure."

"Coffee, not tea?"

"Yes. Why do you ask, Grace?"

"The tea tin used in the bombing was an unusual and expensive variety. Mrs Patterson uses that tea, after being given it by her brother. An odd gift to choose if this household drinks coffee."

"Perhaps he knew she enjoyed fancy tea," Kelly suggested.

"Probably. Shall I take a look at the corpse?"

"I'm not sure that is a good idea, Grace. He shot himself in the head. It's not a sight for the faint of heart."

"Just as well I am no shrinking violet, isn't it? Lead on, Declan."

Kelly knocked on the library door. "DC Kelly, sir, with company."

242

Wallace opened the door a crack, so no unfortunate visitor might glimpse what lay inside. "Pyke, what are you doing here?"

"We have information, sir. Mrs Patterson, Lennox's sister, is Grace's neighbour. We found her in a state of distress. She believed her brother was so disturbed by the allegations being made against him that he might do something reckless. When she added he had a gun, we came to warn you of the danger. Too late, I gather."

"We? You didn't bring Miss Penrose, I hope?" Wallace slipped out into the hall and closed the library door firmly behind him. "Mrs Patterson was right about his state of mind. Suicide is always tough on the family."

"I hope Lennox left a note admitting guilt and telling us whom he paid to plant the bomb," Charlie said.

"Unfortunately, his guilt was expressed in such a loose way, it doesn't really help us," Wallace replied.

"May DC Pyke and I examine the scene, DI Wallace?" Grace asked.

"Not a good idea, Miss Penrose. I have sent a message to the police surgeon."

"Doctor Cranston-Hartfield may take a while to get here. He is at a wedding out of town this afternoon."

Judging by the careful way in which she failed to meet his eye, Charlie felt sure the police surgeon had invited Grace to the wedding. Did she decline the invitation or was it only because of the bombing that she was not sipping champagne under chandeliers right now?

"The duty surgeon lives miles away," Grace continued. "If you want a quick medical opinion, I am willing to oblige, unless you have anyone else to hand with medical experience."

Wallace remained in the doorway, but he was wavering. "There is a great deal of blood and gore."

"Detective Inspector Wallace, you don't know what gore is until you have attended a post-partum haemorrhage involving a ruptured placenta."

243

Wallace hastened to open the door for her in order to hide the sickly shade his face had gone.

Charlie followed her in, close enough behind her to whisper in her ear. "And you accuse me of being a charmer."

Grace stopped so abruptly, he bumped into her. At first, Charlie thought the sight of the body had shocked her, but he should have known better. Like all good investigators, she paused to survey the scene in detail, rather than jumping to conclusions and stomping through the evidence. Charlie was fairly sure that Grace had never attended the scene of a suicide by firearm, but she didn't flinch.

Lennox MacDonald's body was near the French doors, which were latched open. The impact of the bullet had knocked him backwards, leaving him lying on his back with his legs to the open doors. Although the rear of his head was lying on a Turkish carpet, the reds and blues of the pattern could not disguise the mess of hair, blood, brain tissue and shattered bone from the exit wound. An arc of spatter was visible as far away as the desk, which stood close to the French doors.

Charlie kept a tight grip on his stomach contents, as he glanced at Grace to see how she was coping. She had her head forward and nostrils flared, a hunting dog on a scent. His pulse quickened every time he saw her, but never more so than watching her work her medical magic.

Wallace pointed to the firearm, which had dropped to Lennox's right side under his out-flung hand. "Webley .455, standard issue service revolver. Six-shot, auto-eject, one shot taken, one spent cartridge. Shot himself under the chin. Remains of the bullet lodged in the ceiling on the far side of the room. Powder and burns around the entry wound, indicating a close-range shot, as you would expect with a suicide. No sign of struggle or forced entry. Traces of mud at the French doors, matching his boots, suggesting the deceased must have entered the house that way. The key is still in the door."

"A last view of nature's beauty before he shot himself," Kelly murmured.

Outside, the afternoon was balmy for autumn, with a blaze of red and orange leaves in the garden against a backdrop of blue sky. No houses in view, a thick hedge, no one to see or hear the shot. What splendid isolation the rich enjoy, Charlie thought, yet still they find life too much to bear.

Grace prowled around the edge of the room, from the bullet hole to the desk, where she paused before continuing to the French doors. Seconds turned to minutes as she stood there, gazing at the floor, fiddling with the drapes, standing with her head on one side as if listening for clues.

Finally, she bent to examine the body. Wallace released a low grunt of pent-up impatience. But, rather than touch the body, Grace opened her medical bag and extracted a small brush, working her way across the muddy footprints in the doorway. She brushed her way up to Lennox's foot, taking a measuring tape to his boots and the muddy print, before running her hand over his calf. At last, she leaned over his body to examine the fatal wound.

Wallace, who was shuffling from foot to foot by the inner door, could take no more. "Care to hazard a time of death, Miss Penrose?"

"Rigor mortis hasn't set in and there is minimal lividity, so not more than a few hours. More than an hour though, as the blood is clotted and starting to separate. That is consistent with Mrs Patterson's statement that he left before luncheon."

"What else did Mrs Patterson say?"

"Lennox MacDonald was called to his father's house last night," Charlie explained. "According to his sister, Lennox was given a stern lecture by his father for bringing the family name into disrepute, with the threat of cutting him off if he was involved in the bombing. To make matters worse, Mr Patterson found the safe empty the next morning and accused Lennox of stealing the payroll. Lennox was so angry and upset, he stormed out. It must have been a furious argument, as Mrs Patterson was extremely distressed when we saw her. She will be devastated to hear her brother has committed suicide."

Grace looked up from the corpse. "It wasn't suicide. Lennox MacDonald was murdered."

Wallace and Kelly stared at her, unconsciously imitating each other, with jaws thrust forward and eyes narrowed.

Wallace recovered first. "You're telling me that MacDonald allowed his murderer to stroll in here with a revolver and shoot him under the chin, without a single sign of a struggle?"

"Without doubt, it was somebody he knew and trusted. He didn't shoot himself. There is no powder residue or back spatter from the entry wound on his right hand, nor as much as you would expect on the floor in front of him."

"Are you sure that wasn't because of the angle of the shot?" Wallace countered. "His neck and chest are covered in gore."

Grace shook her head. "The murderer cannot have gotten so close without himself becoming sprayed with blood, thus protecting an area of the floor. It is difficult to discern, because of the pattern of the carpet, but a clean area is visible if you look closely."

Wallace thrust a finger toward the typewriter on the desk. "Care to explain the suicide note?"

"It is the suicide note that proves beyond doubt that this is murder, not suicide."

Charlie went over to the typewriter, being careful not to touch anything. The suicide note had a blurred 'e' and an angled 't'. "It's the same typewriter that was used for the bomber's note to Harriet Morison. It's certainly odd for a suicidal person to type a suicide note and not sign it."

"Odd, but not conclusive," Grace agreed. "In fact, I was more surprised by the competency of the typist. A person learning to type, as Lennox was, finds it difficult to maintain an even pressure and avoid mistakes. However, it is the state of the note and typewriter that confirms it is murder."

Charlie looked closer. "I see what you mean. The suicide note and the typewriter are completely clean, yet there is a faint spatter of blood around it, so fine it's nearly invisible." He levered the

246

typewriter up. "There are even tiny droplets of blood underneath it, both on the desk and smeared on the bottom surface of the machine."

Grace nodded. "There can be no doubt about it. The typewriter was not on the desk when Lennox died. It was placed there after his death, while the blood was still wet. The bomber or one of his associates has committed his second murder and forged a suicide note to implicate Lennox. Does the note give any clue as to the writer?"

"All it says is: 'It is my deepest regret that I did not put a stop to this madness. The guilt has become intolerable. Would that God had granted me the grace to be a better man. Society is better off without me.' Other than the obvious – that the writer is literate and knows how to use a typewriter – there is not much to go on. The language strikes me as too florid and apologetic for a man like Lennox."

Kelly came over to the desk to read the note again. "It must be Bertram, trying to make it appear as if MacDonald is to blame. By God, he's a wily one. To kill his own brother-in-law, he must be evil to the core."

Wallace was still standing in the same spot, staring out the open doors as if the few puffs of cloud drifting across the sky might hold the answer. Charlie knew him well enough by now to recognise that he was running through the facts of the case in his head, adjusting his thoughts to the fresh evidence. A lesser man might have been cross at missing the miniscule droplets of blood on the typewriter, but not Wallace.

A full minute passed before he spoke. "I'm convinced Bertram was behind the campaign to disrupt the Women's Franchise League, but I'm not so sure about the bombings. Bertram had no motive to kill Mrs Creswell, and he must have realised that the bombs would only generate more sympathy for the suffrage cause."

"Mrs Patterson was rather incoherent towards the end of our discussion," Charlie said, "but she did say that Lennox suspected Bertram was having an inappropriate relationship with Mrs Creswell. I can't say I think it likely, as she was a pretty, delicate

247

woman, whereas Bertram is unattractive to the point of being repulsive. If I found him creepy, surely it would be worse for a woman. Although, come to think of it, Mrs Vance said he was the only one of the four not to touch her."

"Maybe there is another explanation," Grace said. "Molly Sugden thought Mrs Creswell was about to come into some money. We assumed the money was from Lennox, as a private settlement to pre-empt her compensation claim, but it's possible the money was from Bertram. If so, perhaps the connection between Mrs Creswell and Bertram wasn't a physical relationship, but a payment for services rendered."

"You're thinking Bertram paid her to put the tea tin in the kitchen?" Wallace had lost the faraway stare and was all but pawing the ground. "Destroy the franchise petition, kill his accomplice, and implicate Lennox MacDonald all in one go. Now that is the type of plan a man like Bertram would relish. Time to have another word with him. Kelly, you come with me. Pyke, I know you are not supposed to be working, but I'd be grateful if you would stay here until we can send a constable to stand guard. See what you can find while you are waiting."

"Remember to search Bertram's house for blood-stained clothes," Grace called after them as they raced out the door. "And tea, check for tins of Darjeeling tea."

Kelly saluted her as their carriage rattled along the drive.

Charlie leaned down to whisper in her ear. "Alone at last. How I wish that we might have one moment together without the distracting presence of a jailor, rival, nurse, criminal or corpse."

"Where would the fun be in that?" Grace replied. "Perhaps we ought to concentrate on the search. I'll not rest easy until we get the fiend who enjoys bombing suffragists. Shall I talk to the housekeeper, while you search the house?"

248

Doubts

Grace curled up on the cushioned comfort of the veranda seat. Her thoughts were far from the pretty garden view. There were too many pieces that didn't fit. One or two were to be expected, but the inconsistencies had mounted until a vague itch had become an irritating rash.

Charlie slouched around the corner, kicking a stone. "There you are, Grace. Are you having a nap, or is your body resting while your brain is churning?"

"Come, sit. Tell me this all makes sense to you."

He dropped down beside her, draping his arm along the top of the seat as if they were courting, rather than dissecting another murder. "I wish I could. It feels wrong. Let's talk it through. Facts only, no assumptions. What have you found, Grace?"

"It's only a minor point, but I've asked the housekeeper and checked in the pantry. There is no sign of the type of tea tin used in the bombing. If Lennox or his wife gave it as a present to Mrs Patterson, it was not because it was their tea of choice. In fact, they both drink coffee and kept tea only for visitors. A nice tea, but nothing special, from Ceylon, not Darjeeling."

"I found the missing cartridges of dynamite. It should be conclusive evidence as to his guilt, but I can't help thinking Lennox would have been a fool to keep them in such an obvious place. Dangerous, as well as incriminating."

"The housekeeper says she has never seen a typewriter here before. However, she also said the locked cabinets in the library were not to be touched by anyone but Lennox, so he might have concealed the typewriter. Did you search them, Charlie?"

"I found a space in one cabinet about the size of a typewriter, along with some paper of the same type used for the suicide note.

249

Yet none of Lennox's correspondence is typed. Nor is the handwritten correspondence on that type of paper."

"He hadn't had the typewriter long," Grace reminded him, "and he has been rather too busy to use it."

Charlie shook his head. "His letters prove he is an atrocious speller who rarely uses punctuation. Totally inconsistent with the typewritten notes, which are also neatly typed, suggesting an experienced typist. All the more reason to think he is not the bomber."

"I agree. An action as shocking as a bombing would risk hostility towards their anti-suffrage, pro-liquor cause, even without the death, while providing only a temporary setback for women's franchise. And Lennox had little to lose from Mrs Creswell's official compensation bid, either."

"How so?"

"An action taken by a union would be against the company rather than Lennox personally, despite what Mrs Patterson said. Lennox might have been shamed into promising a private settlement, to save his father's business reputation, but would the amount have been so much that he preferred to kill rather than pay?"

"I can't see it, especially as it seems Lennox was a wealthy man, despite his extravagant tastes. I had a quick look through his accounts. The brewery was far more lucrative than the roading business. He could have paid off Mrs Creswell without losing a wink of sleep."

Grace curled up against Charlie's shoulder, comforted by the steady beat of his heart and the weight of his arm around her. "If that's the case, don't you find it odd that Lennox should stoop to stealing cash from MacDonald Roading?"

"I'm inclined to agree, except that some men never feel they have enough, no matter how well off they are. While others are blissfully content sitting on a sunny seat next to a beautiful woman with an unusual proclivity for solving crimes."

Grace leaned into his warmth. "Don't you ever think it would be nice to live a normal life?"

"Never. You?"

"Absolutely not. That's another oddity of this case. I struggle to believe that a sweet, sensible woman like Violet Creswell could be in league with a man like Harry Bertram, unless she was truly desperate for money."

They sat in silence, content to listen to each other's breathing and the occasional bird call.

"Whatever you have to say, Charlie, just say it. You're thinking so loud, it's like sitting next to a ticking bomb."

He sat forward, avoiding her scrutiny. "It's a bomb I am reluctant to set off."

"I suspect you are thinking the same as I am – that everything odd or misleading seems to come back to the evidence of either Mr Patterson or his wife."

"Grace, you read my mind." Charlie rose from the seat and began to pace. "I liked Mr Patterson. More than that, I believed him. What he said rang true, unless he was a consummate actor. He seems a solid man, with no pretence or subterfuge about him – quite happy living on a moderate salary and grateful for whatever bones the miserly old MacDonald threw his way. Quite the opposite of the prodigal son, who was forever taking and never lifting a finger to work for it."

"And yet, we are taking a great deal on Mr Patterson's word. Do you have any independent evidence that Lennox was stealing from the roading business? Or that he took the old typewriter? Or indeed that he took the explosives?"

The pacing paused, as he considered her questions. "I think Lennox did take black powder for the firecrackers and Patterson knew it."

Grace joined him at the veranda railing, where they watched in silence as a small flock of silvereyes flitted around an apple tree. Too tranquil a scene for dark thoughts.

251

"It comes back to the crucial question of any investigation," Charlie said. "Who had the most to gain by killing Lennox MacDonald and Violet Creswell?"

"Mrs Patterson's maid said that Mr and Mrs Patterson often complained about how much wealth Lennox flaunted, while they struggled along with insufficient income to meet the expenses demanded of their social status. I can't help thinking that they were more likely to take the cash from the safe than Lennox."

"Exactly. It would be easy for Patterson to justify it as a loan against his wife's future inheritance. Not unreasonable, as he was putting in all the work to make the business a success, but not getting the benefit of a fair income."

The idea, once planted, took root quickly, until Grace wondered why she hadn't thought of it before. "With Lennox dead and his father on his last legs, Mr and Mrs Patterson would gain complete control of the roading business. They would feel as if they were getting their fair reward, instead of seeing the majority share go to a useless troublemaker."

"They would also get the father's shareholding in the brewery, but only if Lennox died before the old man. Patterson had to act quickly. What better time than when Lennox was implicated in criminal activity himself?"

"Especially as Mrs Creswell's death could be blamed on Lennox, eliminating the need to pay her compensation and providing a motive for his suicide. Now I think about it, Molly said that Mrs Creswell had noticed the theft of the money. What if she realised it was Mr Patterson taking the cash from the safe, not Lennox?"

"You could well be right, Grace. Mrs Creswell resigned and left in a hurry, so she must have had a good reason." Charlie resumed his pacing, faster this time, thudding along the boards of the veranda until they quivered. "It feels as if we have two separate cases. Bertram and the other three liquor barons nipping at the heels of the Women's Franchise League, with Patterson cleverly using their

252

activities as a diversion to get rid of the people standing in his way of a fortune."

Grace ticked off the points on her fingers. "Patterson had the strongest motive, access to and knowledge of explosives, access to the typewriter, and he fits the description of the man who delivered the bombs."

"The problem is that he was out of town when the bomb was planted at Choral Hall and when the package was sent to Harriet Morison. Patterson's foremen signed off the payroll deliveries he made against specific times, with the last one being late in the afternoon, too late to ride back to a station to get a train."

"Has his alibi been run through the ringer, Charlie?"

His pacing stopped abruptly. If his brain had been a bomb, Grace was sure the timer would be ticking down the last few seconds.

"Maybe there is a way. Imagine a busy foreman, receiving a site visit from the boss. Would he stop to check every detail of the logbook entry before signing his name to it? What if Patterson had entered the time as five o'clock, when it was actually earlier? Perhaps three o'clock, as three and five would be easy to confuse if not written clearly. Patterson could have made it back in time for the late train or ridden back to Dunedin."

Their deliberations were interrupted by the return of Wallace and Kelly, accompanied by two constables who were barely old enough to shave.

The constables were directed to guard the house, while Wallace slumped on the stairs with his back against the veranda post. "This damnable case will be the death of me."

"Bertram has an alibi for Lennox MacDonald's shooting," Kelly explained.

Charlie looked from one to the other, but Wallace was stony-faced, while Kelly was flushed an unnatural shade of magenta. Finally, Kelly whispered in Charlie's ear.

"Would anyone care to let me in on the secret?" Grace demanded.

"Bertram was occupied with a lover. His valet swears Bertram was locked in his bedroom, occupied with thoughts other than murder." Charlie paused. "It would seem our intuition was correct and Mrs Patterson was wrong. Bertram's hatred for women runs far deeper than their intellect and desire for the vote."

"Stop speaking in riddles," Grace complained.

"Kelly was trying to spare your sensibilities, Grace. Bertram's lover was a man. I really did have more reason to fear his unwanted advances than Mrs Vance and Mrs Creswell."

"And Bertram only drinks a cheap tea from China," Kelly muttered.

"One good thing has come out of this sordid state of affairs," Wallace said. "Bertram was so terrified that I'd haul him in on an indecency charge that he made a clean breast of his other offences. He admitted to running an illegal gambling den – you'll get the credit for that, Pyke – and orchestrating the mob and the minor incidents, as well as ordering Vance to plant the evidence in Pyke's lodgings."

"But he denied any link to the bombings, and he swore he had never heard of Mrs Violet Creswell," Kelly added, "so we are no closer to identifying the bomber or the killer of Lennox MacDonald."

"As a matter of fact," Charlie said, "Miss Penrose and I have some thoughts on that very matter."

Burning Issue

Charlie outlined their concerns about Mr Patterson as the four of them headed to Fergus MacDonald's house.

"You see how close the two houses are?" Charlie said. "Patterson could have walked through the trees of the town belt without being seen. With only the deaf housekeeper home at Lennox's house, he could have gone around to the French doors and been let in by his brother-in-law."

The man on the gate told them that Mr Patterson had already left for the day, but Mr Fergus MacDonald was at home.

As they pulled to a halt in front of the house, a drift of smoke hinted at a fire.

"Pyke, you take the outside. Kelly, you take the office. I'll talk to Fergus MacDonald. Miss Penrose, I suggest you stay in the carriage."

Wallace said the last with resignation, as if he had little doubt she would obey. As soon as Wallace and Kelly disappeared into the house, Charlie held out his hand to help Grace down, knowing her too well to believe she would do as she was told. They walked around the back of the house, where a fire smouldered. He prodded through the half-burnt remnants with a stick, hooking out a mass of charred fabric.

"A man's overcoat, by the look of it. Very similar to the long canvas coat Mr Patterson was wearing when I first met him. Split at the back for horse-riding, like this one. Same buttons too." He poked at the mass, revealing a row of metal buttons. "I expect there will be a pair of blood-stained gloves in there as well, not that there will be enough left of them to tell if there is blood or not. Can you think of any other reason a man would burn a perfectly good coat?"

"Not offhand. See if you can unfold it, Charlie."

255

One front panel of the coat was folded underneath the other. When Charlie flipped the charred top layer off, the protected side showed traces of a dark stain. "Could be blood, but it's too burnt to tell, unless you have a clever way of identifying scorched blood."

"There is a test for fresh blood, but I doubt it would work in this case," Grace replied. "I've never had the opportunity to try it."

A man strode towards them, swinging a rake. Charlie had his badge out before he could vent his thoughts. "Detective Constable Pyke. Would you be the gardener?"

"Aye. What do you think you're–" The gardener's question was cut off as he saw the charred remains of the coat. "What's that doing in my fire? Burning dead leaves, I was."

"Have you seen anybody outside the house today?"

"Nobody out of the ordinary. Tramps sleep in the woods from time to time, but it's getting too cold at nights for them now. Don't always spot them, of course, with the woods being so close."

"What about family members or staff?"

"Mr Lennox left earlier today. On foot and in a hurry, looking out of sorts. Must have been late morning." The gardener took his time, raking the fire as his memory chugged slowly through the day. "Mr Patterson came out soon after. Chopping wood with a fury he was. Not his job, of course, but he's a man what likes to be busy, especially when he is vexed." He nodded his approval at this evidence of manly outdoor activity, before adding, "He often chops wood when Mr Lennox has been here."

"Do you know how long he was chopping wood?"

The gardener shook his head. "Went in for me dinner. Didn't see a soul the rest of the day, Saturday being as it is a half day for me."

"So why are you here now, if you don't mind me asking?"

"I live in a cottage on the grounds. Thought I caught a whiff o' smoke and wondered if I'd not put the fire out properly. I'm sure it was down to embers when I left it. Darn fool thing for someone to be throwing wood on it and going off without keeping an eye on it."

They left the gardener to his fire and made a circuit of one end of the grounds. The only item of interest was a large stack of newly split wood. Mr Patterson must have spent a considerable period working out his feelings towards Lennox, before deciding to get rid of him once and for all.

Outside the back door, a pair of boots was drying in the sun, having been scrubbed clean down to the raw leather. Grace picked them up and examined them. "The muddy boot prints by the French doors in Lennox's house. I thought they were Lennox's, but Patterson wears the same type and a similar size."

The exhilaration of the chase gripped Charlie, as the net closed around their suspect. He pointed out the shirt and trousers hanging from a line. "What innocent man would wash his own clothes and boots so thoroughly at his father-in-law's house, rather than going to his own home and having a maid do it?"

"Patterson seems to be a practical man who prefers to keep busy. I'd wager he has a workshop, where he does his own carpentry and mending. Perhaps he even shoes his own horses?" Grace nodded towards the gable end of a building they hadn't yet investigated.

"And makes his own bombs?" Charlie tucked his arm through hers. "I've missed working with you, Grace."

She nudged him. "Two brains are better than one, even if one is only the smaller and feebler brain of a woman."

"Ha! Those anti-suffrage fools don't know what they are talking about. They must walk around with their ears closed, if they don't know the value of a woman's thoughts."

They found what they were looking for in the stables. A work bench, surrounded by enough tools to supply a hardware store, and everything needed to shoe horses. A battered old tea tin stood at one end, full of used horseshoe nails. The tin had long since lost its label, but it was the same size and shape as the one they had seen in the kitchen storage room at Choral Hall.

Charlie pulled out the nail he'd kept from the bomb. It was a match. "It's probably the same type of nail used by farriers everywhere, but it does show Patterson had access to plenty of them. Bent when the old shoe is pulled off, same as this one."

Boots plodded across the wooden floor behind them. "Can I help you, sir, ma'am?"

Charlie took in the weather-beaten face, patched clothes and aroma of horse dung. "I'm Detective Constable Pyke. Would you be the stableman?"

"Aye. Mr Patterson ain't here, and he wouldn't care for you poking around neither."

Charlie ignored the reprimand. "Does Mr Patterson shoe his own horses?"

"Aye. By rights it ought to be me, but me back ain't what it used to be, and he likes to do it himself anyways. A fine man, Mr Patterson."

"He keeps the old nails?"

"Oh, aye. Nowt wasted around here. He has them melted for re-use."

"Does Mr Lennox MacDonald ever come in here?"

The ancient stableman snorted. "He ain't the sort to get his hands dirty."

Grace smiled at him. "Didn't Lennox get up to all sorts of pranks as a child? I heard he exploded a chicken with black powder."

The stableman grinned back, showing toothless gums. "Oh, aye, Lennox got the blame for that. Just between you, me and the fence post, it were wee Abigail behind it. Mrs Patterson could run rings around her brother. Clever as a pixie, she were and twice as naughty. Shame she weren't a boy, if you ask me, the way she used to follow her father around. Best decision she ever made, marrying a sensible man like Mr Patterson rather than some useless la-di-dah. Makes my day, when she comes down here to see her husband off whenever Mr Patterson has to go away. True love is grand, ain't it?"

"It is indeed," Charlie agreed. "Thank you for your time."

As Charlie and Grace crossed back to the house, Wallace and Kelly came out the front door.

Wallace headed straight for the brougham, gesturing at them to hurry. "Patterson has gone home. Fergus MacDonald pretended the meeting with Lennox this morning was a minor quarrel – one of many since Lennox was old enough to string a sentence together. Fergus was lying through his teeth. He's still so furious about the argument with Lennox that I thought he might have an apoplectic fit."

Kelly jogged along beside his boss, his eyes bright with the thrill of the chase. "The servants all agreed that there was a lot of angry shouting involving all parties. Most of them ducked for cover, but one maid was trapped in the adjoining room, too scared to move in case they heard her. You won't believe what she overheard."

"Don't keep us in suspense," Charlie demanded.

"Mr Patterson was furious about money going missing from the safe again. The maid said she heard a scuffle as he demanded Lennox return it, while Lennox cursed his brother-in-law and bellowed that he never took any money. Meanwhile, Mrs Patterson screamed Lennox could go to the devil, after shaming the family name, despite having been given the lion's share of everything his whole life. Fergus MacDonald was there too, yelling that Lennox was no son of his and vowing to disown him."

"No wonder Lennox fled the house," Grace said.

"But not before he got in a few choice words of his own. Lennox denied any involvement in Mrs Creswell's death and accused them of setting him up to take the blame. According to the maid, he said something like: 'You must have known that giving me that parcel to deliver to the Tailoresses' Union would implicate me. How could you have been so heartless? Was it any wonder I left Dunedin in a hurry? I'm not putting up with this abuse a minute longer.' With that, he stormed out of the house. From the maid's shocked expression, I gather that is very much the expurgated version."

Charlie and Grace exchanged their own shocked glances as he helped her into the carriage.

"Did you find any evidence, Pyke?" Wallace asked, when they were rattling down the drive, heading for the Patterson house.

259

Charlie dragged his thoughts away from the maid's evidence, trying to emulate Wallace's matter-of-fact tone. "Patterson has some explaining to do, sir. We found a long riding coat burning in a fire. The same as the one Patterson wore the day we met him. Stained on the front, but too badly burned to tell if it was blood. Scrubbed boots and clothes too. Boots matching the muddy prints at Lennox's house, according to Miss Penrose, although Lennox wore the same type. And an old tea tin filled with used horseshoe nails, the same as the ones in the bomb."

A predatory glint ignited in Wallace's eyes. "Excellent. Now all we need to do is break his alibi for the time the bomb was planted."

"He might have faked the times of his payroll delivery. An hour or two earlier, and he could have returned on to the last train to Dunedin. His site foreman probably only counter-signed whatever Patterson had written."

Wallace was silent as they passed the gatekeeper, resuming the discussion only when they were out of earshot. "I've got a man trying to track down the works' foreman to check his alibi. Fergus MacDonald said he bought both Lennox and Patterson a Webley revolver. Patterson needed one for the payroll delivery and Lennox didn't want to be left out. Be on your toes when we interview him, in case he is armed. Follow my lead."

"Will we arrest him and take him to the station, sir?" Kelly asked.

"I rather think it might be useful to start softly in the comfort of his own home," Wallace replied. "See if we can trip him up. After all, he shouldn't know anything about his brother-in-law's death, or the bombs for that matter, if he is innocent."

"If Patterson insists he didn't come back to town to plant the bomb, you could always try accusing his wife instead," Charlie suggested. "He dotes on her. Any hint that we suspect her of collaborating with him and I think our upstanding Mr Patterson might show the tiger hiding within."

"I cannot accuse a lady like Mrs Patterson. Mr Patterson would be well within his rights to take extreme offence. She's the president of Homemakers' Association, for heaven's sake, as well as any number of other charitable organisations."

"Being a society lady takes more money than she has to spare," Grace countered. "Mrs Patterson was one of the few people who could have let her husband in to Choral Hall to plant the bomb. Also, one of the few who knew the petition forms were stored there."

"But we know the caretaker left the door open," Wallace said.

"Mr Patterson couldn't have known that it would be open. He must have had another plan to get in, preferably much earlier in the day, as he had to return to his payroll delivery. Or, he got his wife to plant the tea tin for him."

Wallace gaped at her. "Miss Penrose, you shock me. I am all for women's rights, but I cannot for a single moment believe that a lady of her standing could be involved in such a plot."

Charlie added his support. "Mrs Patterson knows how to use a typewriter and had a key for the safe. She was interested in the business from a young age and knew her way around the practicalities of explosives. Mr MacDonald even said he wished she'd been a boy, as she would have made the perfect heir."

Wallace lapsed into silence. His willingness to put his own views aside and consider all options was one of the things Charlie admired about him.

"All right, I agree that Mrs Patterson might have let her husband in or even planted the tea tin on her husband's orders, not knowing what it contained. But I cannot countenance the idea that she built the bombs or shot her own brother in cold blood."

"I am not saying she did help her husband," Charlie replied, "only that it is plausible enough to shake Mr Patterson into admitting the truth, to save his wife from being implicated and her reputation ruined. I admit it is not the most gentlemanly of ways to achieve a confession, but none of our evidence is unequivocal."

The lines of doubt cleared from Wallace's brow. "I concede it's a clever idea, Pyke. I want you to sit with me and ask any questions you think might shake him, so long as it doesn't break into my line of questioning. Kelly, you stand between Patterson and the door, to give him the hint that this will not be a cosy little fireside chat."

Charlie noted Grace was trying to appear small and harmless, a sure sign that she was going to attempt to infiltrate around the edges. Wallace noticed too, but didn't move to stop her. The more Charlie got to know him, the more he realised Wallace was almost as clever and unconventional as his own boss, DI Stewart, but with a significant difference – he hid it better.

They had no more time to plan, as their carriage had drawn to a halt outside the Patterson house on High Street.

Wallace jumped out with the enthusiasm of a man half his age. "Follow me, team. Time to corner a murderer."

Moves and Countermoves

The police team settled into their places in the drawing room, as if they were part of a stage set, with actors awaiting the raising of the curtain.

Mr and Mrs Patterson were seated together on a sofa, so close they were touching along the length of their bodies. Their heads were held high, their hands identically crossed in their laps. Had there been an audience to this play, they would have been left in no doubt that here was a loving couple facing up to bad news with dignity.

Nor would the audience have any difficulty identifying Wallace as the senior police officer, facing them square on, the focus of attention. Charlie played the junior officer, with a notebook at the ready, seated in an upright chair, slightly back from his boss and at an angle to the action. Kelly had his arms crossed and jaw clamped, the guardian of the exit.

The pretty young woman sitting near the door was the only enigma. An audience might assume she was the couple's daughter, but her alert expression and placement on the police side of the stage suggested another, more unexpected, role.

Act One, Scene One. Tea is poured.

Mrs Patterson picked up a cup, but it rattled so alarmingly in her hand that she put it down. Her husband ignored his cup and patted her hand. Wallace leaned back in his chair, allowing the passage of time to build the dramatic tension, as he sipped his tea. Nobody else was drinking – they simply waited and watched.

Wallace put his cup down. "What delicious tea, Mrs Patterson. Where do you get it, if I might ask? I know my wife would enjoy it."

Mrs Patterson's lips moved, but no words came out.

Her husband covered her white knuckles with his own hand. "Detective Inspector Wallace, you are not here to discuss tea. We have had a trying day, so I beg of you to state your business without further delay."

"If you wish, we will set aside the matter of the tea for now and return to it later. Perhaps you would you care to explain why your day has been trying, Mr Patterson?"

"An unpleasant family argument, Inspector. My wife's brother has been a constant source of trouble. He has brought our good name into disrepute."

Wallace selected a piece of cake. He sliced it into bite-sized chunks so slowly that they all jumped when he finally laid the knife down. "That must be infuriating for you, Mr Patterson. I know how hard you worked to make the roading business a success, only to see its reputation tarnished by the death of Mrs Violet Creswell's husband. And then to have her belatedly seeking compensation. All the fault of your brother-in-law, yet he still takes his share of the profits without doing a shred of work."

Again, Mrs Patterson reacted, but her husband answered. "Yes, I admit it was frustrating. We did a great deal for Mrs Creswell and I truly believed she was grateful to my wife and I. Roading construction is a dangerous business. Accidents do happen occasionally. It is a risk the workers know and accept. Mrs Creswell knew that too, but she fell into the company of radical unionists, who convinced her she was owed more."

"You must have harboured a great deal of anger towards the women of the Tailoresses' Union. Perhaps Mrs Harriet Morison in particular?" Wallace popped a chunk of cake into his mouth, creating a silence begging to be filled.

"The Miners' Union, I think you must mean, Inspector. They were simply doing what they saw as their job, albeit with the aim of damaging the reputation of honest employers. I was not angry at them, so much as annoyed that they would so blatantly manipulate a fragile widow. Mrs Creswell had been an excellent worker and a friend to my wife, before the union got their claws into her."

"Her death must have been a shock for you both," Wallace said.

Mrs Patterson spoke for the first time, so softly they had to strain to hear. "It was a terrible tragedy. I still feel faint at the thought of such a dreadful death."

"My wife and I are advocates of temperance," Mr Patterson added. "We are appalled that the liquor lobby would descend to such violence in a vile attempt to stop those franchise women."

"Your temperance beliefs must be another source of tension between you and your brother-in-law, Mr Patterson."

"Indeed. My wife pleaded with her father not to purchase a brewery for her brother. Becoming a purveyor of the demon drink is the very last enterprise that would help Lennox become a better man. But Lennox insisted. And what Lennox wants, he gets."

"Your wife was actually present at Choral Hall shortly before the bomb went off." Wallace waited for Mr Patterson to nod, before turning to his wife. "How traumatic for you, Mrs Patterson. Of course, your own group – the Homemakers' Association – must have had little sympathy for the Women's Franchise League. The loss of all those signatures on the women's suffrage petition might even be seen as a blessing for a group who believe the role of women is to create a warm home and happy family for their menfolk, rather than meddling in masculine concerns of which they are profoundly ignorant, such as voting."

Mrs Patterson found her old spark at last. "I find your remarks deeply offensive, Inspector. God has directed us to observe the proper role of women. We need only a Bible, not a bomb, to prove our case."

"Merely an observation, Mrs Patterson." Wallace swallowed another morsel of cake. Every eye was fixed on the deliberate way he brushed crumbs off his coat, when he struck again. "Take us through your movements this morning, Mr Patterson, from the moment Mr Lennox MacDonald left his father's house, after you all argued with such fury that the servants ducked for cover."

Patterson leaped from the sofa with his fists clenched, but Kelly was quick to intervene. Patterson sank back, his face a fiery red. "I don't like your insinuations, Detective Inspector Wallace. Every family has its disagreements."

"Would you care to tell me what you did following this disagreement?"

"I admit I was angry at Lennox, but I calmed down quickly after chopping a pile of wood. Nothing better than physical exertion to bring peace to a man."

"You strike me as a capable man, Mr Patterson. You even shoe your own horses, I believe."

Patterson nodded, appearing disconcerted rather than stressed by Wallace's change of tack. "I enjoy such work. A well-tended horse is vital in my business."

"After you chopped the wood, did you walk to your brother-in-law's house to settle your differences?"

Patterson's face turned purple, as he struggled to hold his temper.

"My husband came inside after chopping the wood, Inspector," Mrs Patterson interrupted, her voice icy calm. "Despite it being Saturday afternoon, we had much to do in the office. I myself had had to do all the administrative work in the regrettable absence of Mrs Creswell."

Charlie used the opportunity to remind Mr Patterson of his wife's vulnerability to being charged as an accessory. "You are a passable typist, Mrs Patterson, are you not?"

"Not in the least. I do what I must."

"Come now, no need for modesty. I saw a letter you were working on. Very neatly done, I must say. Perhaps you used the old typewriter for occasional work that needed doing, after Mrs Creswell got her new machine?"

"Lennox decided he wanted the old typewriter, so of course he must have it," she said, through tight lips. "My brother always gets his way."

"He wouldn't want it for himself, surely? I have seen his correspondence. All handwritten. The man can barely spell and has no concept of punctuation. Unlike yourself, Mrs Patterson. You have a fine way with words."

Now it was Mrs Patterson's turn to flush. "Nevertheless, Lennox did take it. He told me he intended to practice on it at home, because in the end it would be easier than writing longhand. Whether or not he used the typewriter, I cannot know. I am not my brother's keeper."

"No indeed, Mrs Patterson. Quite the opposite, I suspect."

Patterson was again out of his seat, lunging at Charlie. "What the devil are you insinuating, you jumped up ne'er-do-well?"

Wallace raised a hand to halt his advance. "Step back, Mr Patterson. I would ask you not to insult my men, who are only doing their duty. Your duty is to answer our questions. Why did you wash your clothes and boots, if you spent the afternoon in the office?"

"It's no business of yours, I'm darn sure. As a matter of fact, I worked up a sweat chopping wood."

"Then why did you attempt to burn your coat in the fire? It appeared to be a superior garment and by no means near the end of its life."

Patterson sat in granite-faced silence, his brow furrowing as he thought of an answer.

His wife was far quicker. "I'm afraid that was my fault. I tripped on the back steps while bringing in some flowers from the garden and ripped the coat beyond repair with my shears. I'm awfully sorry, John darling, I know you liked that coat."

"But why burn it, Mrs Patterson?"

"I … I don't know. An impulse. The coat was ruined, the fire already burning. Guilt at ruining a favourite garment, I expect."

"Guilt. Of all the deception and misdirection I have heard from you both, that is the one thing I can believe, without a doubt."

"Whatever misapprehensions you are labouring under, Inspector, I assure you that my wife and I have no reason to feel guilt. As far as I can see, you have done nothing but spout insinuations, without a single word about what you truly mean."

"All right, Mr Patterson, I shall speak plainly. Did you take explosives from your own store to fashion two bombs, one sent to Mrs Harriet Morison and one hidden in Choral Hall, the latter causing the death of Mrs Violet Creswell?"

Patterson clenched every muscle in his body. "I most certainly did not."

"And did you, after chopping wood today, proceed on foot to the house of Mr Lennox MacDonald, wherein you murdered him in cold blood? After which, you returned in your blood-soaked garments and proceeded to remove all traces of evidence."

"My husband did no such thing," Mrs Patterson snapped. "How dare you come into this respectable house and make such outrageous claims? Please leave immediately and address all further questions to our attorney."

Wallace rose slowly from the armchair. "We have sufficient evidence to arrest your husband, Mrs Patterson. Your attorney will be welcome to visit him in the police cells."

Charlie gathered up his notebook without haste. "Sir, don't you find it odd that neither Mr nor Mrs Patterson expressed any surprise at the fact of Lennox MacDonald's death, only at the accusation against his killer? Indeed, I am at a loss to understand their reaction to your questions, if they did not know of his death."

"By Jove, Pyke," Wallace replied, slipping a wink in his direction, "I do believe you are correct. How remiss of me not to inform them of the death of Mrs Patterson's brother prior to accusing her husband of murder." Wallace sank back into the armchair, adjusting his coat so that he sat comfortably.

Mr Patterson looked ready to kill again, but his wife restrained him.

"If my husband and I expressed no shock that Lennox was dead, Detective Inspector Wallace, it is only because we knew his moods all too well. Lennox has always been impulsive, rushing in to foolish behaviour, before retreating into piteous self-recrimination. This time was the worst yet. I feared he might take his own life, so I was not surprised when you said he had been shot."

Charlie had to hand it to this stalwart woman. She was a quick thinker and a staunch supporter of her husband. But she had made another mistake. "In fact, Mrs Patterson, Detective Inspector Wallace said murdered, not shot. Only his killer would know that he had been shot."

Mrs Patterson glared at him so hard, Charlie felt the scorch marks on his eyeballs. "I merely assumed he shot himself. He owned a gun, as I told you earlier today. If you recall, Constable Pyke, I even warned you about my brother's depressed state of mind."

"Indeed you did, Mrs Patterson. You made quite sure to direct my attention to your brother."

Wallace took up the offensive. "And yet, your brother did not die by his own hand. He was murdered and his killer left a neatly typed note on your old typewriter. How do you explain that?"

"Of course he killed himself." Mr Patterson half-rose, but his wife put out a restraining hand, and he subsided.

Charlie waited for him to settle. "Lennox was murdered, without a doubt."

"That scoundrel, Bertram—"

"Bertram has an alibi, Mrs Patterson. And there are no burning overcoats in his garden."

Mr Patterson jumped to his feet again. He stood there, clenching his fists, but rather than lash out, he forced himself to walk around to the rear side of the sofa, where he placed his calloused hand on his wife's shoulder. He took two more deep breaths before speaking. "You cannot believe I had anything to do with Lennox's death. Whatever you think you know, I'm sure you will find it was suicide, upon proper examination of the facts."

"On the contrary, Mr Patterson," Wallace said. "We have had an expert opinion on the matter. Cleverly staged to appear as a suicide, but a murder nevertheless."

Charlie noted Wallace's subtle shifting of weight towards him and took the hint. "I suppose, sir, that we will be obliged to note that a woman can pull a trigger as easily as a man or wear a long coat to avoid being covered in blood." He shifted his gaze to Mrs Patterson. "Women are so easily overlooked, are they not, Mrs Patterson? How often is their contribution undervalued? An intelligent woman might work her whole life, helping her father, then her husband, to build a business into a success. How aggravating that a feckless younger brother would inherit a majority share, as well as the entire brewery."

Mrs Patterson's face boiled with emotion, but only fury and righteousness, not fear or guilt, as far as Charlie could judge.

"Enough!" Mr Patterson's sudden cry was enough to make them all jump, even though they had been hoping for it.

"I killed Lennox." Patterson swallowed the tremor in his voice and spoke with brisk determination. "The world is a better place without him. I placed the bomb in Choral Hall as well, in order to lay a trail to Lennox, so his suicide would be seen as evidence of his guilt."

Wallace stood and signalled Kelly to take charge of Mr Patterson.

Mrs Patterson launched herself off the sofa at Kelly, clawing at him as she screamed, "Leave him alone. John is innocent."

Dilemma

Grace had sat back in silence throughout the interview, marvelling at the way Wallace played the room as a maestro directs a symphony, with Charlie so perfectly hitting the dramatic top notes. The thrill of watching them work never dimmed.

But suddenly, Kelly and Mrs Patterson were in a tangle at her feet. A symphony ending on an unexpected discordant note.

Mrs Patterson pushed herself to her feet, adjusting her petticoats in an involuntary gesture towards propriety. She stood between a dumbfounded Wallace and her shocked husband, who had retreated to the mantelpiece for support.

"My husband is only trying to protect me, Inspector. You have done all in your power to implicate me in these dreadful crimes. Is it any wonder my loyal husband stepped in to save me, when he had nothing to do with any of it? He was, as you well know, far away from Dunedin at the time of both of the bombing incidents. My father's gardener will vouch that John was chopping wood when Lennox shot himself. If you do not believe it was suicide or murder by another hand, then by all means arrest me, for I am the only one of the pair of us who might have done it."

"No, that isn't true. It cannot have been Abigail. Everyone knows the bomb was delivered by a man." Mr Patterson gazed at his wife with such devotion that Grace couldn't help but admire the strength of their attachment. He moved to his wife's side and took her hand. "Abigail, darling, you are an angel beyond compare, but I beg you to let me take the punishment due to me. I did it all for you, my love, so you could have the life you deserve."

Wallace looked from one to the other with an expression halfway between admiration and vexation. "If you murdered

Lennox MacDonald, Mr Patterson, you will be able to tell us how you did it."

"I shot him with a Webley revolver."

"How did you shoot him?"

"What?"

"It is a simple question. Only the murderer knows exactly how he was shot."

"Clean kill shot through the head. In the library."

"I wouldn't call placing a gun against a man's temple 'clean', Mr Patterson."

"Nice try, Inspector. You know as well as I that he was shot under the chin."

Wallace stepped forward and placed a hand on his shoulder. "Mr John Patterson, I arrest you for the murder of–"

"Wait," Mrs Patterson commanded. "John knew how Lennox died only because he followed me to Lennox's house. We were both worried about Lennox's state of mind. I admit I was there, but only after Lennox had shot himself. John must have seen him dead and mistakenly thought it was me who did it, hence his attempt to take the blame."

"Abigail–"

"No, John, let me handle this. If you arrest my husband, Inspector, I will fight you with such single-minded determination, you will wish yourself dead. My husband was neither the offender, nor an accessory, no matter what he says."

"Do not listen to her, Inspector," Mr Patterson retorted. "I will plead guilty, but only if my wife is freed from any blame."

Mrs Patterson turned to her husband and gave him a smile of such intensity that he bent and kissed her cheek. She turned her smile on Wallace, but this time, it was not a smile of devotion, but a calculated leer. "I see, Inspector, that you are still not convinced by the truth, that Lennox and Bertram were responsible for the bombs. Either Lennox's guilt drove him to suicide or Bertram had him killed."

272

"We know neither of those options is possible, Mrs Patterson."

"Well then, if your refuse to believe the truth, Inspector, you face an impossible dilemma. Which one of us did it? If I tell my husband not to utter a single word more on this matter and I do the same, you will never know for sure. More to the point, what judge and jury would convict either of us, when there remains such doubt as to the perpetrator?"

"I will charge you both," Wallace growled.

"In which case, we will both plead innocent. Your evidence is weak and contradictory. I'm sure you wouldn't wish to become a laughingstock for arresting the wrong person." Mrs Patterson glanced at Charlie. "Again."

"Honestly, I can't help but feel the evidence against Lennox is much stronger," her husband added. "A jury would see that immediately. Or Bertram, an ungodly, villainous type if ever I saw one. Alibis can be faked, after all."

"So true, my dear. What cannot be faked is one's long-established reputation. You, for example, are known throughout the region as a kind, honest, temperate man who works hard and espouses Christian values."

"While you, dearest Abigail, are known for your works for the worthiest charities, supporting family values and helping those who cannot help themselves. You, a murderess? It is unthinkable."

"Detective Inspector Wallace, this interview is over. You have insulted us in every possible way. We have nothing more to say, now or ever."

Wallace stood rooted to the spot. Grace could all but hear the whirl of his thoughts as he attempted to wade through the confusion.

Her own brain had been churning too, sifting through everything she had seen and heard. It was, as Mrs Patterson had said, a devilish dilemma. In order to prove guilt beyond doubt, the police would not only have to make a watertight case against one of them, but also prove the other didn't do it, while they joined together to mount a convincing case against Lennox. The police would be crucified if they put either of these upstanding citizens on the stand and failed to gain a conviction.

Mrs Patterson had been clever enough to admit nothing but possibilities, while her husband was blatantly sacrificing himself for her. Both had motive and access to explosives. Mrs Patterson had the opportunity, but the caretaker's evidence suggested the bomber was a man.

Charlie broke the silence. "Before we go, we need to see the clothes and boots you were wearing earlier today, Mrs Patterson, when Miss Penrose and I saw you outside your house. As you got down from your carriage, I noticed your boots were muddy and stained with what appeared to be a sticky substance."

"It is true I got some mud on my boots – hardly surprising with this wet spell of weather. I may even have spilled strawberry jam on them, during a rather heated argument at morning tea. However, I assure you there is no point in you seeing them, as I cleaned them as soon as I got home."

"No matter how much you try to clean an item, there is always a trace left behind. Isn't that right, Miss Penrose?" Charlie flicked a glance at Grace.

Grace took the hint and ran with it. "Yes, of course. I can test for blood using the Schonbein method. Hydrogen peroxide bubbles when mixed with blood." On boots scrubbed clean? Very unlikely, in her opinion, but it seemed Charlie had a plan.

With sudden blinding clarity, Grace realised that she too had noticed the boots Mrs Patterson had been wearing, because they had unusually sharp toes. Grace specifically recalled thinking how uncomfortable they must be to walk in.

She signalled for Charlie to join her, pulling him into the corridor for privacy. "The toes of her boots were narrow and pointed," she whispered. "Do you recall that I brushed aside some leaves on Lennox's library floor by the door? There was an odd V-shaped patch of mud underneath the man's boot print. I couldn't work out what made it at the time, but now I see it must have been the toe of her boot."

274

"Which means Mrs Patterson was there first. She must have shot Lennox. She was also telling the truth that Mr Patterson must have followed her later and seen the dead body. Clever thinking, Grace."

"Still not conclusive, though. She might have left the boot print after he died, as she claims. I don't think the hydrogen peroxide test will work on cleaned boots."

Their whispered conversation had the desired effect of unsettling Mr and Mrs Patterson. Unfortunately, it also distracted Wallace and Kelly. When they returned to the room, Mr Patterson was back by the mantelpiece, withdrawing a revolver from behind a large clock.

He pointed the revolver at Grace. "Please sit down on the floor, gentlemen, or I will be forced to shoot Miss Penrose. For her sake, I beg you to believe that I would do absolutely anything to protect my wife, as any loyal husband would."

When they didn't move, he barked out an order. "Sit! Do I have to remind you that this revolver contains six bullets and I am an excellent shot?"

Kelly slid his back down the wall until he was squatting, while Wallace resumed his seat in the armchair. Grace started to sit too, but Charlie grabbed her and hurled her through the doorway. He slammed the door and dropped to the floor in front of it.

Unravelling

Grace sprawled across the corridor, terrified that the next sound would be a bullet piercing Charlie's skull. The seconds passed in agonising silence. No scuffling, no shot, no screams. Grace was on the verge of running for reinforcements when the door opened. All she could do was fling her arms over her head and curl into a ball.

Strong arms scooped her up, as if she weighed no more than an infant. As Charlie carried her out the front door, she saw Wallace and Kelly escorting Mr Patterson from the drawing room in handcuffs. Mrs Patterson stood in the doorway wearing an expression of such virtuous fervour that Joan of Arc would have recruited her on the spot.

Grace waited until he placed her gently on a sofa in Anne's house before she spoke. "What happened in there, Charlie?"

"Mrs Patterson simply held out her hand and told her husband to give her the revolver. She assured him that the police would not be able to make a case against either of them, if he held his tongue and trusted her. Honestly, if he had been a dog, his tail would have been wagging."

"Wallace arrested Mr Patterson?"

"Only for threatening a police officer and possession of a stolen weapon, so far."

"Lennox's revolver?"

"Engraved with 'LM'. He must have taken Lennox's revolver, so the murder weapon was the only one left in the house."

"They've been clever," Grace said.

"Unfortunately, Mrs Patterson is too clever by half. She will hire the best attorney in Dunedin and put the blame on Lennox, I'm sure of it."

"But Lennox was murdered."

"I know, Grace, but will the average man on a jury be swayed by the absence of a few tiny specks of blood on a typewriter, when he is faced with beguiling pleas of innocence from a devout, loving, society matron like Mrs Patterson and an honest, hard-working man like Mr Patterson?"

Grace closed her eyes. It had been a long, exhausting day after a long, exhausting week. The lingering effects of concussion closed in on her with as much subtlety as a sledgehammer on a crystal goblet. Charlie bustled around her, plumping cushions, finding a blanket, pouring a glass of water.

She was sure that Wallace would forge ahead and try to make a case, for he was not a man to quit in the face of obstacles. But would the Chief Inspector support him? How easy it would be to accept that the bulk of evidence pointed to Lennox MacDonald and his liquor baron conspirators. Convenient too, that Lennox was dead, allowing the case to be wrapped up expediently, so the press was not left waiting, baying for a sacrifice.

When Grace opened her eyes again, she saw Charlie was sitting on the window seat with his back to her. From the tightness of the muscles in his shoulders and the way his head was propped in his hands, he must be suffering the same frustration.

Grace dragged herself upright on the cushions and sipped the water. "How strong the Patterson's love must be, that they were willing to sacrifice themselves for each other. To think I have spent these past two years believing Mrs Patterson to be a woman who thought of nothing but tea parties and social niceties. How disheartening that she felt the need to hide her intelligence and business skills to fit in with society's view of the perfect woman. She would have been far better served by joining our cause."

"You sound as if you admire her, Grace. Can you not see that she is a woman driven to evil for the sake of maintaining her position in society?"

"You think it was her?"

"On balance, yes. Unless her husband is a consummate actor, I'm convinced he didn't know about the bombs when we first interviewed him. She was the one with the skill to type the notes, she was equally able to make a bomb, and she was on hand to plant it at Choral Hall. If Lennox agreed to deliver the parcel to Harriet Morison, it was more likely for his sister than his brother-in-law. And I doubt Lennox would have let Patterson get near enough to shoot him at close range. Besides, Mrs Patterson strikes me as the stronger of the two and the more likely to choose such an appalling method of solving their financial problems. An entire lifetime of watching a useless brother get everything she deserved must have eaten away at her until she could bear it no longer."

"Do you think you can prove she did it if they maintain their innocence?"

"To a jury? Not a chance."

They lapsed into silence.

When Charlie spoke again, his voice had an odd, harsh ring to it. "Mrs Patterson was right about one thing – her advice to you to marry well. Despite her love for Mr Patterson, marrying beneath her status tore her apart, eventually."

Grace glared at his hunched back on the other side of the room. Even with all the months they had been living hundreds of miles apart, she had never felt so far away from him as at that moment. The silence dragged until she could bear it no longer. "Charlie, I am not Mrs Patterson. I don't care about social status and wealth."

"Mrs Patterson probably said the same in her youth. Let's face it, she couldn't cope in the end, despite Mr Patterson earning a decent wage and her benefiting from a share of the business. How much harder would it be to marry a person with few prospects – perhaps even no prospects at all?"

"I don't understand, Charlie. Wallace wants you on his team, doesn't he? Isn't that enough for now?"

"Wallace may want me, but he will be overruled by the Chief Inspector."

"Why? Can he not admit to making a mistake in arresting you? He had a duty to follow the evidence."

"It's not only that, Grace. I have had a letter from a fellow officer in Wellington, warning me that the Deputy Police Commissioner is furious that DI Stewart went against orders in attempting to clear me of the assault accusation. The real assailant's family has powerful connections. Even if I am cleared of the charge, there will always be a black mark against my name. The Deputy Commissioner will make darn sure that I never rise above the rank I am now. That is, if he allows me to stay in the police force at all."

"Oh, Charlie. Surely he couldn't be so despicable."

"To be honest, I truly wonder if policing is right for me. I'm not good at following orders I don't agree with. With Stewart, it was never a problem, as he trusted me enough to give me free rein. Wallace may allow it occasionally too, but officers of that type are a rarity."

Grace forced herself not to react to the unfairness of it. What Charlie said deserved some consideration. How would she feel if she was forced to give up medicine over a false allegation, after working so hard to become a doctor? Her career was so important to her that she had made it crystal clear to every man and his dog that she would not consider a normal life – marriage and children – before she graduated and established herself as a doctor. How could she expect anything less from Charlie?

"Your silence tells me that you agree with me, Grace. I'm glad. It will make it easier if I must leave you."

"Charlie, you do not understand in the least. I was giving your thoughts the consideration they deserve. I understand that it is hard for you and I don't want to give a trite reply. I know how it will sound if I say not to worry because it might never happen. Or if I insist on stating the obvious – that you are intelligent and hardworking, and young enough to begin a new career, if that is what you must do. These are the facts, but perhaps you need time to come to terms with them. I will be waiting for you when you do, however long it takes."

"No, Grace, I've made up my mind. You must look to a future with somebody like Cranston-Hartfield. He is rich, educated, successful, and he loves you. What more could any woman want? He will never leave you at home alone for days or weeks at a time. He will never risk death or disgrace or abuse." Charlie choked out a weak laugh. "In fact, as the police surgeon, he can't even be accused of harming or killing a patient, as they come to him already dead."

"Charlie, for heaven's sake, look at me." She waited until he turned to face her. Other than a flush of red across his high cheekbones, he appeared unnaturally calm. "I want a future with you."

"You will come to see that would not be in your best interests." The words slid out between tight lips. He looked away.

"What do you intend to do?"

"I will leave for Wellington as soon as possible. I intend to fight the blasted Deputy Commissioner with everything I've got at the disciplinary hearing. If I have to leave the police, I want to do so of my own free will. I refuse to let them throw me out without due cause."

"Please promise me you will come back to Dunedin."

"That depends on the outcome of the hearing. If I am dismissed or not offered an acceptable role in the Dunedin police force … well, I'll cross that bridge when I come to it. Australia, perhaps, after I have paid a long overdue visit to my parents. I need time away to consider my future."

"After everything we have been through together, you would desert me so readily?"

Finally, his face softened, but rather than coming across the room to her, he headed for the door. He paused at the threshold. "My darling Grace, it is because I love you so much that I want only the best for you. If I could stay in Dunedin, knowing I had a decent wage and future career prospects, I would do so in a heartbeat. If I cannot, I must leave you to live the life you deserve."

She waited for the door to slam, but he closed it gently, with such deliberate finality that she felt physically sick.

The minutes ticked by, as she curled up on the sofa, waiting for him to come to his senses.

Grace woke up with her face squashed against a cushion and the dread feeling of being watched. She looked up from underneath a mass of dishevelled hair, seeing Anne's furrowed brow hovering over her.

"Grace, you were dead to the world. I wasn't sure whether or not to wake you." Anne studied her minutely, as Grace hoisted her reluctant body upright and used her fingers to comb her hair back. "Grace, what's happened?"

How to explain to her great-aunt the lifetime's worth of drama she had endured since they had last seen each other? *Oh, just a regular day – the man of my dreams has walked out on me and, by the way, our neighbour is a murderer.* "I don't know where to begin. Perhaps you could tell me what you have been doing instead. Make it cheerful, if you can."

Anne lowered herself onto the sofa beside her, turning Grace so that she could twist her hair into a tidy roll. "The working committee for the Women's Franchise League held its first meeting today. Thanks to the national coverage in the newspapers, we are being flooded with offers of support. Towns across the country are forming their own Franchise Leagues. The government cannot turn a blind eye to women now."

Grace's gloom lifted a notch. "That's wonderful news. Anything else? I need all the good news I can get right now."

Anne turned Grace back towards her, so she could straighten her shirtwaist and sneak in a motherly pat on the cheek. "Donations are pouring in to the Violet Creswell Memorial Fund. We'll be able to pay for her burial and have enough left over for a scholarship fund for promising young women. Mrs Creswell's mother-in-law refused

281

to take any of the money herself. She is going to live with her daughter."

A flicker of a smile formed on Grace's lips, as she tucked her head against her great-aunt's wrinkled neck. "Tell me there is more good news and I will be in your debt forever."

"Sir John Hall has contacted the Public Petitions Committee. They have agreed to undertake an urgent inquiry, based on the signatures you and other suffragists collected, to prove that false pretences were used to get women to sign Fish's petition. Sir John feels certain they will find in our favour."

Could it really have been only a week ago that she and Molly were chased through the streets, clutching their precious signatures? If the petition against suffrage was dismissed, the few minutes of terror would have been worth it. "Henry Fish will be fish paste."

"Totally kippered," Anne agreed.

How blessed she was, Grace reflected, in having an extended family who knew exactly what she needed. When to laugh and tease, when to comfort, when to remain silent. And always understanding what was fair and right, even for the only daughter in a large household of sons. Would Mrs Patterson have become so bitter if she had been treated as fairly as Grace had? One could never know what made people crack under pressure. Grace hoped she would never be pushed into that dark a place.

"Now, Grace, are you going to tell me what is wrong, or do I have to torture it out of you?"

Grace was saved by the ring of the bell at the front door. She ran to open it.

"Charlie, thank goodness–" Grace stared at the man in front of her, unable to believe it was not Charlie coming back to her, full of remorse. "Rory, what are you doing here?"

"Grace, are you all right? I've only just heard about the bombing. They said you were in hospital."

"Only for a few hours. How is it that you didn't hear earlier? All of Dunedin is up in arms." Grace led Doctor Ravenwood into the drawing room, where she flopped into an armchair and waved him to another chair. Anne had disappeared, giving them privacy.

"The clinic has been frantic. A nasty bout of gastro. Not sure if it was contaminated water or food poisoning, but we've had half the local population through Lavender House in the last four days. I tried to find you on Thursday to get some more of Mrs Wu's tonic. My sister said you would be at Choral Hall, so I went to find you there."

"Oh Rory, I'm so sorry that I wasn't there to help you. Is everything all right at the …. wait, did you say you went to Choral Hall? When?"

"Thursday morning. Must have been about eleven o'clock. The door was open, and I was about to ask a woman in the kitchen where you were, when the caretaker grabbed me and pushed me out the door. Extremely rude he was, but I suppose the police must have shut the place tight to stop troublemakers from getting in. I had to buy some medicine from the apothecary instead, not that it was a patch on Mrs Wu's tonic."

Grace stared at him, taking in his ordinary working clothes, the cap in his hand, his regular features, and tall, well-built stature. "The caretaker told us he threw a man out. We thought he was the bomber. Rory, we need to inform Detective Inspector Wallace immediately. The entire case may turn on whether the unidentified man in the hall was the bomber. Were you carrying an empty bag?"

"Yes, my old doctor's bag – the black leather one. I was going to carry the tonic in it." Rory leaned forward, searching her face. "Grace, you don't think I was the bomber, do you?"

She laughed – a weak laugh, but a laugh nevertheless. "Of course not, Rory. You were born to be a healer, not a killer. Tell me everything you saw or heard at Choral Hall."

"I was only there for a moment. I walked in the open back door, as the front door was locked and nobody answered my knock. I only took a few steps inside, as far as the kitchen door, when the caretaker called me back."

"But you saw a woman in the kitchen?"

"I didn't have time to talk to her. I don't think she even noticed me, she was so intent on her work."

"Do you recall exactly what she was doing?"

"I remember she was carrying a tin. Must have been something special, because she was her whole concentration was on it as she walked into the storage room ..." his sentence tailed off as a question formed on his lips.

"If it was a tin with a green and gold label, it was the bomb."

The doctor blew out a long breath. "The tin did have a green and gold label. Good gracious, if only I had known. She seemed quite the lady. I would never have believed she had any involvement in the bombing."

"Describe her, if you would."

Rory closed his eyes, picturing the scene. "Slightly above medium height, strong jawed, age around mid-forties, impeccably dressed, large hat, draped with jewellery."

Mrs Patterson, without a doubt. "Rory, this is crucial evidence. Can you come to see DI Wallace straight away?"

"Of course."

"And, for heaven's sake, tell nobody else about this."

"If you insist, Grace. If you don't mind me saying, you look ill. Can't you stay here, while I go?"

Grace would have been delighted to agree. To sink into her bed and let sleep take her away from the mess that was her life. But if she was with Rory, Wallace would see him, where he might put a stranger off. "Sleep can wait. I will take you and make the introduction, then come home. It's too important to risk a moment's delay."

Future Imperfect

The bell at the front door didn't ring again until that evening. Grace hoped it was Charlie, but news from Wallace or Kelly would be welcome too. Wallace had shaken Rory's hand so hard when he heard his evidence, it was a wonder no bones had been broken.

Mrs Brown opened the door. Grace heard a deep Scottish voice echoing down the corridor. Detective Inspector Wallace. Kelly had come too.

"Don't leave me on tenterhooks," Grace pleaded, when they were all seated. Anne and Mrs Brown had insisted on hearing the news as well, after she had told them what had happened.

"Where's Charlie?" Kelly asked. "He ought to hear this."

"Gone," Grace replied.

"Gone? Gone where?"

Grace tucked her hands in her lap, so they could not see the tremor. "He is going to Wellington to fight for his position. I assume he will not leave until the morning, in which case he is probably still at Mr Drummond's house. More than that, I cannot say. He is talking about going to Australia, if the outcome of the disciplinary hearing goes against him."

Wallace's woolly eyebrows converged into a single exasperated line. "Kelly, go find Pyke and tell him about the Patterson case, while I talk to Miss Penrose."

"I had hoped the case would be solved, with Doctor Ravenwood's evidence," Grace said.

"So it is," Wallace agreed. "Mrs Patterson admitted to putting the tea tin in the storage room when faced with the fresh evidence. Unfortunately, she is as cunning as any back-alley shyster I've ever met. She claimed she and Lennox had agreed that they had no choice but to pay off Mrs Creswell – 'that treacherous little hussy' in her

285

words. Mrs Patterson claimed Lennox gave her the tin of tea, telling her he had arranged for Mrs Creswell to pick it up from Choral Hall. According to Mrs Patterson, the tin was only supposed to contain enough money to halt the compensation bid with the union."

Grace, Anne, and Mrs Brown exchanged horrified glances. She had to hand it to her neighbour. Mrs Patterson had come up with an all too plausible explanation. Then she saw the tic at the side of Wallace's mouth. "You don't believe her, Inspector?"

"The timer switch on the bomb must have been activated by one of them and we are sure Lennox had a solid alibi for the period in which it could have been set off. It couldn't have been Mr Patterson either, as we finally contacted the works foreman and he confirmed his boss was on site all night. I am left with the inescapable conclusion that Mrs Abigail Patterson is a ruthless murderess."

Grace wasn't sure whether to be relieved or appalled.

Wallace studied her reaction. "I must admit, Miss Penrose, that you were right. I will never make assumptions about the capabilities of ladies again, whether it be in their aptitude for committing crime or their aptitude for solving crime."

Grace managed a weak smile. "Has the Chief Inspector agreed to charge her with the two murders?"

"The Chief believes in justice as much as the rest of us. He is pleased to have a resolution so quickly. I'd say he has every right to be satisfied. The murderer is no longer a danger to the public. Lady Stout and the other women are safe and being lauded as heroines. The publicans have been arrested for illegal gambling and their attacks on the suffragists."

"I trust the Chief Inspector is now convinced that Charlie had no hand in the villainy?"

"Absolutely. He recognises how much the police owe to both you and Pyke. Indeed, the Chief is so pleased, he is allowing me to select a successor of my choice to replace my retiring detective sergeant. I don't suppose you know of any worthy candidates?"

286

Grace flew at him, wrapping her arms around his neck and planting a delighted kiss on his cheek. "That's wonderful news."

Charlie burst through the door and ground to a halt at the sight of the unexpected embrace. Grace ran across the room to him, flinging her arms around him, encountering more muscle than warmth.

"I was just telling Miss Penrose I am about to have a vacancy for a detective sergeant. You're the man I want, Pyke, but I don't want to get your hopes up until the appointment can be officially confirmed. You might be an old man by the time I fill in all the darn paperwork."

Anne nudged Charlie with the tip of her walking cane. "For the love of Aphrodite, Charlie, don't just stand there gawping like a simpleton, kiss the girl."

And so he did, throwing propriety to the wind in a moment of reckless joy.

The audience cheered, as the door opened again to reveal Charlie's aunt and his commanding officer, right on cue.

"Lily, Alistair," Grace stammered. "I thought you were in Wellington."

"Our work is done, Grace." Lily looked between Grace and Charlie, her eyes alight with speculation. "What are we celebrating?"

"The possibility of a detective sergeant position for Charlie in Dunedin."

After a round of delighted embraces and introductions, Mrs Brown returned with champagne, which Kenneth Drummond opened and distributed. Anne raised her glass to propose a toast.

Grace had her eye on Stewart, who was showing a marked reluctance to celebrate. "Wait a moment, if you will. I believe Detective Inspector Stewart has news to share."

"I'm plain old Mr Stewart henceforth, which might take a little getting used to. I'd prefer Alistair, as I am amongst friends again. I've resigned from the police force and come south to marry my sweetheart." He took Lily's hand and shared with her a look of such tenderness, that Anne was forced to dab her eyes with a handkerchief, passed to her by a solicitous Drummond.

"What news do you have, Alistair?" Grace persisted.

"The disciplinary hearing has been cancelled. After presenting my superiors with all the evidence we gathered, the case against Charlie has been dropped. The question of charges against the young men who attacked the Chinese shopkeepers is as yet unresolved. I have no doubt that a great deal of political pressure has been put on the police to turn a blind eye. Frankly, I am glad to be out of it. I am looking forward to a life of rolling bandages and making tea at Lavender House, alongside my lovely wife."

"Surely that is good news, Alistair," Anne said. "Why the long face?"

Stewart exchanged a grimace with Lily. Shuffled his feet. Chewed his luxuriant moustache. Finally, he cleared his throat. "The Deputy Commissioner needs a scapegoat to appease a powerful group of politicians. It's not only the Wellington assault. There are accusations of police persecution against the liquor lobby here in Dunedin. Charlie, I'll never forgive myself for putting you in such an invidious position, right in the middle of both cases."

"You cannot be serious," Anne snapped. "Police persecution? Even if those vile publicans are cleared of the two bombings, they will still be charged with the other attacks and threats. Do the lives of Women's Franchise League supporters mean so little to those in power? They attacked Lady Stout, for heaven's sake."

Grace couldn't bear the suspense. She grasped Charlie's hand tightly and felt his grip tighten in response. "What will happen to Charlie, Alistair?"

"I have been given a letter to pass on to you, Charlie. All I know is that you have been offered a new position within the police force. This happened before the position came up in Dunedin, but I doubt that will make any difference. The Deputy Police Commissioner is in no mood to be generous. He is a man who puts political expediency ahead of the welfare of his own men. He told me this position was all he was prepared to offer."

Charlie took the letter, but did not open it. "I want to thank you all, and your families and friends, for the support you have shown me. I'm more grateful than I can express that all the charges against me have been dropped, thanks to your intervention. You have saved my sanity, even my life. No matter what happens, my choices will be guided by the love and respect I have for you. Detective Inspector Stewart, it has been a privilege to serve you. I know you have done everything in your power to help me."

Charlie extended a hand to his former boss, but Alistair pulled him into a hard embrace. "You'd better not be thinking of leaving Dunedin, Pyke. I've got a wedding coming up and I'll be relying on you to stand beside me."

Charlie's fingers fiddled with the letter until he could clear the lump in his throat. "It would be my honour, Alistair. I promise I will be here for your wedding, come what may."

He opened the envelope in complete silence. Not one of them breathed as he drew out the letter and read it. He handed it on to Alistair, who let out an uncharacteristic curse.

"What is it?" Grace demanded.

"I have been offered a reassignment as a uniformed constable in Russell." Charlie spat out the words as if they were hemlock in his mouth.

"Where is that?" Lily whispered.

"It is known as the Hell Hole of the Pacific," Charlie replied.

"That was decades ago," Anne said. "I am sure it is much improved these days."

"No matter how improved it is, it is still at the far end of the North Island, almost as far away from Dunedin as one can get. They might as well have offered me a position at the North Pole. And not even as a detective. The Deputy Police Commissioner couldn't have found a better way to kick my career into the gutter, short of shackling me in stocks in the middle of the town square."

Charlie reached into his pocket, extracting his police badge and a letter. "Can you please see that these are returned to Wellington for me, Alistair? The letter is my resignation from the police force. I suppose I should be grateful they have allowed me the dignity of resigning rather than being dismissed."

When Alistair refused to take them, Charlie dropped his badge and resignation letter on a table beside his untasted champagne and walked out of the house.

Alistair rushed after him, while Lily put her arms around Grace's shoulders. "Charlie will come to his senses, Grace. He's stubborn, but not stupid. You will have to be patient for a while."

Grace slipped out of her embrace. "He has made his choice, Lily. What I need right now is a large dose of laudanum and a soft bed. I have medical school to attend on Monday and I feel utterly exhausted."

"Wait," Anne called after her, as Grace stumbled across the room.

"Please, Auntie, not now. I don't have time to waste on men anyway, if I am to graduate with distinction and prove, once and for all, that it will take more than bombs, abuse and rejection to stop women succeeding at whatever they choose to do."

Lily got to the bottom of the stairs as she reached the top. "He'll come back, Grace, I know he will!"

Grace couldn't bring herself to reply. She went into her room, locking the door behind her.

Charlie Pyke had better find a darned good hiding place if he didn't come back soon. Real life was no fairy tale, but that didn't mean Grace Penrose was going to let a pig-headed former copper get in the way of a happy ending. However long it took.

Read on

In Book 4 of the *Penrose & Pyke Mysteries*, **Murder in the Moonlight**, Grace witnesses the death of a prominent surgeon, struck down during a moonlit walk after a feud over hospital services for women.

Grace has had no time to dwell on the absence of former detective Charlie Pyke. She is busy with her medical studies, a campaign to improve Dunedin's hospital, and fittings for a bridesmaid's dress. Not to mention the little matter of being implicated in the surgeon's murder. As the case becomes ever more baffling, the only thing Grace needs more than Charlie's sleuthing skills is his uncanny knack of appearing when she needs him most.

Thank You

Thank you for reading this story. If you enjoyed it, I would be very grateful if you would leave a rating or review to help other readers discover it.

Find out about other books and sign up for notifications of new releases at https://RosePascoe.com

Historical Notes

This story is entirely fictional. Women's suffrage in New Zealand was achieved by peaceful, democratic means, with a great deal of passion on both sides, but no incidents of major violence (and no explosions!). However, elements of the story were inspired by real events surrounding the campaign to gain the vote for women and the deceitful methods used in opposition to suffrage.

The story is set in Dunedin in April 1892. Women had already come close to achieving the vote in 1891, failing only at the last hurdle, because of political trickery. Universal suffrage had strong support within parliament, thanks to the efforts of powerful men, including Premier John Ballance, Sir Robert Stout, and Sir John Hall. Determined not to be beaten, women went out once again in 1892, into streets, alleys and country lanes across the nation, collecting over 20,000 signatures – by far the largest petition ever presented to the New Zealand Parliament.

Nowhere was support as strong as in Dunedin (over 7000 signatures), thanks to women like Harriet Morison and Helen Nicol, who ensured that the voices of working women were heard, especially through the work of the Dunedin Tailoresses' Union.

But there were vocal and powerful opponents as well. Henry Fish was the epicentre of vitriolic opposition in Dunedin. Considered loud, brash, and obnoxious by most people, but favoured (for a time) by the workingmen of his electorate, Fish did not shy away from either controversy or dubious methods. Fish was supported by the powerful liquor lobby, who feared that women voters would bring in more restrictive liquor licencing, or even the total prohibition of alcohol.

In parliament, the larger-than-life hero of the working man, Richard Seddon, was one of the more noteworthy opponents of votes for women. Ironically, when the vote was finally won in 1893 (after an extraordinary 30,000 signatures were collected – representing one in four adult women in New Zealand), Seddon's Liberal government was the major beneficiary, dominating politics for the next thirteen years. The fear of the liquor lobby that women would vote for prohibition was also unfounded.

Tensions in Dunedin came to a head in April 1892. Henry Fish circulated a petition against extending the franchise to women, which used all the forms of trickery mentioned in this story. Claims that this petition collected signatures by false pretences were later upheld by the Public Petitions Committee, thanks to a counter-petition put forward by Sir John Hall, as in the story.

Supporters countered the anti-suffrage threat by proposing a Women's Franchise League, at a meeting that overflowed City Hall on 12 April 1892. The Women's Franchise League provided an organisation focussed solely on votes for women, open to women from all walks of life, regardless of religion and temperance beliefs. Meanwhile, a series of temperance lectures (17-23 April) heightened the threat to the liquor lobby, which was already reeling from closures to hotels by local Liquor Licensing Committees stacked with prohibitionists.

The first meeting of the Women's Franchise League was held on 28 April 1892 at Choral Hall, with Lady Anna Stout and Marion Hatton elected presidents, Helen Nicol as secretary, and Harriet Morrison and Rachel Reynolds (amongst other stalwart women) as vice-presidents. All these wonderful, under-appreciated women appear in this story, in an entirely fictional capacity, and the real meeting was a success. The cause of women's suffrage was the winner and Henry Fish was trounced in his bid for the Dunedin mayoralty later that year.

However, despite all the hard work, the bill enabling universal franchise again failed at the final hurdle in 1892, after a devious last-minute amendment scuppered it. Women had to wait another year before they could vote (although "wait" is hardly the right word, given the renewed effort and massive 1893 petition). The bill passes only a few weeks before the election, yet 80% of women were enrolled and 83% voted. So much for the opponents' argument that women didn't want the vote!

Thus, New Zealand became the first self-governing nation in the world where women gained the right to vote. For more background on this proud achievement, see Patricia Grimshaw's *Women's Suffrage in New Zealand* (1987, Auckland University Press, Auckland, New Zealand).

For a wider-ranging view of political issues in this turbulent time, I found Tom Brooking's biography of Seddon fascinating (*Richard Seddon: King of God's Own*. 2014, Penguin, Auckland, New Zealand). Erik Olssen's research on Caversham society provided local colour (*Building the New World: Work, Politics and Society in Caversham 1880s-1920s*. 1995, Auckland University Press Auckland, New Zealand).

Choral Hall was not bombed in reality, but the bombing part of this story's plot is not as outlandish as you might think. The world really was up in arms about anarchist plots in Britain and Europe. A search for the term "anarchist" in *Papers Past* revealed 113 articles in the main Dunedin papers between January and May 1892, including dynamite bombs in France and Spain in mid-April 1892 (and in London in early May). Hundreds of thousands of troops were mobilised. The Fenian attacks in London during the 1880s, using dynamite bombs with timers, were also real events.

Meanwhile, an advertisement in the local newspaper, the *Otago Daily Times*, on 19 April 1892, was offering a variety of goods to the public, including blasting powder, dynamite and fuses. How times have changed. The store? Arthur Briscoes, which is still well known to New Zealand readers 160 years after it was established. The *Otago Workman* was a real bi-weekly tabloid, noted for its fervent anti-suffrage and anti-establishment views. However, the letter to the editor from Outraged Gent is fictional, although the language was loosely based on real letters.

I am, as always, immensely grateful for the available online resources. *Papers Past* can't be beaten for insights into daily events, especially when combined with the digitised images and information from the Hocken Library and National Library. Details of buildings were taken from Heritage New Zealand and https://builtindunedin.com. Choral Hall (formerly Temperance Hall) is still at 21 Moray Place, but renamed and significantly altered. City Hall (formerly the Lyceum Theatre) has been demolished. My website has more information and images: https://RosePascoe.com.

About the author

Rose Pascoe writes historical mysteries with a dash of romance, when she isn't plotting real-life adventures.

She lives in beautiful New Zealand, land of beaches and mountains, where long walks provide the perfect conditions for dreaming up plots and fickle weather provides the incentive to sit down and actually write.

After a career in health, justice and social research, her passion is for stories set against a backdrop of social revolution. Her heroines are ordinary women, who meet the challenges thrown at them with determination, ingenuity, courage, and humour.

Visit her at: https://RosePascoe.com

www.ingramcontent.com/pod-product-compliance
Lightning Source LLC
Chambersburg PA
CBHW011458170626
46814CB00008B/2945